"These fifteen robust, timely, intellectually challenging essays explore women's relationships to private time and private space as opportunities that enable creative work, as alternatives to masculine models of creativity, and as sites of ownership and autonomy. Representing energetic, upbeat, and often unconventional feminist approaches to gender theory, personal experience, and literary criticism, they analyze, interpret, and evaluate texts by Charlotte Brontë, Kate Chopin, Virginia Woolf, Zora Neal Hurston, Marguerite Duras, May Sarton, Tillie Olson, Ursula Le Guin, Mary Catherine Bateson, Mary Daly, and others. Each contributor brings insight not only to gendered concerns but also to the divergent responses of different races and classes to conditions of solitude, to its social value, to its accommodation of partners and children, and to its shifting relevance at various stages of life. The cumulative effect is dynamic, disruptive, and wonderfully emancipating."

—William J. Kennedy, PhD
Professor of Comparative Literature,
Cornell University,
Ithaca, NY

"*Herspace* will be a welcome read for all women academics who struggle to find the time to write. These essays are about women and space—intimate space, enclosed space, home space. We are privileged to read here a collection of 'house-work' produced in spaces described and constructed in the essays. Though earlier writers, such as Woolf, Hurston, Sarton, and Duras, are invoked, it is the contemporary voice which dominates. Opening with more theoretical statements, the book moves increasingly into the personal and applied voice. Writers such as Johnson, Mon Pere, Berry, and Rose show us the many sides of solitude: loneliness, solitary confinement, creative solitude, regeneration. They also describe how to create and nurture that solitude. Moving from gender and literary theory to house-owning, this book is finally about the landscape and habitation of the self."

—Carol S. Long, PhD
Professor of English;
Interim Dean, College of Liberal Arts,
Willamette University,
Salem, OR

"In *Herspace: Women, Writing, and Solitude* Jo Malin and Victoria Boynton have gathered an eclectic set of essays probing the meanings of self-sufficiency for women: the cultural representations of the solo woman; the heterogeneous valences of solitude; the struggles to create spaces of writing in the midst of everyday life; and the pleasures of houses, their materiality, and their locatedness at the intersection of interiors and exterior surrounds. Collectively, the essays address these themes through a variety of generic modes—critical inquiry, poetry, meditation, how-to autobiography, and allegorical topography.

Throughout the book, the voices of women writers accumulate into a chorus of exemplars, models, strugglers, and jugglers of the temporal and spatial pressures and pleasures of solitude: May Sarton, Virginia Woolf, Charlotte Brontë, Zora Neal Hurston, Marguerite Duras, Kate Chopin, Alice Koller. Sarton, in particular, emerges as a mythic figure for the woman who writes alone, who writes aware of the materiality and psychic resonances of the home around her.

For those who have been writing, who think of writing, who once wrote and must write again, *Herspace: Women, Writing, and Solitude* will bring hours of reading pleasure in solitude and about solitude and model generic possibilities for imagining women's solitude differently."

—Sidonie Smith, PhD
Martha Guernsey Colby Collegiate Professor
of English and Women's Studies,
University of Michigan

Herspace
Women, Writing, and Solitude

HAWORTH Innovations in Feminist Studies
J. Dianne Garner
Senior Editor

Herspace
Women, Writing, and Solitude

Jo Malin
Victoria Boynton
Editors

Taylor & Francis Group

LONDON AND NEW YORK

First pulished 2003 by The Haworth Press, Inc.

Published 2013 by Routledge
2 Park Square, Milton Park, Abingdon,Oxon OX14 4RN
711 Third Avenue, New York, NY 10017, USA

Routledge in an imprint of the Taylor & Francis Group, an informa business

TR: 8.21.03

"An &/or Peace Performance" by H. Kassia Fleisher and Joe Amato originally appeared in *The Mechanics of the Mirage: Postwar American Poetry,* edited by Michel Delville.

"A Woman's Place" by Anne Mamary originally published as "Home/Work" in *International Studies in Philosophy,* vol. 34, no. 1 (Winter 2002): 127-141.

Cover photograph "Solitude and Waiting" copyright 2002 by Julie Magura.

Cover design by Marylouise E. Doyle.

Library of Congress Cataloging-in-Publication Data

Herspace : women, writing, and solitude / Jo Malin, Victoria Boynton, editors.
    p. cm.
   Includes bibliographical references.
   ISBN 978-0-789-01820-5 (bpk)
   1. American literature—Women authors—History and criticism. 2. English literature—Women authors—History and criticism. 3. Women and literature—United States. 4. Women and literature—Great Britain. 5. Authorship—Sex differences. 6. Personal space in literature. 7. Solitude in literature. I. Malin, Jo, 1942- II. Boynton, Victoria.

PS147 .H47 2003
810.9'8287—dc21

2002012018

CONTENTS

ABOUT THE EDITORS

Jo Malin is a Project Director in the School of Education and Human Development and Adjunct Assistant Professor of English at the State University of New York at Binghamton. She is a writer of autobiography criticism, personal narratives, and grant proposals. Dr. Malin is a member of the Autobiography Society. Her book *The Voice of the Mother: Embedded Maternal Narratives in Twentieth-Century Women's Autobiographies* was published in 2000. Dr. Malin is included in the *Directory of American Women, 10th Edition,* the *World's Who's Who of Women, 14th Edition,* and the *Who's Who of American Women, 20th Edition.* In 1995, she received the Woman of Achievement Award from the Broome County Status of Women Council in Binghamton, New York.

Victoria Boynton is Associate Professor in the English Department at the State University of New York at Cortland, where she teaches rhetoric, creative writing, literature, and multicultural and gender studies courses. She publishes at the intersection of these fields on such figures as Leslie Silko, Rita Dove, and the collaborative teaching of prejudice and discrimination. She has recently published articles on whiteness studies, feminism, and composition in various volumes. In addition to being a scholar, she is also a creative writer. In 2000 and 2001, Sharon Olds invited Dr. Boynton to New Poems Week, a summer gathering of poets. Recently, she has published a short story in *Faultline* and poems in *Poem* and *Blueline.*

CONTRIBUTORS

Joe Amato is the author of *Symptoms of a Finer Age* (Viet Nam Generation, 1994), *Bookend: Anatomies of a Virtual Self* (SUNY Press, 1997), and *Under Virga* (forthcoming, Chax Press). His poetry, scholarship, and prose musings have been published or are forthcoming in *Postmodern Culture, Nineteenth Century Studies, Denver Quarterly, New American Writing, Chain, Jacket, Crayon, electronic book review, Computers and Composition,* and *Voices in Italian Americana.*

Eleanor Berry has published papers on twentieth-century American poetry and the prosody of free verse in edited collections and in numerous journals, including *College English, Contemporary Literature, SAGETRIEB, Twentieth-Century Literature, Visible Language,* and William Carlos Williams Review. Her own poetry has appeared in anthologies and in various magazines, including *Crazyhorse, Kalliope, The Spoon River Poetry Review,* and *Writing on the Edge,* and her book manuscript "Westering Winter Sun" was a finalist for the 2000 May Swenson Poetry Award. She has taught writing and literature at several colleges and universities, including the University of Wisconsin—Milwaukee, Marquette University, and, most recently, Willamette University. She currently lives and writes in rural western Oregon.

Maria Brown is a thirty-six-year-old lesbian who currently lives in central New York State with her life partner and their beloved pets. Since writing about her little house, she has relocated and joined households with her partner. Maria works in the software development industry and is currently employed as a software test engineer.

Annabelle Cone teaches in the Department of French and Italian as well as the Comparative Literature Program at Dartmouth College. Her essay is a chapter from her doctoral thesis, "W(rite) at Home: Representations of Domestic Space in Sand, Colette and Duras." Her essays have appeared in *Simone de Beauvoir Studies* and *Literature Film Quarterly.*

Kristina Deffenbacher is Assistant Professor of English and women's studies at Hamline University in Saint Paul, Minnesota. Her recent research focuses on intersections of architectural, psychic, and narrative spaces. She is completing a manuscript with the working title "The Housing of Wandering Minds in Victorian Literature and Culture." She and her partner-in-many-pursuits, Mike Reynolds, are currently hunting for a house of their own.

H. Kassia Fleisher's essays have appeared in *Z Magazine, Postmodern Culture, American Book Review, Exquisite Corpse,* and *electronic book review;* excerpts from her novel manuscript "Accidental Species" have been published in *Antennae* and *Sugar Mule.* She teaches writing, women's literature, and ethnic literature as an adjunct at the University of Colorado–Boulder.

Suzette A. Henke is Thruston B. Morton Senior Professor of Literary Studies at the University of Louisville. She is the author of *Joyce's Moraculous Sindbook: A Study of Ulysses* (Ohio State University Press, 1978) and *James Joyce and the Politics of Desire* (Routledge, 1990). Her publications in the field of modern literature include essays on Virginia Woolf, Dorothy Richardson, Anais Nin, Doris Lessing, Janet Frame, Keri Hulme, Maya Angelou, Sally Morgan, Samuel Beckett, and W. B. Yeats. Her most recent book is *Shattered Subjects: Trauma and Testimony in Women's Life-Writing* (St. Martin's Press, 1998).

Lisa Johnson is the editor and contributing author of *Jane Sexes It Up: True Confessions of Feminist Desire,* released this spring by Four Walls Eight Windows. After earning a PhD in English from Binghamton University (SUNY), she returned to her hometown in Georgia to live in her very first house of her own (actually it was rented, but still, no thin apartment walls to worry about) and now lives in North Carolina. She quotes Julia Alvarez, "Nothing is as good as stability for getting your work done," and would like to dedicate her essay to Mike and Cheryl Steed for providing this stability by housing her—and her writerly imagination—so generously for the past three years.

Claudia A. Limbert grew up in the Ozarks of southern Missouri. The first person in her family to graduate from high school, she did not begin college until she was thirty-five and had four children. She has a BA with three majors (English, history, and education), an MA in fiction writing, and a PhD in English. She has published scholarly articles in *Restoration, English Language Notes, Philological Quarterly,* and *Papers of the Bibliographic Association of America,* as well as fiction in such magazines as *Country Living, House Beautiful,* and *The Boston Globe*'s Sunday *Magazine.* She is president of Mississippi University for women.

Anne Mamary earned her PhD in the Philosophy, Interpretation, and Culture program at Binghamton University (SUNY). She is Visiting Assistant Professor in the School of Liberal Arts at Clarkson University and so, happily, has been able to move back into her house. Her co-edited anthology (with Gertrude James Gonzalez de Allen), *Cultural Activisms: Poetic Voices, Political Voices,* was published by SUNY Press in 1999.

Claudia Mon Pere directs the Creative Writing Program at Santa Clara University. Her poetry and fiction have appeared in *The Kenyon Review, Prairie Schooner, Calyx, The Spoon River Poetry Review,* and elsewhere. Her essay "Flowers, Bones" was published in the collection *Living on the Margins: Women Writers on Breast Cancer* (Persea Books, 1999). She received the 1997 Georgetown Review Fiction Award and is at work on a collection of short stories set in the San Joaquin Valley.

Christina Pugh has received *Poetry* magazine's Ruth Lilly Poetry Fellowship, the Grolier Poetry Prize, and a nomination for a Pushcart Prize. She is the author of *Gardening at Dusk,* a chapbook of poems published by Wells College Press. Her poems and nonfiction have appeared in *Harvard Review, Hayden's Ferry Review, Verse, Poetry Daily,* and other publications. Her article "Non-Pictorial Mimesis in the Ekphrastic Lyric: Louise Bogan's 'After the Persian'" is forthcoming in *Interrogating Images* (Northwestern University Press). She holds a doctorate in comparative literature from Harvard University and an MFA in poetry from Emerson College. Currently she is Assistant Professor of English at Northwestern University.

Mary Rose writes and sells her antique frames in upstate New York. She has contributed two articles to *Victorian Homes:* "Painting a Shingle-Style House" and "Victorian Frames for Photographs." This is her first published essay.

Lisette Schillig is a PhD candidate at Purdue University, focusing on the relationship between women and solitude, and the ways in which the intersections of gender, space, place, and time work to inform and redefine notions of subjectivity and women's relation to history. Her particular research interest lies in the works of twentieth-century American women writers, ranging from H.D. to the contemporary language poet Lyn Hejinian.

Jan Wellington was born in Philadelphia, has lived in New York and New Mexico, and is now Assistant Professor of English at Utah Valley State College, where she teaches British literature. Her poems have appeared in venues such as *The Prose Poem: An International Journal* and *Connecticut Review.* She hopes to soon give birth to an edition of the works of eighteenth-century English poet and critic Elizabeth Moody.

Acknowledgments

Jo, for both us, wishes to acknowledge the support of Claudia Limbert who first put the idea of *Herspace: Women, Writing, and Solitude* into existence by inviting us to co-author a paper for her panel at the 1998 Midwest Modern Language Association Convention in St. Louis. It was the beginning of our collaboration on this topic, preceded by years of friendship and colleagueship.

She also thanks her family members, who have always believed in her as a scholar and writer; Al Tricomi; Ted Rector; and her staff at Binghamton University for constant and unfailing support.

However, the most important support came from the contributors to this volume, who have become an online scholarly and personal community. Suzette Henke, in particular, was our constant and most ardent mentor and fan.

Victoria, first, would like to thank Jo Malin. Without Jo's invitation to help her edit, her intellectual and emotional support, and her down-to-earth attitudes toward the project, our book would never have come to fruition. She would also like to thank Kathy Russell and Mecke Nagel for their encouragement, and our former teacher, Sidonie Smith, for showing us the path. She also owes her family thanks for their ability to live their lives while she claimed her solitude to work on this book.

Acknowledgments

Introduction

Jo Malin

> It is just the way rooms open into each other that is one of the
> charms of the house, a seduction that can only be felt when one
> is alone here. People often imagine that I must be lonely. How
> can I explain? I want to say, "Oh no! You see the house is with
> me." And it is with me in this particular way, as both a demand
> and a support, only when I am alone here.
>
> May Sarton, *Plant Dreaming Deep*

> At first I just walk from room to room, amazed. At the luxury of
> so much empty space, at my unbelievable luck. . . .
>   Always before a creature of others . . . I'd expected solitude to
> be the challenge, the handicap, the price to pay for the freedom
> to feel and think unencumbered. . . .
>   But now I feel that solitude, far from being the price, is turn-
> ing out to be the prize.
>
> Alix Kates Shulman, *Drinking the Rain*

> She liked to be alone, she liked to be herself.
>
> Virginia Woolf, *To the Lighthouse*

In 1929, Virginia Woolf wrote that a woman must have enough
money and a room of her own, and eloquently described the human
dignity that is the offspring of "privacy and space" (4). Woolf's central concern was a woman's need for her own space and privacy, that
is for solitude, as necessary prerequisite conditions for writing. She
knew from her own history and the history of women who lacked
both the money and the room, that literary silences, despair, and mad-

1

ness are the results when a woman wants to write and is unable. That is, the world would not know her name if Shakespeare had a sister who wrote plays. Woolf very bluntly and concretely wrote that "intellectual freedom depends on material things" (112).

Predating Woolf by almost sixty years, Susan B. Anthony called for an acceptance of a transitional period between her own time of conventional marriages, in which women were subjugated by their husbands, and a new future day when marriages would be built on a model of a partnership of equals. During this period, Anthony prophesied, women would support themselves and have their own houses. In a speech in October 1877, titled "Homes of Single Women," Anthony said:

> If women will not accept marriage *with subjection,* nor men proffer it *without,* there is, there can be *no alternative.* The women who will *not be ruled* must live without marriage. And during this transitional period . . . single women make comfortable and attractive homes for themselves. . . . (Dubois 147)

Although Anthony's vision was embedded in a rationale that made it acceptable to audiences of her time, she was, in reality, describing a small group of self-supporting women, "many of them her friends, whose economic independence was marked by a new level of personal freedom, in particular their ability to own their homes" (Dubois 146). Anthony's very privileged friends had access to incomes or professions that made home ownership possible only for very few women at that time. Nevertheless, her vision and their choices, despite her reassurances that this was the product of a transitional time, were radical. She saw these women, who were perhaps pitied by their communities, creating homes of "exceeding joy and gladness . . . each a little paradise save the presence of the historic Adam . . ." (147). These homes were not only the mark of independent women but, more important, shelter for women's intellect and creative production, a physical and metaphorical "herspace."

In the inspiring, almost religious, rhetoric of Anthony's 1877 speech, she describes women's desire for their own space, "the soul's dream of rest, the one hope that will not die . . ." (147). Using the unique conditions that allowed some of her friends to own their homes and couching her idea in a politically acceptable image of a transitional condition and time, Anthony foresaw the possibility for women, as human beings, to have the aspiration and the right of home ownership. She described this ownership as "the one thing above all others longed for, worked for . . ." (147).

By the 1930s, another unique group of American women, larger than Anthony's group of associates, found themselves independent and eager to possess and shape their own space, including buying their own homes. The history of this group, female faculty members at the "Seven Sisters" women's colleges, is chronicled in *Alma Mater: Design and Experience in the Women's Colleges from Their Nineteenth-Century Beginnings to the 1930s* by Helen Lefkowitz Horowitz. At the turn of the twentieth century, these women began to move out of their required quarters in student resident halls. While this option was available to male faculty members at most of these institutions, female faculty members were expected to serve as guides or "housemothers" for their students. When their independence from required on-campus housing was finally won in the 1930s, many embraced home ownership with great enthusiasm. Vida Dutton Scudder, a Wellesley College faculty woman, wrote in her own book, *On Journey:* "If there is any happier game than building a house, I have failed to play . . ." (272).

According to Horowitz, some faculty women even named their houses. Their unusual professional status and earning power put them in a position that was unique for women in the United States at the time. Home ownership was enthusiastically grasped for the independence it represented and allowed. Horowitz writes, "Home-owning gave to some the most meaningful aspect of their lives. These domestic structures provided them with physical confirmation of their existence, their independence" (190).

Woolf's call for "a room of one's own" and the small but significant examples from Anthony's circle in the nineteenth century and women faculty in the 1930s was taken up by a generation of women in the second wave of the feminist movement. Women, wanting the space to write, struggled to find their own rooms. Today, however, at the beginning of the twenty-first century, many women have surpassed Woolf's fantasy. Some of us now have *houses* of our own. For many, this quite literally is a house; for others, it is an apartment or a similar domestic space.

This luxury is so historically radical that it was forbidden by the Puritans, for both men and women. Some women have entered this state in traditional ways. They have been widowed, divorced, or deserted. However, for a growing number it is their choice to live alone, to experience solitude as a condition of life and a basis for creative work. Such a choice defies the construction of women as "other oriented." In this regard, one of the contributors to this collection, Christina Pugh, writing about the works of May Sarton and Alice Koller, theorizes that:

> with all the choices open to women in our time including a loosening of heterosexual gender roles and the option not to have children, it may well be the "last" frontier for women to explore but also conceivably the choice that is most troubling to the common and even highly theoretical notion of women as predominantly familial and/or relational beings. (Pugh 1)

I came to know this last frontier when my daughter, my younger child, left home for college and I began living alone. I stayed in the apartment where I raised my children, after a divorce, for another nine years, still regarding this housing situation as temporary. I had many rooms of my own and I was writing. When I purchased a house of my own—nearly 2,000 square feet of solitude, including a book-lined study with a fireplace—five years ago, I began to recognize that this was a deliberate choice and one I hoped was permanent. Being a solitaire, a writer, and a home owner is definitely the most enjoyable lifestyle I have experienced or can imagine. Yet why do I sometimes feel, as a woman and an academic who happens to live alone, that I don't "have a life" if I spend weekend hours at my desk? What keeps me and others like me from valuing the lives we have for the freedom and space they provide us to work creatively?

These are the questions that propelled me to find other women—some academic and some not—who value solitude and private, claimed space, as well as writers who autobiographically describe their experiences with solitude and/or with inhabiting their own homes. These conversations and my reading have provided some tentative answers to several major issues, such as reconciling a love of solitude with core feminist values of connection, affiliation, and collaboration; claiming solitude for academic work; realizing my privilege as compared to the lives of most of the women in the world; increasing focus and productivity in our academic or nonacademic work as a function of living alone and having plenty of solitude; appropriating space and physical beauty as they affect the enjoyment or comfort of solitude.

Speaking for myself, I love my work and the freedom to write on a Sunday afternoon in blissful uninterrupted solitude. I have a typically busy academic life. I work full-time in an administrative position and at the same time continue to pursue writing and scholarly interests. When I leave my crowded and hectic workplace, I retreat to solitude, serenity, and visual beauty in my house. I am in love with the house as an architectural structure as well as a protected, intimate space that nurtures my solitude. When I unlock the door and walk in, I see calm, peaceful, orderly spaces all around me. I feel very privileged, and sometimes even guilty, to have such good fortune. I have feelings similar to those Alix Rates Shulman describes in *Drinking the Rain*: "now I find that solitude, far from being the price, is turning out to be the prize" (51).

For me, it is no accident that my academic career has been most successful in the years since I started living alone. My children are grown and I have not lived with an adult partner in many years. I am also aware that many of my married or partnered friends and colleagues, especially those with children at home, envy aspects of my lifestyle and my status as a solitaire. They envy the quiet, the structured routine, and the freedom I have. Quite simply, my life of solitude works, both personally and professionally.

The notion of women and solitude, women living alone and liking it, is askew with the feminist values of connectedness, relationality, and collaboration. Beginning with Nancy Chodorow's work, the self-in-relation model of feminine personality has been used to understand gender differences and to analyze women's texts. Carol Gilligan's work also describes women in webs of relationship and connection. For this image of the web to make sense for me, I visualize my placement in a social web, but the web is once-removed; there is a neutral, peaceful space between the web and me. In her introduction to *The*

Center of the Web: Women and Solitude, Delese Wear describes a time in her own life when she struggled with her need for solitude and her feelings about this need. She writes: "the idea of solitude and my pursuit of it became an important focus of my life. As I am apt to do, I thought I was an irregularity in this category Woman . . ." (xii). Twenty-five years ago, Nina Auerbach, in *Communities of Women: An Idea in Fiction,* wrote: "In British idiom, a manless woman is by definition an 'odd woman'" (30). However, even in the beginning of the twenty-first centry, I struggle for self-acceptance of my chosen life as a solitaire without a partner, man or woman.

As a child I loved being alone, especially to read in uninterrupted silence. Probably many academic women share such childhood memories. In *An American Childhood,* Annie Dillard describes her early pleasure in books. She remembers "reading books to delirium . . ." (80). She continues: "Books swept me away, one after the other, this way and that . . ." (85). It is still difficult, however, to find models of women who live alone and women writers who write from quiet and peaceful solitary spaces.

May Sarton is my major inspiration and touchstone as I live and work alone. Her *Plant Dreaming Deep* and *The House by the Sea* un-romantically chronicle the life of a writer who loves her house with great passion and comes to depend on it for companionship. In the life she describes, she also represents herself as a model of female self-sufficiency. Auerbach notes that "female self-sufficiency is not a postulate of this or that generation of feminists, but an inherent and powerful component of our shared cultural vision" (6). The mere fact of a woman owning or occupying her own house is always tied to female self-sufficiency to some extent. As the home owner or its sole occupant she alone does the "housework" in the most essential meaning of the word.

As long as publication is a necessity of success in academia—that is, for tenure, promotion, and job security—it is vital that academic women have some hours alone to read, think, and write. It is important to state, however, that this is also a great privilege. Because of poverty and/or the status and expectations of women in many cultures, it still remains a very elusive dream for many. Many women do not know what Virginia Woolf described as "the dignity which is the offspring of luxury and privacy and space" (*Room* 24). Nevertheless, all academic women must negotiate the issue of solitude in their lives in order to flourish in their jobs. Women who live alone often have an easier task. In *The House by the Sea,* May Sarton describes a particular bonus that solitaires often have. Sarton writes, "It is not that I work all day; it is that the work needs space around it. Hurry and flurry break into the deep still place where I can remember and sort out what I want to say . . ." (157). I'm very aware of the open space to think "around" all the ordinary activities I do, such as cooking or bathing. I have this undisturbed time and space because I live alone.

Despite what Jane Austen accomplished writing in a "common sitting room," I find it very difficult to write with noise around me and with interruptions. In fact, it's hard enough to focus amid my own interruptions, such as the "things-to-do-list" in my head. One academic I spoke with fights her own working-class family's values that define work as something that makes one appear busy and physically tires the body. She constantly struggles with her own demons when she wants to enjoy her solitude to think or to write. In addition, her friends, especially the ones with partners and dependent children, tend to think it's permissible to interrupt her time alone in a way she thinks they wouldn't interrupt a man's time. She recollects that her father was allowed to close his study door to "just think," but her mother never had the same opportunity.

Again, it is the open space "around" the work that living alone gives me and that I find so valuable in helping me to achieve focus and be more productive. I often get some of my best ideas while doing the everyday chores of domestic life. When I lived with others, this space was often filled with thoughts of the relationship I was "working on" at the time. My life is also much more orderly, now that my surroundings remain orderly. When I place a book or a file somewhere, it remains in that spot for me to find it. To quote Doris Grumbach in *Fifty Days of Solitude:* "Order, sequence, is a secret of being alone" (6). These orderly qualities are also, for many, essential ingredients in the writing process. To be able to clear a work space and create a pattern for one's work supports writing and allows the academic woman to engage in the conversation of scholarship.

Grumbach asked herself: "Would I have been as content alone if it were not for the beauty of this place?" (26). I enjoyed solitude before, but now the beauty of my house is an extra enrichment of the experience. Like Grumbach's beautiful place, my house, in addition to being a shelter, is a lovely piece of tangible beauty that enhances my life as a solitaire. May Sarton described a feeling for her house in *Plant Dreaming Deep* that matches my own.

> It is just the way rooms open into each other that is one of the charms of the house, a seduction that can only be felt when one is alone here. People often imagine that I must be lonely. How can I explain? I want to say, "Oh no! You see the house is with me." And it is with me in this particular way, as both a demand and a support, only when I am alone here. (59)

In order to broaden this conversation, we proposed this volume and advertised a call for contributions. We were overwhelmed by the response, both the number and the range of the content of the pieces. From what we received, we chose fourteen essays and one poem by fifteen contributors, in total. The prose poem is written "concurrently" by a man and a woman.

To organize the text, we've used the image of Virginia Woolf's dream of a woman, sitting at her own desk, alone in her own room, writing. The first section of this book focuses on the fact that she is alone. In the second section, the essays center on the writing that the woman is doing in her own room. The writers in the second section speak not only of their writerly desire for solitude, but also of their experiences of accommodation and of alternatives to the history of class-bound, masculine models of the creative process. The third and final section is built around the fact that she "owns" the space and what this ownership means. This section is devoted to personal essays about the authors' relationships to their homes, what herspace has meant to them as home-owning women.

Our book is like its subject: multidimensional, a mixture of genres. From literary theory to autobiographical narrative; from textual analysis to cultural critique; from literary citation to personal testimony— our book looks at women claiming and occupying herspace. But herspace has a variety of expressions and is variously inflected. Sometimes herspace is women's "owned" space; sometimes it is a specially structured setting, and the solitary time within that setting to engage in writing. Sometimes herspace is a mental state in which women meditate about their writing processes and thus about the spaces in which they write—a physical and a "metaphysical" space—i.e., a space produced through a reflection on space, a metaphorical space within, which corresponds to the actual physical room (or house) of one's own but is also a complex set of signals for autonomy, creativity, productivity, revolution, and other gender-inflected concerns. Her space is richly productive of meaning, and its complexity instigates multiple expressive agendas.

Section I, Women Theorizing Herspace—Solitude and Writing, commences with Suzette A. Henke's essay, "Women Alone: The Spinster's Art." Henke places her analysis of literary texts and the 1987 film *Fatal Attraction* within feminist discourse that has demanded a complete reassessment of narrow cultural assumptions concerning the spinster. She cites Mary Daly in *Gyn/Ecology: The Metaethics of Radical Feminism,* who provides new etymologies for the word *spinster* and attempts to reclaim the term in its radical suggestion of a bold, freethinking, independent woman, passionately spinning mysterious webs of creative selfhood. Henke also cites Daly's *First New Intergalactic Wickedary,* in which she offers a definition of a spinster as a "woman whose occupation is to spin, to participate in the whirling movement of creation; one who has chosen her Self, who defines her Self by choice neither in relation to children nor to men; who is Self-identified; a whirling dervish, Spiraling in New Time/Space" (*Wickedary,* 167). Throughout her essay, Henke uses *spinster* not in its pejorative connotation of lack, failure, barrenness, or impotence; but rather, in the discourse of Mary Daly, to designate a fiercely independent woman who chooses to remain husband-free and child-free.

In "Women Alone," Henke interrogates issues of spinsterly creativity in literary texts by Kate Chopin, Virginia Woolf, Gail Godwin, and Margaret Atwood, and she ends her study with a feminist analysis of Adrian Lyne's film, *Fatal Attraction.* She concludes that, even at the dawn of a new millennium, the independent creative woman remains a deviant, even dangerous figure in the mainstream American imagination.

Following Henke's contribution is "With Sure and Uncertain Footing: Negotiating the Terrain of a Solitude in May Sarton's Journals," by Lisette Schillig. Schillig's contribution is one of several that deal with May Sarton's autobiographical works. Sarton is a touchstone and a major example for women living and writing in their own homes. Any examination of the issue would necessarily have her at its center. To the extent that Sarton speaks to her inability to ever truly be "alone," this piece navigates the precariousness of *Sarton's* solitude, complicated as it is with the material realities and this essay also explores the responsibilities that position her not only as a woman alone, but as a writer who took on the burden of being a beacon of hope for other women who desire to seek themselves out fully as she does, but who also must fulfill the compromising roles of wife, mother, and nurturer. This sense of responsibility that Sarton has to her large following of readers reveals the dynamics of her own mythmaking propensities as a kind of lighthouse keeper, while it simultaneously heightens the tension between what she calls her "real life" and the life she performs for others.

Always for Sarton, Schillig notes, the house of solitude is both the physical and psychological place that makes it possible to start again, such that a journal becomes less (or as much) a means for diurnal reflection than a means to creatively work through her constant struggle for sanity. In experiencing and practicing such moments through her journal writing, Sarton works to subvert the possibilities of being contained in any permanent way by other cultural forces and institutions that operate upon her, whether these are evident through discourses of sexuality, aging, health, and death, or are borne out by the economic reality of living alone and needing to write a book a year in order to survive financially.

Christina Pugh's critical piece, "Unknown Women: Secular Solitude in the works of Alice Koller and May Sarton," pairs the autobiographical works of Sarton with those of philosopher Alice Koller, examining the culturally subversive portrayal of solitude and solitary space. By presenting solitude as a woman's choice, these works challenge our cultural scripting of women as predominantly relational beings. The essay shows the way in which both Koller and Sarton employ the tropes of pilgrimage and religious conversion in order to describe their secular choice. This borrowing of religious vocabulary reveals not only the dearth of secular metaphors for women's solitude, but also the authors' struggle with exemplariness. The essay goes on to discuss Koller's conceptualization of solitude as commensurate with analytic thinking, as well as Sarton's articulation of the "aesthetics of solitude" based upon the conflicts within the solitary state.

Lisa Johnson has lived alone for five years and "A Veritable Guest to Her Own Self" tells the story of that journey, the challenges of solitude, and the pride she takes in it. Her autobiographical narrative is mediated through the books she has read along the way. Authors such as Nancy Mairs, May Sarton, and Nancy Venable Raine provide a set of imagery and philosophies for her as a solitary woman. What the authors of these texts and Johnson have in common is the struggle to learn how to make lives of their own amid cultural forces that coerce women into partnerships, marriages, institutions of enclosure, and dependency.

Living alone, for Johnson, requires attention to the details of her body rhythms and surroundings. She makes use of the phrase "felicitous space," which comes from Judith Fryer's study of American women writers' treatments of their surroundings. Fryer, she notes, finds that women deal creatively with the spheres accorded to men and women by reconceiving enclosures as refuges, recasting the imprisoning house as a space of creativity; domesticity, long associated with women's inferior social status, instead becomes associated with spiritual growth, autonomy, and continuity. Johnson weaves autobiography and reflections on other women's words on solitude and creativity to explore, in positive terms, her relationship to the space of her own house and to her efforts to become a complete enough self to fully occupy the space. Like her writing, she says, learning to live alone takes practice and rapt attention.

Kristina Deffenbacher's "Woolf, Hurston, and the House of Self" engages domestic space as a metaphor for identity, discussing the history of male-owned houses and the relationship between theories of a unitary, stable individual and "a fortified space of property." Patriarchal enlightment subjectivity, for Deffenbacher, is challenged by Woolf and even more so by Hurston, as these authors bring their gender as well as race and class identities to bear on the theory of space. Patriarchal constructions of the individual and the house must maintain the illusion of self-control and self-possession, of distinct divisions within the house, and of a clear and strong separation between inside and outside.

Deffenbacher analyzes Woolf's rejection of this version of the house and the parallel identity, illustrating how Clarisa Dalloway dissolves both the illusion of "a fortified space of property" and the autonomous and unified individual. Then the essay turns to Hurston, arguing that *Their Eyes Were Watching God* transcends and thus revises the opposition between superstructured space and dissolved space, and between the autonomous (masculine) individual and Woolf's famously diffuse subject. The essay describes this revised home space—this her space—as "shelter in motion and motion in shelter," and the subjectivity that parallels this revised space as a fluid and productively transient one.

Deffenbacher makes important distinctions between how privileged white women occupy space in contrast to those women who have historically been subjected to race and class oppression. And it is Hurston who is able to imagine and transform the ways in which she and her characters occupy space and thus how they occupy their own lives.

The final contribution in Section I, is Annabelle Cone's "The Domestic Politics of Marguerite Duras." Cone notes that in the autobiographical works of Duras, the home figures as a site of confrontation between the political and economic necessities of the patriarchal order and the desire of woman, whether it be sexual, intellectual, or otherwise. Cone attempts to unravel the complex web of Duras's fictional and nonfictional accounts of the/her home. The autobiographical trilogy, *Un Barrage Contre le Pacifique, L'Amant,* and *L'Amant de la Chine du Nord,* set in French colonial Indochina, are contrasted with Duras's film *Natalie Granger* and several essays that include her country house as a setting or backdrop.

The home takes on a more paradoxical dimension as Duras attempts to reconcile her "poetical" agenda with a more universal political one that addresses the domestic needs of all women. For Duras, Cone asserts, the act of writing about the home renders the private public, and politicizes it by deconstructing the bourgeois ideology that has come to dominate it.

Section II, Women's Writing Spaces—Solitude and the Creative Process comprises three contributions about women who write. These authors describe the demands of the writing process, especially as it requires herspace. Their desire for solitude and space to pursue their writing amid peopled spaces leads them to a variety of negotiated and constituted sites of creativity.

Victoria Boynton writes about the split life of the white, middle-class female academic enmeshed in familial relations but attempting to do solitary intellectual work. This academic work requires effort, concentration, and time—requirements that she finds difficult to meet. Yet meeting the challenges of the writing life and claiming the necessary solitude are possibilities for contemporary women who do not live alone. Though troubled, the writing life can be a reality for women who occupy a domestic space peopled with partners and children. Boynton cites articulate women who have testified to the difficulties and the successes they have encountered attempting to live this split life.

Boynton describes the social and historical forces at work to construct middle-class women's identity as the good wife and mother in opposition to the image of the successful writer. She goes on to argue that the image of writer could usefully be revised for feminist purposes. However, it is not only women whom Boynton wants to include in the revised version of the writer in her writing space. More important, she complicates the notion of solitude itself, including a more critical take on the concept. The essay draws parallels between the valuable and mythic solitary state that writers and creative workers of all sorts crave, and the solitary confinement that women prisoners experience in contemporary prisons. Through this unconventional deconstruction of the notion of "solitary," Boynton offers a view of creative production and the space in which this process occurs as particular to privileged women.

In "Car, Kitchen, Canyon: Mother Writing," Claudia Mon Pere explores her own attempts at achieving solitude for her poetry and fiction as a teacher, director of a writing program, and mother of young children. Grounded in details of domesticity, baby-sitters, broken appliances, grocery shopping, and dishwashing, this personal narrative addresses Mon Pere's shifting notions of solitude at different life stages and her contradictory responses to the interior world of her house and the natural world outside. She also contrasts the collaborative nature of composition studies with the solitary nature of creative writing.

In "Between the Study and the Living Room: Writing Alone and with Others," Eleanor Berry draws on a variety of texts and her own experience as a poet to convey the value, for women writers, of a rhythmic alternation of solitude and society, of movement back and forth between the solitary space of the study and the social space of the living room.

The essay locates the value of a work space of her own for the woman writer in a combination of the freedom from the demands of family and society that Virginia Woolf stresses in *A Room of One's Own* and the conduciveness to daydream and creativity that Gaston Bachelard explores in *The Poetics of Space*. Berry looks to May Sarton's *Journal of a Solitude* as an expression of both these values, and also considers the interruptibility and responsiveness exhibited by Sarton and discussed by Mary Catherine Bateson in *Composing a Life* as potentially positive for writers.

Berry considers the origins of one of her own poems and draws on Woolf's representation, in *To the Lighthouse,* of Lily Briscoe's struggle to maintain confidence in her artistic vision and on Anne Ruggles Gere's analysis of the functions served by writers' groups outside of academe. She finds in an effectively functioning writers' group a space of permission to complement the space of brooding, to which the writer returns to compose and revise.

Section III, Women Writing Herspace— Personal Takes on Home, begins with Jan Wellington's essay "What to Make of Missing Children (A Life Slipping into Fiction)." In her own words, it issues from the pen of a woman who has, in her forty-plus years, lost several children, suffered from writer's block, found her writer's voice, and, in the process, treasured and lamented her plentiful solitude. The time-honored metaphor that marries writing and procreation is central to her essay, which plays variations on the "womb/tomb" nature of solitude, its "Janus-faced" potential to nurture and strangle.

The essay begins with an autobiographical narrative that centers on the loss of children and ends with a critical-poetical meditation on what it means (to the woman, the teacher, and the writer) to read a work of fictional autobiography, such as Charlotte Brontë's *Jane Eyre,* while one is losing a child. Linking and infusing these parts is the notion of fiction. Lurking within Wellington's text is the thesis that fiction or, more properly, the marriage of fact and fiction, is an antidote to solipsism that enables the solitary woman writer to "people" her solitude with creativity and hope.

In Claudia A. Limbert's contribution "The Little Gray House and Me," she tells a very personal story of her childhood dream of a little gray house and the eventual realization of this dream. In describing her house, Limbert writes:

> When I was a child growing up in poverty in the Missouri Ozarks, I enjoyed drawing. In particular, I would draw a house that I drew as any child would when asked to depict his or her idea of "home." It was a little gray house with a dark roof, white trim, a big brick chimney on one end, and a sidewalk right up to the front step. I drew endless versions of that house, but they were basically the same and they all meant "home" and "security" to that little girl in that time and place. (231)

Limbert's narrative of her love affair with the little gray house she now owns reads like an adventure story. The reader feels caught up, along with the writer, in the process of remodeling, painting, and furnishing the house. Now an occupant of the house, she relates the difficulty of explaining how much the house means to her. Despite her expressed self-doubts, Limbert most certainly has found the right words. Each room is described lovingly with expressive and concrete detail.

Maria Brown's personal narrative, "The Colors and the Light," also tells the story of purchasing her own home, including all the concrete details of the process, from looking at properties with a real estate agent, to her first night sleeping on an air mattress, to do-it-yourself projects. Her decision to be a home owner was reached at age twenty-six and was very much a decision based on a desire for security and stability, in contrast to the turbulent homes of her childhood. She tells the reader that it was "one of the best decisions" she has ever made.

Anne Mamary's "A Woman's Place" weaves descriptions of her nineteenth-century red brick house with her multicultural feminist work at a small undergraduate college. Refusing the dualism of public/private and work/home, Mamary's essay moves seamlessly from house to garden to classroom. Although it may no longer be true that a woman needs a husband to buy and live in her own house, the piece suggests that academia still demands a wifelike loyalty—in thought, word, and deed—from its female employees. The essay describes the women-centered work of the author at the college, work that did not offer unconditional loving support of individual men or a white patriarchal academic project, work that ultimately made it impossible to stay at her job and, therefore, in her house.

Mary Rose's autobiographical essay, "Reframing My Life," chronicles the fifth decade of her life, following a divorce, in which she learned to live by herself and love her space, finding that it was just as fulfilling as married life might be. Her contribution is divided into three general areas. In the first part she deals with how she built a life for herself in a new space and learned to be content in her own company. In the second section she explores her connection with the outside world, how she changed from seeing herself as a woman who was financially supported and taken care of to a woman capable and confident of supporting herself. In the third part she discusses her relationships with the men in her life and her growing sense of independence from the authority they represented for her, especially as a woman who has entered a relationship to her own space.

The last entry is this collection is what its authors, H. Kassia Fleisher and Joe Amato call a collaborative piece on collaboration. In "An &/or Peace Performance," two voices talk down both sides of the pages simultaneously. Fleisher notes that a major issue for her in collaborating with a man in a heterosexual partnership is the problem of finding space for her own voice within that collaboration. The lack of space in the house in which they live and work is a metaphor for the lack of "headroom" for the woman in the partnership. The Bride, in the prose poem, faces this rather pedestrian concern while the Groom hovers in abstraction, which is to say he doesn't face the concern and barely registers it, and so has the leisure to abstract. In this way, what the piece does is enact a primary issue of feminist history, the question of whether and why women and men write differently.

This book represents the culmination of several years of thinking and writing on three conjoined topics of personal interest: women and solitude, women as writers, and women claiming and designing their own spaces to support creativity. The topics are conjoined in the book and similarly conjoined in our own personal experiences: emotional, intellectual, and financial. The fifteen contributors convey their respective interest in the topics, in general, and in deconstructing its meanings through literary criticism, feminist theory, and personal narratives. They represent the diverse feminist approaches to the topic. Most work within academia, but some do not. Also, several of the academics write narratives that are entirely personal and autobiographical. Herspace—its mode, materials of construction, as well as its meaning to the user—is richly diverse and yet unique to the women who occupy it.

WORKS CITED

Auerbach, Nina. *Communities of Women: An Idea in Fiction*. Cambridge: Harvard U P, 1978.

Daly, Mary. *Webster's First New Intergalactic Wickedary of the English Language*. Boston: Beacon Press, 1987.

Dillard, Annie. *An American Childhood*. New York: Harper & Row, 1987.

Dubois, Ellen Carol, ed. *The Elizabeth Cady Stanton-Susan B. Anthony Reader: Correspondence, Writings, Speeches*, Rev. ed. Boston: Northeastern U P, 1992 (Parts One–Three, 1981).

Grumbach, Doris. *Fifty Days of Solitude*. Boston: Beacon Press, 1994.

Horowitz, Helen Lefkowitz. *Alma Mater: Design and Experience in the Women's Colleges from Their Nineteenth-Century Beginnings to the 1930s*. New York: Alfred Knopf, 1984.

Pugh, Christina. "Re: Solitude/Women's Autobiography." E-mail to Jo Malin. August 4, 1999.

Sarton, May. *The House by the Sea*. New York: Norton, 1977.

_____. *Plant Dreaming Deep*. 1968. New York: Norton, 1996.

Scudder, Vida Dutton. *On Journey*. New York: Dutton, 1937.

Shulman, Alix Kates. *Drinking the Rain*. 1995. New York: Penguin, 1996.

Wear, Delese, ed. *The Center of the Web: Women and Solitude*. Albany: State U of New York P, 1993.

Woolf, Virginia. *A Room of One's Own*. New York: Harcourt, 1929/1957.

_____. *To the Lighthouse*. New York: Harcourt, 1927.

SECTION I:
WOMEN THEORIZING HERSPACE—
SOLITUDE AND WRITING

In a photo above the month of June on the 1998 Pomegranate calendar, *The Writer's Desk,* Toni Morrison sits on a couch in an elegant bathrobe. She has her pen in hand, a spiral notebook propped on her lap in a sparsely furnished room with glowing wood floors. Under the photograph are Morrison's words describing her writing process: "I always get up and make a cup of coffee while it is dark—it must be dark—and then I drink the coffee and watch the light come. . . . For me this ritual comprises my preparation to enter a space that I can only call nonsecular." This space is the locale of the solitary woman writer, a special place where the creative mind is invited to open; it is herspace.

Definitive aspects of herspace are privacy and singularity. The woman who occupies it is alone, able to concentrate on the dance of thought and emotion, able to funnel that dance into creation—writing along with her thought, making art out of the quiet. She most often seems like a hermit, taking satisfaction from her lone standing and nourishment from solitude. However, women alone have often been viewed from a different angle, have experienced their reflections in the mirror of culture in frightening ways. As Mary Anne Ferguson argues, "Throughout history women who have lived alone have been looked on with suspicion, either as unnatural or as having failed: the witch has been feared and persecuted; the 'old maid' treated with contempt or, at best, viewed with pity." Women without men become targets (339). As the institution of the family exerts its power, women who wish to live differently must be courageous and passionate to choose writing as an alternative to beauty competitions and baby production. Not only is the writing life a radical alternative to the cultural default settings, but it is a solitary occupation, requiring, for most, a life independent of the typical heterosexual plot. All serious writers crave solitude and uninterrupted time, and ideally plan for it. But solitude in herspace takes many shapes.

In their variety, the essays in this opening section, titled Women Theorizing Herspace—Solitude and Writing, set up the book as a whole. They look at women alone who claim and occupy their own space for the purposes of creative production. These women write about writing and about the space in which they write. This very special space is physical and metaphorical, an external space mirrored and refracted internally. As a result, the actual physical room (or house) of one's own stands for a complex set of signals for autonomy, creativity, productivity, and revolution.

The space functions in multiple ways and evokes other gender-inflected concerns and agendas. Though the first section is the most theoretical and scholarly of the three, it deviates from the writing conventions that have traditionally governed scholarship as it mixes voices, especially the personal voice, bringing a writerly identity intentionally forward. By including such strategic essays, we hope to make explicit how solitary locales feel in their particularities as they are inhabited by productive women living alone and tethered by complex social and historical positionings.

WORK CITED

Ferguson, Mary Anne. *Images of Women in Literature,* Fifth Edition. Boston: Houghton Mifflin, 1991.

Women Alone: The Spinster's Art

Suzette A. Henke

SPINSTER—1. A woman who has remained single beyond the conventional age for marrying. 2. A single woman. 3. A woman whose occupation is spinning. *(Webster's II: New Riverside University Dictionary)*

One cannot begin to touch the *Stabat Mater*—the image of woman as specular object, the invaginated container of masculine seed and male fantasy. The ideology of woman invariably sees her as *le deuxieme sexe*—not only secondary to man but perpetually defined by virtue of a sexual potential that can be fully acceptable only if actualized through fertility and childbearing. "Ripeness is all" in the implacable (male) Western construction of the female body as specular object—an invaginated container whose reproductive capacities endow the "other" sex (feminine) with maturity and womanhood and valorize empty uterine spaces through the legitimate production of offspring that assure the continuation of patriarchal blood/power/genes/genius.

As Julia Kristeva observes, "we live in a civilization in which the *consecrated* (religious or secular) representation of femininity is subsumed under maternity. Under close examination, however, this maternity turns out to be an adult (male and female) fantasy of a lost continent" (99). The Madonna informs every archetypal construction of the female subject in a world based exclusively on what Gayatri Chakravorty Spivak calls a philosophy of "uterine social organization."[1] The womb that remains empty is defamed as sterile and barren, a bodily organ whose menstrual roses signify flowers without fruit, a metaphorical wound scorned by the dominant requisites of social production.

Historically, women have chosen either to be sexually active within or outside of the social institution of marriage, or to remain celibate for religious, social, or psychological reasons. Until the past hundred years, a woman's voluntary engagement in copulation usually implied her tacit agreement to accept the maternal responsibilities engendered by pregnancy. Surely some women under these conditions, when faced with the reproductive urgency of the species, must either have gone mad or steadfastly guarded their virginity, choosing witchery or the nunnery over conventional societal expectations. The aging spinster was liable to charges of communal hostility that indicted the unsheltered crone with such contemptuous epithets as "hag," "witch," or "harridan." As Mary Daly explains, "witch-hunters sought to purify their society . . . of these 'indigestible' elements—women whose physical, intellectual, economic, moral, and spiritual independence and activity profoundly threatened the male monopoly in every sphere" (*Gyn/Ecology* 184).

The term *spinster* has long been used as a derogatory label to marginalize the superfluous woman, whose role in society is perceived as liminal and, by its very idiosyncrasy, perplexing. The spinster is, by definition, *"de trop"*—a supplement to traditional community organization and an outsider whose disruptive and subversive behavior might, indeed, make her an outcast, a rebel, or a bohemian artist. The unmarried woman, in order to remain part of the society that shuns her, must spin a palpable web of social productivity. As the exchange value of her sexuality diminishes over time, she feels obliged to compensate the collective economy for the reproductive function suppressed or denied by her refusal of nature's biological imperative.[2]

Until the twentieth-century resurgence of the feminist movement, the term *spinster* served as a universal label of denigration and opprobrium. Well into the nineteenth century it was common knowledge that a dutiful daughter was expected to bide her time until she was claimed as a possession by the Prince Charming who captured both her heart and her dowry. At some indefinable age, the ripe young woman displayed on the marriage market became overripe—spoiled, rotten, and unmarketable. Unclaimed, she withered and shriveled.

What was left was the husk of a strong and husky woman—a maiden aunt or self-sufficient crone who, unprotected by husband or family, degenerated into a curious *isolée.*

Current feminist discourse has recently demanded a complete re-assessment of narrow cultural assumptions concerning the category of spinster. In *Gyn/Ecology: The Metaethics of Radical Feminism,* Mary Daly provides new etymologies for the word *spinster* and attempts to reclaim the term in its radical suggestion of a bold, freethinking, independent woman, passionately spinning mysterious webs of creative selfhood. In her Webster's *First New Intergalactic Wickedary of the English Language,* Daly describes the spinster as a "woman whose occupation is to spin, to participate in the whirling movement of creation; one who has chosen her Self, who defines her Self by choice neither in relation to children nor to men; who is Self-identified; a whirling dervish, Spiraling in New Time/Space" (*Wickedary* 167). Throughout the following essay, I have used the word *spinster* not in its pejorative connotations of lack, failure, barrenness, or impotence, but rather in the discourse of Mary Daly, to designate a fiercely independent woman who chooses to remain husband-free and child-free in the interest of personal, spiritual, vocational, or creative self-development.

The spinster is there, always, as society's well-kept secret resource—a woman whose life is devoted to the spinning of cloth or the spinning of tales, to the weaving of Penelopean tapestries that, in the communal fantasmatic imagination, implicitly recall and call out to an absent Odysseus. The spinner of language and poetry, of music and art, anxiously gives birth from her entrails to magnificent fabulations, intricate spiderwebs of solitary creativity that exude an oddly Circean *odor di femina.* Located on the margins of cultural discourse and exiled from the seamless web of domestic organization, she purposively spins herself an emotional cloak of vocational enterprise to keep off the chill of man-free winter nights. The productions of this brashly unreproductive female spin themselves out of a deracinated consciousness, a space beyond the seemingly inexorable webs of domestic responsibility. Often alone and sometimes defenseless, she continues to spin wheels and words, webs and visions, fantasies and frustrations—all collected in the marginal spaces allotted to the outcast curiously at odds with contemporary society's prominent domestic center.

Her forerunners in the nineteenth century were independent artists or madwomen wandering through the pages of a family-oriented fiction made for an audience of middle-class burghers. Only artistic talent could justify a woman's radical separation from tightly knit enclaves of class and capitalistic production in the Victorian era. The aloof and extraordinary Mademoiselle Reisz can play beautiful sonatas that orchestrate Kate Chopin's novel *The Awakening*. But this piano-plunking crone has paid a heavy price for investing all her talents in a life devoted exclusively to music. Friendship and love are both unknown to her. Art, demanding all, has condemned her to emotional bankruptcy.

The twentieth-century spinster cuts a somewhat better figure, though she is still sketched deliberately in enigmatic tones.[3] No hag or harridan, she hangs on the edge of social configurations that would, if she let them, engulf her. She laughs at the charms of comfortable domesticity and mocks its glittering power. The contemporary spinster has often chosen to remain childless or unmarried for the sake of marshaling her own creative resources: first, in the interest of self-creation; then for the sake of art, beauty, freedom, relationship, or political power. I do not mean to invoke the age-old antithesis between maternity and art but rather to suggest that, for some women, the redemptive egotism often claimed as a valorization for male genius might provide a necessary haven from societal expectations. If Eve spanned and Adam delved in the postlapsarian world of productive labor, the spinster heeds the call to a vocation of intellectual or artistic production free of the reproductive urgency of the species. Though detached from sex-stereotyped domestic responsibilities, she feels, like any nun or mother, passionately committed to the life choices that determine her situation. Spinning like a whirling dervish, she is likely to forget the world and take refuge in fruitful contemplation.

Virginia Woolf's Lily Briscoe emerges in *To the Lighthouse* as one of the great spinster-artists of twentieth-century literature. Compared to Mrs. Ramsay and her eight angelic children, Lily feels like an unspoiled virgin, pure as a lily and as ingenuous as an adolescent schoolgirl. In awe of the ripe maternity of a woman she adores, Lily perceives herself as a fragile and diminished being. An "unmarried woman has missed the best of life," chirps Mrs. Ramsay, thus "presiding with immutable calm over destinies which she [has] completely failed to understand" (77-78). The injunction of this inveterate matchmaker undermines Lily's self-confidence and threatens her tenuous self-esteem. She desperately wants to please the surrogate mother whose words are internalized in the shape of a female imago. There they sit, those words—to rile and rot at the heart of Lily's spinsterly soul. But Lily cannot, finally, please the imaginary mother of her dreams by sacrificing all in order to embrace the mandates of maternity.

Like a child pleading for exemption from a homework assignment, Lily begs for release from the universal law that legislates the inexorable scripts of gender—marriage, mating, and motherhood.

> Oh, but, Lily would say, there was her father; her home; even, had she dared to say it, her painting. But all this seemed so little, so virginal, against the other. Yet . . . gathering a desperate courage she would urge her own exemption from the universal law; plead for it; she liked to be alone; she liked to be herself; she was not made for that; and so . . . confront Mrs. Ramsay's simple certainty . . . that her dear Lily, her little Brisk, was a fool. (77-78)

Despite feelings of timidity and impotence in the face of Mrs. Ramsay's gospel of marital bliss and her insistent proselytizing, Lily courageously marshals all her psychological resources in a timorous defense of spinsterhood—her art; her needy father; her own marginality; and, finally, herself.

Relishing a succulent morsel of *boeuf en daube* at the family dinner and contemplating the awe-inspiring spectacle of possessive rage flaring up in the newly betrothed Paul Rayley, Lily feels overwhelmed by a sense of melancholy when she envisages the two lovers, Paul and Minta, led like lambs to a socially sanctioned nuptial altar. She casts a skeptical gaze on the testosterone-driven male who "turn[s] on her cheek the heat of love, its horror, its cruelty, its unscrupulosity" (154). The eruption of Eros, it would seem, gives rise to implacable atavistic drives toward swaggering domestic appropriation and conjugal jealousy. Frightened by the imaginary fangs of lust, Lily takes refuge in aesthetic meditation. "For, at any rate, she said to herself, catching sight of the salt cellar on the pattern, she need not marry, thank Heaven: she need not undergo that degradation" (154). Years later, she remembers having "only escaped by the skin of her teeth. . . . She had been looking at the tablecloth, and it had flashed upon her that she would move the tree to the middle, and need never marry anybody, and she had felt an enormous exultation" (262).

Lily's psychological triumph constitutes a centering of her decentered life in the roots of artistic creativity. Like the symbolic tree in the middle of her painting, art provides the virginal spinster with a spiritual and emotional ground for the blossoming of her talent and personality. Although her pictures might eventually be stashed in closets and hidden under couches, they nonetheless construct a meaningful focus for an otherwise deracinated, fluid, and fragmented set of experiences. Mrs. Ramsay, the matriarch haunting Lily's sentimental imagination, was, quite simply, wrong in her assessment of little Brisk. In opting for lifelong spinsterhood, Lily finally lays to rest the Victorian "Angel in the House" still stalking the female consciousness at the beginning of the twentieth century.

By the end of the novel, Lily comes to realize that she has constructed Mrs. Ramsay as a false antagonist—a maternal imago self-consciously introjected as a defense against emotional insecurity and atavistic fears of social disapproval. Remembering a beach excursion ten years earlier, Lily pictures herself on the shore with Charles Tansley and understands, for the first time, that Mrs. Ramsay had succeeded in fashioning out of "their miserable silliness and spite" a unified "moment of friendship and liking" that recurs "almost like a work of art" (240). In a sudden flash of recognition, she acknowledges the older woman as an artist of human relations who has remained, all along, both a compatriot and a friend:

> Mrs. Ramsay saying, "Life stand still here"; Mrs. Ramsay making of the moment something permanent (as in another sphere Lily herself tried to make of the moment something permanent)—this was the nature of a revelation. In the midst of chaos there was shape; this eternal passing and flowing . . . was struck into stability. . . . "Mrs. Ramsay!" she repeated. She owed it all to her. (240-241)

Through a fantasmatic process informing the artistic act, Lily nostalgically apprehends the benevolent shade of Mrs. Ramsay sitting by her side and encouraging her work in progress. Thinking of this foremother as a silent spiritual guardian, the artist struggles to identify "the human apparatus for painting or for feeling." She observes:

> Love had a thousand shapes. There might be lovers whose gift it was to choose out the elements of things and place them together and so, giving them a wholeness not theirs in life, make of some scene, or meeting of people . . . one of those globed compacted things over which thought lingers, and love plays. (286)

Mrs. Ramsay has been one kind of creator, Lily another. Each has devoted her life to one of the numerous protean shapes of art—painting, sympathy, or love. By remaining true to her own inspired vision, Lily gives birth to a "globed, compacted thing" (286) that will prove to be a gift and an offering to the memory of her maternal muse.

In *The Reproduction of Mothering,* Nancy Chodorow examines the female child's preoedipal attachment to the mother and concludes that women, in adulthood, can survive only by learning to nurture their own egos. Never fully separated from a narcissistic attachment to the mother figure, the mature female must transfer preoedipal dependence from her biological mother to an authentically mothering self in adult life. A dependent woman who looks for mothers everywhere—in husband, children, and female friends—may nonetheless find herself alone and motherless if she does not learn to feed and foster her own creative talents in the interest of empowered subjectivity.

Some spinsters create art; others, only themselves. The protagonists in two of Gail Godwin's novels, *The Odd Woman* (1974) and *A Mother and Two Daughters* (1982), are both spinsters from the academic ivory tower. Like the Lady of Shalott, they spin webs of romantic illusion reflected in mirrors of emotional need. Can a gifted and intelligent woman remain happily unmarried in contemporary society? The question is fraught with ambiguities and riddled with indeterminacy—especially if the female subject emerges from Gail Godwin's richly provocative feminist imagination. After reading *The Odd Woman,* a 1970s' visitor to earth from another planet might reasonably conclude that the entire supply of interesting middle-aged male human beings was limited to semiavailable university professors whose academic lives focus on the pursuit of fellowships and the production of scholarly articles, and whose careers are facilitated by shoe boxes full of notes tended by docile wives who solicitously index the contents of the shoe boxes. (Fortunately, this last job has now been rendered obsolete by the advent of more efficient word-processing systems).

Why, one might wonder, doesn't "plain Jane" Clifford, also a university professor, write her *own* book? Apply for a Fulbright grant or a Guggenheim Fellowship? Stuff her *own* shoe boxes (or computer files) with notes and her mind full of exciting ideas? A professional spinster, she obsessively spins around a patriarchal figure who subtly exploits her but resolutely refuses the prize of emotional commitment. Her egotistical lover needs psychologically to separate the durable mommy/wife from the ephemeral hetaera/mistress. Godwin's protagonist refuses her lover's secretarial assignments but seems curiously maladroit in organizing her own creative and scholarly future. She spins wheels of emotional frustration rather than the kind of computer "daisy wheels" that might offer more palpable intellectual and scholarly rewards.

Love, too, has its pitfalls in these days of casual sex and truncated romance. Cate Strickland, the thirty-nine-year-old protagonist of Godwin's *A Mother and Two Daughters,* is an academic woman perched on the brink of middle age—at the height of her career and with everything ostensibly under control, until she suddenly discovers that her ingenuous illusion of mastery is nothing more than a naive fabrication. When her diaphragm fails, Cate finds herself unexpectedly pregnant, and her bubble of complacency abruptly shatters. Her sense of mastery gives way to the shock of acknowledging that her body has been colonized by the species. Caught between nature's generative drive and her cherished dream of solitude, Cate must choose between the pleasures of self-sufficiency and the emotional satisfactions of maternal attachment. "A baby's not a symbol," she insists. "A flesh-and-blood baby means you have to go back into the fallen world and take what you can get till that baby grows up. The baby keeps you a hostage in the world" (*Mother* 408-409).

In the end, the need for solitude triumphs in Cate's life and future, but not without exacting a significant psychological price. In explaining her reasons for terminating an unplanned pregnancy, Cate offers a passionate and pellucid manifesto of contemporary spinsterhood:

> I want to be free to conduct my own sustained inquiry into this maddening, fascinating, infuriating world I was born into. . . . I can stand being obscure. I can stand being by myself. I can even stand growing old alone, without an "admiring bog," or a man to love me, or children to "invest my unfulfilled dreams in." . . . I think I can forego the luxuries if I have the freedom and mobility to investigate things as they are. (*Mother* 335)

Godwin's cerebral protagonist realizes that personal sacrifices have taken such a toll on her emotional resources that she can no longer dream of an endlessly absorbing future. "How infinite the possibilities had seemed; how limitless the frontiers! But now, many of the possibilities had been exhausted, or tried and found wanting. . . . And the frontiers were shrinking. Deterioration had set in" (*Mother* 434). In her fiercely guarded privacy, Cate joins the marginalized crones and purported witches of women's history, the Hester Prynnes and the mute, inglorious Jane Austens who startle by their queerness and sheer inscrutability.

Queerest of all, perhaps, is the spinster protagonist of Margaret Atwood's mythic and lyrical novel *Surfacing,* a text that Cate Strickland appears to be reading in *A Mother and Two Daughters,* about a woman "down on all fours naked in the forest . . . trying to get back to her basic instincts and wondering if she could grow hair over her whole body" (*Mother* 401). Although Godwin's character is somewhat perturbed by the extravagance of this feminist utopian fantasy, she reflects that "at least these writers are trying to stretch the limits of communal imagination and envision new ways to live" (*Mother* 401-402).

Margaret Atwood's protagonist in *Surfacing* is haunted throughout the novel by nightmare recollections of a loveless affair that culminated in traumatic abortion.[4] "He said it wasn't a person, only an animal. . . . I let them catch it. I could have said No but I didn't" (*Surfacing* 170). Screening the unbearable event in fantasies of marriage and childbirth, she gradually plunges into the unconscious and recuperates buried fragments of guilt and remorse. Her private meditations border on madness as they articulate a long lamentation, a cry of bereavement for a "section of my own life, sliced off from me like a Siamese twin, my own flesh canceled" (56). Bitterly, she recalls: "I stank of salt and antiseptic, they had planted death in me like a seed" (169).

The horror of pregnancy loss and the pain of longing for a fantasized child drives Atwood's heroine in the direction of loveless mating, a man-free pregnancy, and aspirations toward an amorous union with a protective Mother Earth. This primitive Amazonian purity imbues the notion of spinsterhood with utopian dreams of an exclusively female and matriarchal territory. In response to a psychological wound that she interprets as symbolic castration, only one solution seems plausible for Atwood's bereft survivor—the atonement offered by pleasureless sex and a celebratory, pleasure-filled pregnancy. In fantasmatic expectation of healing through recuperation of the lost fetal life embedded in melancholia, she triumphantly proclaims:

> I can feel my lost child surfacing within me, forgiving me, rising from the lake where it has been prisoned for so long, its eyes and teeth phosphorescent. . . . The baby will slip out as easily as an egg, a kitten, and I'll lick it off and bite the cord. . . . In the morning . . . it will be covered with shining fur, a god. (*Surfacing* 191)

Although this scene of rutting and premeditated maternity would seem to border on the margins of madness, the heroine who surfaces at the end of Atwood's mythic narrative gives evidence of psychological lucidity and a sense of feminist resolve: "This above all, to refuse to be a victim. Unless I can do that I can do nothing. . . . But I assume it; if I die, it dies, if I starve it starves with me. It might be the first one, the first true human" (*Surfacing* 222-223).

Such mystical/maternal exultation is later inverted in Janus images as the parodic center of Atwood's 1986 novel *The Handmaid's Tale*. In the dystopian world of Gilead, women are pampered for their reproductive possibilities and either exploited for their childbearing capacities or damned for their infertility and barrenness. Those rebellious "unwomen" who cannot or will not reproduce are sent off to the

Colonies to clean up toxic waste dumps and radiation spills until they themselves waste away and succumb to cancer. Women must either consent to fertility or kill themselves. In a society that has virtually obliterated the legitimate category of spinster, self-destruction becomes the only possible exit and an existential mode of revolutionary behavior. Lascivious or self-willed females function as parodies of pornography, living dolls who caricature temptresses and tease the commanders in pantomimes of sexual titillation. Scapegoats are maimed or torn to pieces in a bizarre ritual of savage "particicution." Terror reigns. Ripeness and obedience are all.

Alice Walker's protagonist in her 1977 novel *Meridian* exhibits a different kind of feminist defiance when she abandons her infant son in favor of personal healing and political agency. Meridian Hill self-consciously chooses spinsterhood in lieu of maternal bonding and the domestic commitments of child rearing. Relinquishing the child of her body, she adopts the role of nurturer and surrogate mother to emotional waifs such as Truman and Lynne, who participate in a collective but personally disastrous struggle for social revolution. Separated from her infant son, Meridian succeeds in giving birth to herself as a politically efficacious being in the world—a saint, a mystic, a prophet, and a communal hero. When Truman expresses concern over her solitary ascetic life, Meridian protests that it is precisely her isolation that validates the power of her commitment. Female autonomy testifies to her revolutionary act of noncompliance.

Even at the beginning of a new millennium, the spinster remains something of a social anomaly, often perceived as marginal, threatening, mysterious, and subversive. A surprisingly recalcitrant conservatism continues to relegate the unmarried woman to a position of deviance by characterizing her as weird, crazy, sinful, or, at the very least, unhappy. The "new free woman" of the late twentieth century is still considered suspect if she remains resolutely detached from the rapidly disintegrating nuclear family. Society's judgment is certainly less brutal than in the days of witch burning, but it continues to evoke subtle censure everywhere in popular culture.

As a final example of the denigrated and dangerous single woman, I have chosen the female protagonist of Adrian Lyne's 1987 box-office thriller *Fatal Attraction*. Glenn Close stars as the infamous Alex Forrest; Michael Douglas plays Daniel Gallagher, a successful and happily married lawyer; Anne Archer rounds out the cast in her role as Beth Gallagher, the outraged but victorious wife. If film be a mirror of popular social consciousness, then James Dearden's melo-dramatic screenplay offers a remarkable reflection of reactionary mores at the end of the twentieth century. Although Glenn Close gives a stirring performance, the movie manipulates its audience into accepting age-old stereotypes about the predatory single woman. De-spite her professional accomplishments in the publishing world, Alex Forrest is quietly going crazy for lack of a man. Part witch, part nym-phomaniac, she lures the unsuspecting Dan Gallagher to her lair in an urban meatpacking district, where both proceed to pant and paw at each other in bestial frenzy. This modern-day Circe feels rejected af-ter a one-night stand and compulsively slits her wrists to lengthen the liaison. Several weeks later, on a subway station platform, she an-nounces the fertile results of their heated encounter. From this mo-ment on, the chaos—and the chase—begins.

The message of the film is clear. Women of a certain age who lack a legitimate partner are at best evil temptresses who prey on other women's mates; at worst, psychotic killers who fight to the death to gain possession of their inseminators. Glenn Close emerges as a terri-fying projection of the American male's Freudian nightmares. She is a witch (dressed in black) who seduces a cocksure but naive philan-derer, then turns on him like a spider, to appropriate and devour. She is the mental patient (dressed in white) whose isolation gives birth to psychotic fantasy. Alone in her garret, she obsessively switches a lu-minous lamp on and off, playing it like a visual metronome to eerie strains of *Madame Butterfly* (the death scene, of course). James Dearden and Adrian Lyne have offered us a remake of Alfred Hitch-cock's *Psycho* done in drag. The terrifying phallic mother, wielding her penile dagger, rises like a vampire from a blood-filled bathtub and is finally defeated by the loyal, dutiful, long-suffering wife. Leonard Maltin acerbically comments that the thriller "telegraphs most of its suspense payoffs and features a finale that seems more appropriate to RAMBO" (414).

Fatal Attraction is so riveting, however, that as members of the au-dience we have little time to analyze its psychosexual strategies. We are programmed from the start to feel contempt for Alex Forrest with her black dress and Medusa locks.[5] Our reactions are Pavlovian.

Frozen in spectatorial horror, we are seized by atavistic impulses to kill, maim, and obliterate this nympho-psycho character, get rid of the monster (Scylla and Charybdis rolled into one), and go home to Mommy. Unsuspecting males in the audience have undoubtedly grasped the transparent moral of this celluloid fable: "Don't play around. The predatory spinster/spider woman might catch you unawares." Females leave the theater with an analogous subliminal imperative: "Trap your conjugal mate early and cling to him with Amazonian ferocity."

Here is contemporary America's most vicious stereotypical projection of the "swinging spinster" (a deliberate oxymoron). Only the most sensitive of viewers will interpret Dearden's script critically, from a feminist perspective, and raise objections to his celluloid scapegoating of the central female character. "To reread as a woman," explains Nancy Miller, "is at least to imagine the lady's place; to imagine while reading the place of a woman's body; to read reminded that her identity is also re-membered in stories of the body" (355). Although Alex Forrest is no Hester Prynne, one might discern in the film's phallic modeling a shadow of the kind of puritanical repugnance and hypocrisy reminiscent of Hawthorne's *Scarlet Letter*. Underneath all the glitter and horror of this ghoulish psychodrama lurks America's perennial contempt for women who challenge the social order by conceiving children outside the legal sanctions of marriage. Alex Forrest is guilty of the unforgivable sin of accidental pregnancy, implicitly caused by her ruthlessness and irresponsibility. For this, no punishment seems too harsh—desertion, battering, strangling, drowning, and finally a fatal shooting.

What gets obscured in this suspenseful witch-hunt is the genuine pathos of the antagonist's victimization by an age-old female dilemma. After all, this woman did not apparently plan to get herself knocked up. A spinster in her late thirties, she believed herself infertile after a midlife miscarriage. She might, in fact, have been suffering from post-traumatic stress disorder evinced by the trauma of pregnancy loss—a dimension of her unstable psychology never explored on-screen. The lady has, in effect, been impregnated and abandoned. If she weren't so crazy and vindictive, one would probably feel sympathy for this curiously vulnerable female vomiting in the bushes and demanding recognition from the man whose child she is carrying.

What about the moral obligations of Dan Gallagher—an arrogant attorney who appears to be upwardly mobile, self-satisfied, and just a trifle narcissistic? Why, one might ask, in the age of AIDS, herpes, and syphilis, does this smart professional chap not pop into the local drugstore and arm himself (the wrong appendage, to be sure) with a dozen condoms? Couldn't he at least take a moment to inquire about contraception before banging away in that freight elevator? Shouldn't this mature, sexually active male take some responsibility for the fate of his sperm? And why is the urbane Gallagher so shocked to discover, in the sepulchral environs of a subway tunnel, just exactly how it is that babies are made? Not once does he empathize with Alex in her potentially challenging role as single mother. Nor does he offer to help support his future offspring. According to his self-righteous rationale, only a child born within the institution of marriage deserves acknowledgment as property/progeny. No bastards need apply to call *this* man "Daddy."[6]

The subliminal sign system of *Fatal Attraction* is alarming in its rhetorical message. It valorizes the tacit assumption that a woman is singularly responsible for sexual activity and the consequences thereof. Pregnancy is *her* problem, since the harassed lawyer can flee the femme fatale, confess to Mommy, and deny the child he engenders. The implicit moral agenda of this film depends on an age-old double standard of adultery, which Christine Brooke-Rose attributes to the physical reality that "*pater semper incertus est,* and therefore the only method of being *certus* is social: lock up your wives or hedge them about with equivalent taboos, lies and terrors; men could sow as many bastards as they had women but woe to the women who bore them" (307). Even the most chivalric male, Brooke-Rose insists, has historically distinguished between his respectable ladylove and those unprotected women exploitable as "testicle-emptiers, *le repos du guerrier*" (313).

Fatal Attraction offers the 1980s' American public a mirror image of the dreams and nightmares fostered in the reign of Ronald Reagan, and a celluloid vindication of conservative "family values." Even at the end of the twentieth century, the nuclear family posits a uterine social organization legitimized exclusively by marital appropriation and sexual fidelity. A woman (self) excluded from this circle is suspicious, even dangerous. Beware the sex-starved spinster: in another incarnation, she might rise from a steaming, amniotic bathtub wielding a bloody dagger. And what would an outraged mommy say to *that?* To the extent that Alex Forrest is a woman of independent means who has chosen to remain husband-free, she fits into the broadly defined category of spinster—though her rapid decline from self-sufficiency to psychotic dependence and murderous hysteria bolsters the fragile psychopathic skein mysteriously unwound in the anxious frames of Dearden and Lyne's engaging melodrama. (Surely the repulsive bunny-boiling scenario is so grotesque that it irreparably demonizes the film's distraught antagonist.) *Fatal Attraction* appeals to a deeply embedded societal fantasy that female sexual libido, unrestrained by monogamous marriage, might suddenly erupt in an insatiable, orgiastic frenzy that could threaten not only the foundations of the nuclear family but the entire structure of bourgeois capitalism.

Fatal Attraction reflects a late twentieth-century antifeminist, antispinster backlash that is not, unfortunately, new. In a 1913 volume titled *The Truth About Women,* Mrs. C. Gasquoigne Hartley compares human society to the organization of a beehive and the spinster to a dangerous worker bee "left the possessor of the stinging weapon of death" (Jeffreys 142). Such random intertextuality, thematically echoed in A. S. Byatt's *Angels and Insects,* suggests the perdurance of archetypal figures of feminine vindictiveness and Scyllan chicanery. Despite what television advertisements and current situational comedies would have the American public believe, the independent woman who chooses lifelong spinsterhood apparently remains an implicitly deviant and dangerous figure—even at the dawn of a new and ostensibly more enlightened millennium.

NOTES

1. See Gayatri Chakravorty Spivak. For a historical discussion of the role and function of the spinster in Britain, see Sheila Jeffreys, who notes that any "attack on the spinster is inevitably an attack on the lesbian. . . . When lesbians are stigmatized and reviled, so, also, are all women who live independently of men" (100). The following essay takes a literary and theoretical stance rather than a historical one and, for reasons of space and praxis, does not deal directly with the issue of the spinster as lesbian. Implicit throughout this discussion, however, is a celebration of the op-

tion of loving and bonding with women as an alternative to traditional heterosexual coupling. My focus is limited primarily to those dimensions of isolation, independence, and solitude that marginalize the spinster and cast a shadow of mystery around her person. With the single exception of my final cinematic example, I have restricted this discussion to texts authored by women.

2. Sheila Jeffreys tells us that in the late Victorian era, "almost one in three of all adult women were single and one in four would never marry." In fact, the "1851 census revealed that there were 405,000 more women than men in the population. They were described in the press as 'excess' or 'surplus' women and in the 1860's to 1880's the 'problem' of 'surplus' women caused great alarm amongst male commentators. Those men who saw women as being superfluous if they were not servicing men suggested emigration as a solution" (86-87).

3. An early twentieth-century response to the enigma is captured in an article entitled "The Spinster," authored "By One" and published in the *Freewoman,* November 23, 1911. The essay begins with the following description: "I write of the High Priestess of Society. Not the mother of sons, but of her barren sister, the withered tree, the acidulous vessel under whose pale shadow we chill and whiten, of the Spinster I write. Because of her power and dominion. She, unobtrusive, meek, soft-footed, silent, shamefaced, bloodless and boneless, thinned to spirit, enters the secret recesses of the mind, sits at the secret springs of action, and moulds and fashions our emasculate society. She is our social nemesis" (Jeffreys 95).

4. For a discussion of post-traumatic stress disorder evinced by pregnancy loss, see Henke, *Shattered Subjects.*

5. See film reviews by Roger Ebert and Laurie Stone, the latter of whom also notes the prominent Medusa quality of Close's snaky coiffure.

6. Roger Ebert distinguishes himself as one of the few film critics cognizant of this movie's flawed moral perspective. He asks: "Although he [Douglas] grows to hate Close, is he really completely indifferent to the knowledge that she carries his child?" Indicting the film's exploitation of a " 'Friday the 13th' cliché that the villain is never really dead," Ebert notes that this "conclusion . . . operates on the premise that Douglas cares nothing for his unborn child."

WORKS CITED

Atwood, Margaret. *The Handmaid's Tale.* 1986. New York: Fawcett Crest, 1987.
_____. *Surfacing.* New York: Popular Library, 1976.
Brooke-Rose, Christine. "Woman As a Semiotic Object." In Susan Rubin Suleiman, ed., *The Female Body in Western Culture* (pp. 306-316). Cambridge: Harvard University Press, 1978.
Chodorow, Nancy. *The Reproduction of Mothering.* Berkeley: University of California Press, 1978.
Daly, Mary. *Gyn/Ecology: The Metaethics of Radical Feminism.* Boston: Beacon Press, 1978.

_____. *Webster's First New Intergalactic Wickedary of the English Language.* Boston: Beacon Press, 1987.

Ebert, Roger. Review of *Fatal Attraction. Chicago Sun-Times,* September 18, 1987. Online: <http://www.suntimes.com/ebert/ebert_reviews/1987/09/253587.html>.

Godwin, Gail. *A Mother and Two Daughters.* London: Pan Books Ltd., 1982.

_____. *The Odd Woman.* New York: Berkley Publishing Corp., 1974.

Henke, Suzette A. *Shattered Subjects: Trauma and Testimony in Women's Life-Writing.* New York: St. Martin's Press, 1998.

Jeffreys, Sheila. *The Spinster and Her Enemies: Feminism and Sexuality 1880-1930.* London: Pandora Press, 1985.

Kristeva, Julia. "Stabat Mater." In Susan Rubin Suleiman, ed., *The Female Body in Western Culture* (pp. 98-118). Cambridge: Harvard University Press, 1978.

Maltin, Leonard. *Leonard Maltin's Movie and Video Guide.* New York: Penguin Signet, 1996.

Miller, Nancy K. "Rereading As a Woman." In Susan Rubin Suleiman, ed., *The Female Body in Western Culture* (pp. 345-362). Cambridge: Harvard University Press, 1978.

Spivak, Gayatri Chakravorty. "French Feminism in an International Frame." *Yale French Studies* 62, 154-184; 1981.

Stone, Laurie. "The New Femme Fatale." *Ms. Magazine.* December 1987.

Suleiman, Susan Rubin, ed. *The Female Body in Western Culture.* Cambridge: Harvard University Press, 1978.

Walker, Alice. *In Search of Our Mothers' Gardens.* London: The Women's Press Ltd., 1984.

_____. *Meridian.* New York: Simon & Shuster Pocket Books, 1977.

Woolf, Virginia. *To the Lighthouse.* New York: Harcourt, Brace & World, 1927.

2

With Sure and Uncertain Footing: Negotiating the Terrain of a Solitude in May Sarton's Journals

Lisette Schillig

Solitude was that, too. A kind of writing.

Marguerite Duras

Only when she built inward in a fearful isolation
Did any one succeed or learn to fuse emotion

With thought. Only when she renounced did Emily
Begin in the fierce lonely light to learn to be.

from Sarton's "My Sisters, O My Sisters"

A recent book, titled *The Clock of the Long Now* (2000), addresses the late twentieth-century experience of a technological "rush" for information, the culture of speed that surrounds it, and the resultant need for a long-term sense of both time and responsibility toward the future. What author Stewart Brand and other members of the Long Now Foundation propose, and what the book describes, is a millennial clock, a computer designed to keep perfect time for the next 10,000 years. This, argues Brand, will bring about awareness of the need to slow down and take personal and collective stock. As well as inviting readers to participate in the guideline setting and design of the clock and of the proposed adjacent library, the book outlines the "candidate guidelines" that the Long Now Foundation has come up with to date, including: "Serve the long view (and the long viewer), Foster responsibility, Reward patience, Mind mythic depth, and Leverage longevity" (53-54).

In interesting though different ways, May Sarton's decision to live a life of solitude and her journal writings about that experience parallel what the Long Now Foundation seems to promote, which is a perceptual change in the way one's personal relationship to time and history might be viewed, and how "a long view" might be sustained as part of daily life. The differences by which the Long Now Foundation and Sarton initiate this change in perspective are revealing, as they relate largely to issues of gender and culture, particularly in terms of how solitude has historically been and continues to be scripted not as a free space but as an already culturally dominated sphere that nevertheless presumes itself to be neutral ground.

For the founding members of the millennial clock project, the address for change ultimately locates itself in a familiar male-scripted terrain, meaning it operates on the notion of forward movement (or progress) that has its grounding in a phallologocentric binary system of naming, the distorting effects of which prioritize product, or object, over process. This dynamic unfolds in spite of the project authors' well-intentioned desire to maintain the project's "neutrality," as evidenced by their invitation for multiple readers' input into the design of the clock itself. Certainly the use of binary terms here to describe this distortion falls into an easy kind of gender stereotype in the sense that they play on an essentializing system of meaning, wherein "male" constitutes product and progress, and "female" constitutes process and the defiance of object. But this is the point, for the Clock of the Long Now precisely does reinforce this binary and referential mode of thinking, however much its authors are trying to resist it. As long as the project insists as it does on "What is it?" questions such as "What is the present?", "What is history?", and "What is time?" it assumes there are definitive ways to answer, hence a "truth" to be found. It then posits that there is a way to represent that truth in objective form, at the expense of other simultaneous possibilities for what a "long view" experience might be. It does not help matters that the form of choice is a clock, itself a profoundly Western mechanism of dominance and control, and also of equalizing, for clocks ignore difference. They register one minute as no different from the one before or after it, just as the time clock in a factory punches one person "in" in the same way it punches another person "out," thus accounting only for a cumulative value as the Clock of the Long Now hopes to do, though perhaps with more mysticism and a prescribed sense of awe attached.[1]

In the case of the millennial clock, progress is of a particularly technological and commercial kind, for while the aim may be visionary to some, the ideas surrounding the project are tied up in a language of Disneyesque profit, as if the clock constituted an e-ticket ride to attract paying customers with the intriguing opportunity to be momentarily surprised.[2] To quote Stewart Brand:

> The main characteristic of the Clock is its linearity. It treats one year absolutely like another, oblivious of Moore's Law accelerations, national fates, wars, dark ages, or climate changes. . . . For the Clock to be such a point of reference it must *deliver an experience.* After an encounter with the clock a visitor should be able to declare with feeling, "Whew. *Time!* And me in it." It is not so much a conversion experience as a deep pause, like coming upon the Grand Canyon by surprise, where you simply want to sit and watch for a while and let your life adjust to two million years visible in one glance. Yet the Grand Canyon, like the night sky, is crushing in scale; *there is no way to engage it personally.* The Clock's time frame of four hundred generations is human scale—it should invite you to engage it personally, by doing something, leaving some mark." [italics mine] (49)

The Clock project indeed invites questions about what it actually might mean to engage something personally, about how and what it means "to take pause," to feel connection to something else, someone else, something larger than yourself in the movement that is time and space, and whether doing so would be measurable in any quantifiable way. It raises the questions of whether the experience of solitude ultimately serves the purpose of "leaving a mark," of whether it requires a monument to be erected, and if so, of what kind, and for whose benefit. Does the erection of a monument, ostensibly a male act, effect the kind of memory necessary to sustain a "long view," one that speaks to the duration of living as dictated by the small, patterned and repeated acts of day-to-day living? Does it recognize the minor-keyed, daily eruptions and erosions of life, those out of which the depth of a grand canyon evolves? To what extent does it deny or submerge them? Should we expect that the eruptions and erosions of each person's daily living will create canyons that all look the same?

For May Sarton, the experience of solitude was *all* about engaging it personally and engaging it as a woman, the "it" not being a monolithic sense of time but rather the ambiguities and complexities (including the push-pull nature of her relations and responsibilities to friends, lovers, and readers) of her own life and sense of self as she moved *with* and *through* time. Solitude was also, equally important, her writing. Her experience of it was intended to have (and had) duration, and so, unlike a visit to a millennial clock to achieve the trick of momentary reorientation as prescriptively envisioned and chosen by someone else (and in the case of the Long Now project, it's prescribed by a nearly all-male group), Sarton's was a long-lived and continuous reorientation based upon her decision at age forty-five to live alone (although in many respects, never alone).[3]

This chapter examines Sarton's journal writings on and out of solitude on multiple levels: (1) Sarton's dismissal as a writer by the critical literary establishment—a dismissal that in part informed her decision to live alone; (2) the phenomenon of Sarton's large and loyal following of readers, this in spite of her dismissal by critics and *because* of the experience of solitude that she writes about in her journals; and finally, (3) the experience of solitude itself that Sarton describes—an experience that questions traditional notions about the relationship between women and solitude, and the ways in which that experience initiates a different set of parameters by which time and space might be lived and viewed. The "inside" and "outside" realities of Sarton's experience, which these categories of analysis explore, and the dynamics of her emotional/psychological state juxtaposed with the public status of her image as a writer/solitary, converge on her solitude. Considered mutually, as they must be, and informed as they are by her racial and class status that informs the experience of solitude, they point to the intersecting parameters within which Sarton attempted to define her solitude for other women as ultimately an act, not of submission or separation but of agency and of constant negotiation between what is inside and outside, the terms for which she creates, and in which is manifested both pleasure and rage. By negotiating through writing what a life alone means to her, Sarton reveals and simultaneously attempts to shatter notions of women's powerlessness against social systems and institutions which position women and which serve to alienate them from themselves by distorting and depleting their sense of possibility. The expression of possibility is a transgressive act; it establishes power on a different plane and it does so by allowing for the continual renegotiation and speculation about one's own mythmaking acts, however destabilizing and unsafe constant renegotiation might be for the person, someone similar to Sarton, who is continually driven to mythmaking practices and by a need to maintain psychic self-control.

Although Sarton's oeuvre certainly encompassed more than her journals, it is her journals that speak most to the daily rhythms, requirements, and madnesses (often in the form of a deep loneliness) of solitude. Although *A Plant Dreaming Deep* was written as the first of such works, *Journal of a Solitude* and *The House by the Sea,* following immediately after, initiated the exploration into a solitude that was more open and cognizant of Sarton's pain and struggle over the experience of living alone. In these works solitude becomes defined as more than what traditional notions of it may imply to most, namely a peaceful escape safe from emotional upheavals, outside forces, and daily interruptions.[4] Although Sarton's solitude is certainly studio space for her artistic work, it is also a pattern of living on all levels—artistically, emotionally, socially, intellectually, spiritually, imaginatively, and physically. Its parameters encompass Sarton's material realities as well—her gender; her identity and practice as a writer; her sexuality; her class, race, and education; her New England upbringing and ties to Europe; her economic realities; her community of friends and neighbors; her relationship to the critical literary establishment; her following of readers; the culture of the period in which she was born (marked by major wars abroad and the dynamic advances of the first and second waves of the feminist movement); and the ever-changing daily circumstances out of which she was continuously writing. Solitude thus cannot be isolated from personal, cultural, or historiopolitical contexts.

Although the experience of living alone and writing about it garnered for Sarton a large following of mostly women readers, her work attracted little sustained critical attention or praise from literary critics. As friend and critic Carolyn Heilbrun put it, Sarton was never part of the established literary network. "Even when she had an influential friend," she writes, "the friend . . . was unable to commit herself professionally to May. What would the men think? May and I used to joke that after she had published seventeen or some such number of books, the only good review she had in *The New York Times Book Review* was for a children's book about a parrot" (Heilbrun 5-6). This lack of critical reception frustrated and angered Sarton throughout her entire life. In interviews, she often spoke of her dismissal by critics, either about the rage she felt at being consistently ignored; about the depression she endured after bad reviews, particularly of her poetry; or about feeling like an outsider, someone who has felt that she never belonged to a society, at least one that would be validated by the mainstream culture. "I think it's just that I feel an outsider and a stranger in every respect," she explains in a 1982 interview. "And I'm a lesbian. That also makes me an outsider" (Bonetti 101-102). In a 1989 interview, she explains the other ways in which she felt marked: "In America, I think I'm pushed aside as that awful thing called a sensitive feminine writer. The very ingredient that makes me universal has kept me from being interesting to the critics. You can't say that I'm a Maine writer, or a New England writer. I'm not regional. I can't be labeled as a lesbian writer because only one of my books deals with that subject" (Rosenthal 191).[5]

Although critical attention to Sarton's work has grown in recent years, the attention remains largely confined to the realm of university women's studies courses. This realm remains "partitioned off" and unintegrated (and therefore isolated from the mainstream literary canon). It tends also to sustain a limited readership (of women) and winds up grouping the writings of women, no matter what diverse and often experimental genre forms they deploy, into one gross category of "women's texts." Texts such as *Journal of a Solitude* and *The House by the Sea* are likely to fall under the category of "personal writing" and are ones that many contemporary literary critics and theorists might deem insignificant, simple, and dated, *because* they are too personal. "On the surface my work has not looked radical," admits Sarton, "but perhaps it will be seen eventually that in a 'nice, quiet, noisy way' I have been trying to say radical things gently so that they may penetrate without shock" (*Journal* 90).

In spite of the disappointment she felt at the hands of critics, the devotedness of her great number of readers kept her continually buoyed, for her work indeed penetrated. As she attests in a 1989 interview, W.W. Norton, her publisher, "keeps twelve to fourteen of my books in print at any one time. They've told me they've made a million dollars selling my work. . . . *Journal of a Solitude* has sold 2,000 books a year for twenty years. I receive so many letters from people who tell me my books have changed their lives. I feel loved by so many people" (Rosenthal 192).[6] When one interviewer asked about her feelings "in regard to . . . the feminist movement," prefacing her question with the statement that "Many women in the movement must ally themselves with you whether they're homosexual or not," Sarton's response was: "Yes. It's also because I live alone. I have proved that you can do it and have a wonderful life . . ." (Shelley 71).

Indeed, the popular following that Sarton's writings have garnered, particularly in response to her journals and novels, has much to do with what many have cited as the courageousness of her resolve to live alone as a woman and to write about the experience with honesty (although, as I argue below, there is much that is left concealed). It is that honesty and her popular following that have made her a figure of curiosity and attraction, not only for a long list of interviewers but for other writers, including her contemporaries Carolyn Heilbrun and Doris Grumbach, both whom have come out recently with their own accounts of solitude and the aging process, subjects which Sarton certainly set a precedent for, making them possible for women to talk and write about.

Sarton herself wrote often in her journals of the letters and visits she received on a continual and sometimes overwhelming basis (about fifty letters a week, she claimed) from admiring readers who expressed gratitude for the courage and sense of comfort they received from reading her work.[7] That sense of comfort and courage is derived largely out of a shared yet often unspoken awareness of the particular burden women carry—a burden that is directly borne out of their inscription in a reproductive economy, with all the constraints that this economy continues to exercise. Because of that burden, the relationship between women and solitude is contextualized differently, for the courage with which women practice solitude is not scripted in the same way as the courage that Henry David Thoreau (whose *Walden* Sarton kept near her writing desk) speaks to in "front[ing] only the essential facts of life" (Thoreau 343). For Sarton, it is much more the matter of attempting to front only the essential "facts" of the many dimensions of her own self. Because Thoreau already has license to enter the woods alone, there is a certain confirmation of identity that is already implicit. Precedence is already established for male wanderers; they are expected to wander, to live alone, to "go out on a limb."

Such an endeavor, for women, invites guilt, for it is anything but an expectation. Although the social roles and expectations of women today are expanded so that women have more possibilities for defining themselves outside the home, a guilt factor nevertheless persists for many if not most. This guilt factor is tied up with the iconic position women hold as nurturers, comforters, and sustainers of others. If women choose solitude, then they are perceived to be irresponsible; it means they are not paying enough attention to children, partners, parents, or loved ones. If they are single and pursuing a career, then they are being irresponsible in not carrying out their duties fully as women. In addition, if a woman does pursue a career, she is met with the criteria that she distinguish herself by reaching heroine or role-model heights.

Sarton was keenly aware of the roles women were scripted to play, and she wrote particularly of how these roles proved hazardous to the opportunities women had for solitude. In *The House by the Sea,* she expresses concern for women who are duty-bound to husband, house, and/or children, and she simultaneously challenges the idea that a life of solitude for women must be equated to a life of loneliness. In speaking of a woman friend, she writes:

> The greatest problem of my young married friend is really fatigue . . . this seems the insuperable *fact* about bringing up small children. There is no rest. If there is hostility toward a husband who is not at home enough to take his share of simply being human, then it all becomes doubly hard to handle, and the "bone loneliness" eats its way into the psyche. (59)

Conversely, at another point in the journal, she writes of how women without children experience a sense of guilt.

> Thinking so much these days about what it is to be a woman, I wonder whether an ingrained sense of guilt is not one feminine characteristic. A man who has no children may feel personally deprived but he does not feel guilty, I suspect. A woman who has no children is always a little on the defensive. (*House* 66)

With or without children, a woman is embroiled in an economy that emphasizes husband, household, childbearing and child rearing, and the creation of "home" for the sake of the family unit, of which she is often viewed less as a member than as a caretaker. The feminist movement made (and continues to make) tremendous strides in promoting and emphasizing possibilities *outside* of the household, but the process of cultural role making and maintaining is slow to change. Women still remain marked in terms of their value in a reproductive economy.

Nurturing for the sake of others' well-being, though this can indeed be a pleasure and a joy, has also always been, because an expectation, a burden for women. Sarton knew this burden, as evidenced by her sense of responsibility to answer all the letters she received from admirers who in many ways idolized her as a role model—as someone who had the resolve to defy and openly declare against, through her writing, prescripted expectations of what her sexuality should be, what her role should be as a woman and as a woman writer, and what her relationship should be to various communities, lesbian and literary. Sarton accepted the letter writing and admirers' visits to her home as responsibilities (and in many respects they affirmed her hopes that her words mattered), but these responsibilities induced anger and resentment. Her purposes for solitude were not motivated by her desire to set herself up as an example of solitary possibility only to address for the rest of her life the success of her achievement. And unlike Thoreau, whose defense of his solitude was at least partly caught up in the sense of its performing "a higher obligation," Sarton's desire for solitude was also a need, and the need was interwoven with her need to write and her impulse to create form. In discussing the conflict between the sense of obligation to one's own conscience and the obligation to perform higher good, Philip Koch, in his book *Solitude: A Philosophical Encounter*, recalls that "the traditional monastic interpretation of the story of Mary and Martha also insists upon higher duties: Christ was reminding Martha that although there is an obligation to be 'busy with much serving' there is a higher obligation to worship God" (236). Sarton's response: ". . . the chief problem women have, even now, is that they have to be both Martha and Mary most of the time and these two modes of being are diametrically opposite" (*House* 57). In light of this conflict, Sarton's solitude is a creative act of form(ing) and of fighting a New England, duty-filled impulse to be productive, an impulse that she equates, interestingly, with her father, writing:

> I am still pursued by a neurosis about work inherited [from him]. A day where one has not pushed oneself to the limit seems a damaged damaging day, a sinful day. Not so! The most valuable thing we can do for the psyche, occasionally, is to let it rest, wander, live in the changing light of a room, not try to be or do anything whatever. (*Journal* 89)

When Sarton first moved from Cambridge, Massachusetts, to her newly purchased Wild Knoll house in the small village of Nelson, New Hampshire, she was forty-five and already an established poet and novelist. There was likely no principal reason for her moving, in spite of what Sarton herself may have claimed at various times. The reason she most often gave was that the move was an attempt to escape the literary establishment's negative (sometimes absent) treatment of her work, a decision to get away in order to lick her wounds before she went crazy. The decision may also have been based on her desire to extricate herself from complicated relationships with friends and lovers for whom she felt passions that threatened to overwhelm her, and/or a desire to retreat from an experience of unrequited love.[8] Whether in matters of money Sarton was her own worst enemy or her greatest source of capital,[9] her financial situation was precarious, making her ability to choose and maintain a life of solitude simultaneously privileged and forever in jeopardy. Particularly given the era (early 1970s) in which Sarton first moved to Wild Knoll and began writing journals, a woman living alone without the financial support of a male breadwinner was far from the norm, and this contributed profoundly to the nature—and the myth—of the solitude she both created and knew.

Certainly, too, being a poet and writer, Sarton's need for quiet and for a space where her concentration was less likely to be compromised must also have been a motivating factor for her move to Wild Knoll, not to mention the fact that she was raised by parents whose intellectual and artistic endeavors would likely have required a home life where the need for study and concentration mandated few interruptions.[10] Sarton also attributed her own sense of emotional imbalance to her need to be alone, writing in *Journal of a Solitude:*

> I live alone, perhaps for no good reason, for the reason that I am an impossible creature, set apart by a temperament I have never learned to use as it could be used, thrown off by a word, a glance, a rainy day, or one drink too many. . . . I go up to Heaven and down to Hell in an hour, and keep alive only by imposing upon myself inexorable routines. (12)

The internal tension borne out of this temperament, which Sarton often characterized as childlike, both fueled her writing and challenged her need for self-control, and made daily routines a structural necessity.

Indeed, much of what Sarton writes about in *Journal of a Solitude* and *The House by the Sea* are her routine, day-to-day practices and experiences—her gardening, her setting a table for a friend who is coming to visit, her sitting admiring a bouquet of flowers she has arranged and brought into the house, her chasing out of the house in the middle of the night a mouse her cat Bramble has carried in. These seeming surface doings are what make solitude tangible to the reader. They offer a daily rhythm that is concrete and imaginable. They establish form. A reader can see herself performing similar acts, and in many ways these acts are recognizably and stereotypically "women's doings." They constitute reproductive work in the sense that they are reenacted on a daily or weekly basis (making the bed, washing dishes, pulling weeds). Women working in the domestic sphere perform such actions, though certainly the actions themselves are not restricted to women. In describing them through her writing, however, Sarton requires their significance differently, away from the traditional connotations that these actions might otherwise have to female domesticity, and thereby to the caretaking of family. Certainly the class implications of home ownership cannot be ignored here, for *as* a single home owner, Sarton can assume and enjoy the privilege of space that the majority of women historically, and at the specific period in which she was writing, did not have the financial independence to entertain, let alone enjoy. For a vast majority of women, a house was (and still is for many) a compromised domain, shared as it often was by a woman's children, and/or owned by a husband whose income was usually the principal one of the household.

Sarton's insistence on the significance of these routine tasks through her writing about them can be considered in another important way, for their significance is not unlike the historical and even national significance afforded to Thoreau's hoeing a beanfield, for example. The difference is distinct, however, in terms of how Sarton's and Thoreau's tasks are valued. For Thoreau, there was already a historical precedent for why farming, even on the more minor level of growing beans at Walden, had national relevance. Thoreau's hoeing had a foundation of support, for it harkened back to the beginnings of an agrarian economy, one that was tied to America's sense of its own self-sufficiency and survivability, a self-sufficiency that was scripted as male. Sarton's practice of solitude, and all the forms of work that she performs within its walls in support of that solitude, have no precedents for women. For her, unlike for Thoreau, solitude and writing (particularly as a woman) serve no recognized national or historical purpose and there is, consequently, no support for the kind of survival she is trying to establish at Nelson. For her, these acts are anything but "simple" or "simplifiable" as readers of Thoreau might have mythologized them to be.

What may nevertheless be off-putting for some and simultaneously attractive to others about Sarton's "doings" has as much to do with her recording them as it does with what the recording also performs, namely a continuous attempt at control over demons in an almost desperate desire for "order and beauty," a phrase that resurfaces repeatedly in Sarton's journals.[11] These "demons" can come in a host of forms: loneliness, frustration, fear, anger, shame, guilt, or disappointment. The daily recordings witness what is indeed beautiful for Sarton, reflecting an almost Keatsian sensibility for order that a satisfyingly arranged bouquet of flowers affords. But order here means a kind of promise and assurance that is sensual and kept physically close but also purposefully at bay, for herein lies necessary and troubling tension. This tension is between what is desired (the finished work—a well-arranged bouquet, a well-crafted poem, a successfully productive day, a well-controlled temperament, for instance) and the personal and creative pain out of which what is desired is wrought. The tension also lies in the possibility of disappointment that the arrangement will *not* satisfy, that the vision of the poem will *not* materialize in words, that the day will *not* be well managed. In writing, for instance, of not yet knowing how she will juggle three writing projects at once, she says, "the only thing is to immerse oneself very fast as if a plunge into icy waters and hope to find one can swim one's way to safety! And that I am about to do" (*House* 50).

This energetic anxiousness to "plunge," marked by "icy" trepidation, is followed immediately by a meditation on the cyclamen she has in her window, and the question as to whether she will sink or swim gets displaced. "The way the sun shines through the petals of pink and white cyclamen . . . and lights up a scarlet and pink poinsettia is one of the rewards of *getting up* [italics mine]," she writes (*House* 50). Here, "getting up" is another way of suggesting, via juxtaposition to the "reward" of flowers, the trepidation that confronting a new day—a clean slate—entails. She will reference the cyclamen several times in *The House by the Sea,* and usually in terms of how the light is striking it and making it transparent or how it reveals patterns and colors not readily seen unless truly studied. The promise of what a flower brought inside holds for Sarton is as much founded in the rich multiplicity of ways it can change and be seen as it is in what it will help mask over and keep at bay, namely the messiness of her own emotions and thoughts and the insecurities she feels over the possibility that her own self-created forms (her poems, principally) will fail to entrance readers or critics in the same way that the flower occupies her. The assurance afforded by "order and beauty" is not invulnerable, for clearly Sarton references the rages that can intrude. Nevertheless, these rages are never performed outright on the pages of her journals, and this tends to leave both rages and Sarton confined to the silence of the margins. In spite of this silence, however, and perhaps because of it, a space is created, which is the struggle itself between the text and what lies outside it. In essence, this struggle is where the heart of the reader's and Sarton's conversation lies, however "invisible," for here the reader can recognize and place her or his own frustrations, chaos, and madnesses and not be constrained by Sarton's refusal to perform or let "spill out" her own. The references to rage alone—in spite of their being references only—offer their own brand of assurance.

Other forms of solitude come in other repetitions of the day for Sarton, such as her daily walks with her dog, Tamas, always along the same path. Such physical practices as walking invite their own rhythms, and underpin and open up the multiple dimensions of consciousness, of time, and of the walker's meditations. This dynamic of walking is not unlike that of Sarton's poetry writing wherein Sarton works within the structure of the lyrical form but determines the context for herself, which will vary with every poem. While walking, Sarton keeps to the same path by choice, but with that choice she establishes anew her relationship to the space around her by virtue of coming to that familiar terrain with an attitude, emotions, a set of worries, hopes, or outside circumstances that differ from those of the day before. The familiarity of the path then, and certainly the luxury of time she can take to walk it every day, affords a thread of continuity and a sense of reliability that is not static or imposed from the outside. That reliability gives Sarton a sense of safety, which in turn gives her the psychic space to wander freely in her own head; as a result, she becomes more acutely aware of her own multidimensional presence. Thoreau described a similar awareness, writing in *Walden* of a feeling of doubleness when he was alone.

> I only know myself as a human entity; the scene, so to speak, of thoughts and affections; and am sensible of a certain doubleness by which I can stand as remote from myself as from another. However intense my experience, I am conscious of the presence and criticism of a part of me, which, as it were, is not a part of me, but spectator, sharing no experience, but taking note of it; and that is no more I than you. (386)

In spite of how fragmented or confused a feeling this doubleness may describe, Thoreau remarks that he finds it "*wholesome* to be alone the greater part of the time" (italics mine) (386), a conclusion to which Sarton no doubt ascribed.

Such wholesomeness suggests confidence, health, and reliability that comes from within, though arguably it is enhanced, perhaps even locatable *only* given the freedom and continuity of available space and time that both Sarton and Thoreau enjoy. As Susan Alves points out in reference to a poem from Sarton's *Letters from Maine,* "Sarton seemingly encodes the more positive function of being alone as a reliable presence in the temporal" (108). As with Thoreau, whose solitude enlists the dual acts of thinking and observing, both of which afford him an awareness of presence in time, Sarton's solitude is caught up in the parallel creative and positive acts of writing and reading. As Marguerite Duras writes, both acts are a part of solitude: "A kind of writing. And reading was the same as writing" (19). These acts, indistinguishable, afford Sarton a sense of her own presence that is reliably bound up with her in all her dimensions, all her voices.[12]

As with the act of writing, which requires solitude, reading gives agency; it affords the reader a space that she or he in part creates. In *The Practice of Everyday Life,* Michel de Certeau points to the daydreaming otherwhereness that reading places one in, away from the social milieu, calling reading "an initial, indeed initiatory, experience: to read is to be elsewhere, where *they* are not, in another world; it is to constitute a secret scene, a place one can enter and leave when one wishes . . ." (173). This is not to say that de Certeau sees reading as a strictly privatized act that escapes the outside world absolutely. Even though one reads alone, reading itself is always informed by "a relationship of forces (between teachers and pupils, or between producers and consumers) whose instrument it becomes" (de Certeau 171). Reading, in other words, occurs in the context of larger cultural relationships of authority. Pupils read what teachers tells them to; consumers read what publishers or *The New York Times Book Review* dictate as worthwhile. Such forces influence the reader's perspective. Certainly the "text" of her own thoughts that Sarton "reads" and interprets as she is out walking alone is informed by the larger cultural forces that have shaped her—forces bound up with issues of race, class, gender, and sexuality, for instance, of which Sarton may not always be fully conscious. Nevertheless, Sarton sustains an autonomy through "reading"/writing/walking that not so much denies as subverts the control these forces have in scripting her identity in any absolute way. In a sense, the simple act of taking a walk takes on greater significance, for it becomes an act of agency and choice that allows Sarton the freedom to explore and question, to become temporarily and temporally lost in a matrix of emotions and thoughts, but lost in familiar terrain.

Although offering tangibility, these daily activities that Sarton describes also insist on something simultaneously elusive to words, more like something written out of but also within a form that has its own unpredictable dimensions. It is a form Sarton nonetheless participates in creating and must struggle constantly to maintain. "My solitude is everywhere," she writes, "and sometimes I don't speak to anyone, except just to say good morning to the post mistress, for days, for days literally in the winter. And this is hard to handle, to not get unbalanced and not let depression get hold of you. Everything becomes more intense, you see, which is partly why it's marvelous. There's nothing to break the intensity. The great flow from the subconscious to the conscious is the good thing about solitude" (*A Self-Portrait* 22).

This intensity of consciousness affords possibility, a kind of salvation from but also a potential inducer of madness. She can feed and nourish herself on it, but the intensity can be painful. She speaks at one point of a friend, Danny, "a man of twenty who has grown a lot of wisdom through suffering. We recognize each other as fellow sufferers, possibly suffering for the same reason, an acute awareness beyond what we are able to put into action or to *be,* as it were" (*Journal* 43). Thus the potential of the everywhereness of solitude to turn into a kind of overwhelming internal chaos is what Sarton is forever striving to avoid. When she doesn't succeed, it can throw her into a rage or depression, because the chaos will sap her ("Depression eats away psychic energy in a dreadful way"), and she'll cease to be able to write (*Journal* 27). Not writing is a kind of death. Being without solitude is a kind of death also, for without it there is no means for stepping back and observing, for seeing the kinds of changing patterns (such as the cyclamen's or the seasons') that provide a constructive context in which to view one's life.

In her book *Stigmata,* Hélène Cixous speaks about the relationship between death and writing, describing writing as forever a matter of "lateness," a mourning process in which the writer is always trying to catch up to what is passing by him or her every instant, internally and externally. Writes Sarton:

> It is next to impossible, I find, to go back into the immediate past when one is keeping a journal. I suppose the very nature of a journal is catching things on the wing . . . and by the time one has an hour in which to look back, so much else has already happened—such as seeing a kingfisher, a review of Woolf's letters—that one has no interest in the immediate past. (*House* 151)

A "journal has to do with 'what I am now, at this instant' " (*House* 79). There is a desperation that underscores this process of "lateness," for in one sense mourning suggests regret at having failed to capture the instant, or oneself. It connotes the unacceptable death of something, the death of the person who passed by before she or he could be experienced. The motivation in writing, however, is always toward life. For Cixous and for Sarton (in terms both of solitude and of writing), writing is also continuity. It is what anticipates itself, but is what never arrives. Writing is, therefore, not so much a safe middle position between life and death but a kind of hope, something that moves frenetically backward and forward between both forces and that defies their canceling each other out. For Cixous, writing is always a matter of loving the process of creation more than the created but realizing both. It is the anticipation she favors, for the *process* of writing is a kind of instant where everything is allowed, everything remains, and where truth and identity are still in flux. "I want to draw the present, say da Vinci, Picasso, Rembrandt, the fools for truth," writes Cixous. "How to make the portrait of lightning? At what speed draw speed? We have all cried out stop! to the instant. . . . This is why we desire so often to die, when we write, in order to see everything in a flash, and at least once shatter the spine of time with only one pencil stroke" (30-31). For Cixous, shattering the spine is to write the flux, not to stop it; the flux itself is what is critical.

When one thinks about the ways in which time, as relayed chronologically in history books, has effectively effaced the dynamic presence of women, this "shattering" takes on an even deeper resonance, for women have not historically had the luxury of even pretending to write their own stories, let alone get them into official print. Shattering the spine of time (and, metaphorically, the spines of body and of book) is particularly painful for women who have had literally to break into the language of a history that has simultaneously identified and confined them to silent roles like so many Helens of Troy. In shattering, there is promise of possibility and freedom that comes with acknowledging a present that cannot effectively be scripted, constrained, or "set down," because it is always passing; it is a kind of truth that is unpredictable, unannounceable. It is desire itself, desire for an open-endedness and unforeseeability that is transgressive for women, because it defies the power to be statically positioned. And yet, as Cixous suggests, there is still the desire to write, but to write in a way that "escort[s] the unseized thought, without limiting its free course" (82).

Sarton's writing out of solitude moves toward this same idea of not wanting to limit the free course of her own being, and in this sense her recognition of solitude *as* writing, and *as* continuity anticipates Cixous' desire for a language that allows for flux. Ultimately, however, Sarton's desire for "order and beauty" and her need to displace the flux of her own becoming into objective form disrupt the possibilities of ever truly shattering the spine of time, inasmuch as form connotes freezing an object, thought, experience, and even person into some kind of permanence that affords Sarton a sense of self-reliability rather than vulnerability. She writes in *The House by the Sea* of the value of writing a journal, stating, "If [it] is to have any value either for the writer or any potential reader, the writer must be able to be objective about what he experiences *on the pulse*. For the whole point of a journal is this seizing events on the wing" (78-79). Even in light of this desire to write on the wing, Sarton is at cross-purposes with herself, simultaneously driven as she is by her desire to experience and write the instant (as in that instant when she looks at the light that falls on a flower), and her need as a poet to objectively reduce an event to its essence through the placement of words. Sarton knows the light's patterning across the petals of a flower is only momentary and she celebrates it, but she celebrates it in writing, and writing, as Cixous points out, is a matter of "advancing backwards" (30). "We live more quickly than ourselves, the pen doesn't follow," writes Cixous. "To paint the present which is passing us by, we stop the present" (30). Although solitude for Sarton affords her the means to write on the pulse and to start anew, she also sees it and the journals as a means for sorting out her life and of reflectively making sense of it, such that the instant, or pulse, gets continuously displaced and Sarton along with it. If solitude serves as allowance for Sarton to make sense of things, then the making of sense is something that escapes her grasp continually. In essence, Sarton herself is a text that eludes, even as she tries to shape it, and the contradiction that is apparent in her dual purpose of "writing on the pulse" and the impulse to order becomes apparent. This does not suggest defeat, however, for the act of continually writing is an act of striving, and striving itself is a continual process that defies death. "All we can pray is not to outlive the self," Sarton writes. "Yet my guess is that we make our deaths, even when senile" (*House* 72).

However restful it can be ("I woke to . . . a serene pale blue satin sea") or tormented ("I slept badly, a night of flotsam and jetsam moving around in my head"), solitude for Sarton is a process that has no end point (*House* 123, 156). It is a space intimately opened up, which makes words possible by virtue of solitude's allowing for the duration of thought(fulness) required for a writer's words, for writing, for the connection that writing makes possible between writer and reader. In this sense, solitude is a personal and moving act of nurturing—Sarton nurturing herself, Sarton nurturing her writing, her writing nurturing her and ultimately her readers. There is also a reciprocal nurturing that Sarton requires from her readers (and arguably from her female readers, principally) as evidenced by the very fact that she writes her journals for publication. She is obviously writing *to* someone, and there are occasions when she addresses her readers more directly, as in *The House by the Sea* where she informs the reader why she hasn't been writing: "(Except for two entries from March 16th to May 27th there are blank pages because I was too ill to keep the journal going . . .)" (86). The nurturing (Margot Peters frames it as "approval-seeking," which is also accurate) necessarily allows in the voices, the histories, and the actions of others, even to the point of bombardment. Sarton writes in *Journal of a Solitude:* "When I talk about solitude I am really talking also about making space for that intense, hungry face at the window, starved cat, starved person. It is making space to *be there*" (57). On the one hand, that space to "be there" refers not to static moment/place, but to *process,* with its own lasting endurance, a pattern that repeats, a room for seeing what's inside and what's out, what's both restful and tormented. These are abstract descriptions, but solitude requires them, as does the act of writing. There is nevertheless tension evidenced in Sarton's description, for solitude is never uninterrupted; it implies someone else, someone who requires, who even demands at times. The "intense, hungry face at the window" can be someone outside looking in or inside looking out—an admiring reader, an annoyed critic, a letter that seeks to be answered, a stray cat who seeks shelter, food, or trust. It is also Sarton herself, or some dimension of her, who is antsy, unrequited, or demanding, or who feels the tug and pull of responsibility, the need for connection. "I have the time to think," she writes of her solitude.

> That is the great, the greatest luxury. I have time to be. Therefore my responsibility is huge. To use time well and to be all that I can in whatever years are left to me. . . . The dismay comes when I lose the sense of my life as connected (as if by an aerial) to many, many other lives whom I do not even know and cannot ever know. (*Journal* 40)

Solitude, in this sense, becomes a kind of burden, both agonizing and impossible to avoid or escape.

It is the simultaneity of tumult and quiet that Sarton's descriptions of solitude speak to. The few feet of distance that she creates in living at Nelson, and later in Maine, do not assure her a safe place of refuge. "Here in Nelson I have been close to suicide more than once," she writes, "and more than once have been close to a mystical experience of unity with the universe. The two states resemble each other: one has no wall, one is absolutely naked and diminished to essence" (*Journal* 57). The fragility of this psychic state is one writer Marguerite Duras also shares:

> Living like that, the way I saw I lived, in that solitude, eventually means running certain risks. It's inevitable. As soon as a human being is left alone, she tips into unreason. . . . [A] person left to her own devices is already stricken by madness, because nothing keeps her from the sudden emergence of her personal delirium. (21)

Sarton's honesty about solitude—that it is not necessarily or even ever idyllic or tame but often wild and treacherous and unpredictable—is what makes her description of her experience particularly attractive to women, for it speaks to what is nevertheless desirable about solitude's disorderliness, and how that disorderliness sparks desire to creatively structure that disorder on self-created terms, even at the risk of losing oneself in it, or in being unable to anticipate what abysses it may lead her to confront.

Little if anything has been written about the journals' photographs, but Sarton's placement of them throughout is a testament to her structuring attempts to "freeze-frame" into form at least one aspect of her experience of solitude. It is also to project an experience to her readers through representations of arrested scenes and moments that she herself can relish, like desire, pleasure, safety, and assurance. The photographs seem chosen to invite readers/viewers into the sculpted serenity and possibility of her space—both at Nelson and at Wild Knoll. They are personal photographs—of her house (interior and exterior), pets, neighbors, the surrounding landscape. One photograph, for example, is of her house in Nelson at night, the lights on outside, snow all around. A seemingly safe-looking place that *is* her (even as it contains, or hides, her rages), that reminds her of who she is, of her own sense of self-reliability, of what she's decided for herself, and what she is *being*. "[I]t can be meaningful," she writes in *Journal of a Solitude,* where the photograph appears.

> It is an age where more and more human beings are caught up in lives where fewer and fewer inward decisions can be made, where fewer and fewer real choices exist. The fact that a middle-aged, single woman, without any vestige of family left, lives in this house in a silent village and is responsible only to her own soul means something. The fact that she is a writer and can tell where she is and what it is like on the pilgrimage inward can be of comfort. It is comforting to know there are lighthouse keepers on rocky islands along the coast. Sometimes, when I have been for a walk after dark and see my house lighted up, looking so alive, I feel that my presence here is worth all the Hell." (*Journal* 40)

Certainly her remarks here serve in part as her statement of purpose. They suggest her awareness of the role she was playing (and simultaneously creating) as a "lighthouse keeper" for her readers. In making her own personal journey inward and in publicizing it, she declared her journey—and anyone else's—to be valid and worthwhile, and to have meaning on a much broader scale than may have otherwise been mapped. She offers no guarantees, however, that the journey will be anything but rocky (though here, too, as in the prose, the potential for wrecks is not depicted in the frame); nevertheless, she positions herself as the one who keeps the light, and therefore shows others—particularly other women—the way.

Many of the photographs showing the interior of her house testify, like another kind of witness with the words, to her need for an orderliness of space, and for control of a physical and psychic inside, and a control against any infringement of the outside on the in. Two simple chairs. A table. A vase of flowers from her garden atop it, a bottle of wine, her cat. Light coming through a window, a door. Hardwood floors, swept neat. A mat at the door. These photographs have a family album feel. They provide a record, a history linked to a space, a time, a certain *feel*—of beauty, light, composure—that assumes the power of legacy. Although the "neatness" and beauty of these photographic compositions can and ought to be enjoyed and appreciated on their own terms, they also need to be considered critically, for their very presence in the journals contributes decidedly to how Sarton wished her solitude to be viewed, and on what terms the viewer-reader might actually engage it. For one thing, the photographs *do* assume the power of legacy, and that legacy is inescapably tied to privilege. It is difficult not to view the photographs of the interior of Sarton's house, for instance, and not feel, as a reader, a desire to have that kind of space for oneself, whether it be for writing or for sanctuary, or both.

Certainly the connection of home to women's solitude has historical precedence. Koch, in identifying the features of women's solitude, notes the connection for women between the interior of the house and writing, "for what women often did, safe in their own room, was to write, and moreover a particular kind of writing. . . . Writing in a diary was a 'permission for solitude' given to girls who could not go off fishing at dawn alone as I used to do" (266). What Koch fails to point out is the extent to which the connections of safe home, solitude, and writing were principally true historically for white, privileged women who had access to books, an education, and the physical space in which to write. Inasmuch as the composition(s) of photographs in Sarton's journal are tied to her need to establish a legacy, the idea of legacy is itself tied up with privilege, such that Koch's notion of women being "safe" in their writing space borders on a clichéd romanticism that Sarton can participate in by virtue of her racial and class heritage. Thus the privilege of Sarton's "private" life is already predetermined by a wider social system that automatically validates her because she is a white, well-educated, middle-class, taxpaying property owner—a rural property owner at that. This validation alone grants Sarton a certain social space and with it a certain agency to be let alone in the physical space she chooses to occupy, to move as she chooses inside and outside of that space, and to enjoy the possibilities for constructing a legacy through writing of her experience within that space.

Even though Sarton did not take the photographs, she presumably chose which ones would be in the journals and may have even directed the photographers as to where, and on what, to aim the lens.[13] In this sense, the photographs, too, are meant to testify to a kind of solitude that she enjoys only sporadically and can maintain only inconsistently; nevertheless, it's one she desires constantly. Thus, even if the photographs taken together offer only a sometimes real but otherwise mythic representation, it is a myth that steadies her and gives her courage, and one that she hopes will steady the reader. That desire for steadiness necessarily reflects, too, the upheavals of world events such as the painful aftermath of Vietnam and the civil rights movement, and the "sheer constant pain at the violence and hatred that seems to be the chief motor power" with which "we are confronted every day on the TV screen and in every newspaper . . ." (*House* 191).

In her book *Family Frames,* Marianne Hirsch explains how family photographs often provide the viewer (and here that is both Sarton and the reader) with what she wants to see. Photographs initiate a collaboration between photographer and viewer in creating and perpetuating an ideology, or mythology, of family cohesion, whether or not the cohesion is real. "Between the viewer and the recorded object," explains Hirsch, "the viewer encounters, and/or projects, a screen made up of dominant mythologies and preconceptions that shapes the representation. . . . Since looking operates through projection and since the photographic image is the positive development of a negative, the plenitude that constitutes the fulfillment of desire, photographs can more easily show us what we wish our family to be, and therefore what, most frequently, it is not" (7-8). Although Hirsch's project specifically studies the ways in which family photographs construct and define familial relationships, her analysis of how photographs become a means for self-representation has application to the way in which photographs operate in Sarton's journals. Although the photographs in the journals are not of Sarton's biological family, they fall into the categories of either neighbors/friends (or pets), or the interior/exterior of her house (with Sarton sometimes in the frame). These categories suggest Sarton's need to at least appear to belong to a communal "family," and the simultaneous need to show the house of solitude as haven/home, which often it is not, as her writing establishes. In fact, Sarton is oftentimes her own worst enemy in thwarting the social relations she otherwise establishes. She describes one episode, for instance, in which she admits to having flown off the handle at a friend's small remark about the flowers in a vase being faded. "I must have screamed terribly loudly as I have lost my voice today!" she writes. "Tension had built up simply by my trying to cope with the mundane side of having a guest. . . . But the reaction was wildly out of proportion, and that was what made it frightening" (*Journal* 27-28).

Although the description offers only a glimpse of the rage and disappointment that underscores much of her solitude, this "glimpse" comes in words that follow only after the fact. There is no photograph that depicts the rage unfolding "on the pulse" of the moment. The fact that there are no photographs of Sarton's longtime friends (such as Eleanor Blair, the guilty party of the faded flowers remark), but only of neighbors she has become friendly with, connotes a necessary distance that Sarton likely wishes to maintain, such that the friends who intimately know of, and therefore remind her of, her rages are not the ones pictured. There is only Sarton attempting to make sense, through writing, at a saner point in time, of what happened and why. She writes of her "anger" as "a Laocoon struggle *between anger and my life itself,* as if anger were a witch who has had me in her power since infancy, and either I conquer her or she conquers me once and for all through the suicidal depression that follows on such an exhibition of unregenerate behavior" (italics mine) (*Journal* 27). Sarton's careful distinction between the "anger" and "my life itself" suggests her denial in allowing that anger to *be* a defining force, even though the verbal reference to such episodes reveals an honest willingness to go naked in front of the reader. Nonetheless, by describing her anger as coming in episodic fits, Sarton further isolates it as something apart from "her real life," lest she reveal too much of her underlying emotional vulnerability in a way that would counteract the calm image of the tidy house. Even her reference to the "Laocoon struggle" underscores a need to present her vulnerability through heroically mythological, and therefore distancing, terms. Ultimately, text and photographs do not so much betray each other as reveal each other.

Another photograph depicts a table, set for a dinner guest. All arranged and ready. Waiting. Expectant. An invitation to visitors to experience vicariously, but in a way that transfers the creative possibilities into their own hands. An allusion to writing. "I envy painters," Sarton writes, "because they can set their work up and look at it whole in a way that a writer cannot, even with a single page of prose or a poem. . . . I suppose I envy painters because they can meditate on form and structure, on color and light, and not concern themselves with human torment and chaos. It is restful even to imagine expression without words" (*Journal* 127-28).[14] For Sarton, the images in her journals provide this kind of restfulness in a way that won't reveal her inadequacy as a potential disrupter. They "promote forgetting," at least temporarily.[15]

Sarton's feelings of inadequacy were certainly not restricted to the anxiety she felt about her temperament. What she no doubt also wished to forget, but couldn't, were those pressures she faced as a single woman living alone in a heterosexist social system that valued marriage and children for women over singlehood and independence. Such pressures motivated her desire for solitude, for self-assurance, and for a "a safe place" to be. But if Sarton's solitude was motivated by these pressures, it was also intricately influenced by the materiality of her sexuality, and by the passionate and spiritual connection with women that she found both painful and simultaneously necessary to her writing. It would be a mistake not to see her need for solitude as connected not so much with her being a lesbian, as to her anger and frustration over the way "lesbian" as a label restrictively marked her as a woman and as a woman writer. Such labeling fueled her resistance to being called "a lesbian writer," and informed her desire that her writing be recognized for appealing to universal, human

emotions and not just to emotions that might be stereotypically identified by others as "characteristically lesbian." Of her one and pro-
fessedly hardest-to-write novel, *Mrs. Stevens Hears the Mermaids
Singing* (1965), whose protagonist is a lesbian, she said:

> the fear of homosexuality [was] so great that it took courage to
> write [it], to write a novel about a woman homosexual who is
> not a sex maniac, a drunkard, a drug-taker, or in any way repul-
> sive; to portray a homosexual who is neither pitiable nor dis-
> gusting, without sentimentality; and to face the truth that such a
> life is rarely happy, a life where art must become the primary
> motivation, for love is never going to fulfill in the usual sense.
> (*Journal* 90-91)

As K. Graehme Hall points out, it is vital that any discussion of
Sarton's novel acknowledges the generation in which Sarton was
writing, for "lesbian protagonists were rare and provided a risk to
their creator's career" (167). By dealing openly with the subject of
homosexuality in 1965, "Sarton was making a political statement"
(167). Although such labels as "sex maniac" and even "crazy" were
more likely to be prevalent in their association with homosexuality at
the time Sarton was writing, vestiges of those pejorative terms still
operate today.

Interestingly, some critics of Sarton's novels and poetry took issue
with her for not offering more sexual details, insinuating that she was
sexually repressed in not being emotionally honest enough in her portrayal of sexual relationships, regardless of whether her characters
were involved in a heterosexual or homosexual relationship. As Phyllis Chesler notes in her 1972 hallmark text *Women and Madness,*

> Most psychoanalytic theorists either sincerely misunderstand or
> severely condemn lesbianism. Some do both. The "condition,"
> they say, is biologically and/or hormonally based. No, say oth-
> ers, it is really an environmental phenomenon. In any event, all
> agree, it is maladaptive, regressive, and infantile: even if it isn't,
> it leads to undeniable suffering, and is *therefore* maladaptive, re-
> gressive, etc. (210)

Conversely, "Male homosexuality," she goes on to argue, "is often perceived, even through tears, as having a more 'glorious' tradition and a more legitimate or valued meaning than lesbianism" (212). Chesler's 1972 analysis still resonates, as with Peters' use of pejorative terms in commenting on Sarton's novel *We Aren't Getting Anywhere,* arguing how it reveals "Sarton's infantilism (Susie calls herself 'an embryo') as well as her pathological sense of isolation and lack of identity. It also reveals a confused sexuality" (330). Peters follows with her observation of the novel's character Susie (presumably she means Susie and not Sarton, though it's unclear) that "male sexuality terrifies her. Sarton's novels contain almost no sex; it is startling when Liesel's husband kisses Susie hard on the mouth. Susie is devastated—a young woman who feels unfeminine, thus preferring masculine women and neutered men" (330). Perhaps Peters is right about Sarton's being "confused" about her sexuality, and Peters is not the only one who uses the word "infantile" to describe Sarton. Sarton uses it, too, but she uses it to describe her "tantrum" behavior at times; she does not relate her "infantilism" to her sexuality in the way that Peters seems to do. Rather, for Sarton, it is her rages generally that she defines as infantile, and over which she confesses to feeling shame and guilt. However unconscious Peters may have been in making the kind of association that Chesler speaks to, the deleterious effects such associations can have in positioning such women as Sarton are no doubt felt still.

Perhaps it is these and other associations (and their positioning effects generally) that explain, in part, why Sarton did not particularly wish to be remembered either for her journals (in spite of their popularity) or for her decision to live her life by solitude. Indeed, the decision itself to live alone had its own disabling consequences. She writes in *Journal of a Solitude* that "It did not cheer me that Carol Heilbrun . . . feels that what I have done best—and what she thinks altogether new in my work—is to talk about solitude. I cried bitterly last night, as if a prison door were closing. But this is a mood, of course. Solitude here is my life. I have chosen it and had better go on making as great riches as possible out of despair" (134). At other times, Sarton made more subtly disparaging remarks about her "fame" along these lines, responding in one interview with veiled cynicism when asked about a column she had written for *Family Circle* magazine:

"Oh, that was heaven! I loved it. It was like being Colette. *Why* did they ever have me? I mean, FAMILY Circle? All the pieces were about living alone. They pushed the column to the back of the book and surrounded it with advertisements of bread so nobody could find it. But I enjoyed it" (Shelley 69). Undoubtedly, the publication of her work in a magazine such as *Family Circle* confirmed even for Sarton the kind of familial economy she was embroiled in—an economy that was willing to engage her solitude only on the merits of its appeal to matters of "home and hearth," and even then, only in terms of its reflecting—at least in the safe venue of the back pages—an older, middle-class white woman's hearth. It was yet another kind of marginalization that Sarton no doubt had gotten used to though was unlikely to have fully accepted, even though her being positioned in this restricted way translated into her name and work getting publicized. In the end, at least to some degree, the very process of solitude, which she did not desire to commodify, only to write, ended up commodifying, and writing, her. In her journal *Daybook* (1982), artist Anne Truitt explains why this commodification process unfolds, stating: "The public, themselves deprived of the feeling of community that grants due proportion to everyone's self-expression, yearn over the artist in some special way because he or she seems to have the magic to wrench color and meaning from their bleached lives. The artist gives them themselves. They can even buy themselves" (115).

Certainly in an age that still thrives more than ever on production/consumption, the commodification process seems even more unavoidable, and in the increasing absence of the kind of communal belonging that does provide "color and meaning" to people's lives, Truitt's recognition of the public's need for an artist to reflect back something real about itself assumes even more validity. But, as Truitt argues, there is nothing that can keep what is "real" from being purchasable so long as it can be packaged in some way, to the point where the artist herself can get in on the game. May Sarton's "story of solitude" ultimately became a purchasable myth in the form of published journals. In this respect, it is perhaps no different from the ticket price that the Clock of the Long Now project will issue for experiencing "the long view" of the next 10,000 years. As a commodity, however, the Clock of the Long Now fails to engage personally, for with the Clock there can be no possibilities for consumers' self-expression, let alone for their engagement and embroilment in the complexities and contradictions of human life and human interaction that do get revealed by Sarton, though perhaps not as fully as they might be. Unlike the process of solitude that Sarton writes, a process that *requires* individual agency, the Clock of the Long Now can be nothing more than a symbol that is without capacity for reflecting in any real way the people who come to visit it. It can reflect only the slow tick of time, and only in linear terms; thus it can serve only as a technological postmark of the technological age itself, emptied out of the people who interact within its spatial and temporal boundaries.

As stated earlier, and as Peters makes clear in the biography, May Sarton contributed to the myth of May Sarton's solitude, reluctant as she was to display fully all the frustration and anger operating within it. But whatever myth her journals create, it should not discount the agency that Sarton's solitude affords. Certainly, both myth and agency are inescapably tied to the privileges that come with Sarton's being white, well educated, and with the independent means to live protected on her own property that is both house, and house with a garden and a view. "What would I do without this calming open space to rest my eyes on?" she writes (*Journal* 31). Indeed, what would or does a woman do who doesn't have such open space? What possibilities for solitude might she realize? What agency does she have to choose a solitary life? How would she value it? What would her account of solitude describe? Sarton described her own solitude as "the great, the greatest luxury," because, she wrote, "I have time to think" (*Journal* 41). That time to think—to meditate and to write—is informed and fueled as much by the space around her as by its quality, which is hard to separate out from the class and racial privileges she knows. On coming back from a trip to Dallas, a place she thought had "too much luxury" and therefore "too little quality," Sarton's points of comparison are "dear old shabby Cambridge" and the "Heaven" of Nelson, themselves predominantly "white," middle-to-upper-class towns, whose "quality" Sarton does not associate with class but with age (*Journal* 51-52). "I saw it freshly, saw the beauty of wooden clapboard painted white, of old brick, of my own battered and living maples, as a shining marvel, a treasure that lifts the mind and the heart and brings everyone who sees it back to what *quality* is" (51-52).

Acknowledging (where Sarton may not) the significance of racial and class privileges should not take away from appreciating the agency that Sarton exercises in choosing and creating a life of solitude in the first place. In fact, it is important to recognize *how* such privileges inform that agency. Not acknowledging privilege as a significant factor—indeed not focusing on it enough—is to somehow risk Sarton's solitude becoming *the* unquestioned and unexamined model for all women. It would mean failing to recognize the multiple ways solitude might be defined but also limited and denied, given the different social and cultural realities that can adversely affect women's lives. To see Sarton's solitary lifestyle as somehow selfish because of the privileges she knows is not the answer, certainly not to the question of how women's relationship to solitude might also be written. But to fail to see agency as influenced by privilege is to fail to see how agency, when realized both in and because of solitude, might be performed differently by those without the same privileges and/or with different ones.

Ultimately, if Sarton does create a myth of herself, and of her world at Nelson or by the sea in Maine, then that myth is significantly *her* myth, and *her* agency that the processes of solitude allow her to establish for herself. It is this agency that is important, more than the idyllic impression some readers may walk away with (or even, through their *own* sense of agency as readers, assist in creating themselves) of what a life of solitude might mean. Instead, it is the personal agency that Sarton achieves that is the magnet, particularly for women readers who, for whatever personal and cultural circumstances, may find themselves without.

NOTES

1. The connection I am drawing here between the Clock of the Long Now project and male centeredness has foundation in Lucy Sargisson's *(Contemporary Feminist Utopianism)* reading of Derrida and his examination of the logocentrism of Western thought and the system of naming, wherein she writes: "Naming, for Derrida, is claiming. Naming, asking and deciding 'What is it?,' is central to philosophical discourses and relies upon the possibility of attaining the truth. It assumes the (possible) presence of truth, hence logocentrism. This project for Derrida is corrupt, not a neutral quest of inquiry, but rather an imposition of an order which is normative and repressive. There is no such thing as a neutral quest of inquiry, as the question itself

('What is it?') is phallo-logocentrically loaded" (89). As Sargisson points out, the implications of this logocentric system for feminism and utopianism run deep, for such a system operates on exclusion—something validated as "good" over its opposite, which is "bad"—and disallows a different feminist utopian paradigm based upon inclusion and positive difference.

2. According to the book's Appendix note, the millennial clock project maintains alliances with several organizations, with Disney listed among them. Others include the National Park Service, the Global Business Network, and the Getty Center.

3. I say "never alone" here in light of Sarton's ongoing sense of responsibility to others, particularly to other women, and because of the obligations that responsibility resulted in, namely to an attentive, lifelong following of loyal readers, whose letters Sarton felt duty-bound to answer.

4. Sarton wanted to correct what she saw as an incomplete or "false view" depicted in *Plant Dreaming Deep*. She writes in *Journal of a Solitude,* in reference to the earlier work, that "[t]he anguish of my life here—its rages—is hardly mentioned. Now I hope to break through into the rough rocky depths, to the matrix itself. There is violence there and anger never resolved" (12). Interesting to note is Sarton's claim that the book's "false view" was written "without my own intention" (12).

5. Though the majority of Sarton's growing-up years were spent in New England, she was not a native New Englander and did not feel like one. Sarton was born in Belgium. Her Belgian-born father moved the family to the United States at the outbreak of World War I, and eventually to Cambridge, where he found a position at Harvard. Sarton's mother was English. This feeling of neither belonging wholly to an American culture or to a Belgian one also contributed to Sarton's sense of being an outsider.

6. See Carol Virginia Pohli's illuminating essay "Saving the Audience: Patterns of Reader Response to May Sarton's Work" in the collection *That Great Sanity* (pp. 211-238), Susan Swartzlander and Marilyn R. Mumford, eds. (1995).

7. The popular attention her journals acquired came as a surprise to Sarton, who states in *A Self-Portrait:* "The journals, funnily enough, have brought me a whole new audience of the young which is extremely charming and amusing to me . . . [they] seemed to have a rather wide appeal, I don't know why. I've tried to be honest" (24).

8. See Margot Peters' discussion in *May Sarton: A Biography* of Sarton's reason for leaving, namely over frustrations she experienced in her love relationship with Cora DuBois, a professor of anthropology at Harvard. Of Sarton's reason for leaving, Peters writes: "With her biographer, however, she was frank: 'I did it for Cora' " (217). Finally, Sarton's move to Nelson may also reflect a transient history that began in childhood. Sarton was Belgian-born, but at the onset of World War I she was forced to move, initially with her mother to her mother's native England and later to America, where they rejoined her father who had already established residency in Cambridge. From that point on, Sarton's life would be marked by continual trips back and forth between America and Europe, the bills for which were, more often than not, footed at Sarton's request by her parents or through the generosity of friends. Although Sarton's parents were by no means rich, Sarton nevertheless en-

joyed the luxury while they were alive of being able to take off on her own at their expense.

9. Margot Peters points out, perhaps uncharitably, that while Sarton indeed struggled to support herself financially, often, as Sarton claimed, by having to produce at least a book a year to meet the demands of her publisher, the struggle was in no way helped by Sarton's penchant for reckless spending. Writes Peters: "[Sarton's] excuse that she had to write to support herself is true—but only because she gave so much money away" (317).

10. Sarton's father, George Sarton, was a Harvard professor of the history of science; her mother, Mabel Sarton, was a designer of furniture and of women's clothing.

11. In her discussion of the critical reception of Sarton's *The House by the Sea,* Peters references a male Chicago critic who "admitted he could be 'impatient with her [Sarton's] chatter about dogs, cats and flowers' " (324).

12. Christina Pugh (see Chapter 3, "Unknown Women: Secular Solitude in the Works of Alice Koller and May Sarton" in this book) calls Sarton's solitariness a state of "incompletion" that involves Sarton's ongoing self-dialogue with what may be "versions of her own voice or echoes of others." As Pugh argues, these versions of Sarton's own voice may not be distinguishable from others', for others bear influence on Sarton, not simply in terms of their presence in her life but in terms of the roles Sarton, in turn, plays in relation to them.

13. The photographs were taken either by Sarton's friends Eleanor Blair and Beverly Hallam, or attributed to Mort Mace or *The New York Times.*

14. Sarton's taste in art gravitated to works by such painters as Vermeer, whose scenes were often portraits of persons (often women) in private, still moments. I believe such works are what she has in mind when she makes this statement. Someone thinking of Picasso's portraits, for instance, or of many of van Gogh's paintings would no doubt reject Sarton's description of the artist's experience as not involving some aspect of chaos or of pain.

15. The complete quote, "Photographs promote forgetting," comes from Marguerite Duras *(Practicalities),* as quoted by Marianne Hirsch *(Family Frames)* in her discussion of Duras's use of photographs in *The Lover.*

WORKS CITED

Alves, Susan. "A Poetry of Absence: May Sarton's Use of the Sentimental." In *A Celebration for May Sarton,* 105-117. Constance Hunting, ed. Orono: Puckerbrush P, 1994.

Bonetti, Kay. "An Interview with May Sarton." In *Conversations with May Sarton,* 85-107. Earl G. Ingersoll, ed. Jackson: UP of Mississippi, 1991.

Brand, Stewart. *The Clock of the Long Now: Time and Responsibility.* New York: Basic Books, 2000.

Chesler, Phyllis. *Women and Madness.* New York: Four Walls Eight Windows, 1972/1997.

Cixous, Hélène. *Stigmata*. London: Routledge, 1998.

de Certeau, Michel. *The Practice of Everyday Life*. Trans. Steven Randall. Berkeley: U of California P, 1988.

Duras, Marguerite. *Writing*. Trans. Mark Polizzotti. Cambridge: Lumen Editions, 1998.

Grumbach, Doris. *Fifty Days of Solitude*. Boston: Beacon P, 1994.

Hall, K. Graehme. "'To Say Radical Things Gently': Art and Lesbianism in *Mrs. Stevens Hears the Mermaids Singing*." In *That Great Sanity: Critical Essays on May Sarton,* 167-186. Susan Swartzlander and Marilyn R. Mumford, eds. Ann Arbor: U of Michigan P, 1995.

Heilbrun, Carolyn. "The May Sarton I Have Known." In *A Celebration for May Sarton,* 3-12. Constance Hunting, ed. Orono: Puckerbrush P, 1994.

Hirsch, Marianne. *Family Frames: Photography, Narrative, and Postmemory*. Cambridge: Harvard UP, 1997.

Hunting, Constance, ed. *A Celebration for May Sarton*. Orono: Puckerbrush P, 1994.

Ingersoll, Earl G., ed. *Conversations with May Sarton*. Jackson: UP of Mississippi, 1991.

Koch, Philip. *Solitude: A Philosophical Encounter*. Chicago: Open Court P, 1994.

Peters, Margot. *May Sarton: A Biography*. New York: Ballantine Publishing Group, 1997.

Rosenthal, Lois. "[Interview with] May Sarton." In *Conversations with May Sarton,* 183-192. Earl G. Ingersoll, eds. Jackson: UP of Mississippi, 1991.

Sargisson, Lucy. *Contemporary Feminist Utopianism*. New York: Routledge, 1996.

Sarton, May. *A Self-Portrait*. Marita Simpson and Martha Wheelock, eds. New York: W. W. Norton and Co., 1982.

_____. *The House by the Sea: A Journal*. New York: W. W. Norton and Co., 1977.

_____. *Journal of a Solitude*. New York: W. W. Norton and Co., 1973.

Shelley, Dolores. "A Conversation with May Sarton." In *Conversations with May Sarton,* 64-73. Earl G. Ingersoll, ed. Jackson: UP of Mississippi, 1991.

Swartzlander, Susan and Marilyn R. Mumford, eds. *That Great Sanity: Critical Essays on May Sarton*. Ann Arbor: U of Michigan P, 1995.

Thoreau, Henry David. *The Portable Thoreau*. Carl Bode, ed. New York: Penguin Books, 1982.

Truitt, Anne. *Daybook: The Journal of an Artist*. New York: Penguin Books, 1984.

– 3 –

Unknown Women:
Secular Solitude in the Works
of Alice Koller and May Sarton

Christina Pugh

In the photograph, a woman raptly reads in bed by the light of a small lamp while a man sleeps beside her. Above this soft-focus domestic scene, a page from the woman's book is legibly reproduced: "Chapter 5: A Right to Peace, Solitude, and Half the Blankets." The text continues: "Her bed was a haven. The last stop of the day. A place to be alone, even with her husband snoring softly beside her." This woman longingly reads a storybook tale of solitude's impossibility: a truth her photograph itself "proves" by the very presence of the man next to her.

This recent ad for Lexington Home Brands is utterly consonant with the predominant cultural view of women's solitude: if it exists at all, solitude is seen as a breath a wife and mother catches for a few rare minutes as her husband or partner snores by her side.[1] For the struggling single mother, solitude may indeed be an impossibility. But what of the woman who chooses to live alone? Where will she find the storybook that rings true to her own life? More than seventy years after Virginia Woolf's imaginary sketch of the interrupted Jane Austen in *A Room of One's Own,*[2] it would appear that the phrase "women's solitude" continues to function as an oxymoron in Western culture at large. Filmic renditions of women's solitude, such as Kieslowski's *Bleu* or *An Unmarried Woman,* invariably depict this state as either precipitous—brought about by tragedy or divorce—or ephemeral, and sometimes both.

Clearly, women who have chosen to take solitude and its concomitant silences seriously—women, that is, who have chosen solitude as something other than an illusory, continually interrupted state—will find few models or inspirations in the media representations surrounding them. This is the void that the autobiographical "how-to" works of May Sarton and Alice Koller fill with their descriptions of a woman's right and choice to live alone. Though neither writer works specifically from feminist concerns, both offer a unique perspective on a life choice that remains virtually unrepresented in American culture: the possibility that the solitary existence can constitute a viable, even rewarding option for modern women who are pressured both to mother and to relate unstintingly to others. And it is because there are so few models for solitary women that the question of their own exemplariness haunts both of these writers' autobiographical works.

Perhaps even more transgressive of common assumptions about solitude, both Koller and Sarton represent this life choice as *secular* in its orientation. Indeed, these texts rely notably upon religious metaphor, or the vocabulary of monasticism and pilgrimage. The creeping of the monastic model into these works shows the dearth of secular images and vocabularies from which we may draw metaphors for women's solitude: the aloneness of the saint or mystic, even if considered an aberration, still depends on a somewhat familiar paradigm. The chosen aloneness of the atheist or agnostic—particularly the female atheist or agnostic—does not.

Yet even if the choice of the word *pilgrimage* remains problematic, there are many ways in which these writers may be seen as pioneers. The secular solitary life arguably constitutes the last frontier for women in the new millennium, transcending issues of sexual orientation (Koller is heterosexual, Sarton lesbian) and even class. Regardless of the widely trumpeted new options open to American women at the end of the twentieth century—delayed childbirth or childlessness, arguably more openness than ever before to the options of lesbianism and bisexuality as life choices—the choice of solitude remains the last taboo for women who have been theorized as predominantly relational, regardless of their sexual orientation. Carol Gilligan's argument for women's relational morality in *In a Different Voice* has informed works ranging from the highly influential *Women's Ways of Knowing* in the late 1980s to the recent concept of "emotional intelligence."[3]

French feminists Luce Irigaray, who has located such relationality in women's labial anatomy itself ("Quand nos levres se parlent") (203), and Julia Kristeva, who has defined "women's time" as essentially the cyclical ticking of women's biological clock ("the majority of women today see the possibility for fulfillment, if not entirely at least to a large degree, in bringing a child into the world," [206]), have only conferred a more intellectual patina upon the popular myth of the selfless superwoman who will make any degree of sacrifice for her family.

Though neither Koller nor Sarton addresses the woman reader primarily nor bases her work in overtly feminist claims (Koller, somewhat problematically, calls herself a member of "that third gender: a human person, the being one creates of oneself" [*Stations* 23]), both Koller and Sarton begin from the premise that, in Sarton's words, "a middle-aged, single woman, without any vestige of family left, lives in this house in a silent village and is responsible only to her own soul means something" (*Journal of a Solitude* 40). At the very least, this meaning is differential in kind, since the choice of solitude is deeply troubling to the predominant cultural portrayal of women as bearers of greater sociability and emotional accessibility than men.

The Personal Is Philosophical: Alice Koller and the Benisons of Reason

Alice Koller's project is to reveal what she calls the "benisons" of solitude as a personal and secular choice. For Koller, this choice was commensurate with a form of conversion experience, as I shall show. Koller's desire for solitude is also commensurate with her desire to write, and both are inextricable from the larger drive toward meaning she feels in her life—in particular, the definition and "use" *(mode d'emploi)* of the self. In this sense, her companion pieces *An Unknown Woman* and *The Stations of Solitude* are as much about the discovery of true philosophy as they are about discovering solitude. Koller calls this philosophy "writing my thinking," or a thinking-through-writing that becomes a manner of self-fashioning.

An Unknown Woman chronicles Koller's three months wintering in isolation on the island of Nantucket in 1962, soon after completing her PhD in philosophy at Harvard. She made this trip at a particularly low point in her life—after a series of failed love affairs, the death of a beloved therapist, and with no academic job prospects on the horizon—in order to find out what she wanted and how to divest her own desires from the expectations of others: "On Nantucket I slashed away everything that was preventing my seeing, my hearing, my feeling, my understanding" (*Stations* 8); "One principle served me as knife: I had to know what was true" (*Stations* 15).

Although *An Unknown Woman* was rejected thirty times over thirteen years by publishers who criticized it as "too personal" (*Stations* 66), its personal narrative is subordinated to a central philosophical, even phenomenological problem: what does it feel like to want, from one's own point of view?[4] Is it possible, and how is it possible, to distinguish one's own desires from the desires of others? How can one move from desire to the living of a true life? Koller could only broach these problems from a position of physical isolation. When she landed on Nantucket, she was sure of just three desires she could name as hers: "Logos [her dog] was of my heart. I had to live near the sea or other wildness. I possessed a passion and perfect eye for color" (*Stations* 8). Through its trajectory of, in Koller's words, "tale and explication," *An Unknown Woman* comes both to expand and to consolidate these three certainties (*Stations* 66).

Koller's narrative of her time in Nantucket reenacts an often brutal self-searching, a series of flashbacks and probing questions that seem almost painfully imbued with the difficulty of women's experience, certainly resonant even in the "postfeminist" twenty-first century. In hindsight made dramatic through her terse use of present tense narration, Koller describes her failing of general exams at Harvard, her brief study of theater, and, most frequently, her dependence upon a series of love affairs with men. What distinguishes the narration is the intense self-scrutiny to which Koller subjects the self she is trying to save: the "knife" of analytical reason cutting cruel, ultimately, to be kind:

> . . . it took me until yesterday to discover that I never knew whether I wanted to act. I wasn't acting because I wanted to act. I was acting for the applause. Even studying philosophy was all part of the same thing: I just transferred the action from the theater proper to a university. I've never known whether I *wanted* to do philosophy either.

> But why have I *needed* other people's eyes? I must not have
> trusted what I could see, and so I turned to what they could see.
> And yet, not every "they." I chose which ones I'd believe. I must
> have had some reason for choosing Dr. Gnesin's opinion over
> David's, for instance. Or for believing the people who told me I
> was beautiful, even though I suspected them to be wrong. . . . Of
> course, being beautiful isn't something you get an opposing
> opinion about. People don't walk up to you and say, "You're not
> beautiful." (*Unknown* 96)

Koller's searching appraisal of her own narcissism—and the text's
preoccupation with the themes of feminine role-playing and feminine
objectification—predates not only such scholars of the heterosexual
gaze as Deleuze and Mulvey, but also the grassroots struggles of second-wave feminism itself. Hers is a struggle between a historically
bound model of femininity as passivity and a hunger for knowledge
that is concomitant with the need to act in the world as an independent agent.

The preceding two passages' self-indictment, certainly more sca-
thing than her indictment of the men she loved, may seem to us—certainly after the work of feminist writers from Susan Brownmiller to
Naomi Wolf—an extreme instance of victim self-blame. But we
should keep in mind that this narrative took place in 1962 and the
years before.[5] As she describes in *An Unknown Woman,* her energy
and assertiveness were not in keeping with the times, especially in
such a traditional academic setting as Cambridge. The passivity associated with traditional femininity required a different, loathsome education to which she could not truly subscribe: "To wait. That was
what I hated most to do. To wait for the phone to ring, to wait to be
asked out, to wait to be kissed. Every man who tried to educate me began with waiting" (126).

Koller's time on Nantucket constituted a third education, one separate from but informed by both Harvard academia and the emotional
demands of the men she knew. Perhaps paradoxically, this unflinch-
ing gaze at peculiarly "feminine" embarrassments and disappoint-
ments enables her story to become exemplary for others—to gain, in
a sense, the universality that the "impersonal" discipline of philosophy claimed for itself in the academy. Ultimately, Koller's strategy is

to examine the subjective facts of her life from a position of disinterest, not to embrace one particular philosopher's worldview; and it is this fitting of reason to the varying (but heretofore formless) matter of experience that enables her story to become universal: ". . . it is not a novel, not a journal, not ultimately about me, but that in tandem with the narrative about coming to understand myself it is an account of the *process* of coming to understand oneself" (*Stations* 66; emphasis Koller's). In Koller's view, then, readers who engage in a vicarious experience of reasoning become her unwitting coconspirators: "Those readers [of *An Unknown Woman*] have let themselves do philosophy along with me, even though some of them did not know to call it by that name" (*Stations* 66). Yet the tease of reason Koller holds out to the reader—the lure of the seamlessness she wants to claim between logos (not coincidentally, the name she gave her first puppy) and praxis—is also the discovery that virtually saved her life: ". . . without my being a philosopher I might merely have found Nantucket the most congenial shore from which to walk into the water" (*Stations* 44).

Indeed, the Nantucket retreat described in *An Unknown Woman* has become the fulcrum for Koller's entire autobiographical oeuvre: the "tale," as she says, to whose exegesis she eternally returns. In this sense, the choice not to walk into the water nevertheless approximates baptism, or an experience similar to religious conversion: "I often say, 'before Nantucket' or 'since Nantucket'" (*Stations* 1). And her commitment to philosophy, or to the "knife" of analytic thinking that enabled her to slice through her own web of tangled relationships and desires, remains a sentiment almost religious in its enthusiasm. For this reason, the language of faith strenuously abuts the language of philosophy in her narrative, even when she most vehemently denies its influence: "I am not a saint; I am only a philosopher" (*Stations* 195). A confirmed atheist, Koller is nevertheless fully aware that her vocabulary shades into the religious, even down to the choice of title for her second book: "I am not Catholic. I am not religious in any sense of the word. . . . So the stations of solitude that I shall be displaying to you do not imitate those of the cross" (*Stations* x).

Yet *The Stations of Solitude* itself operates through a loosely allegorical structure, the gerunds of its chapter "stations" comprising integral and active aspects of the solitary life ("Working," "Loving," "Singling," "Moneying," etc.). Koller's life-made-universal becomes a challenge set before the unconvinced reader, similar to Bunyan's hortatory "apology" beginning his *Pilgrim's Progress:* "This book will make a traveler of thee, / If by its counsel thou wilt ruled be. / It will direct thee to the Holy Land, / If thou wilt its *directions understand:* / Yea, it will make the slothful active be, / The blind also delightful things to see" (48, emphasis mine). Like Bunyan, Koller emphasizes understanding as a motive for change. Indeed, she credits understanding rather than reader identification with the effect her *Unknown Woman* has on readers: "The philosophical skill I deliberately cultivated of being able to say exactly what I mean lets me articulate my own thinking in *such a way that readers believe I am articulating theirs*" (203, emphasis mine). Yet philosophical treatises as such operate through precept rather than through reader identification; they are not mimetic in the classical sense. Thus in her very enthusiasm for reason, Koller may mistake reader identification elicited by skillful *narrative* for a winning of the reader through "philosophical skill."

Koller's promotion of a fiercely secular journey in *Stations* echoes Bunyan's in tone and temperament, equally promising self-transformation as a reward for the choice of activity rather than "slothful" pursuing of a stifling and too-familiar world of human relations:

> That route toward yourself that you pursue by yourself is your reflective occupation of the first station of solitude. The journey is almost totally one of looking back. When you leave the station, you will probably never look back again. There will be no nostalgia for the life you used to live: it belongs to someone you no longer are. (*Stations* 7)

The stations of this reading experience, much as the allegorical topography of Christian's journey in Bunyan's text, promise a form of salvation born of choice, though Koller refuses to provide specific instructions: "Your circuit of the stations of solitude will thereby differ from mine. Not only in detail, as is to be expected, but in principle as well" (364). She continually returns to the trope of blindness and vision in a way that is reminiscent both of Bunyan and of the New Testament he allegorized: "For now we see through a glass, darkly; but then face to face; now I know in part; but then shall I know even as also I am known" (I Corinthians 13:12). And in a similar way, she exhorts the reader to true sight: ". . . you cannot see only because of the encrustations you have let seal your eyes. You have only to rip them away" (13). Of the many allegories at her disposal, from the survivalist's dream of climbing Everest (198) to the storybook tale of Alice's fall down the rabbit hole ("like Alice's doorway, you cannot enter it until you are the right size" [12]), it is the font of religious metaphors that enables Koller's "eternal return."

Why this return to the language and tropes of faith, on the part of an archrationalist such as Koller? As I suggested earlier, it may have much to do with the paucity of other discourses that would describe the solitary enterprise or voyage—the secular solitude that seems to elude our vocabularies and means for conceptualization:

> Not all ecstasy is sexual. Or religious. And yet not *ekstasis:* standing outside oneself, out of control. I hereby invent *instasis:* standing inside oneself, in full and rapturous control begotten in doing one's work. (56)

The drive toward neologism is entirely appropriate in this context: if we read "rapturous control" as an oxymoron, perhaps it is because we have yet to adapt our perceptions, and thereby our language, to Koller's experience.

But the link between conversion and philosophy is also an old and forgotten one. As Gerald Peters points out in a study of conversion narratives titled *The Mutilating God,* the concept of conversion itself originated with Plato's specific use of logic:

> The fact that the concept of conversion may have come to fruition first in the philosophical schools may seem somewhat surprising to many who have claimed the term for religion alone. But if we consider that conversion presupposes *a unity of consciousness only possible with the advent of an integrated and systematic form of expression,* the link between conversion and philosophy should cause no surprise at all. (31, emphasis mine)

Above and beyond the specific arguments of any philosopher she quotes, it is the methodological "knife" of reason that has enabled Koller to become herself most fully; and this self is indistinguishable from the unified postconversion self to which Peters refers. Far from the abstract and purely cerebral enterprise sanctioned by the academy, Koller sees the practice of philosophy as enabling the flowering of a whole, purposeful, and viscerally defined self that is inseparable from the actions of a solitary agent in the world: "The philosopher I am is inextricably entwined with the person I am" (*Stations* 224).

As Koller has shown from the beginning, however, the knife of reason may be reinterpreted as a pen; the writing process itself is neither tangential nor incidental to this enterprise of "writing her thinking":

> By the time I have written something, the words on the paper exactly as I wish them to be, I understand the matter they crystallize. . . . Understanding some matter, I have in effect detached it from envy, anger, pride, shame, dismay, perhaps even grief. Writing of it is a mark of the distance from which I can ever after view it. (67)

Certainly worlds away from the notion of "women's ways of knowing," undeniably Cartesian in its orientation, Koller's renegade drive to render everyday life commensurate with philosophical text has paradoxically revalued the Derridean trace or mark absent from discussions of philosophical "presence." And yet this very writing necessarily "detaches" itself from the polyvalence that would necessarily elude the perfect understanding she describes.

Indeed, good poststructuralists may well see Koller's devotion to reason as itself a blind spot replacing the ocular "encrustations" she earlier mentions, as well as her near collapse of the often warring faculties of reason and desire. Her inspirational if dubious confidence in the power of the self to reconstruct itself based on will alone ("On Nantucket I dismantled one self. Since Nantucket I have been designing, constructing, another" [22]) is surely an atypical example of the second-wave feminist adage, "The personal is political." By effectively denying the role of the unconscious in human endeavors, and by upholding a faith in self-re-creation, Koller does champion an existentialist approach to living that risks eliding the very richness of complication that psychoanalysis has revealed to us as operative in quotidian human interactions. Her universalist approach to the solitary life in *The Stations of Solitude* also risks underestimating the gender differentials that drove her to her crisis in Nantucket in the first place. Has the solitary life, or the writing of it, required Alice Koller to "unsex herself"?

Clearly, Koller's relationship to feminism, and indeed to women as a gendered category, remains problematic. After her departure from Nantucket, she lived solitarily for decades, supporting herself—and a series of houses and dogs ("I who belong no specific where make my home wherever I happen to live" [*Stations* 257])—with a variety of teaching and freelance writing jobs. Indeed, both books would be notable achievements only on the basis of their portrayal of loving, respectful relationships between human beings and animals.[6] Yet there is an important way in which Koller has not fully negotiated the heterosexual role she found so painful, even though, as she states in *Stations,* her sexual orientation did not change: "My life without human beings has not changed my sexuality: I want only a man's body next to mine" (*Stations* 196). In this sense, the joint import of *An Unknown Woman* and *The Stations of Solitude* constitutes, I believe, a much harsher critique of relations between the sexes than Koller herself is perhaps willing to admit. The relationship between sexuality and autonomy, between agency and the theater of gender expectations, remains imperfectly articulated; and the implications of Koller's celibacy for women in particular certainly bear further exploration.

But if we return briefly to the spurious notion of women's "solitude" as "a right to half the blankets," we can perceive both the courage of Alice Koller's writings and the immense cultural need for such an exemplar. Though she claims that, apart from those three inaugural months in Nantucket, she never consciously planned to live a solitary life ("It was not part of my plan to become solitary. . . . I wanted only to write my thinking, to teach and to learn. In a house of my own in the country" [*Stations* 95]), Koller is a pioneering woman in many senses of that word. Her own particular version of instasis, or of "loning," as she calls it elsewhere—her joy in the dawn and in the personalities of her dogs—becomes itself a benison to the woman reader who has set out on a similar course, who has been made to "see reason" in solitude, and who might follow in her wake.

May Sarton: Sociability, Solitude, and Nakedness

> I made my song a coat
> Covered with embroideries
> Out of old mythologies
> From heel to throat;
> But the fools caught it,
> Wore it in the world's eyes
> As though they'd wrought it.
> Song, let them take it,
> For there's more enterprise
> In walking naked.
>
> W. B. Yeats (*Collected Poems* 127)

Like Koller, May Sarton appreciates color and the outdoors, the companionship of neighbors and animals, and the solitary state as a life choice. It is her profound distrust of exemplariness that distinguishes Sarton's autobiographical works most dramatically from *An Unknown Woman* and *The Stations of Solitude.* If we take Sarton's *Plant Dreaming Deep,* a narrated memoir, and *Journal of a Solitude,* written in diary format, as companion pieces mirroring Koller's two texts, we find that each pair of books is inversely proportional to the other. While *The Stations of Solitude* expands upon and teaches the self-denuding thinking process so painfully hammered out in *An Unknown Woman,* Sarton wished the immediacy of her *Journal* to correct what she felt was the illusion of a too-smooth life trajectory, a too-celebratory portrait of solitude in her earlier book. The very title of *Journal of a Solitude,* with its indefinite article before the vexed noun in question, bespeaks an aloneness that refuses to be universal. Sarton's struggle between solitude and sociability is less a treatise than an ongoing, nonlinear narrative resembling the disorderliness of our days themselves; yet her charting of this particular "nakedness," including her minute attention to her surroundings as both material and symbol, elucidates a reluctant aesthetics of solitude.

When the poet and novelist Sarton bought a house in Nelson, New Hampshire, at the age of forty-six, her purposes were from the beginning more deliberate than Koller's. Sarton chose this solitude over a domestic partnership she had long maintained with another woman, a

partner her narrative describes in only the most loving of terms (and
to whom Sarton dedicates her account of moving to Nelson, titled
Plant Dreaming Deep). This choice suggests another motivation for
choosing solitude, one that is unrelated to heterosexual demands on
women but has much to do with the need for developing the self outside the rubric of intimate human relations. And, in fact, for Sarton,
solitariness constitutes her most authentic being-in-the world: "I am
here alone for the first time in weeks, to take up my 'real' life again at
last" (*Journal* 11).

In a metaphor that is extended throughout *Plant Dreaming Deep*
and *Journal of a Solitude,* Sarton equates this new solitude with the
Yeatsian nakedness described in the poem serving as epigraph to this
section:

> . . . my demons will, perhaps, never be exorcised entirely. But I
> had made the decision to move into the country out of powerful
> need, the need to try at least to come to terms with them. I was
> deliberately cutting life back to the marrow, and this meant that I
> had cut myself off from all that helps us balance acute depres-
> sion against the gentle demands of day-to-day living—from
> family life, in my case the dear rites and traditions of my life
> with Judy, getting a meal together, going for a walk, playing
> with the cat in the evening, from all that clothes the naked soul
> and comforts it. (*Plant* 87)

Nakedness, and its concomitant depressions, become part and parcel
of the challenge Sarton sets for herself by choosing to live alone. By
stripping away the comforts of routine and everyday sociability—including the sometimes luxurious trappings of human intimacy, to
continue the metaphor—Sarton must contemplate her own emotional
anatomy, or the grim countenances of what she terms her "demons."
By depicting this struggle as ongoing, Sarton portrays the naked self
as continually in flux, stitched and unraveled on a veritable Penelope's loom.

Tellingly, Sarton reverses the metaphor later in the *Journal,* when
she asserts that "[we] must find a balance between going naked (in
the Yeatsian sense, 'There's more enterprise in walking naked') and
being tough enough to survive such intensity of caring and such

openness, between a driving need to share experience and the need for time to experience, and that means solitude" (75). The reversibility of the nakedness metaphor, as the vulnerability of solitude becomes the vulnerability of intimacy, speaks to a doubled set of vulnerabilities—a double helix, as it were—that entwines both of these narratives.

Carolyn Heilbrun has championed Sarton for the nakedness of her text as a whole, claiming that the publication in 1973 of *Journal of a Solitude* marked a turning point for women's autobiography because "Sarton deliberately retold the record of her anger," thus raising the bar on the degree of honesty expected from women's autobiography (13). Certainly the diary format allows for more minute swings of consciousness than does the retrospective memoir; it refuses the teleological thrust of *The Stations of Solitude* and even of the chaptered *Plant Dreaming Deep*. In contrast to Koller, Sarton does not portray herself as representative of an exemplary life choice; on the contrary, she claims to have relatively few lessons to teach: "Mine is not, I feel sure, the best human solution. Nor have I ever thought it was" (*Journal* 123). The palinodic relationship of the *Journal* to her earlier book reflects this refusal to act as model for her readers:

> . . . I have begun to realize that, without my own intention, that book [*Plant Dreaming Deep*] gives a false view. The anguish of my life here—its rages—is hardly mentioned. Now I hope to break through into the rough rocky depths, to the matrix itself. There is violence there and anger never resolved. I live alone, perhaps for no good reason, for the reason that I am an impossible creature, set apart by a temperament I have never learned to use as it could be used, thrown off by a word, a glance, a rainy day, or one drink too many. My need to be alone is balanced against my fear of what will happen when suddenly I enter the huge empty silence if I cannot find support there. . . . It may be outwardly silent here but in the back of my mind is a clamor of human voices, too many needs, hopes, fears. (*Journal* 12-13)

Living alone "for no good reason" would be a foreign notion to Alice Koller, whose self-criticism essentially disappeared from her work after what I have termed her conversion experience in Nantucket.

Sarton's intent to capture the vicissitudes of the moment—replete with self-recrimination and often baleful self-doubt—lets her reside in the stubborn incompletion or constant imperfection of the solitary state, in which the need to be alone is met with an "empty silence" that is nevertheless "clamoring" with the sometimes overwhelming needs of what Sarton calls "human voices"—whether versions of her own voice or echoes of others', she does not tell us in this passage. Indeed, perhaps the two categories cannot be so easily separated out. Unlike Koller, who was driven to divest herself of others' voices, to become a version of *vox clamantis in deserto,* Sarton, even in her solitude, conducts an ongoing dialogue with other voices that she clearly cannot—and sometimes does not wish to—quiet.

This often painful vacillation between the experience of solitude as isolation and the experience of the-other-within-solitude is often expressed in the terms of either-or extremes or insoluble dilemmas: "It would be a real deprivation to have no phone here, but on the other hand how devastating a voice can be!" (*Journal* 107). Such a dilemma also becomes a vocational conflict for a writer who deems herself at times "fatally divided in loyalty between two crafts, that of the novel and that of poetry" (*Plant* 88). Such a division between Bakhtin's heteroglossia of the novel, as opposed to the "loning," in Koller's terms, of the lyric voice, haunts Sarton both personally and professionally: "the poem is primarily a dialogue with the self and the novel a dialogue with others" (41).

Yet it would be a mistake to read *Journal of a Solitude* as a journal of pain and conflict only. Despite Heilbrun's valid claim, there is measurable continuity between the *Journal* and *Plant Dreaming Deep*—down to the very format of these books, including the W.W. Norton edition's integral series of photographs showing flowers gracefully arranged in vases, austere and beautiful empty rooms, the exterior of the house, and sometimes Sarton herself at work. Even with a heftier dash of more immediate anger, Sarton's pleasure as "author" of her surroundings is not so easily erased or corrected by the later book. This pleasure is inextricable from what I earlier called her "aesthetics of solitude," an aesthetics deeply informed by the conflict *within* the solitary state that I have just described.

There is a particular sociability within solitude that governs Sarton's relationship to her environment in Nelson from the very beginning. She opens *Plant Dreaming Deep* by describing an ancestral portrait of Duvet de la Tour she hung in her house eight years *after* moving in. This choice to begin the text with a symbolic act rather than a linear chronology characterizes her larger relationship to the house: ". . . I knew I was performing a symbolic act, and this is the way it has been from the beginning, so that everything I do here reverberates, and if, out of fatigue or not paying attention, I strike a false note, it hurts the house and the mystique by which I live" (15).

In a limited, self-contained space, one can arrange symbols as one chooses, but the result of such arrangement may be startling: an atmosphere that is considerably more than the sum of its parts. Sarton's choice of the word "mystique" to describe her interior decoration suggests the spiritual life that loved objects can assume. Her pragmatic arrangements become both theatrical and spiritual acts, as she wonders at the particular and even mystical way in which her house's atmosphere coalesces. Her metaphor of playing the house as an instrument ("everything I do here reverberates") is both precisely visual in its orientation and mnemonic with respect to her family history, for absent familial presences constantly inhabit her and the house, informing both the materiality and the aesthetics of her everyday life: "My mother is most with me as a living presence when I go out to weed" (127); "My mother tasted color as if it were food, and when I get that shiver of delight at a band of sun on the yellow floor in the big room, or put an olive-green pillow onto a dark-emerald corduroy couch, I am not so much thinking of her as being as she was" (184). For Sarton, then, there is always a familial and historical element that humanizes the disinterested feel for color that Koller also shares. Visual, aesthetic pleasure—here in synaesthesia as taste—returns her to her family lineage.

Sarton's aesthetic is also intimately related to negotiation, or "demands" she feels the house makes on her: ". . . the house demands that everywhere the eye falls it fall on order and beauty"; "The white walls are a marvelous background for flowers, and from the beginning I have considered flowers a necessity, quite as necessary as food" (*Plant* 57). When she sets her table for dinner, she is the house's guest; but at other moments, she feels her own negligence almost in a masochistic way, as if the house has become a metonymic projection of her own feelings: "I knew when I walked in here last

Sunday that this house dies when there are no flowers. It felt desolate and I ended the day in tears, as if I had been abandoned by God" (124).

Indeed, Sarton oscillates between intimacy and pure identification with her house, which she names metonymically as "Nelson." Her abiding metaphor of nakedness allows her to express this sense of unity:

> I feel sometimes like a house with no walls. The mood is caught in a photo Mort Mace took of this house all lighted up one March evening. The effect is dazzling from the outside, just as my life seems dazzling to many in its productivity, in what it communicates that is human and fulfilled, and hence fulfilling. But the truth is that whatever good effect my work may have comes, rather, from my own sense of isolation and vulnerability. The house is open in a way that no house where a family lives and interacts can be. My life, often frightfully lonely, interacts with a whole lot of people I do not know and never will know. (*Journal* 114-115)

Perhaps another version of Koller's chapter on unexpected nonsexual "connecting," this passage moves beautifully from the opening metaphor to the photograph of Nelson included earlier in the book. Sarton identifies with the photographic vision of the house, which her friend captured: a luminescence she has "seen" as a house with no walls, unprotected, like a human being without clothes. Yet a house with no walls is a house that has, literally, fallen apart—one step beyond the "enterprise" of nakedness espoused in the Yeats poem. The passage thus envisions a vulnerability that would threaten a person's very anatomical structure—one, in fact, that would eclipse architecture itself. Earlier in the *Journal,* she brings architectural and anatomical metaphors together in a single sentence addressing the similarity of mystical experience and suicidal impulses: ". . . one has no wall, one is absolutely naked and diminished to essence" (57). This slippage into perfect identification with metonymic surroundings recalls Michelet's description of nesting which Bachelard quotes in his *The Poetics of Space:* "The house is a bird's very person; it is its form and its most immediate effort, I shall even say, its suffering" (101).

But at times Sarton also conceptualizes the house, the shelter of her solitude, as a significant other—both a bridegroom and a host. Indeed, she compares her purchase of the house to marriage: "I was not wrong in divining that for me . . . this step would mean radical change and so might be compared to marriage. No woman in her forties can afford to marry the wrong person or the wrong house in the wrong place!" (24). Whether intentionally or not, Sarton's preservation on this theme ("It is a strange marriage and its like does not exist anywhere else on earth . . . and just that has been the adventure," [25]) sheds a more humorous light on the second-wave feminist joke about housewives being "married to their house." Clearly, marriage has been an apt metaphor for all sorts of devotions throughout literary and intellectual history—one only has to look back at the Song of Songs—but it keeps Sarton within the play of solitude and sociability that the two journals animate, as well as within a curiously heterosexual vocabulary: "My friends realized that my whole relation to the place was a little like that of an old maid who suddenly gets married" (39).

Despite this lapsing into conventional heterosexual metaphors, Sarton is clearly conscious of her distance from the lives of her more conventional and usually heterosexual readers. In contrast to Koller's work, Sarton's writing evinces at least a topical awareness of the second-wave women's movement of the 1970s, and she provides some commentary on its heady concentric ripples. Published in 1973, the *Journal* periodically finds Sarton pondering letters she has received from women readers since the publication of *Plant Dreaming Deep* in 1968. One significant excerpt from a letter written by a struggling artist—also a wife and mother—reads, "Can one *be* within the framework of a marriage, do you think? I envy your solitude with all my heart" (122). This phenomenon of solitude envy—also observed by Koller in *Stations*—causes Sarton to balk at the idyllic cast with which the women's movement may have colored her life: "But there is something wrong when solitude such as mine can be 'envied' by a happily married woman with children" (123).

Yet the phrase Sarton uses to describe these wives' and mothers' yearnings—"[they] feel they are missing their 'real lives' all the time" (122)—is exactly the same phrase with which she began her book: "I am here alone again for the first time in weeks, to take up my 'real' life again at last" (11). In both of these instances, Sarton puts the word *real* in quotation marks, as if the boundaries of realness may very well be fluid: is a woman most "real" when she is married to a man or to another woman? Or is she most authentically herself when she conceives herself as married to a house of which she is the sole inhabitant? Clearly, for Sarton, there is not much of a contest:

> I have found it useful also these past days to say to myself, "What if I were not alone? What if I had ten children to get off to school every morning and a massive wash to do before they got home? What if two of them were in bed with flu, cross and at a loose end?" That is enough to send me back to solitude as if it were—as it truly is—a fabulous gift from the gods. (*Journal,* 109)

A breath of even fresher air today than it was at the time of the journal's publication—America in 2003 being the terrain of mothers, would-be mothers, and a larger culture obsessed with "putting children first"—this passage is nevertheless steadfast in its refusal to "prescribe" solitude as a panacea for all women, particularly for the "fragmented lives" of which they complain. Indeed, for Sarton, solitude is no healer of wounds, no restorer of unitary consciousness.

As I have been trying to argue, Sarton is a much more reluctant pilgrim than Koller, even though her relationship to the concept of deity is considerably more complex: as she states, many of her poems speak of God's presence as well as his absence (13). Yet like Koller, Sarton also makes use of religious imagery and tropes to describe her state of mind and her solitary life. She sees the sky in her window as stained glass (". . . the transparent blue sky behind a flame-colored cyclamen, lifting about thirty winged flowers to the light, makes an impression of stained glass, light flooded" [*Journal* 81]); she describes her house as "this nunnery where one woman meditates alone" (*Journal* 73), and she inevitably employs the pilgrimage metaphor to describe her solitude:

> The fact that a middle-aged, single woman, without any vestige of family left, lives in this house in a silent village and is responsible only to her own soul means something. The fact that she is a writer and can tell where she is and what it is like on the pilgrimage inward can be of comfort. It is comforting to know

there are light-house keepers on rocky islands along the coast. (*Journal* 40)

The metaphor of pilgrimage, recalling both Bunyan's progress and Koller's stations, lacks here the teleological sense with which both of those works imbue it. As is clear from the vicissitudes of the *Journal* as a whole, Sarton's "pilgrimage inward" recalls the Latin root of *pilgrimage,* or *peregrinus:* a wanderer or stranger. Refusing second-person address, Sarton also exchanges instruction for the notion of temporary comfort, much as the anonymous lighthouse keeper comforts by virtue of his stationary light alone. On some level, at least, as the passage makes clear, Sarton sees her life and her solitude as a comfort to those who are not writers, who cannot as aptly "tell where they are."

Yet Sarton wished not to be remembered predominantly for her journals and memoirs. Like many writers, she ghettoized this work as marginal with respect to her "real" work of writing novels and poems, as the following quotation makes clear: "It did not cheer me yesterday that Carol[yn] Heilbrun, up here from Columbia yesterday, feels that what I have done best—and what she thinks altogether new in my work—is to talk about solitude" (134). Yet this is exactly the difficulty: women's solitude must be taken seriously enough that its life representations are seen as viable, whether as guides or simply as possibilities.

Inevitably, we must consider what Koller and Sarton omit: that is, the populations to whom they cannot speak. As Delese Wear writes in *The Center of the Web,* it is easy to focus on the limitations of these white, educated, and privileged women:

> The women I've described are women of privilege, and none has the dailiness of dependents . . . they are writers or academics, not bound by timecard or rigidity of being here or there for this person at that time. They are white, apparently well-educated, middle class. I worry that it is my position, like theirs, that allows me even to raise the issue of solitude. (10)

Though Wear's point is crucial to keep in mind, I would raise another question: by expecting the work of Sarton and Koller to resonate for all women, are we not imposing a familiar (though nominally "feminist") burden of universality on their work? It is important to bear in mind the limitations of Koller's and Sarton's lives and thought. But if we disqualify their experience because it does not speak to all women, are we not falling into the very trap of the relational model their work challenges?

Though I identify to a certain extent with Wear's disclaimer, this very response also suggests to me just how threatening women's solitude still is—indeed, how very far we have to go in studying the variations of race and class within it. Like Christian's burden in *Pilgrim's Progress,* the weight of exemplariness would fall from the metaphorical "backs" of Koller's and Sarton's work only if more varied representations of women's chosen solitude existed. This is certainly not to imply that every solitary woman must be a writer; it is only to suggest that the solitaires who do write begin to consider their lives as a viable subject of nonfiction. Until then, women's solitude will continue to be seen as a default mode of living, a last-ditch effort, inconceivable as a choice. This, precisely, is what women's autobiography can work to change.

NOTES

1. This ad for Lexington Home Brands appears in *Sunset* magazine, September 1999.

2. In order to imagine the everyday conditions of Austen's writing life, Woolf quotes James Edward Austen-Leigh's *Memoir of Jane Austen:* ". . . she had no separate study to repair to, and most of the work must have been done in the general sitting-room, subject to all kinds of casual interruptions" (70, n. 1).

3. Carol Gilligan's reworking of Lawrence Kolberg's model of moral development, emphasizing women's privileging of specific relationships to others rather than logic or abstract ideas of right and wrong, has been widely influential in academia. The publication of *Women's Ways of Knowing* (ed. Blythe McVicker, et al.) used the relational model to describe women's acquisition of knowledge.

4. *An Unknown Woman* was finally published in 1981 by Holt, Rinehart and Winston, still significantly prior to the current memoir trend in publishing.

5. Susan Brownmiller's *Femininity* (1984), as well as Naomi Wolf's *The Beauty Myth* (1991), discuss the way in which cultural pressure on women to conform to an ideal of physical attractiveness has robbed them of their own power—or, in the words of Wolf's subtitle, *How Images of Beauty Are Used Against Women.* Research into this particular topic—though copious, in 2003—is still a fairly recent phenomenon. At the time *An Unknown Woman* was written, departments of women studies did not yet exist in American universities.

6. Indeed, Koller's chapter titled "Mourning," treating her dog Logos's death, is one of the most moving descriptions of grief I have read.

WORKS CITED

Bachelard, Gaston. *The Poetics of Space*. Trans. Maria Jolas. New York: Orion, 1964.

Bunyan, John. *The Pilgrim's Progress*. Middlesex, England: Penguin, 1965.

Heilbrun, Carolyn G. *Writing a Woman's Life*. New York: Ballantine, 1988.

Irigaray, Luce. *Ce sexe qui n'en est pas un*. Paris: Minuit, 1997.

Koller, Alice. *An Unknown Woman*. New York: Holt, Rinehart, Winston, 1981.

_____. *The Stations of Solitude*. New York: Bantam, 1990.

Kristeva, Julia. *The Kristeva Reader*. Ed. Toril Moi. New York: Columbia UP, 1986.

Peters, Gerald. *The Mutilating God*. Amherst: U of Massachusetts P, 1993.

Sarton, May. *Journal of a Solitude*. New York: Norton, 1973.

_____. *Plant Dreaming Deep*. New York: Norton, 1968.

Wear, Delese, Ed. *The Center of the Web*. Albany: State U of New York P, 1993.

Woolf, Virginia. *A Room of One's Own*. New York: Harcourt Brace, 1929.

Yeats, W. B. *The Collected Poems of W. B. Yeats*. Ed. Richard J. Finneran. New York: Collier Books, 1989.

– 4 –

A Veritable Guest to Her Own Self

Lisa Johnson

Like Hester Prynne, I embroider my A's and days . . .

Diane Freedman, An Alchemy of Genres (43)

Usually the idea hits me out of nowhere, like a craving or something exciting suddenly remembered: it's time! Time for one of those nights I giggle to myself as I trot around the house getting my things together. Ten tea lights in frosted sea-green glass holders, matches from Bally's in Las Vegas, a glass of merlot, a book I'm reading just for fun (no pencil in hand)—something such as Denise Levertov's *Tesserae* or Katherine Dunn's *Geek Love*—bath salts (the romance mix of juniper-berry essence I once saved for boyfriends), terry-cloth bath pillow from Victoria's Secret, portable CD player and disc (something that resonates with my mood—The Jesus & Mary Chain's *Stoned & Dethroned,* Natalie Merchant's *Ophelia,* Me'shell Ndegeocello's *Peace Beyond Passion*—nothing hard or sad or anxious). The water runs hot, candlelight flickers on the pages, summoning memories from girlhood of reading by flashlight under the covers. Will this ruin my eyes I wonder—then banish the thought, banish all thoughts of health (I tend toward hypochondria most days) or work (my dissertation lingers like an illness) or love (a long-distance boyfriend sometimes feels worse for my health than reading by candlelight).

These are the nights I remember myself, what I'm made of, what gives me pleasure. This tub-reading time, often combined with self-administered spa day treatments of lotion, facials, and deep conditioning, is time when I'm not working for anyone but myself. Not working for my dissertation committee, or for the suffocating image I

95

hold over my own head, that string of committees for whom I will perform for the rest of my life: job search committees, tenure committees, the conglomeration of book editors out there screening my writing, and, worst of all, the committee I host of internal critics. In the tub I'm not working for love, not making myself beautiful or fascinating or indispensable. I'm not following "the rules": not drawing him out in conversation by tapping into *his* interests, not working on my domestic skills of cooking and cleaning, not cultivating my sex kitten side. Instead, I'm sweaty, absorbed, and deeply happy. Usually so "good" at playing the girl for people, I take deep pleasure in these moments of being "bad" (cultural shorthand for "autonomous woman seeking pleasure").

I have lived alone for four years. The first one was the hardest. I lived in a drafty apartment with an orange-striped Salvation Army couch where I laid and thought nightmarish thoughts about the flakes of other people's shedded skin embedded in the upholstery beneath my head. Lonely, depressed, and alienated, I watched too much TV and ate too much bad food, skimped on cheap tuna fish and restricted rental movie nights. What was the point of a good movie, a good dinner, with no one there to share it? I was waiting for something—pining for the day I'd have a boyfriend again, someone to make nice evenings for me, someone to filter my day through. I was too small a life for the space accorded me. That was Ohio.

The second year still found me floundering, gasping at the surface of my days like a drowning woman. I had moved to Binghamton, New York, a depressed (and depressing) northeast factory town known for its diffuse light (movie term for gray and dreary). My new apartment was larger and dirtier than the last and in a bad (ugly, poor) part of town. I rattled from room to room in my pajamas with dirty hair and headaches from the weight of responsibility bearing down on me to order whole days and weeks on my own, still not used to the freedom of leading my solitary life. Part of the problem was that I had not yet learned to self-indulge, blind to the possibility of happiness as a single woman as I forayed into a life we see few models of, except sad, pathetic ones, such as Sandra Bullock in, well, any of her movies; but in particular I'm thinking of *While You Were Sleeping,* sharing a bowl of breakfast cereal with her cat at the table, or Elizabeth Wurtzel's epilogue to *Bitch: In Praise of Difficult Women.* Lifting the title of a popular country song she asks, "Did I Shave My Legs for This?" and writes exasperatedly, "Here I am trying to live a life in which man is not my destiny, but the powers that be have done all they can to stymie any burst of joy this self-determination might give me" (386). Like them, I had not yet learned what I now consider the cardinal rule of living alone: nourish your pleasure.

Judith Fryer, a professor of English at the University of Massachusetts at Amherst, reflects on the impact of spatial configurations on women's imaginations in her 1986 work, *Felicitous Space: The Imaginative Structures of Edith Wharton and Willa Cather*. Her central argument is that the American configuration of separate spheres for men and women in the nineteenth century did not serve women well, enclosing them inside houses like prisons and barring them from the liberatory American landscape. However, within this context, Fryer maintains, women nevertheless moved about with greater latitude than was explicitly accorded them. In fact, in their imaginative structures, women turned the rules of space and gender on their heads, both by refusing separate spheres and, when accepting them, by working within women's domains to create "felicitous spaces." Fryer takes the concept from Gaston Bachelard's *The Poetics of Space*. Paraphrased, felicitous space refers to a mode of inhabiting space successfully, experiencing aloneness with one's surroundings. Bachelard explores the poetics of inside spaces—houses and nooks—as well as outside spaces, in terms of their resonance with the human imagination. As Fryer notes, these spaces have distinctly gendered meanings in American culture, and women who write about houses in liberating ways revise a historically negative relationship to space.

One example that stays with me comes from Nancy Venable Raine's memoir, *After Silence: Rape and My Journey Back*. Rape is one of the reasons women fear living alone, fear being single and moving in solitude through the world. The lone woman is a woman in danger, a woman asking for trouble, according to the logic of patriarchal culture. Raine's rape occurred in her home, invading her personal space on many levels. Two nights ago I dreamed I was in my living room and realized somehow that someone had raped and abducted me, but I could not quite remember, just felt it somewhere in my guts, somewhere just around the corner of my conscious mind. The feelings of fear and invasion woke me in a panic. I rose from my

bed to go to the bathroom and left the light on when I returned, an ac-
quiescence to vulnerability that I resented and yet found unavoidable
at that moment. By the time my third and fourth years of living alone
rolled around, I began to love it; yet I still know at every moment, on
rational and deeply subconscious levels, that I am still in danger.
Raine's journey back to herself and her sense of home, her exploration of what comes "after silence," struggles against the sense of vulnerability the penetration of her house and body rent on her.

In particular, her chapter "Under the Eaves" holds lessons for creating felicitous spaces as a method of establishing authority over
one's emotional landscape and taking pleasure in one's immediate
environment, acts that resist the position of women as vulnerable and
dependent. In this chapter, Raine describes her first living arrangement after the rape. She took an attic apartment above a family out in
the country—a fixer-upper. Much smaller than the home she left behind, this apartment reflected Raine's shrinking sense of safe space,
her room shaped in the posture of a defensive animal, balled up tight.
She needed a home like a membrane to cover her bruised body and
spirit. She needed a shell to withdraw inside. What she also needed,
though, was light. She set about making this enclosure nourish her,
stripping the grungy wooden floor and refinishing it with a bright,
glossy white paint. She made it shine. I remember the floor in my first
apartment alone, dark chipped wood like Raine's; I remember looking at the dirt between the slats, never thinking of trying to get rid of it,
just recoiling from my environment in the same way I'd recoiled from
the world as an unsuccessfully solitary woman. What force and vision
Raine brought to bear on that small space—what elbow grease. There
was soul-making going on in each jab of the scraping tool, each swipe
of the paintbrush. As she refinished the floor of her apartment, she began to refinish the walls of her spirit, taking control over her life one
slat at a time. "Under the Eaves" functions for me as a parable of the
practical and metaphysical work of being a woman who lives alone, a
parable that helps me take pride in being the kind of gal who owns her
own (literal and figurative) toolbox. I may once have looked impo-
tently at the materials beneath my feet, but no longer.

I live in a small white clapboard house now, going on six months.
In it, I have discovered a number of felicitous spaces. The tub, of
course, but also the porch, where I am both at home and outside at

once. Sitting on the steps between the red begonias my grandma planted to welcome me home this summer, I feel so solidly connected with the motions of the earth and the living world. The feeling I once expected to arrive only in the form of a man comes to me now in the shape of a house, warm porch wood under my legs, blooming myrtle trees in my yard, wind chimes above my head, snails with their miniature houses at my feet. I added some permanent arrangements of ivy last week to brighten up the front of the house as the weather is getting too cold for live flowers. The woman at the flower shop told me she lives alone too, and that flowers make such a difference. I know just what she means, how making your surroundings aesthetically pleasing, even just for little old you, means determining that you deserve pleasures of your own, approaching each day as an exercise of the senses and the spirit. It means producing a sacredness in the ordinary routines of life. I have found that the sink brings me surprising pleasures. Washing dishes (gifts from family and friends)—small soapy swipes, one after the other to the bottom of the pile, bright sun a haze outside my window—I fall into a reverie, the kind of meditation where tangled ideas unloosen and lines flow to fill in the spaces of writing that baffled and frustrated me earlier in the day. I run to my desk and jot them down with wet hands.

May Sarton published *Journal of a Solitude* on the experiences of living alone, the work, the small pleasures. I taught this book in a course on women's life writing last spring, but the students—young girls fresh from their parents' houses—could not yet see the value of Sarton's struggles. They rejected her journal as too much complaining. Let them spend a year living alone and see how far they get on this journey of the spirit—full of rewards but the details of the map remain unwritten for each to fill in herself; it's not easy. I see *Journal of a Solitude* (sequel to *Plant Dreaming Deep,* written upon the purchase of Sarton's first house) as a guide to this journey, hinting at strategies for not going insane from the headiness of so much self. Although her biography suggests that life turned out messier than the journal reveals, Sarton recognizes some of what it takes to manage the days. I recognize my own struggles in hers: "I am in a limbo that needs to be patterned from within. People who have regular jobs can have no idea of just this problem of ordering a day that has no pattern imposed on it from without" (53). And similar solutions: "Each day, and the living of it, has to be a conscious creation in which discipline and order are relieved with some play and some pure foolishness" (109). Sarton acknowledges the importance of seeking out joy, listening to one's bodily rhythms, and most important, taking responsibility for creating one's days and spaces in response to these needs. A day in the life of a woman who lives alone must be treated as a work of art. We approach it, elusive as a good idea, and craft it like a poem, drawing out the organic form of breaks and pauses, building a structure around unifying images. Sarton's work of creating a personal mythology—telling herself a particular story about her life—is a way of ordering experience and making life inhabitable, a project that corresponds with her desire to break with cultural myths that position women infelicitously. In this work I see the internal aspect of felicitous space, how we must learn to inhabit not only our homes but also our lives and bodies more successfully.

Nancy Mairs does this in her memoir, *Remembering the Bone House: An Erotics of Place and Space*. With an epigraph from Bachelard—"Not only our memories, but the things we have forgotten are 'housed.' Our soul is an abode. And by remembering 'houses' and 'rooms,' we learn to 'abide' within ourselves"—Mairs begins her meditative account of her life as a female body, housed in various places and positions. The concept of the body as bone house, enormously evocative, gets at the idea that women must overcome Western culture's division of soul from flesh in order to truly possess either. Citing French feminist Hélène Cixous, Mairs asserts that women's bodies have been colonized as a space which men inhabit, but that "[t]hrough writing her body, woman may reclaim the deed to her dwelling" (7). Each woman must write the stories of her body in order to live inside it with felicity. The relationship between houses and female sexuality unfolds as Mairs ruminates on the spaces in which she experienced, dissociated from, and struggled back toward her body as an erotic being and a woman. In *Carnal Acts: Essays,* she writes that bodies—all bodies, men's and women's—need to be rescued from Western philosophy's abuse and neglect: "Bodies get treated like wayward women who have to be shown who's boss, even if it means slapping them around a little" (85). In *Remembering the Bone House,* she works against this ideology, returning to the felicitous spaces of her childhood—her first home, the beach house where her family retreated in summer—and coming for the first time to a sense of her body as a felicitous space. Like Sarton, Mairs recognizes that dwelling with felicity in one's body means attending to what brings her joy, attending to the needs and desires of her body—making oneself at home in the bone house first and foremost. More, she advances the idea that inhabiting the spaces of one's life successfully—the houses, the relationship configurations, the architecture of bones—means facing the reality of embodied consciousness, acknowledging the lived entanglements of gender, sexuality, and, in her case, the disability of multiple sclerosis. Bodies, like wayward women, need something other than abuse before they (be)come home. Here is why I take to the tub, then: to submerge myself in a comfort of my own creation, to attend to the spirit through my very capillaries.

In addition to writing the stories of our bodies, we must return to the stories of our mothers' bodies, bodies of the women who came before us. I remember reading Mary E. Wilkins Freeman's "A New England Nun" for a college American literature course. The story centers on Louisa, a woman whose fiancé left her waiting for over a decade while he made his fortune before marrying her. He finally returns, but his big man-body seems utterly out of place in her house, with its tea and china and lace, its feminine order and peace. The reader gets the sense that Louisa has grown comfortable with her space and solitude, that perhaps she no longer wishes to marry. Long story made short, she discovers his affections lie elsewhere and since both she and he bind to the other out of duty and not love, she ends the courtship affably. When we read this piece for Dr. Murphy, an older gentleman scholar and a group of eighteen-year-olds, we took it for granted that Louisa was psychically deformed, that she had grown unnatural in her preference for solitude over the company of a man, that her distaste at Joe Dagget's bungling presence as he knocks over her sewing tray was a matter of fussiness and distorted priorities— preferring trivial woman things over big bad man love. I recently re-read this short story, remembering it vaguely as I set up housekeeping in my first whole house (small as it is), and this time I found Louisa remarkable, far from the weird spinster we made of her. I laugh now at our assumptions, realizing from my current vantage point that Louisa was really on to something, that she had answers way back then for questions I've only lately formulated: how to fill this life; how to be large; how to be enough.

The story opens with an atmosphere of well-being. "There seemed to be a gentle stir arising over everything for the mere sake of subsidence—a very premonition of rest and hush and night" (1). Louisa's homemaking performs the courtship she missed (but didn't really miss at all) while her man was away. "Louisa was slow and still in her movements; it took her a long time to prepare her tea; but when ready it was set forth with as much grace as if she had been a veritable guest to her own self" (2). Understanding, unlike many women—unlike myself for far too long—that she deserves finely orchestrated experiences even when alone, "Louisa used china everyday—something which none of her neighbors did. They whispered about it among themselves" (2). Joe Dagget mars this performance of feminine self-pleasuring. "He seemed to fill up the whole room," (3) changing the dynamics inadvertently and irreparably to Louisa's detriment, for if he filled the room, she would have no choice but to shrink and disappear. Danzy Senna describes this masculine effect in her essay on kinds of female power: "In walked huge, serious, booming creatures who quickly became the focus of attention. The energy of the room shifted from the finely choreographed dance of women talk, where everyone participated in but no one dominated the conversation, to a room made up of margins and centers. The relative kindness of men didn't change the dynamic of their presence" (6). Joe makes it impossible for Louisa to remain at the center of her house or life, just by his simple presence.

I think certain parts of Wilkins Freeman's descriptions of Louisa were more visible to our American literature class than others were. Phrases that described her life as "so narrow that there was no room for anyone at her side" (7) sounded to us like rigidity and small-mindedness (evil traits to eighteen-year-olds with all their aspirations toward worldliness). This may be what brought about our readings of Louisa as emotionally crippled. We took it as strange how sewing a linen seam could make her feel like "peace itself" (9), believing she was settling for a tame life by preferring stasis over adventure (unforgivable in American literature). What we missed, though, was the daring involved in setting up house as a solitary woman, and daring to enjoy it. We missed this: "Louisa had almost the enthusiasm of an artist over the mere order and cleanliness of her solitary home. She had throbs of genuine triumph at the sight of the window-panes which she had polished until they shone like jewels" (9). We read as a joke this elevation of housework to art, but I think now of Gail Griffin's comment on Penelope's weaving (in *The Odyssey*), that housework "traditionally amounts to remaking and reordering their worlds daily, ensuring that life goes on against and through constant destruction. As it happens, that's the gods' work too" (259). A culture antagonistic to independent women coerced us subtlely into hearing Louisa's art as aberrance. We policed her with our readings. We policed ourselves. The serenity she achieves stands for me at the pinnacle of my desires, to be peace itself. "She gazed ahead through the long reach of future days strung together like pearls in a rosary, every one like the others, and all smooth and flawless and innocent, and her heart went up in thankfulness" (17). Perceiving Louisa as an artist of days, pioneer of solitary American womanhood, makes this practice of living days as prayers seem finally admirable. Gaston Bachelard writes, "if I were to name the chief benefit of the house, I should say: the house shelters daydreaming, the house protects the dreamer, the house allows one to dream in peace" (6). I like reading Louisa (and myself) through his words: "the passions simmer and resimmer in solitude: the passionate being prepares his explosions and his exploits in this solitude" (9). Through this simmering, the solitary woman becomes what Elizabeth Grosz calls a "volatile body," someone whose performances of gender unsettle traditional roles of femininity. I see Louisa fingering her days like a rosary, simmering in American literary history, volatile as a teakettle. She offers an alternative picture of womanhood and waits patiently for her readers to understand.

What I understand is this: women have to figure out how to take up the space around us, to take it up like a craft or a stiff drink. Because we cannot learn the poetics of living alone from the culture we live in—it can come only from inside, and from one another.

WORKS CITED

Bachelard, Gaston. *The Poetics of Space*. Trans. Maria Jolas. New York: Orion, 1964.

Freedman, Diane. *An Alchemy of Genres: Cross-Genre Writing by American Feminist Poet-Critics*. Charlottesville: UP of Virginia, 1992.

Fryer, Judith. *Felicitous Space: The Imaginative Structures of Edith Wharton and Willa Cather.* Chapel Hill: U of North Carolina P, 1986.

Griffin, Gail. "Penelope's Web." *The Intimate Critique: Autobiographical Literary Criticism,* pp. 255-264. Eds. Diane P. Freedman, Olivia Frey, and Frances Murphy Zauhar. Durham: Duke UP, 1993.

Grosz, Elizabeth. *Volatile Bodies: Toward a Corporeal Feminism.* Bloomington: Indiana UP, 1994.

Mairs, Nancy. *Carnal Acts: Essays.* Boston: Beacon, 1996.

_____. *Remembering the Bone House: An Erotics of Place and Space.* Boston: Beacon, 1989.

Peters, Margot. *May Sarton: A Biography.* New York: Fawcett Columbine, 1997.

Raine, Nancy Venable. *After Silence: Rape and My Journey Back.* New York: Crown, 1998.

Sarton, May. *Journal of a Solitude.* New York: Norton, 1973.

Senna, Danzy. "To Be Real." *To Be Real: Telling the Truth and Changing the Face of Feminism,* pp. 5-20. Ed. Rebecca Walker. New York: Anchor, 1995.

Wilkins Freeman, Mary E. *A New England Nun and Other Stories.* New York: Harper, 1891.

Wurtzel, Elizabeth. *Bitch: In Praise of Difficult Women.* New York: Doubleday; 1998.

Woolf, Hurston, and the House of Self

Kristina Deffenbacher

The master's tools will never dismantle the master's house.

Audre Lorde

[W]e all of us, grave or light, get our thoughts entangled in metaphors, and act fatally on the strength of them.

George Eliot

In the first chapter of *A Room of One's Own* (1929), Virginia Woolf describes the experience of standing outside the Oxbridge chapel, from which women are excluded: "As you know, its high domes and pinnacles can be seen, like a sailing-ship always voyaging never arriving" (9). In the pages following this depiction of patriarchal structures, Woolf explores the difficulty of distinguishing truth from illusion (15), fiction from facts (16), and reality from dream (17). The opening paragraphs of Zora Neale Hurston's *Their Eyes Were Watching God* (1937) begin, "Ships at a distance have every man's wish on board. For some they come in with the tide. For others they sail forever on the horizon," and conclude with the idea that for women, "the dream is the truth" (1). Hurston's lines seem to "signify upon" Woolf's essay (to turn Henry Louis Gates Jr.'s phrase) as much as they do upon Frederick Douglass's *Narrative*.[1] Regardless of whether Hurston was directly responding to Woolf, reading *Their Eyes Were Watching God* alongside *A Room of One's Own* and *Mrs. Dalloway* (1925) lends a better understanding of the extent to which each writer signifies upon, or repeats with a signal difference, the dominant culture's spatial models of selfhood.

Both Woolf and Hurston envision the psyche in spatial terms. In *A Room of One's Own,* in defiance of those who would turn her out of patriarchal structures, Woolf declares: "I refuse to allow you, Beadle though you are, to turn me off the grass. Lock up your libraries if you like; but there is no gate, no lock, no bolt that you can set upon the freedom of my mind" (75-76). Hurston, who cannot declare with Woolf that "Literature is *open* to everybody" (Woolf, *Room* 75; my emphasis), describes the black writer's "tactics" in *Mules and Men* (1935):

> The white man is always trying to know into somebody else's business. All right, I'll set something outside the door of my mind for him to play with and handle. He can read my writing but he sho' can't read my mind. I'll put this play toy in his hand, and he will seize it and go away. Then I'll say my say and sing my song. (3)

Although each writer faces a different set of spatial negotiations determined by her race and class position as well as by her gender, for both Woolf and Hurston a self defined in relation to domestic space seems necessary to the creative process. In her psychic home, especially if not in her actual house, a woman writer seems to need four walls, a door, and perhaps some decoys or other defenses outside that door. Such psychic architecture protects against certain contingencies—from family members making consuming demands to white men threatening to penetrate and colonize one's space.

Woolf and Hurston were not the first to employ the psyche-as-domestic-space metaphor. Sigmund Freud noted in 1916 that "The one typical—that is regular—representation of the human figure as a whole is a *house*" ("Lectures on Dreams" 153), and he often employed figures of domestic space to represent the differentiated functions of a coherent mind.[2] After building his house at Bollingen, Carl Jung reflected upon the model of selfhood that the home enacts: " 'It is thus a concretization of the individuation process. . . . Only afterward did I see how all the parts fitted together and that a meaningful form had resulted: a symbol of psychic wholeness' " (quoted in Marcus xv). In *The Poetics of Space* (1964), French philosopher Gaston Bachelard remarks that "the house image would appear to have become the topography of our intimate being" (xxxii). But this image is not as innocent as Jung's and Bachelard's explorations of it suggest; as John Agnew has noted, in capitalist societies the privately owned home is both a sign of autonomous individuality and a prerequisite of full political subjectivity (60). Bachelard's *Poetics* draws to the surface a conception of selfhood so natural to us, so fundamental to many of our institutions (psychoanalysis, philosophy, the law, and literature, to name a few), that we tend to take it for granted. But, as Fredric Jameson reminds us, "the structure of the psyche is historical, and has a history" (62).

The at once unitary and partitioned psychic structure described by Freud, Jung, and Bachelard is as historically determined as is the domestic architecture through which they understood it; these twentieth-century thinkers inherited the self-as-house model from Victorian culture. In the 1840s and 1850s, as the theory that architectural space helps to shape consciousness gained in influence, and as physiological studies of the mind achieved credibility, the mind came to be understood as a constructed and internally structured space.[3] One measure of the success of this idea is the enormous popularity of phrenology—the theory that the mind is a physical space comprised of localized faculties—in the first half of the nineteenth century. This work of spatializing and apportioning the mind corresponded with contemporary efforts to redefine the ideal home as a self-contained, rigidly divided space, with specific functions confined to specific areas (Spain 112). Members of the housing reform associations that arose in mid-Victorian England attempted to translate this middle-to-upper-class ideal to the working classes, for they believed, as George Godwin succinctly put it, " 'As the Homes, so the People' " (quoted in Hole 1). Their hope was that properly structured homes would produce self-contained and self-regulating individuals. The self-as-house ideal, born of a particular cultural moment, thus relies upon a particular conception of "home"—one largely unchanged to this day, and one that continues to communicate certain assumptions about self-construction (Hayden 23). As British historian Carolyn Steedman asserts, the myths and the fairy tales of modern Western societies "show the topography of the houses" belonging to those who stand "in a central relationship to the dominant culture," and these stories have "become

the stuff of our 'cultural psychology,' the system of everyday metaphors by which we see ourselves" (17; 75).

Woolf and Hurston thus inherited the psyche-as-domestic-space
metaphor and the conception of selfhood that it reproduces, though
each woman necessarily had a different relationship to this cultural
ideal than did white men such as Freud, Jung, and Bachelard. Woolf,
as were many modernists, was influenced by Walter Pater's late-nine-
teenth-century materialist theories of subjectivity; as Perry Meisel
notes, "the figure of the dwelling or manmade enclosure is [central]
to both writers' notion of selfhood as a fortified space of property"
(Meisel 173). I would add that unlike Pater, Woolf takes account of
the costs of this model; Hurston goes further to address the exclusions that such a structure produces and to envision other possibilities.

Selfhood, as a unified, circumscribed space, requires some psychic
housekeeping; as Woolf's Clarissa Dalloway muses, "That was her
self when some effort, some call on her to be her self, drew the parts
together . . . into one center, one diamond, one woman who sat in her
drawing-room and made a meeting point" (Woolf, *Mrs. Dalloway*
37). Clarissa's socially recognized self is an individuated collection
of diverse parts defined in relation to domestic space. This construction of selfhood is problematic for both sexes in *Mrs. Dalloway;*
Septimus Warren Smith cannot compose his parts into a coherent
structure, and, significantly, jumps out of a window to his death in order to protect his dissolute self from the doctors' attempts to squeeze
and prune it into proportion (151). Clarissa accepts the sanctuary and
privacy of housed selfhood but also recognizes that such a structure
cannot accommodate certain parts of her, and that its outer walls define a space of sterility and isolation. The self that she draws together
in her drawing room is "a meeting-point, a radiancy no doubt in some
dull lives, a refuge for the lonely people to come to, perhaps; she had
helped young people, who were grateful to her; had tried to be always
the same, never showing a sign of all the other sides of her" (37). In
order to act in her social world, in order to "create" (122), Clarissa
has to construct her self as a finite, unitary space—as a house, or
rather, as a room within a house. Unlike Septimus, Clarissa achieves
unified selfhood, but at the cost of isolation from the common life beyond her doors. Withdrawing "like a nun" to the attic, to the only

room in the house other than the drawing room that is "hers," Clarissa "paused by the open staircase window which let in blinds flapping, dogs barking, let in, she thought, feeling herself suddenly shriveled, aged, breastless, the grinding, blowing, flowering of the day, out of doors, out of the window, out of her body and brain" (31).

It is important to note that the space of Clarissa's self is not equated with the house as a whole but is rather limited to a room—to the drawing room, to her attic room. The notion of selfhood as a fortified space of property is more problematic for women than for men, for as Woolf notes in *A Room of One's Own,* up until very recent history English women could not own property, and in fact *were* property (21-23). Houses are largely man-made and man-owned; as Meike Bal asserts, " 'In the house fatherhood establishes itself; the house becomes fatherhood's synechdochic metaphor' " (quoted in Geyh 106). In his exploration of this poetic image's centrality to Western thought, Bachelard observes that "In the life of man, the house thrusts aside contingencies, its councils of continuity are unceasing. . . . It is body and soul" (6-7). In this formulation for "man," the house, body, and soul are coherent and contiguous structures whose well-defined borders protect him from the undifferentiated, from the contingent. But for Clarissa Dalloway, selfhood is constructed *within* domestic space; her "body and brain" are equated with the house only at the moment that she ebbs and flows "out of doors, out of the window," out of the culturally delineated space of self. Although she has a room of her own, Clarissa Dalloway is ultimately isolated within a larger structure that is not her own, that is not *her.*

As Hurston's short story "Sweat" (1926) opens, Delia Jones' body and soul, "her tears, her sweat, her blood," have melded with her house into one "spiritual earthworks" (199). This house is woman-made; when her husband Sykes threatens to throw her out, she bravely defies him: "Mah sweat is done paid for this house and Ah reckon Ah kin keep on sweatin' in it" (198). The problem is that both she and her house are under her husband's jurisdiction, and as Joe Clark points out, " 'Taint no law on earth dat kin make a man be decent if it ain't in 'im' " (201). Like the previous generations of English women that Woolf describes in *A Room of One's Own,* Delia does not have the right to possess what she has earned. Even if a woman manages to construct a space, such as Delia's spiritual earthworks, that produces a sense of self and a sense of protection, a man can always make that space oppressive, or put her out of it. Bachelard asserts that the house "concentrates being within limits that protect" (xxxii), and Woolf seems to make similar assumptions about the power of a room. But as Chou Ying-Hsiung reminds us, "Space can, in fact, be used as a means of domination" (190).

The collision and collusion of the privileges of house ownership and self-possession in American culture, evident in the society Hurston portrays in *Their Eyes Were Watching God,* preclude the possibility of an ex-slave woman such as Nanny ever fully achieving what the dominant culture defines as selfhood. But that does not keep Nanny from desiring for her granddaughter what she herself could not achieve: " 'Ah was born back in slavey times so it wan't for me to fulfill my dreams of whut a woman oughta be and do. . . . Ah been waitin' a long time, Janie, but nothin' Ah been through ain't too much if you just stand on high ground lak Ah dreamed' " (Hurston, *Their Eyes* 16). As a slave, neither Nanny's cabin nor her body were her own; her owners could break into both at will (17). Once free, Nanny tries to " 'throw up a highway through de wilderness' " for her daughter, but " 'somehow she got lost offa de highway' " (16); she connects their transient state of existence to her daughter's vulnerability to outside forces. Nanny recognizes the dominant culture's equation of house ownership and self-possession; she tells Janie that " 'Ah raked and scraped and bought dis lil piece uh land so you wouldn't have to stay in de white folks' yard and tuck yo' head befo' other chillun. . . . Ah wanted you to look upon yo'self' " (19-20). When she sees "Johnny Taylor lacerating her Janie with a kiss" over her front gate (12), she realizes that neither her house nor her fence can protect Janie. Because her concern for Janie's self-possession is secondary to her concern for her survival, Nanny insists that she marry against her will, explaining that " 'Tain't Logan Killicks Ah wants you to have, baby, it's protection' " (15). Without the shelter of a male-owned home Janie would be left open to what Bachelard blandly refers to as "contingencies," to what Nanny knows can destroy her, body and soul: " 'Ah can't die easy thinkin' maybe de menfolks is makin' a spit cup outa you' " (20).

For Janie, the walls of Logan Killicks's house and the fence around his sixty acres come to represent not the means of protecting herself, but rather the forces which isolate her from the sense of self that she discovered under her grandmother's pear tree, in sexual and spiritual connection with the world around her (Hurston, *Their Eyes* 10-11). After Nanny's death, Janie attempts to escape the limited notion of selfhood passed on to her by her grandmother, then represented and reproduced by Logan Killicks's fenced-in property.

But Janie does not escape. She cannot simply set out on her own, and Jody Starks rescues her only to enshrine her in structures that more closely resemble those that her grandmother desired. Jody reduces Janie's life to the inside of a house and a store; he demands that she stay inside the store and refuses to let her participate in the story-telling sessions on the porch—a liminal space between the realms of private and public in which a community consciousness is created. As "the wife of the Mayor," Janie's identity is collapsed into Jody's public persona (Hurston, *Their Eyes* 46), for which his house stands as a synecdochic emblem:

> It had two stories with porches, with banisters and such things. The rest of the town looked like servant's quarters surrounding the "big house." And different from everybody else in the town he put off moving in until it had been painted, in and out. And look at the way he painted it—a gloaty, sparkly white. (75)

The external structure of the house, which encompasses the domestic sphere and thrusts itself into public space, clearly represents the man. Its walls differentiate Jody from everyone else; its verticality and luxuriousness relative to the rest of town indicate his position in the class hierarchy, which he and his house; its "gloaty" whiteness signifies a sway over others that is, at least superficially, akin to that of white power structures. Just as Jody's "big voice" initially silences Janie's (43), his "big house" encompasses and annexes the space of her identity, as she later realizes. Just moments before his death, Janie tells Jody that " 'Ah run off tuh keep house wid you in a wonderful way. But you wasn't satisfied wid me de way Ah was. Naw! Mah own mind had tuh be crowded out tuh make room for yours in me' " (86).

Unlike Clarissa Dalloway, Janie initially has no space that she can call her own within the walls of the man-made and man-owned structures that define the limits of her existence. From the beginning,

Clarissa has not only a room of her own, but also an identity which— because constructed *within* the dominant model of selfhood—is equated with that contained inner space. To the extent that Clarissa, as a member of the dominant class, at least symbolically possesses the space of home and self, she is free to move in and out of it. She recognizes the social identity defined by domestic space as her "self" ("That was her self when some effort . . . drew the parts together . . . one woman who sat in her drawing-room"), and yet outside of that space realizes a less bounded, more fluid experience of selfhood: "somehow in the streets of London, upon the ebb and flow of things, here, there, she survived . . . part of people she had never met; being laid out like a mist between the people she knew best, who lifted her on their branches as far as she had seen the trees lift the mist, but it spread ever so far, her life, herself" (Woolf, *Mrs. Dalloway* 9). The construction of identity represented by the house exists in a state of tension with Clarissa's experience of dispersal, of a self claimed in its connectedness and represented by organic imagery. Bachelard asserts that "Without [the house], man would be a dispersed being. It maintains him through the storms of the heavens" (7). For Janie, who is utterly trapped within Jody's house and store, the two senses of self that Clarissa alternately experiences exist in the state of radical opposition that Bachelard's model suggests. Janie is completely cut off from the organic world, in and through which she glimpsed sexual and spiritual selfhood under her grandmother's pear tree.

Janie has no more access to private space than she has to the outside world: the "spirit" of her marriage with Jody soon "left the bedroom and took to living in the parlor" (Hurston, *Their Eyes* 71), a public space within the home, and she has no space to call her own within the house or within herself. Although Clarissa's "self," as assembled in the drawing room, is reduced to "being Mrs. Richard Dalloway" (Woolf, *Mrs. Dalloway* 11), both her forays into the streets of London and her access to private, protected spaces within the house and within herself enable her to remain in contact with the parts of her that are left outside of this construction. Janie's world has been reduced to structures that represent Jody, body and soul, and she feels " 'de walls creepin' up on me and squeezin' all de life outa me' " (Hurston, *Their Eyes* 112).

Although trapped within these structures, the only way for Janie to achieve a sense of self distinct from Jody's all-encompassing identity is to re-create the inside/outside divide within the only space that she can silently, surreptitiously reclaim—her mind: "She found that she had a host of thoughts she had never expressed to him, and numerous emotions she had never let Jody know about. Things packed up and put away in parts of her heart where he could never find them. . . . She had an inside and an outside now and suddenly she knew how not to mix them" (Hurston, *Their Eyes* 72). In order to survive, in order to keep the fight from going out of her soul (76), Janie has to adopt the master's strategies and adapt them to her own needs. Her replication of the inside/outside dichotomy—so instrumental in her own oppression—enables her to maintain a sense of self but also radically divides her within and isolates her from the world beyond.

Before Janie can gain access to the life depicted in the storytelling sessions on the front porch, she must first claim a social identity apart from Jody's engulfing public persona. As his aging body falls apart on him, Jody renders the house and especially the store even more oppressive for Janie: "The more people in there the more ridicule he poured over her body to point attention away from his own" (Hurston, *Their Eyes* 78). When Jody's public belittling of Janie gets to the point that it "was like somebody snatched off part of a woman's clothes when she wasn't looking and the streets were crowded," she "took the middle of the floor to talk right into Jody's face" (78). Janie claims a space of her own in the center of the store, asserts her own voice, and thereby transgresses far beyond the limits of what Jody has defined as her identity. His first shocked reaction is to tell her " 'You must be out yo' head' " (79). In the exchange that follows, Janie turns Jody's language against him: " 'You big-bellies around here and put out a lot of brag, but 'tain't nothin' to it but yo' big voice. Humph! Talkin' about *me* lookin old! When you pull down yo' britches, you look like the change of life' " (123). In *A Room of One's Own,* Woolf asserts that "Women have served all these centuries as looking-glasses . . . reflecting the figure of man at twice its natural size. . . . For if she begins to tell the truth," as Janie tells Jodie, "the figure in the looking-glass shrinks; his fitness for life is diminished" (35-36). Or as Gates describes this scene, it is "a Signifyin(g) ritual of the first order because Janie signifies upon Jody's manhood, thereby ending his dominance over her and the community, and thereby killing Jody's will to live" (201).

As Jody lies dying, Janie reveals the emptiness of the structures that have held him up and held her in. Jody, whose identity had become coextensive with the social position emblematized by his house and store, dies after " 'all dis tearin' down talk' " (Hurston, *Their Eyes* 87). After sorting through her thoughts about Jody, Janie "thought about herself":

> Years ago, she had told her girl self to wait for her in the looking glass. It had been a long time since she had remembered. Perhaps she'd better look. She went over to the dresser and looked hard at her skin and features. The young girl was gone, but some woman had taken her place. She tore off the handkerchief from her head and let down her plentiful hair. The weight, the length, and the glory was there. (Hurston, *Their Eyes* 87)

After forcing Jody to see himself for what he is, Janie looks at her own reflection for the first time since she was a girl—the last time she was herself. This symbolic act gains in significance when read in the context of Hurston's account of her mother's death in *Dust Tracks on a Road*. Her ailing mother trusted a then nine-year-old Zora to see that the mirror was not covered at the moment of her death (Hurston, *Dust Tracks* 62). The Eatonville community "believed that a person's dying hard was a bad sign," and that "the looking-glass should be covered because a reflection of the corpse might attach itself permanently to the glass" (Hemenway 16). Zora tried to carry out her mother's wishes, but her father "restrained [her] physically from outraging the ceremonies established for the dying" (Hurston, *Dust Tracks* 64). After Jody dies a hard death, Janie not only fails to cover the looking glass (in defiance of custom and the law of the father) but also supplants the corpse's reflection with her own. Rather than veiling the mirror, Janie unveils her hair and delights in her own image.

Janie uses the mirror first to reclaim herself, then, as does Clarissa Dalloway, to formulate herself: "She took careful stock of herself, then combed her hair and tied it back again. Then she starched and ironed her face, forming it into just what people wanted to see" (Hurston, *Their Eyes* 87). Clarissa similarly "looked in the glass. It

was to give her face point. That was her self—pointed; dart-like; defi-
nite . . . composed so for the world into one center" (Woolf, *Mrs.
Dalloway* 37). Through Jody's death and Janie's subsequent possession of self and home, Janie acquires an identity that resembles
Clarissa's. She then has access to the liminal space of the window,
which she opens to declare that " 'Mah husband is gone from *me*' "
(Hurston, *Their Eyes* 87; my emphasis). Although she is now free of
Jody, the "me" that Janie presents to the public is one assembled according to the design sanctioned by the dominant culture.

Janie realizes Nanny's wildest dreams: she owns both a house and
a self that is coextensive with that property. Although she now has access to windows and porches, Janie, like Clarissa Dalloway, feels ultimately isolated by this construction of selfhood. Janie questions this
isolation: "at night she was there in the big house and sometimes it
creaked and cried all night under the weight of the lonesomeness.
Then she'd lie awake in bed asking lonesomeness some questions"
(Hurston, *Their Eyes* 89), questions that end in a folk account of creation. Jealous angels, a communal narrative voice tells us, chopped
the first, glittering man into millions of pieces, then covered each little spark over with mud, "And the lonesomeness in the sparks make
them hunt for one another, but the mud is deaf and dumb" (90). This,
Clarissa muses, was "the supreme mystery": "here was one room;
there another. Did religion solve that, or love?" (Woolf, *Mrs. Dalloway* 127). Or as Clarissa's friend Sally Seton poses the question, "Are
we not all prisoners? She had read a wonderful play about a man who
scratched on the wall of his cell, and she had felt that was true of life"
(Woolf, *Mrs. Dalloway* 192). In both novels, human isolation is imposed by the material barriers between individuals, walls that are re-
inforced by the notion of selfhood as a fortified space of property.
The question that looms throughout *Mrs. Dalloway* is whether one
can exist as a socially recognized self or "subject" without being
"squeezed, pared, pruned" into such structures (101).

In *Their Eyes Were Watching God*, Hurston both incorporates and
imagines a way beyond the model of selfhood described by Pater and
reinscribed in Woolf's work, just as Janie first internalizes and then
moves beyond the model of selfhood privileged in white culture and
reinscribed in Nanny's wishes for her granddaughter. Tea Cake is the
vehicle for this move; Janie tells Pheoby that before, " 'Ah'd sit dere

wid de walls creepin' up on me and squeezin' all de life outa me. . . . Ah wants tuh utilize mahself all over. . . . Dis ain't no business proposition, and no race after property and titles. Dis is uh love game. Ah done lived Grandma's way, and now Ah means tuh live mine" (Hurston, *Their Eyes* 112; 114). Perhaps Hurston, through Janie, is able to envision another "way" because for African-American women, self-possession has never been a given, and house ownership has been almost unheard of. Hurston was born into her father's "sound eight-room house on his five acres," but after she left home, "the only dwelling she ever owned was an old houseboat bought during World War II" (Hemenway 15; 5). As Mary Helen Washington points out, Hurston "worked most of the time without a door of her own on which to put a lock," let alone the fixed income that Woolf insisted was necessary to write (Washington 24). I have no wish to romanticize the poverty that, as Alice Walker argues, "made all the difference. Without money of one's own in a capitalistic society, there is no such thing as independence" (Foreword xvi). But perhaps Hurston's ability to imagine a way of being a subject in the world beyond the static structures of identity deemed necessary, if not natural, by the dominant culture was, in part, a result of her position as one always to some extent outside of those structures. At the end of her account of her mother's death in *Dust Tracks on a Road*, Hurston describes how she began to live in a more transient mode even before she left home: "life picked me up from the foot of Mama's bed, grief, self-despisement and all, and set my feet in strange ways. . . . That hour began my wanderings. Not so much in geography, but in time. Not so much in time as in spirit" (64-65).

Both Jody's death and the appearance of a man who can more fully embody her dreams help Janie to break away from the house and begin her wanderings; she leaves the vertical space of the two-story house at the center of Eatonville, in which Jody had "classed [her] off" (Hurston, *Their Eyes* 112), for the horizon, for the horizontal— for a journey to the plane of the muck with Tea Cake. The crucial difference between their house in the Everglades and the one Janie leaves behind is that this one-story house is "the *unauthorized* center of the 'job' " (132; my emphasis) and is "full of people every night" (133). Janie and Tea Cake are leaders among equals, just as their house is both central to the community and level with those around it.

They maintain individual identities while immersed in their relationship and in the "mingled people" around them (141), just as their house remains their space even as the community continually moves through it. Janie's experience of selfhood on the muck, as emblematized by the house that she and Tea Cake share, is significantly different from her experience of being submerged in the space of Jody's house and identity. This new construction of selfhood does not separate and isolate, but therefore also does not provide much protection from external forces. In the end, the house in the Everglades does not maintain them "through the storms of the heavens and those of life" as Bachelard asserts a house should do; a hurricane destroys their house and leaves them defenseless against the rabid dog whose bite takes Tea Cake from Janie long before she shoots him in self-defense.

After Tea Cake's death, Janie ends her wanderings in geography but not in time and spirit, and thus returns to her house in Eatonville without regret: " 'So Ah'm back home agin and Ah'm satisfied tuh be heah. Ah done been tuh de horizon and back and now Ah kin set heah in mah house and live by comparisons' " (Hurston, *Their Eyes* 191). For the first time, Janie refers to her house as "home"; this space is no longer oppressive, for it is hers and *is her*. This does not represent a return to the model of selfhood as a fortified space of property, but rather a significant revision of it. The walls of the house that is her(s) are no longer "deaf and dumb," but are rather alive with her experiences of the people and the world outside of that time and space:

> [A] sobbing sigh [sang] out of every corner in the room. . . . Then Tea Cake came prancing around where she was and the song of the sigh flew out of the window and lit in the top of the pine trees. Tea Cake, with the sun for a shawl. Of course he wasn't dead. He could never be dead until she herself had finished feeling and thinking. The kiss of his memory made pictures of love and light against the wall. Here was peace. She pulled in her horizon like a great fish-net. Pulled it from around the waist of the world and draped it over her shoulders. So much of life in its meshes! She called in her soul to come and see. (192-193)

Janie now moves freely between past and present, inside and outside, self and horizon, dream and truth. She is "living by comparison," in metaphor, in the space between poles. The fact that she is alone in a room on the second story of a house in the center of town does not mean that she is isolated or separated from the world outside, as is Clarissa Dalloway up in her attic room. Janie realized selfhood and remained herself while immersed in the transient existence of the muck; she can now realize the life at the horizon and have it remain motion and light within the peaceful and protected space of her house. Hurston, through Janie, envisions the possibilities of shelter in motion and motion in shelter—a reimagining of selfhood much like that at the heart of Rosi Braidotti's recent theorizing of a "nomadic subject" (4).[4] Such "political fictions" not only challenge the dominant culture's construction of selfhood but also radically remodel it.

Feminists still question whether to claim, reconstruct, deconstruct, and/or escape altogether "the master's house" (Lorde 110). In *Their Eyes Were Watching God*, Hurston seems to reach the same inclusive conclusion that, according to Paula Geyh, Marilynne Robinson reaches in *Housekeeping* (1980):

> [O]ptions for women don't have to be limited to either vagrancy or inscription within the household. . . . What Robinson's [or for that matter, Hurston's] conception of the transient subject seems to suggest is that the feminine subject might be constituted, at least in part, by an interaction between the two. We must continually cross and recross the bridge in both directions, for we can no longer really stay "at home," but neither can we depart to some utopian realm beyond all patriarchal structures. (Geyh 120-121)

Hurston herself continually "crossed and recrossed the bridge in both directions," becoming in that continual process what Trinh T. Minh-Ha refers to as an "Inappropriate Other/Same": "Not quite the same, not quite the Other, she stands in that undetermined threshold place where she constantly drifts in and out" (74). The socioeconomic conditions that this position entailed gave Hurston the standpoint from which to signify upon the dominant culture's model of selfhood. The only house that she ever owned was a houseboat—a house in motion, a private space that was part of the natural world: " 'I have achieved one of my life's pleasures by owning at last a houseboat. Nothing to delay the sun in its course. . . . The Halifax river is very beautiful and the various natural expressions of the day on the river keep me happier than I have ever been before in my life'" (quoted in Hemenway 298). Hurston realized a possibility between those presented in Woolf's *Mrs. Dalloway,* in which one either is a unified, "housed" self, or is dispersed in the experience of "ebb and flow," as is Clarissa on the streets of London. As Hurston describes herself in "How it Feels to Be Colored Me" (1928), "I am a dry rock surged upon, and overswept, but through it all I remain myself. When covered by the waters, I am; and the ebb but reveals me again" (154).

NOTES

1. In *The Signifying Monkey,* Henry Louis Gates Jr. argues that Hurston's opening lines in *Their Eyes* revise or "signify upon" Frederick Douglass's " 'apostrophe to the moving multitude of ships' " in his *Narrative* of 1845 (quoted in Gates 170-172).

2. For instance, Freud described the unconscious as that space to which thoughts are relegated when ordered out of the "drawing-room" or "front hall" of consciousness ("Repression" 153).

3. In England in the 1840s, Augustus Pugin's theory that architectural design helps to shape consciousness profoundly influenced not only religious leaders and Gothic Revivalists (Curl 40-41) but also social thinkers such as Thomas Carlyle and Benjamin Disraeli. In the 1850s, Alexander Bain established " 'the physiological basis of mental phenomena' " (Bain, quoted in Hergenhahn 139). Rather than occupying a world apart, the mind became widely viewed in terms of its place in the material world (Danziger 120).

4. In *Nomadic Subjects* (1994), Braidotti explains that the "nomadic subject" is a "myth, that is to say a political fiction, that allows me to think through and move across established categories and levels of experience: blurring boundaries without burning bridges. Implicit in my choice is the belief in the potency and the relevance of the imagination, of myth-making" (203). Hurston, I would argue, was engaged in a similar project.

WORKS CITED

Agnew, John. "Home Ownership and Identity in Capitalist Societies." *Housing and Identity: Cross Cultural Perspectives* (pp. 60-97). Ed. James S. Duncan. New York: Holmes and Meier Publishers, Inc., 1982.

Bachelard, Gaston. *The Poetics of Space.* 1964. Trans. Maria Jolas. Boston: Beacon P, 1969.

Braidotti, Rosi. *Nomadic Subjects.* New York: Columbia U P, 1994.

Curl, James Stevens. *Victorian Architecture.* London: David and Charles, 1990.

Danziger, Kurt. "Mid-Nineteenth-Century British Psycho-Physiology: A Neglected Chapter in the History of Psychology." *The Problematic Science: Psychology in Nineteenth-Century Thought* (pp. 119-146). Eds. William R. Woodward and Mitchell G. Ash. New York: Praeger Special Studies, 1982.

Freud, Sigmund. "Lectures on Dreams." 1916. *The Complete Introductory Lectures on Psychoanalysis* (pp. 83-242). Trans. and Ed. James Strachey. New York: Norton, 1966.

_____. "Repression." 1915. *Complete Psychological Works* (pp. 146-158). Trans. James Strachey. Vol. 14. London: Hogarth, 1953.

Gates, Henry Louis Jr. *The Signifying Monkey: A Theory of African-American Literary Criticism.* Oxford: Oxford UP, 1988.

Geyh, Paula E. "Burning Down the House? Domestic Space and Feminine Subjectivity in Marilynne Robinson's *Housekeeping.*" *Contemporary Literature* 34 (1993): 103-122.

Hayden, Dolores. *The Grand Domestic Revolution.* Cambridge, MA: MIT P, 1981.

Hemenway, Robert E. *Zora Neale Hurston: A Literary Biography.* 1977. Urbana: U of Illinois P, 1980.

Hergenhahn, B. R. *An Introduction to the History of Psychology,.* Second edition. Belmont, CA: Wadsworth, 1992.

Hole, James. *The Housing of the Working Classes, with Suggestions for Their Improvement.* London: Longmans, Green and Co., 1866.

Hurston, Zora Neale. *Dust Tracks on a Road.* 1942. New York: Harper, 1991.

_____. "How it Feels to Be Colored Me." 1928. *I Love Myself When I Am Laughing . . . A Zora Neale Hurston Reader.* Ed. Alice Walker. New York: Feminist, 1979. 152-155.

_____. *Mules and Men.* 1935. New York: Harper, 1990.

_____. "Sweat." 1926. *I Love Myself When I Am Laughing . . . A Zora Neale Hurston Reader.* Ed. Alice Walker. New York: Feminist, 1979. 197-207.

_____. *Their Eyes Were Watching God.* 1937. New York: Harper, 1990.

Jameson, Fredric. *The Political Unconscious: Narrative As a Socially Symbolic Act.* Ithaca, NY: Cornell UP, 1981.

Lorde, Audre. "The Master's Tools Will Never Dismantle the Master's House." *Sister Outsider* (pp. 110-113). Freedom, CA: Crossing P, 1984.

Marcus, Clare Cooper. *House As a Mirror of Self: Exploring the Deeper Meaning of Home.* Berkeley: Conari P, 1995.

Meisel, Perry. *The Absent Father: Virginia Woolf and Walter Pater.* New Haven: Yale UP, 1980.

Minh-Ha, Trinh T. *When the Moon Waxes Red: Representation, Gender and Cultural Politics.* New York: Routledge, 1991.

Spain, Daphne. *Gendered Spaces.* Chapel Hill: U of North Carolina P, 1992.

Steedman, Carolyn Kay. *Landscape for a Good Woman: A Story of Two Lives*. New Brunswick: Rutgers UP, 1987.

Walker, Alice. Foreword. In Robert E. Hemenway, *Zora Neale Hurston: A Literary Biography* (pp. xi-xviii). Urbana: U of Illinois P, 1980.

Washington, Mary Helen. "Zora Neale Hurston: A Woman Half in Shadow." *I Love Myself When I Am Laughing . . . A Zora Neale Hurston Reader* (pp. 7-25). Ed. Alice Walker. New York: Feminist, 1979.

Woolf, Virginia. *A Room of One's Own*. 1929. San Diego: Harcourt Brace, 1989.

_____. *Mrs. Dalloway*. 1925. San Diego: Harcourt Brace, 1990.

Ying-Hsiung, Chou. "A Room of One's Own: Between Individual and Collective Identity." *Proceedings of the XIIth Congress of the International Comparative Literature Association* (pp. 187-193). Volume 2. Munich, 1988.

– 6 –

The Domestic Politics
of Marguerite Duras

Annabelle Cone

Charting out her identity both as a woman and as a writer, Marguerite Duras rewrites the family history from the daughter's perspective by reliving her past, her childhood origins, and her passage to adulthood through the act of writing. In doing so, she assigns a great deal of importance to the mother's influence on her female subject formation, both as a model with whom to identify and from whom she must depart. For her subject formation necessitates an initial exit from the stasis of the mother's house to a life of mobility, from passive domestic ennui to acting on her sexual desire and her desire to write. Hence the Durassian "heroine's" access to subjectivity can occur only through her departure from the mother's house, whose endemic "poverty, boredom, bitterness and hostile environment" as exemplified in one of Duras's earliest works, *Un barrage contre le pacifique,* eventually drives her away (Selous 157). As Marcelle Marini puts it, woman must exit the "cave": "finie 'l'histoire' 'l'enferme,' dans la non-vie, la tendresse étouffoir du mari-père-mère" "finished is the 'story' in which she is locked in by the suffocating tenderness of the husband-father-mother" (25).[1]

This exodus operates on a spatially symbolic level, as Duras describes autobiographically in *L'amant* her own passage from the mother's asexual house to the lover's bachelor flat, one of many sites of her "apprenticeship of desire," along with the streets of Saigon, the cinema, the bordello for which she always had a fascination, the sea, the jungle, all those spaces located outside, in the public sphere (Vircondelet 190).

The discovery of desire, operating through a passage from the private to the public sphere, is paralleled by what Duras calls in *La vie matérielle* the ability to dominate speech, "dominer la parole," brought about by her successful encounter with public school education. Having spent the first years of her life in that province which lies beyond France's national boundaries, the French colonies—in this case, Indochina—Marguerite Duras will not only leave the mother's house but also her mother's adopted homeland in order to complete her education and pursue a career as a writer in Paris. Yet Duras does not abandon the home and the colonies altogether, as she returns to her mother's house by telling and retelling the story of her adolescence in what shall be loosely termed the "Lover" series.[2]

On a material level, Duras will also become a home owner, purchasing an old country house outside of Paris in Neauphle-le-Château with the publication rights of *Barrage,* a novel that tells the story, in part, of a young woman who liberates herself from a life of domesticity. Ironically, with the house in Neauphle, Duras reenters a domestic space.[3] Yet Duras lives in her house on her own terms, having acquired, quite literally, a home of her own, where she can come and go as she pleases, moving back and forth between the kitchen table, where she is known to make *confitures,* to the writing table. Henceforth, Duras will experience real moments of peace that only a house can provide, "une vraie maison, à la campagne" "a real house, in the country" (Vircondelet 231).

There is in fact a tripolarity in Duras's adulthood, as she gravitates from the more public rue Saint-Benoît apartment in Paris to her seaside apartment in Trouville to her house in Neauphle. The Paris apartment seems the most political space of her life, the *lieu de l'évènement,* with Duras presiding over it like a *"Précieuse révolutionnaire"* as if it were a *salon,*[4] particularly during wartime when Duras held clandestine Resistance meetings with a young François Mitterrand in attendance. Yet her bucolic country house is less politically innocuous and uneventful than it might appear. Upon closer examination of Marguerite Duras's many topographies, the house in Neauphle stands out because it represents, as she puts it, the only place where she can be relatively "à l'aise." Furthermore, the home in Neauphle lies at the origin of much of her writing, as a metonymic space, for example, whose scents and sounds she associates with Indochinese nights, or whose architectural layout houses the nucleus for the film, *Nathalie Granger.* In *Les Lieux de Marguerite Duras,* she says,

> One always thinks that one has to begin with a story in order to make a film. It's not true. For *Nathalie Granger* I started completely with the house. Really, completely. I had the house in my head, constantly, constantly, and then a story came to live in it, you see, but the house, it was already cinema. (36)

In elaborating a Durassian version of *écriture féminine,* the home lies at its very heart, in her use of her domestic space not just as a departure point for her writing, but as the very physical site of cinematic representation.

More important, she politicizes the uneventful in the lives of women in her representation of the/her home. The home for Duras is a space for women only or, at least, dominated by women, with men being assigned a secondary role. She says about her house in Neauphle, "All the women from my books have lived in this house, all of them. Only women inhabit these places, men, never" (*Lieux* 12). Duras goes further in making the home a specifically female space as she eradicates the possibility of a male presence within the space and outside it, on its voyeuristic fringes. Taking *Nathalie Granger* as an example, a film about a mother who waits with her friend for news concerning her daughter's need to be sent to reform school, Duras explains to Xavière Gauthier in *Les Parleuses* the necessity for preventing men from witnessing what goes on inside the stone walls, in the house and the adjoining garden:

> If the house in *Nathalie Granger* wasn't a house of women and only that, a house of women . . . if a man, of whatever kind, had been living there, in the house, the film wouldn't have been possible. It would have been as if there were a witness. Because I have this feeling about *Nathalie Granger* that men shouldn't see what happens there. A very strong feeling. (*Woman to Woman* 48)

Whether men witness the goings on inside the home or not, the possibility of a voyeuristic gaze is eradicated and replaced by a new point of view, more respectful of the "fundamental difference, the basic alterity and mystery of the *Other,* the character" (Papin 91). For critic

Liliane Papin, this new point of view hinges on a different relation between narrator and reader when she writes that "[the] narrative voices [in Duras] are all an invitation for spectators/readers to let themselves be guided toward Difference, to love without knowing and without controlling" (Papin 91). Hence *Nathalie Granger* posits a new form of visual pleasure, for it is a film "in which a markedly female universe is created and then sustained . . ." (Portuges *Remains* 220).

In rewriting both her homes of childhood and adulthood, Duras's act of politicizing the home goes even further as she attempts to give meaning to her roots that have been erased or even eradicated by the violence of patriarchy and colonialism. The disaster of her mother's *barrages* surfaces and resurfaces as a metaphorical reminder of the impotence of women, children, and the colonized natives in the face of the monolithic colonizer. Of her mother and her childhood in general, Duras tells Xavière Gauthier:

> You know, my mother ruined herself because of the dam. I've told the story. I was eighteen when I left to take the second part of my *philo* here, and to go to the university, and I didn't think about childhood anymore. It had been too painful. I completely blocked it out. And I dragged along in life saying: *I* have no native country; I don't recognize anything around me here, but the country where I lived is atrocious. (*Woman to Woman* 98)

The insistence on the home in so many of her works signifies an attempt at salvaging, or at least giving herself the illusion of, an origin, a site of departure, albeit a violent and paradoxical one. In filling a personal void with a refabricated home, whether it be her mother's battered bungalow on the edge of a floodplain or her own bourgeois country house, Duras universalizes the endemic victimization of women at the destructive hands of patriarchy and colonialism. In doing so, she tries to recapture, not the Eden of childhood, but rather the violence, the hatred, and the poverty, not just of her family, but of an entire culture (Hirsch 149).

In the context of politicizing domestic space, Jane Riles Wamsley makes the connection between writing and the interior layout of the home in Duras's fictional works. For a recurring theme in Duras's analysis of the writing process is this idea of a sweeping-out process, mirrored in her texts which "advocate 'sweeping out' and 'washing out' old houses stuffed with unnecessary trappings and cumbersome baggage accumulated through years of ritual and custom" (Wamsley 40). On Duras's writing Wamsley concludes,

> Duras' writing style, intended to bring about rupture and reversal in a theoretical mode of thinking, returns to origins: to simple words, ideas and archetypes which have been misconstructed and misinterpreted with usage and time. The created confusion of her simple language points to the need to "get back to the basics" of the meanings of life and literature—to return to the ground floor or the zero point of writing. (Wamsley 43)

Hence the "cleaned-out swept house," a recurring theme in her writing, stands in as a metaphor for a Durassian brand of *écriture féminine*. For Duras, both the house and women's writing must experience an act of destruction followed by a return to *"le basique,"* to *"la matérialité de la vie"* "basic things," "the materiality of life":

> Between themselves [women] talk only about the practicalities of life. They're not supposed to enter the realm of the mind. . . . For centuries women have been informed about themselves by men, and men tell them they're inferior. But speech is freer in that situation of deprivation and oppression just because it doesn't go beyond the practicalities of life. (*Practicalities* 39)

In her introduction to *Les Parleuses,* Xavière Gauthier herself uses architectural metaphors to describe how a feminine language in Duras begins to emerge through the cracks of masculine words when she says,

> If whole and well-established words have always been used, aligned, and stacked up by men, it is quite likely that the feminine might appear like the grass, which, at first a little wild and scraggly, manages to spring up between the chinks in old stones and ends up—why not?—breaking through the surface of cement slabs, no matter how heavy they may be, with the force of what has been long restrained. (*Woman to Woman* x)

If the architectural materials that make up the house, the container, are aligned with the male, then the contained, the contents of the house must slip through the cracks of the patriarchal walls and foundation in order to open up a space, "pour ouvrir un espace" as Marini puts it, "à l'émergence sur le corps et le désir des femmes . . ." "for the emergence of the body and the desire of women" (Marini 49)

But the house is more than a metaphor for the act of writing. Duras makes analogous the woman's body to the house, calling the former an echo chamber that witnesses and records like a "bottomless well," a receptacle, before sending back the story, her story. The woman's body, like the house, listens to and accumulates stories passively:

> . . . there are people whom I was near, whom I knew, who gave me this, that and the other thing until the story was fabricated. But I draw it out of you; I draw it out of others. (*Woman to Woman* 161)

The act of writing is not individual or autonomous but rather happens communally with others, and her role is to give a "sound" (un "son") to what flows through her. Yet unlike a more male-centered vision of the home, which also associates the house with the body of woman but only to make her the facilitator of the writing process (thanks to the presence of woman, man can write), Duras makes woman both the subject and object of writing. By contrast to Emmanuel Lévinas, for instance, who considered the home to be a refuge for the *moi* in need of *recueillement* or quiet contemplation, a contemplation *facilitated* by a female presence, Duras activates a female-centered *recueillement*. In fact, invoking Lévinas and his ideas on the relationship between the home and writing provides a noteworthy contrast to the Durassian vision when he writes, "Et l'Autre don't la présence est discrètement une absence et à partir de laquelle s'accomplit l'accueil hospitalier par excellence qui décrit le champ de l'intimité, est la Femme. La femme est la condition du recueillement, de l'intériorité de la Maison et de l'habitation" "And the Other, whose presence is a discrete absence and from whom the hospitable welcome *par excellence* that describes the field of intimacy is accomplished, is Woman. Woman enables quiet contemplation, the interiorization of House and Home." (128). If *"la Femme"* is associated with *"l'Autre,"* then one has to assume that *"l'Homme"* is the *"Moi"* that is speaking, and it is of *his* home that he is speaking. Duras, as we shall see, activates a female interiority, enabling a female *moi* to emerge, thereby reversing the terms of alterity.

Finally, her act of writing as a woman, returning to the basics of everyday existence through the gaps of male language, gives space to the uneventful, to the so far unrecorded interstices of women's daily existence. For instance, *Nathalie Granger* gives expression to a new kind of realism, not copying reality but rather saying something about it (*Parleuses* 93). Moreover, the film tells us something about women's time and women's work, for it shows two female friends going about their domestic chores as though "something were happening." In the film, women's work is represented as a "harmonious activity" and not a monotonous chore performed by servile women (*Parleuses* 97). Such an alternative representation revalorizes women's work, giving space to Duras's belief that a house is like a ship, and "the women are in the machine room, down below. Without this, everything would stop" (*Parleuses* 105). For Duras, women, and by that she means married women with children, are the only ones to make full use of their time.

This definition of woman, so closely associated with domesticity and the maternal, does verge on essentialism, a tendency to define woman in terms of a preassigned maternal, biological function, which many feminists argue falls within the realm of patriarchal ideology.[5] Yet its cinematic representation in *Nathalie Granger* theorizes a new form of visual pleasure for the female viewer through the familiarity of the mise-en-scène, which represents a break from visual narratives created heretofore exclusively for the masculine gaze (Portuges *Remains* 226). Duras herself articulates the idea of a unique "regard féminin" that permeates the house when she says,

> I think that I never walk through this house without looking at it and I think that this look, is a *feminine look.* A man walks into it in the evening, he eats there, he sleeps there, he warms himself there, etc. . . . A woman, that's something else. She has a sort of ecstatic gaze, an inward gaze of the woman on the house, and on her dwelling, and on the things that are obviously the container of her life, her reason for being, practically even, for most of them, that a man cannot share. (emphasis added, *Lieux* 20)

For Duras, to look, *"regarder,"* means both to look out, to look outside oneself, a form of visual pleasure aligned with the male gaze,
and to look in, inwardly. Duras, in fact, fuses the mental or psychical
and the physical or architectural meanings of the word *intérieur* in
her positing of a specific female gaze associated with her domestic
"interior."

The Durassian home examined so far releases a polyvalence of
meanings. Yet a meaning that emerges above all the others is the notion that the home is the paradigmatic woman's space. The following
section of this essay will attempt to sort out the various meanings
Duras has assigned to the home, for they are numerous and often confusing, if not contradictory. Particular emphasis will be placed on the
home as the site of an anthropology of women, giving special attention to the relics of woman's history, as well as notions of waiting and
silence.

"Femme/Maison"

While men have most often been associated with the physical and
material aspects of the house, being quite literally their architects and
engineers, for Duras, women are the ones that make the house a home
through the more intangible attributes they bring to it, notably the
emotive and the spiritual. In her essay titled appropriately, "La maison," Duras writes, "men can build houses, but they cannot make
homes" (*Vie Matérielle* 58). In fact, she nuances the distinction
bâtir/créer by aligning the "outside order" of the house with the
"aménagement *visible* de la maison" "the *visible* management of the
house" (emphasis hers) associated with men, and the inside order of
the home with the realm of ideas "emotional phases and endless feelings connected with children" (*Vie Matérielle* 57). With a perhaps
clichéd but apropos metaphor of a bird's nest, Bachelard also makes
the distinction between male and female architectural functions when
he writes:

> The female . . . digs her house. The male brings from the outside
> unusual materials, solid twigs. From all of that, the female makes
> a felt-like nest by applying some pressure. (Bachelard 101)

But while Bachelard essentializes the female architectural function by connecting it to the biological, Duras downplays the dominant male function of material colonizer of space only to revalorize the mother's act of creating, of making the home a sacred but secular temple for her children. Invoking once again the memory of her mother, Duras writes,

> A house as my mother conceived it was in fact *for* us. I don't think she'd have done it for a man or a lover. . . . As a general rule, men don't do anything for children. Nothing practical. . . . The child is put into their arms when they get home from work—clean, changed, ready to go to bed. Happy. That makes a mountain of difference between men and women. (*Practicalities* 50)

In a typical Durassian twisting of language, she renders immaterial—the irrelevant—the material associated with the father (the actual structure of the house) while materializing the immaterial—the intangible—contribution of the mother.

Duras is relentless about the intimate, symbiotic relation that exists between the house and its female inhabitants. The entire first section of *Les Lieux* articulates repeatedly the connection between "la femme" and "sa demeure," "woman" and "her home," a connection that Duras makes akin to a woman and her own body. About Isabelle Granger, she writes, "C'est comme quand elle déambule là, dans la maison, c'est comme si elle passait autour d'elle-même, comme si elle contournait son propre corps" "It's as if, when she walks there, in the house, it's as if she were walking around herself, as if she were circling her own body" (*Lieux* 20). The porosity of woman and her house extends to all the other female inhabitants of the house, those who came before her and those who will follow her: "Et quand je parle des autres femmes, je pense que ces autres femmes me contiennent aussi; c'est comme si elles et moi on était douées de porosité" "And when I speak of other women, I think that these other women contain me as well; it's as if they and I were endowed with porosity" (*Lieux* 12). Hence the house tells the story/history of women, starting with the objects that have been left behind, buried in a dresser drawer, or underneath the floorboards. With an archaeologist's scalpel, Duras digs the ground beneath her house in Neauphle in search of written traces of its past, only to find two centuries of "ordures ménagères," marking the unremarkable passage not so much of "famous" men but rather of anonymous women and children (*Lieux* 19).

In her apartment on the rue Saint-Benoît, Duras the archaeologist finds tortoiseshell hairpins and a flea comb, but very little else that would give significance to its prior female inhabitants. In an antique dresser that she had purchased with her royalties from *Barrage,* she does discover a woman's slip, a *"caraco,"* which upon closer inspection, reveals faded red traces of its former female owner. This yellowed piece of women's lingerie sends Duras speculating about the piece of furniture in which it was found, the number of times it was moved without the undergarment being disturbed, and of course, the woman to whom it belonged. Duras concludes,

> The first thing you think when you realize what it is, is: "She must have hunted for it all over the place." For days and nights. She couldn't think where it could have got to. . . . (*Practicalities* 122)

Tracking down woman's (corporeal) history, Duras searches in the banal "underside" of woman's everyday existence.

In the same vein, Duras deciphers women's history by partaking in specifically female activities that continue silently and seemingly effortlessly through time and space. One such activity is the "crafting" of *confitures,* that quintessentially French woman's concoction (a famous commercial brand, Bonne Maman, connotes through its very name and its "handwritten" label, kitchen-cooked savory jam that mom used to make). Xavière Gauthier ends her "avant-propos" in *Les Parleuses* on the statement, "And, between the recordings of our interviews, we made jam[,]" as though women naturally gravitate back and forth between the mundane material tasks of the everyday and more intellectual pursuits. Making jam, writes Jacqueline Lévi-Valensi, is a female type of alchemy, "even if the jam pan is an inferior, utilitarian, domestic, feminine version of the still" (Lévi-Valensi 137). Hence, the anthropology of women is situated in the kitchen, over a simmering pot, with the step-by-step procedure of jam preparation symbolizing female domestic ritual being passed along through the generations.

It would appear so far that Duras is writing a positive history of women, idealizing the communal act of cooking in the kitchen or the narcissistic ritual of making themselves aesthetic objects of desire alone in their bedroom, as they comb their hair and put on sexy undergarments. Accused by Jérôme Beaujour of idealizing women, Duras responds in *La vie matérielle,* "Women could do with being idealized. . . . The main thing is to talk about them and their houses and their surroundings, and the way they manage other people's good" (*Practicalities* 53). But she is quick to point out that the history of women goes beyond a seemingly gratifying management of the household. For behind the walls and the closed doors of the house, another tale unravels, namely the story of women's silence, and of her loneliness, her alienation, and, generally speaking, of her despair. Just as her body is entrapped by the demands of maternity, the home, that quintessential woman's space, entraps women's unfulfilled desire, as they are destined to a life of endurance and abandonment in a shroud of silence:

> Men and women are different, after all. Being a mother isn't the same as being a father. Motherhood means that a woman gives her body over to her child, her children; they're on her as they might be on a hill, in a garden; they devour her, hit her, sleep on her; and she lets herself be devoured, and sometimes she sleeps because they are on her body. Nothing like that happens with fathers. (*Practicalities* 54)

Beginning with her early work, *La vie tranquille,* Duras sets out to record the domestic ennui of everyday existence compounded by the constant deferral of the satisfaction of desire inhibited by a suffocating family life (Murphy 33). Duras writes of the discontinuity of women's time, made to seem invisibly and silently continuous: "From the man's point of view, a woman is a good mother when she turns this discontinuity into a silent and unobtrusive continuity" (*Practicalities* 45). Through the apparently seamless continuity of women's domestic work, Duras concludes, woman erases the traces of her own existence, thereby making herself transparent or invisible. She writes,

> The silent continuity seemed so natural and lasted so long that in the end, for the people around the woman who practiced it, it no

longer existed at all. To men, women's work was like the rain-
bringing clouds, or the rain itself. The task involved was carried
out every day as regularly as sleep. So men were happy—men in
the Middle Ages, men at the time of the Revolution, and men in
1986. . . . (*Practicalities* 45)

From an historical standpoint, nothing has changed for Duras as far
as the invisibility of women's work and, by extension, of women
themselves.

   This is perhaps why Duras sets out as a proponent of a poetics/pol-
itics of discontinuity associated with women's work and women's
time. Such a poetics/politics could be disruptive to the patriarchal order, as women take control of their time, rendering the seemingly
continuous discontinuous, and subsequently less repetitive and alienating, as women take their time and break up the execution of various
tasks. Yet a housewife's ability to be productive in her housework, her
ability to get something accomplished, precludes the multiple daily
interruptions (over which she has little control) that interfere with her
work (the children's cries, the ringing of the telephone and of the
doorbell), thereby rendering her unproductive. Finally, the housewife
is still performing housework, an unpaid, devalued and hence *non*-
productive task in the economic sense of the term, making her work
all the more alienating in a society that only valorizes productive
work. It seems then that a Durassian politics of discontinuity works
better in the realm of poetics, meaning in the elaboration of a specifically feminine writing process, as the woman writer, unlike the woman *tout court,* has more control over her use of time. This is precisely what Duras has chosen to do by appropriating the discontinuity
of women's time in the writing process, by stopping, for example, the
interview to make jam.

   Yet the invisibility of woman associated with continuous time also
finds an echo in Duras's writing, in her famous blanks that critics
have isolated as the marker, the standard bearer of the Durassian
style. Just as she has made a presence out of the absence of speech associated with the silence of women's work, Duras creates an alternate
speech through the blanks in her writing. It is through these blanks
that her writing subverts traditional (white male) ideology by showing up women's silence, "constructing it as more 'true' or 'real' than

the meaning produced in language, perforating and disturbing the dominating chatter of men" (Selous 249-251). The sequestering of women in silence and emptiness becomes for Duras a subversive act that enables her to, in a first moment, kill the interminable flow of words that mystifies and alienates woman (Marini 53). This act of sequestering enables woman to lock herself up "in silence as in a fortress, in order to escape conventional language that another wants to violently impose upon her" (Marini 22). The second step in this subversive act is to make a language out of this silence, by showing, as in *Nathalie Granger,* what is never shown in "male" language, namely the quiet ritualistic gestures of women sealed off from men in the domestic fortress.

The only man allowed to penetrate the woman's fortress is hardly a man at all in the "masculinist" sense of the term, for the traveling salesman is, as Duras puts it, an *"Homme pour rire,"* a far cry from the parental model of the "responsible" man (*Nathalie Granger* 91). In a footnote to the script, Duras explains the analogous oppression of women and traveling salesmen, both forced to speak a language that is not their own.[6] Hence the traveling salesman is forced to emasculate himself, rendering himself powerless through his mimicry of the language of the powerful.[7] This humiliating emasculation is exacerbated by the necessity to penetrate the home as an uninvited guest, an unwelcome stranger, who more often then not is turned away, only to leave him feeling completely annihilated. This annihilation of self aligns him with the housewife, to whom he must sell the machines designed for her by men on the outside intent on perpetuating the smoothness, effortlessness, and invisibility of domestic labor.

It ensues that the Durassian theme connected to domestic space of waiting and abandonment, which Julia Kristeva characterizes as "the insurmountable trauma inflicted by the discovery . . . of the existence of a 'not-I' " also finds expression in much of the work of Duras (Kristeva 145). Film expresses best the duration and the experience of waiting, which Duras associates intrinsically with the history of women, for, as she puts it, women have always waited quietly and dispassionately for their men to come home, whether it be from war or from work.[8] One of her favorite mythical figures to metaphorize the "waiting woman" is Michelet's sorceress, whom she cites again and again in many of her works. In *La Sorcière,* Michelet, the nineteenth-century historian, theorized that women in the Middle Ages were accused of sorcery because they were so often left alone that they began wandering around in the forest and talking to the trees, the animals, the flowers, and the plants. For Duras, this woman of the Middle Ages, left alone in a hut or in a castle, developed a "parole féminine" that men eventually eradicated with the witch trials because of their fear of the "folies des femmes":

> In the Middle Ages, men were off to war for their lord or on a Crusade, and the women in the countryside remained completely alone, isolated, for months at a time in the forest, in their huts, and that is how, starting with this solitude, unimaginable to us nowadays, they began speaking to trees, to plants, to wild animals, meaning that they began inventing an understanding with nature, reinventing it. (*Lieux* 13)

For Duras, women today face the same dilemma of abandonment and solitude, for, whether men are out waging war or earning a wage, these are strictly male occupations. Women, on the other hand, are left alone inside the house, waiting for their men to come home from the outside. Duras's mission as a writer is to revive the sorceresses' mystical and almost incomprehensible "parole féminine" through the special rapport she has with her house and the solitude she experiences within its walls:

> We're still there, we women . . . we're still there . . . yes. We are there. Nothing has really changed. Me in this house, with this garden, I have a relationship that men will never have with a dwelling, a place. (*Lieux* 14)

Hence Duras's mission as a writer is to act as a modern day sorceress, singing her domestic incantations of loneliness, abandonment, and confinement.

Hermetically sealed off from the outside world, the Durassian home is also a space of plenitude and hygiene. If the author herself cleans her home so voraciously, it is in order to wash away the madness of civilization. Similarly, the act of writing can only begin after an evacuation of all thought, after an emptying out which comes about through mindless domestic labor, such as polishing the floors and the furniture in order to dissolve into "the great indifferenciation of the world, in these billions of live and anonymous molecules." (Vircondelet 329).[9]

But Duras will be the first to admit that the hermetic home is doomed to failure by its very vulnerability. The outside "contaminants" always find a way to filter in through the cracks. Even in *Nathalie Granger*, the most utopian of Durassian spaces, the outside world makes its way into the woman's house, from the street noise, to the *voix-off* of the male radio announcer who diffuses the outside violence in news announcements, to the very presence of the stranger, the traveling salesman, forced to speak the language of the father within the female interior. Children themselves contaminate the home, for they must be relinquished to the outside world and enter the institution of the school, where they must adhere to an emotional and intellectual coded norm of behavior. The school forces its patriarchal language onto women who must affix names onto their children's clothing, are compelled to read the monthly report card, and, more generally, are responsible for keeping their children within behavioral boundaries that are always/already there, and over which they have very little power. It is through the child, Nathalie Granger, that the violence of the outside world enters the mother's house, although her violence results from a deviation from that norm, a deviation that signifies, in the end, a forced separation from the mother.

Thus the home fails in its attempt at acting as an alternate intrinsically female site, sheltering its inhabitants in an abundance of food, love, and hygiene. The forced separation of the daughter from the mother by an outside institution more powerful than the women who have banded together inside the home recurs throughout much of Duras's writing. Among other tales, *Un barrage contre le pacifique* and *L'Amant* tell the story of the incapacity of the mother, in this particular case, Duras's own mother, to push back the violent forces of the ocean and the corrupt colonial regime, not to mention the self-destruction that comes from within, from the hatred that family members come to feel for one another. The futility of the mother's rebellion against social injustice points to a bigger theme related to Duras's domestic politics: the failure of women's passive resistance, of their silently banding together in a community of women, sealed off from the violent world on the outside.

In the 1970s, at the height of an era that experimented with revolution and reform, Duras felt more optimistic about a passivity associated with silence and waiting that could inaugurate a feminist politics so long as this passive voice was "completely informed about itself, completely" (*Parleuses* 146). She confides to Xavière Gauthier,

> This great passivity, which seems to me fundamental—it's only women really who can impose it, who can provide the example of it. (*Woman to Woman* 108)

Yet the only way in which the passive voice of women can become effective is if it is spoken outside the home, by taking it to the streets, or by writing it, as Duras does. However, such "passive action" faces major obstacles from the very start because of the difficulty of banding women together and calling them to action when, unlike their male proletarian counterparts who work together in factories, they are isolated each in their own homes (or they, increasingly, by joining the workforce, do not want to disrupt the male status quo). More important, a Durassian brand of passive revolt is ineffective at subverting the social order through transgressive action because of its intrinsic weakness stemming from its very passivity, its very silence.

The passive revolt of Durassian women, which Duras sees as another trajectory of female history, often culminates in the violent use of or destruction of language.[10] Such acts of "violence," such as the women ripping, in a symbolic gesture of destruction of the controlling language of men, the papers on which is written Nathalie Granger's negative report, or the mother's angry letter to the colonial officials in *Barrage,* are of course powerless in affecting change.[11] The temporary chaos that takes over the Granger house, symbolized by the ripping of papers and signifying a taking control of the house by its female inhabitants, does not prevent the more long-term removal and institutionalization of the daughter by outside forces.

Thus the optimism expressed briefly in her interviews from the 70s gives way to an overall feeling of pessimism regarding female passive resistance in a literature that some like Kristeva have characterized as "non-cathartic." The Durassian utopia in which the world, having undergone total destruction and chaos, is guided by a feminine psyche, "without authority, without the all powerful figure of the Father and . . . God," and "no longer dictated by social conventions . . ." can only take shape in the author's imagination (Papin 92). For, in the words of Marcelle Marini, woman will always remain marginalized "whether she chooses total obedience or revolt, which turns out to be as powerless as it is violent" (Marini 47). If women, explains Marini, are to abandon a preestablished value system, it is only to retreat into a system of countervalues, thereby assuring the continuation of the dominant system, which eliminates or "digests" the undesirable without any difficulty.

Because woman is not the subject of her own history, she cannot disrupt by one iota the socio-symbolic system by pointing out its inherent contradictions through her transgression as a female subject. But, as Marini points out, this does not mean that women should give up the revolt, which Duras finds much less alienating than submission to the existing order. Woman's access to subjectivity can solely come about through transgression, for only crime can make a subject out of woman (Marini 22).

A Durassian brand of domestic politics may seem ineffectual, the social order having been left unchanged, women having found access to a subjectivity of their own, but only at the cost of their own destruction brought about by their transgression of the law.[12] This does not mean, however, that Durassian poetics/politics should be abandoned altogether. What should be retained from her politicization of domestic space is its *interpretative* capacity, in the model she puts forward to understand and interpret women's lives, perhaps even their history. In order for women to carve out identities not just as supports of the social order, they must develop, as Elizabeth Grosz puts it, "a framework appropriate to them," in which to locate "a history, a genealogy, a recognized and validated past" (Grosz 180). In the words of Luce Irigaray, women must reappropriate a female genealogy that has long been forgotten in the father's house:

> This genealogy of women, given our exile in the family of the father-husband, we forget somewhat its singularity, and we even repudiate it. Let us try to situate ourselves in this female genealogy in order to conquer and retain our identity. Furthermore let

us not forget that we already have a history, that certain women, even if it was difficult culturally, have marked history, and that too often we do not know them. (Irigaray 31)

Duras's brand of *écriture féminine* does just that, digging up the residues of a female domestic lineage, rewriting the family history, not so much from the study or the library, but from the kitchen table. Through a reevaluation of domestic time, domestic work, and domestic space, Duras has developed a distinctive style of writing, rendering conspicuous women who would have remained otherwise unnoticed.

NOTES

1. All translations, unless otherwise noted, are mine.

2. In the "Lover" series I include *Un Barrage contre le pacifique, L'Eden Cinéma,* the film script based on that novel, *L'Amant,* and *L'Amant de la Chine du Nord.*

3. Gaston Bachelard writes of a "maison rêvée" "a dreamed of house" or "maison de l'avenir" "a house of the future" meaning "un simple rêve de propriétaire, un concentré de tout ce qui est jugé commode, comfortable, sain, solide, voire désirable aux autres" "the simple dream of a home-owner, containing all that is judged practical, comfortable, healthy, solid, meaning desirable to others" (68). What this essay will attempt to demonstrate, however, is ways in which Duras's more feminocentric house is a departure from the Bachelardian standard.

4. I borrow this expression from Vircondelet.

5. Toril Moi sums up the essentialist dilemma by stating that "it still remains *politically* essential for feminists to defend women *as* women in order to counteract the patriarchal oppression that precisely defines women *as* women" (13).

6. I will quote it in its entirety, for Duras articulates so clearly in her unaffected style the connection between power and language. She writes, "La situation du voyageur de commerce—je parle de ceux qui sont au plus bas de l'échelle, qui font du porte-à-porte—m'apparaît toujours comme étant la plus terrible de toutes. C'est en général un dernier boulot, celui qu'on se décide à faire quand on n'a plus d'autres recours. Mais l'aspect terrible de ce travail, c'est surtout qu'il oblige celui qui le fait à en passer par le mensonge fonctionnel qui, en général, est réservé aux patrons. Ordinairement c'est le patron qui vante sa camelote, et non l'ouvrier. Les ouvriers ont au moins le droit de se taire. Et justement, le voyageur de commerce, lui, ne l'a pas: il est tenu d'*imiter* le patron, de *se dégrader,* de rejoindre les rangs des patrons—et cela pour survivre. Il est tenu d'imiter son langage, son maintien, son aisance—même s'il monte quarante étages par jour pour faire un seul repas." "The situation of the traveling salesman—I mean those who are at the bottom of the lad-

der, who go door to door—seems the most terrible of all. It's generally a last recourse type of job. But the worst part of this type of work is mostly that it forces the one who does it to resort to lying, the kind of lying a boss usually does. Usually, it is the boss who boasts about his junk, not the worker. Assembly-line workers have the right to stay quiet at least. But the traveling salesman, he can't: he has to *imitate* the boss, he has to *degrade himself,* in order to join the ranks of the bosses—and he does this in order to survive. He has to imitate his language, his attitude, his ease—even if he climbs forty stories a day in order to earn just one meal." (*Nathalie Granger* 51)

7. Lheureux in *Madame Bovary* travels also from door to door, penetrating the home of many a bourgeoise, seducing them with fabric swatches in this case. But in contrast with the traveling salesman in *Nathalie Granger,* Lheureux is his own agent of "material" seduction, working perhaps as a middleman between suppliers and clients, yet always adeptly encoding language in his sales pitch, to borrow Naomi Schor's terminology (see *Breaking the Chain*).

8. Although Duras does not make mention of this, it is significant that in French women "wait for" a baby as well (on *attend* un bébé) in the sense of "expecting," thereby associating the female biological function (pregnancy) with the psychological (waiting).

9. This theme resurfaces in her fiction as in *Le Ravissement de Lol V. Stein,* in which the female protagonist is a compulsive cleaner and maintainer of order of her house and the surrounding garden.

10. Duras points out in the script to *Nathalie Granger* that women have always been "dolentes et silencieuses," and that from 1672 to 1972 nothing has changed (93).

11. The French word, *"impuissance,"* brings the point home more "potently," for it means both powerlessness and impotence, pointing to the absence of the phallus that afflicts both women and "effeminate" men.

12. An example outside Duras's oeuvre of a woman's unsuccessful access to an alternate subjectivity through resistance in the domestic sphere can be found in Claude Chabrol's *Une affaire de femmes,* a fictionalized account of the last woman ever to be executed in France. Having been left behind, like so many other women during the Occupation, with no money to feed her children (quite the Durassian theme), Marie Latour decides to perform abortions in her kitchen, and rent her spare rooms out to prostitutes. This double transgression, one could almost say triple, since she violates the sacrosanct space of the home by using it as its flip side, a whorehouse and a back alley, will cost her her life, as the Vichy tribunal, in an effort to compensate for its "emasculation" by the occupying German forces, will judge her a traitor to the French nation.

WORKS CITED

Bachelard, Gaston. *La poétique de l'espace.* Paris: PUF, 1958.

Duras, Marguerite. *Des journées entières dans les arbres.* Paris: Gallimard, 1954.

_____. *La vie matérielle.* Paris: P. O. L., 1987.

_____. *L'Amant*. Paris: Minuit, 1984.

_____. *L'Amant de la Chine du Nord*. Paris: Gallimard, 1991.

_____. *Nathalie Granger*. Paris: Gallimard, 1973.

_____. *Practicalities*. Trans. Barbara Bray. New York: Grove Weidenfeld, 1990.

_____. *Un barrage contre le Pacifique*. Paris: Gallimard, 1958.

_____. *Woman to Woman*, Trans. Katharine A. Jensen. Lincoln: U. of Nebraska Press, 1987.

Duras, Marguerite and Gauthier, Xavière. *Les Parleuses*. Paris: Minuit,1974.

Duras, Marguerite and Porte, Michelle. *Les Lieux*. Paris: Minuit, 1977.

Grosz, Elizabeth. *Sexual Subversions: Three French Feminists*. Sydney: Allen and Unwin, 1989.

Hirsch, Marianne. *The Mother/Daughter Plot: Narrative, Psychoanalysis, Feminism*. Bloomington: Indiana University Press, 1989.

Irigaray, Luce. *Sexes et Parentés*. Paris: Minuit, 1987.

Kristeva, Julia. "The Pain of Sorrow in the Modern World: The Work of Marguerite Duras." *PMLA 102* (March 1987):138-152.

Lévi-Valensi, Jacqueline. "Les confitures de Marguerite Duras." *Roman, réalités, réalismes*. Paris: PUF, 1989.

Lévinas, Emmanuel. *Totalité et infini*. La Haye: Martinus Nijhoff, 1961.

Marini, Marcelle. *Territoires du féminin avec Marguerite Duras*. Paris: Minuit, 1977.

Moi, Toril. *Sexual/Textual Politics: Feminist Literary Theory*. London: Methuen, 1985.

Murphy, Carol. *Alienation and Absence in the Novels of Marguerite Duras*. Lexington: French Forum, 1982.

Papin, Liliane. "Place of Writing, Place of Love." In Sanford Scribner Ames, ed. *Remains to Be Seen: Essays on Marguerite Duras* (pp. 81-94). New York: Peter Lang, 1988.

Portuges, Catherine. "Attachment and Separation in *The Memoirs of a Dutiful Daughter*." *Yale French Studies* 72 (1986): 107-118.

_____. "The Pleasures of Natalie Granger." In Sanford Scribner Ames, ed. *Remains to Be Seen: Essays on Marguerite Duras* (pp. 217-230). New York: Peter Lang, 1988.

Schor, Naomi. *Breaking the Chain: Women, Theory and French Realist Fiction*. New York: Columbia University Press, 1985.

Selous, Trista. *The Other Woman: Feminism and Femininity in the Work of Marguerite Duras*. New Haven: Yale University Press, 1988.

Vircondelet, Alain. *Duras, biographie*. Paris: François Bourin, 1991.

Wamsley, Jane Riles. "Marguerite Duras: Revamping the Living-Room." *Journal of the Pacific Northwest Council on Foreign Languages 6* (1985): 34-51.

SECTION II:
WOMEN'S WRITING SPACES—
SOLITUDE
AND THE CREATIVE PROCESS

The acts of reading, thinking, and writing have only recently been serious occupations for women. In 1873 Dr. Edward Clarke, professor of medicine at Harvard University, opined that "A woman cannot afford to risk her health in acquiring knowledge. . . . Too many women have already made themselves permanent invalids by overstrain of study at schools and colleges, resulting in monstrous brains and puny bodies, flowing thought and constipated bowels" *(Sex in Education)*. This attitude toward women as scholars and writers prevailed, and though a few women were able to overcome this popular notion that intellectual exercise would make women sick, most were persuaded about women's place being at home; in general, the domestic sphere circumscribed woman's space and occupied her mind and spirit.

The history of writing, too, rests on the dominant cultural assumptions that serious textual production has been a man's domain. Canon formation has been defined by gender, race, and class prerequisites, and the conservative nature of institutions. However, over the last century, women have appropriated and revised intellectual activities, attitudes, and settings that have been habitually assigned to men; have intruded into metaphorical locales formerly coded masculine; and have challenged the long standing, exclusionary practices of sexist institutions of dominant culture. These challenges include women's intrusion into physical locales—the university, the library, and the study—the man-lands of the past. These places have metaphorically represented the head, in which resides the instruments of intellection as well as the sense on dominance—as in head of household. Women have begun claiming these heady spaces, owning, possessing, keeping their own space sacred, going against the cultural call to minister to others, loving the intimacy with themselves in their solitary spaces. And they have also reinvented space for themselves.

Herspace is space, physical space, space claimed by women for themselves and themselves alone. The obvious example is that famous room that Virginia Woolf described, the actual place. But this setting also takes on metaphorical aspects, important to women's shift into creative work: herspace is like a stage for a single actor; a house of soliloquy; a studio of rich, internal echoes; a closet of expression; a safe cell for the incubation of ideas. It is the particular, gender-inflected space that women writers dream of, struggle to create, testify to inhabiting when they discuss their creative lives, especially their writing. It is occupied by women exploring the edges of their agency as they compose and by women meditating on what that agency and that freedom might mean.

To enter herspace isn't a singular experience with a single meaning: it could be to pass from one room into another or to leave the social world out there for the private world in here or to shift from one internal state into another. This often empty and quiet space supports the dance of reflection and production; it is a site at which the furnishings of the inner life take on weight. For instance, in the physical world of the woman writer's study, one would probably see a desk and chair, writing utensils, and objects of inspiration, including the books of others. But this space in the material world of Woolf's *A Room of One's Own* also contains an internal psychic space. To access this space entails more than simply entering a material locale (though this claiming of the space is surely a crucially important part of the process); it means also entering a metaphorical territory in which the imaginative, generative, and creative powers become more palpable, internal, real.

This private setting of a writer aware of her gender and of the history of spaces with which she has necessarily come to be associated vies with the dominant culture's ideal of women as other-centered. Herspace is created through women claiming space outside of these associations, an out-of-the-ordinary space in which a woman (historically dependent) may cultivate independent thought, in which a woman (always already oriented toward others) may affirm autonomy, in which a woman (always already passive) can act. This sense of agency that herspace allows women to cultivate and affirm may account at least partially for the creative manifestations of women who occupy herspace. The solitary space itself enables the writing process, protects it. And women, more than men, need this enabling protection. Women need to claim their own space, to bargain and plan and keep sight of that solitary space in which to commune with their thoughts and feelings, to experience their creative process intimately.

Writing Women, Solitary Space, and the Ideology of Domesticity

Victoria Boynton

"You are a writer," I say to myself as I eye the tempting stack of interior design catalogs on the coffee table. "You are a scholar." I visualize my vita, my list of intellectual accomplishments. I am using these assertions and visualizations to trick myself into confidence, to beckon my muse, to protect myself against the historical sense that, as a woman, I am an academic outsider, a dilettante unable to work seriously, a "scribbling woman" who breaks off her work to wander the house, straightening, adjusting a chair, moving a potted plant from one dark spot to another sunnier one, digging old candle wax from its jammed holder while dreaming up new arrangements, new furnishings, new additions, or whole new expansive houses—the diversions of my culture, my class, my race, my gender. I could do this dream dance through home space endlessly, polishing the long mirror at the entry to get a better look at myself as I pass. "Write," I tell my reflection. "At least sit down." I go to my little room to get my book, pencil, pad. But when I open the door, I catch sight of the empty wrought iron curtain rod that my husband made and put up for me six months ago. The delicate material for the curtains lies carefully folded in a basket. I want to pick it up and begin the curtain now, stitch myself into a trance, forget the pressure of writing, my desire to write—so like infidelity, so solitary, so antisocial. To be faithful would be to pick up the needle. To be unfaithful means observing my desire to write, no matter how troubling; it means picking up the pen, holding it gently between my fingers, and beginning to draw this desire's outlines; it means struggling against those compulsions to abandon the pen's pleasures in order to maintain a conventional fidelity to a complex of homemaking histories; it means finding myself in the difficult woman-welter of what has made me, what is always exerting force through the social forms of identity.

In this chapter, I turn to myself as a writing problem and as a political problem. Though I see this subject in relation to its larger contexts, I am making a home for myself in, through, and by writing. Significantly, my personal experience of writing is deeply connected to my sense of being contained in physical space—my writing setting, my gendered body, the *where* of myself, even as physicality is inscribed as feminine and set in clichéd opposition to masculinized mentality. I turn to myself as subject, authorized in the project by such theorists as Linda Alcoff and Laura Gray:

> We need new ways to analyze the personal and the political as well as new ways to conceptualize these terms. Experience is not "pretheoretical" nor is theory separate or separable from experience, and both are always already political. A project of social change, therefore, does not need to "get beyond" the personal narrative or the confessional to become political but rather needs to analyze the various effects of the confessional in different contexts and struggle to create discursive spaces in which we can maximize its disruptive effects. (283-284)

Alcoff and Gray's *discursive space* which can create a *disruptive* politics begins, for me, with an interrogation of my own identity as it manifests in set urges, ideological concretions, and cultural scripts. But this interrogation doesn't stop with myself, doesn't stop with my own temptations and urges and compulsions, but asks, "Who else is out beyond me? Who else holds a pen? Can we reach each other, pens in hands? Can I extend beyond my own discursive space, my own writing desire and my own middle-class upbringing and privilege to hear other voices, other desires?"

My best student ever is an African-American woman, a summa cum laude with a diamond-hard work ethic and a passion and talent for writing; she also happens to be gorgeous. The last time I saw her, back from an ivy graduate school for a visit, she had lost so much weight that I was afraid to hug her. She spoke to me through the angles, lines, and hollows of starvation. "I'm writing well, but I'm stressed," she told me. I worry: if she cannot pick up a fork, how can she pick up a pen? I soothe my worry about her by remembering her power to write and recalling that she has turned her life around before, as I, myself, have. We have both been mired in abusive heterosexual relationships, and we have both saved ourselves, have propelled ourselves out of those relationships, and have gone back to writing. I was lucky enough to have academic mentors who showed me the solitary pleasures of writing and offered me support, and I felt that positive energy move through me toward this student as she escaped her troubled relationship in order to write. However, Quiana Allen, another young woman, girlfriend of a student at my school, wasn't able to end her abusive relationship. She, too, is a promising African-American poet who uses writing to reflect on her life, but she has struggled with a difficult economic situation that my Ivy League student was spared. Quiana was intent on making a life different from the one she occupied (or that occupied her). However, tragically, one night in January 2000, when her boyfriend again began to abuse her, "she defended herself with a knife to keep him from choking her to death." She was subsequently "charged with second-degree intentional murder," despite the strong case that she suffered from battered woman syndrome (Nagel 7). Quiana is now in the Albion Correctional Facility.

According to the e-mail messages that pass among faculty and students concerned about her, Quiana says that the prison is like a halfway house. The word *house* in this networked message has a settling effect on me. I read the space that Quiana occupies through my own maze of feminized, middle-class, white subjectivity: prison must not be as bad as I imagined because, of course, my kind of woman makes a *house* into a *home,* a comforting image, the homemade prison space. Certainly, in prison, Quiana must be spatially constrained, I think, but not locked away in a dull cell on which she can make no impression. I want to save myself the trouble of thinking of Quiana in prison, so I think of her at home, although I know that prison can never be home and that her apartment was a violent and unsafe place for her.

It is difficult for me to imagine Quiana. I project my own efforts to make a writing space onto Quiana's prison world. I think of my own diverting dreams of homemaking and my project of finding a safe place to write, a private place for myself, alone, where I can sink into my work without distraction. As a married white woman academic, I complain about the difficulty of this project. (I do not think, as I complain, of the extent to which I have benefited from middle-class and academic support systems.) I am not the first privileged woman to describe how hard it is to construct or appropriate a space for my writing. For instance, I think of Virginia Woolf who also documents my trouble, writing in *A Room of One's Own* of the vast distinction between men and women, between their histories, their bodies, and their habits of life. She goes so far as to say that "the nerves that feed the brain would seem to differ in men and women . . ." (81). Woolf explains what seems to be an essentialist division between men and women, but then she turns around to argue that with money, time, and private space, this division need not lock a woman into a subordinate position in which she is unlikely to create.

However, most women lack these essentials and are thus locked within the confines of gender conventions that define women through connections with others—i.e., as always already self-in-relation. This "woman" is set in contrast to the stereotype of the autonomous, heroic individual, a figure who underwrites the mythic character of the creative man—with solitude as the site of his creation. He has the luxury of uninterrupted time to pick up his pen in his quiet, well-appointed study as he waits confidently for his muse. I want his site, his heroic confidence, his muse, his pen, his space. Would it be possible for me to occupy this site? Woolf predicts that I could. On the last page of *A Room of One's Own,* Woolf marks out her hope and desire that women may have what male creators have had:

> For my belief is that if we live another century or so—I am talking of the common life which is the real life and not the little separate lives which we live as individuals—and have five hundred a year each of us and rooms of our own; if we have the habit of freedom and the courage to write exactly what we think; if we escape a little from the common sitting-room and see human beings not always in their relation to each other but in relation to reality; . . . if we face the fact, for it is a fact, that there is no arm to cling to, but that we go alone and that our relation is to the

world of reality and not to the world of men and women, then the opportunity will come and the dead poet who was Shakespeare's sister will put on the body which she has so often laid down. (117-118)

It is 2003, seventy-four years after Woolf wrote *A Room of One's Own.* A century has not yet passed. We still have more than two decades to go. But right now the man I am married to helps me paint a desk and a bookshelf from a thrift store. We work quietly, covering the surfaces with a sturdy oil base white, then trimming with a golden brown. I stencil leafy vines up the drawers while he and my children admire my decorations. He's glad that I've decided to try to work at home sometimes, though he knows the problems, the distractions, the temptations. And he knows the odds against professional growth for academic women who cannot shake loose that historical identity which horrified Woolf—the Angel of the House. The nineteenth century embraced this wifely identity, whose historical presence in the home parallels the fact that in this period "only 18% of all women over 14 years of age were employed, most of whom were unmarried" (Gini and Sullivan 283). Kate Chopin's 1899 novella *The Awakening* illustrates the Angel identity with its ironic portrait of the "mother-woman":

> The mother-women seemed to prevail that summer at Grand Isle. It was easy to know them, fluttering about with extended, protecting wings when any harm, real or imaginary, threatened their own precious brood. They were women who idolized their children, worshiped their husbands, and esteemed it a holy privilege to efface themselves as individuals and grow wings as ministering angels. (9)

Throughout this *kunstlerroman,* Chopin contrasts this image of the mother-woman with that of the woman artist struggling against the Angel of the House and for the solitude she needs to work. In *"The Awakening:* Tradition and the American Female Talent" Elaine Showalter puts the matter simply: "A writer needs to cultivate solitude and independence" (319). Indeed, the model of the woman artist, Mademoiselle Reisz, is a solitaire who keeps people at a distance through a stinging disdain. This genius who understands the neces-

sary solitude of the artist's life encourages Edna—the novel's evolv-
ing hero—to follow the artist's independent and unconventional path:
"to succeed, the artist must possess the courageous soul. . . . The
brave soul. The soul that dares and defies" (Chopin 61). As Edna pur-
sues her desire to be an artist, she increasingly refuses the identity of
the mother-woman: the social arrangements and niceties, the household designs, the managing of servants, the child care. As she lets
these pieces of her feminized identity fall away, her husband begins
to believe that she is going mad. But Chopin makes clear that Edna, as
she sinks into a serious relation to her art, is becoming herself, "cast-
ing aside that fictitious self which we assume like a garment with
which to appear before the world" (55). These garments are the drap-
eries of the Angel of the House, the metaphoric identity of middle-
class white women's domesticity.

As Edna establishes a strong mentor relationship with Mademoiselle Reisz, Edna learns that she must be able to distance herself from
convention. She reports to her would-be lover, Alcée Arobin, a conversation she's had with her powerful mentor: "When I left her today,
she put her arms around me and felt my shoulder blades, to see if my
wings were strong, she said. 'The bird that would soar above the level
plain of tradition and prejudice must have strong wings'" (79). In this
interchange, Edna is absorbed in thoughts of her mentor and the life
of the artist—a life toward which Edna is working. It is a life of solitude and independence. Interestingly, it is at this very point in the
novel, as she clearly articulates her desire to be an artist, that Edna
acts on her sexual desire. A paragraph after her thoughtful remarks
about the courage required to become an artist, she participates in
"the first kiss of her life to which her nature had really responded. It
was a flaming torch that kindled desire" (80). Directly after this kiss,
the chapter breaks. In the next chapter—only a single paragraph—
Edna experiences an awakened understanding of "The significance
of life, that monster made up of beauty and brutality" (80). This understanding marks Edna's brave break from her conventional life to pursue her desires—both artistic and sexual. As a woman, she has broken
the codes of heterosexual monogamy—a serious breach—and as an
artist, she has gone beyond what Showalter calls "woman's art," which
"is social, pleasant, and undemanding. It does not conflict with her duties as a wife and mother . . ." (315). Originally titled *A Solitary Soul,*

Chopin's novel tells the story of an artist struggling with and tragically frustrated by gender, for finally Edna cannot connect to the energy of her mentor in order to survive her socialization. She both craves and fears solitude, as do many creative women.

Edna's ambivalence about solitude is not uncommon, especially in women. Investigating the terms *solitary and solitude,* we find a number of negative associations: introverted, retiring, inaccessible, concealed, remote, desolate, secluded, withdrawn, apart, detached, isolated, lonely (as opposed to peaceful, productive, meditative, inspiring, self-controlled, independent, free). In a capitalist culture that depends on constant attention to social relations and discourages sitting still and keeping one's own company—especially for women—many of these negative terms point to feelings of being ostracized, disconnected, depressed. The discourse of solitude frequently signals situations in which an individual retreats from social intercourse, and this retreat is characterized as either pitiable or pathological. Although the idiom "give me some space" is a contemporary formulation of the desire for solitude, more frequently individuals fear feeling unconnected.

I witness this fear semester after semester when I ask my women's literature classes about their futures, what they imagine for themselves; semester after semester, all but two or three women students express their desire for marriage and children and say that these desires do not seem incompatible with a full working life. However, as they read and research the statistics about men's resistance to shared domestic responsibilities on top of the horrific facts about spousal abuse, rape, infidelity, divorce, sexual objectification, and mental illness in women, they begin to wonder about the heterosexual promise, especially those who recognize their own creativity and intelligence. Even in the face of their new acquaintance with sexism, more than half of my students who read *The Awakening* judge Edna harshly for being a bad wife and mother, i.e., for craving the solitude to work and the courage to act freely on her body's desires. In short, they condemn her for being a traitor to the heterosexual plot. When I call these inevitable inconsistencies to my students' attention, they are baffled, and some are defensive when I challenge them with their own ideas about the need for social change.

Terri Apter in *Working Women Don't Have Wives* argues that our gendered attitudes about work are slow to change because of a circuit of "interlocking structures wherein one does not budge because the other does not budge because the other does not budge" (61). She suggests that "[I]f we want to change these interlocked structures we should . . . push at the points of weakness, seek out the inconsistencies of outlook and practice, find out where there is the greatest ambivalence, and push on that" (80). Women in the twentieth century began to "push on that," but the trade-offs and punishments have been terrible. In Chopin's novel, for instance, the main character kills herself, torn between her artistic, iconoclastic impulses and her isolation and guilt at being unable to conform to this "Angel" identity. In 1929, Virginia Woolf reverses Chopin's tragic plot—invoking the Angel of the House archetype of exclusive domesticity—in *A Room of One's Own,* and then murdering this Angel in order to write.

I know this murderous impulse. I have almost murdered, have held a knife tight in my fist as an irruption of domestic violence threatened to turn physical. But I didn't take the plunge. Now, in a much safer marriage, I can still identify Woolf's wish to murder the Angel, ironically that very same Angel of the House who probably stayed my hand and kept me out of prison. Today, the ghost of this Angel inhabits my home, a wafting presence of compelling "feminine" forces that lure me, often unaware, into series of questions and choices. Do I pick up the kids' shoes and school papers or do I sit down at my desk? Do I answer my kids' questions about homework or do I continue to read my draft for revisions? Do I sink into the mindless pleasure of peeling apples to make a pleasing dessert or do I pursue my online library search? How about the laundry or the toilet or the everlasting dishes as they stack up against rereading Virginia Woolf? As a serious academic woman who lives within a family, I'm plugged into the cultural connections that keep these high-tension questions alive.

But in an attempt to follow my writing desires while preserving some functional family dynamics in this third marriage, I have kept my work out of the house. Terri Apter offers one explanation: work done at home "allows one to be available in case of need, women who work at home are constantly interrupted" (247). In fact, I could rarely manage "real work" at home, the stewing in thought, the brain hot with it, time compressed with this boiling mentality, the steaming open of my ideas—that intense process, and my impatience with its interruption. And I love the energy of that "real work," the work that takes me out of myself and away from others. My second husband and I had the same fight over and over, the one about how work was more important to me than he was, how I'd rather write than fuck; how he felt like I was cheating on him, excited by books, fondling papers, stroking the pencil, running my mental fingertips over thought after thought—getting off. He would accuse me of having a lover when I was late getting home from writing in my office. Sometimes we would turn on each other in stupid fury. And, occasionally, he was right about the lover. But much more often, I was writing. In any case, when I look back, I have to agree with him: I was, and still am, a work slut.

My first husband didn't hit, but he thought I was a workaholic. Gini and Sullivan in their study of women and work, discuss workaholism, noticing that it is more appropriate for men than for women. They cite studies that claim workaholics are surprisingly happy. "They are doing exactly what they love—work—and they can't seem to get enough of it." But, say Gini and Sullivan, those living with workaholics often suffer, especially if the workaholic is the woman; women are supposed to be able to put down their work in order to be there" for the ones they love (267). In "The Fisherwoman's Daughter," Ursula Le Guin describes the same phenomenon—that women writers in families feel the pressure to put the family first—but she presents us with a picture of her unusual partner, contrasting him to the norm:

> If I needed help he gave it without making it a big favor, and—
> this is the central fact—he did not ever begrudge me the time I
> spent writing, or the blessing of my work.
>   That is the killer: the killing grudge, the envy, the jealousy,
> the spite that so often a man is allowed to hold, *trained to hold,*
> against anything a woman does that's not done in his service, for
> him, to feed his body, his comfort, his kids. A woman who tries
> to work against that grudge finds the blessing turned into a
> curse; she must rebel and go it alone, or fall silent in despair.
> (my italics; 233)

Tillie Olsen's *Silences,* which Le Guin and others writing in this area often cite, is a classic account of literature lost through the social circumstances of gender and class. Olsen describes the reasons that women's writing does not get done: "It is distraction, not meditation, that becomes habitual; interruption, not continuity; spasmodic, not constant toil. . . . Work interrupted, deferred, relinquished, makes blockage—at best, lesser accomplishment" (19). Early in the title essay, Olsen cites author after author on the necessity of "solitude," "silence," and "spaciousness" (11-13). She draws the connection between a meditative life and artistic inspiration. Olsen's guiding question is: "What if there is not that fullness of time?" She answers "Where the claims of creation cannot be primary, the results are atrophy; unfinished work; minor effort and accomplishment; silences" (13). She enumerates examples of our literary loss, "the damage to the creative powers . . . of having to deny, interrupt, postpone, put aside, let work die" (14). However, in the second part of the essay, Olsen looks at women who managed to be productive writers. Most were unmarried or if married, childless and "all had servants."

Olsen's discussion of the social circumstances "which oppose the needs of creation" brings to mind my most enviable colleague, a woman who takes great care to fulfill these creative needs (17). Recently, as we traveled together, she described her study—a large and beautiful room with plenty of work surface and light, the latest computer, good pens, and the most comfortable and expensive chair in the house for reading. She has no encumbering relationships and uses her extraordinary concentration and discipline to maintain her solitude so that she can act on her writing desire. She is never in her office at school on Mondays and Fridays; she is in her study, writing.

Unlike my colleague, I have had trouble balancing and negotiating my work and home life. In the past, my office has been my most productive work space: an escape, a sanctuary for mentality—a pure territory. I call home from my office to say "I'm late" and "Sorry." But now the urge to bring my work life and my home life together, to make a work nest in my house, has risen in me—like a muse, a surprise visitor. Now I want to merge my two lives, experience myself as superimposed upon myself—a postmodern, pentimento woman. This wish leads me to ask myself, as so many other creative women have asked themselves, whether living and working at home helps or hinders me professionally, enriches or impoverishes my creative thinking and my scholarly writing. Gesa Kirsch notes this confusion in *Women Writ-*

ing the Academy: our "stories grow out of ambivalences toward academic life and practice . . . tales of the conflicting loyalties, everyday dilemmas, and contradictory feelings that go into the production of academic knowledge and the construction of individual careers in the academy" (x).

I remember when I was writing my dissertation, I thought that I had to get yet another divorce because I couldn't get the work done. As I was complaining that I needed, but was unable to get, long stretches of quiet, uninterrupted time to finish my work, my dissertation director told me that I could learn to work *with* interruption, could adapt my work habits, could pick work back up after an interruption, in short, could work in the fitfulness of my life. She implied that I didn't have to be a slave to one idea about writing production. She claimed that I could revise my unhelpful idea that a writer must conform to the male myth of the artist as heroic Promethean—aspiring, isolated, rapt in his mysterious relation to his muse. Especially from a feminist perspective, this Romantic image of the artist as requiring a special privacy and a special care to produce could be usefully challenged, or at least complicated. When I was having trouble generating text and would think that it was because my life and space did not meet the specifications, I would remember Virginia Woolf who says, "The book has somehow to be adapted to the body, and at a venture one would say that women's books should be shorter, more concentrated, than those of men, and framed so that they do not need long hours of steady and uninterrupted work. For interruptions there will always be" (81). And then I read Ursula Le Guin's answer to the question "What is the one thing that a writer has to have?" Her answer is simple: "The one thing that a writer has to have is not balls. Nor is it a child free space. Nor is it even, speaking strictly on the evidence, a room of her own, though that is an amazing help. . . . The only thing a writer has to have is a pencil and some paper" (236). Initially, this answer sounded as if it underestimated the power of the Angel of the House—that feminized complex of domestic ideology personified and installed in an alarming number of women. This simple answer also doesn't give sufficient weight to the fact that women have to push harder than men in order to get the room and the time and the support that they need to be productive outside of a narrowly circumscribed domestic sphere, though thankfully as men become feminist allies, this dynamic is slowly shifting.

There is no doubt that intellectual and creative workers of all sorts need time to think and to create. But what does this assertion really come down to? On one hand, it could mean that writers require extended, quiet, uninterrupted time—the op timal condition for creation. On the other hand, it could mean that intellectual and creative workers can produce effectively when they are immersed in the *interbeing* of life—when their lives are full of others and of things to do with and for others in relationships of many sorts. The first assertion assumes that the creative process is fragile; the second assumes that it is robust. In any case, though, the myth of the creator as a man in protected isolation holds sway in the ideology of creativity. In contrast, Le Guin points to Louisa May Alcott as an example of a woman writing in a peopled setting, contrasting this scene of creativity to the Romantic concept of the male genius writing in solitary silence. Le Guin exclaims, "it's shocking. . . . [Alcott] can't be a real writer. Real writers writhe on solitary sofas in cork-lined rooms, agonizing over *le mot juste*—don't they?" (221). These prescriptive pictures of the artist are important to our ideas of how intellectual production is gendered. Le Guin makes this clear: "I ask my friends: 'A woman writing: what do you see?' Her women friends answer 'A woman is taking dictation.' . . . 'She's sitting at the kitchen table, and the kids are yelling' " (213).

The myth of creative geniuses as sealed off in their hermitage stems from Romantic and scholastic traditions. The ultrasensitive Romantic artist must court *his* muse—that illusive phantom who visits only when the artist has cloistered *himself. He* invites her through a rigorous privacy. For the Muse is jealous. She will be courted only by those absolutely devoted: their isolation proves their devotion and thus their worthiness to be visited. These visits are delicious but unpredictable; inspiring but exhausting. Medieval scholastics, too, locked themselves away in cells, studying and copying in silence, closeted, cloistered, safely sealed away from distractions and temptations of the mundane. Priests and hermits have given us models of the creative man. But what about the creative woman? Adrienne Rich's famous notion of revision allows me to rethink these two characters.

> Re-vision—the act of looking back, of seeing with fresh eyes, of
> entering an old text from a new critical direction—is for women
> more than a chapter of cultural history: it is an act of survival.
> Until we understand the assumptions in which we are drenched
> we cannot know ourselves. And this drive to self-knowledge,
> for women, is more than a search for identity: it is part of our re-
> fusal of the self-destructiveness of male-dominated society. (35)

Through Rich's revisionary lens, the artist and his or her muse would
become quite a different couple.

The Muse revised would become a nonstandard muse, a lowercase
muse in several versions. For instance, the muse could be a supportive presence who reminds the writer that she *can* produce in the midst
of teenagers' phone conversations, car pool deadlines, neighborhood
dish-to-pass dinner preparations, and it could help her do so. Or the
muse revised could be like the huge copper statue of Diana in the
Philadelphia Museum of Art, balanced on a sphere, one foot lifted behind her, perfectly poised, her bow drawn, caught in a Keatsian moment. She is at once in motion and exactly still. Certainly her arrow
will find its mark. But she is the embodiment of energy and interruption, and its gorgeous synthesis—just how I feel working with partners interrupting, students interrupting, children interrupting, new
e-mail waiting on the computer screen while I train my sentence on a
thought. These exercises in dreaming up the muse differently are important. But how about revising even further the old conceptions of
intellectual production in solitary space? How about extending this
thinking into a political space beyond these middle-class, feminist revisions targeted at women academics suffering from work paralysis?

Women writers with access to educational and economic power often testify to the importance of constructing their spaces carefully—
May Sarton positioning a blue vase in just the right place and working
at an antique writing desk; Woolf scanning her shelf space full of the
books that support her work and mark the past path of production on
which she meditates; Dickinson in her room, her door closed to maintain this sacred space to write. This space is a necessary prerequisite
for inspiration, we believe; it invites the muse. Though we cannot
snap our fingers and expect that the muse will appear to serve us, we
believe that we can induce the muse's visit if we perform in particular

ways, often ritualized and superstitious. Maintaining quiet is one of these rituals. Also, we observe the writing space as sacred, as special. It closes out the social world and opens the mind's interior. Solitary writing space acts as a container, allowing the writer to meet the extraordinary potential of words.

But solitary space has other political dimensions. In "Crimes of Punishment: An Interview with Christian Parenti," Jensen and Parenti cite the historical roots of solitary confinement in Quaker prison theory (Jensen 11). Meditative, solitary time would lead to a prisoner's mental and emotional clarification and thus to a reformation of thought and action. Similarly, meditation practitioners (including artists) emphasize solitude and silence as a means to gain insight into the self and the world. But when Parenti describes how this theory is practiced through the SHUs (Security Housing Units), we see the horrible reversal that prison solitude effects. Jensen calls these places "prisons within prisons," solitary places in which prisoners are isolated. The occupy heavily walled cells. Their food comes through a slot. The closed circuit television camera in their cells is always on; someone is always watching them (11).

A jailed woman—usually poor, often black or brown, and a member of the fastest growing U.S. prison population in an oppressive, racist system—is one of 2 million prisoners already incarcerated. An additional 5 million are being "supervised" by the justice system, e.g., on parole or probation (Jensen 6). Joy James reports on the 1999 Amnesty International statistics "documenting the abuses of women in U.S. prisons and jails. By June 1997, there were 138,000 women incarcerated in the United States; triple the number since 1985 . . ." Most are nonviolent offenders who are poor mothers and women of color. The violent offenses that have resulted in women's incarceration have frequently been connected to domestic violence (2). If an imprisoned woman challenges the institution that contains her, she is sent to the SHUs, solitary space that has a different meaning than for the academic woman writer who longs for the luxury and privilege of solitary space.

Commonly, prisons control their inmates through spacial and property restrictions because officials understand the pressure they can exert in this way. For instance, in response to protests, officials exercise power through space control: "strip cell status" allows guards to reconfigure prisoners' space, leaving them "with no property, no clothing, no sheets, towels, or blankets for up to three days, though often guards are slow to return property" (Lomax 195). In *Criminal Injustice: Confronting the Prison Crisis,* Karlene Faith comments on prison space from testimonies of women prisoners, listing "the claustrophobia of confinement . . . craving fresh air, nervousness from being under constant scrutiny . . . lack of privacy . . . the inability to escape from the cacophony of radios, television, people hollering at one another, the rattle of keys, and the clanging of electric doors" (171-172). The paradox of both too little human activity and too much characterizes this setting. But the worst spaces for women within prisons are the isolation units.

White, academic women writing in the "free world" crave solitary space and desire to "do time" in that isolation in order to engage in their creative process, but the image of women prisoners in solitary confinement turns the idea of this academic yearning back on itself. In "Women's Control Unit," Silvia Baraldini, Marilyn Buck, Susan Rosenberg, and Laura Whitehorn describe "a physical layout and day-to-day regimen that produce inwardness and self-containment." Space in these units is "severely limited" with the object of controlling and isolating and neutralizing those who are subject to occupying this space (187). Susan Rosenberg's story "Lee's Time" in the recent PEN anthology of prison writing, *Doing Time,* also pictures this sense of space in an isolation unit: "We call the hole 'three hots and a cot.' Actually it's three of everything: cold food, cold water, cold weather; three hours a week outside and three showers a week. . . . Segregation's rec yard is the size of a basketball court. . . . You walk into the cage one at a time, then the gate is locked." The narrator speaks the result of this solitude: "I feel like a fucking corpse" (Rosenberg 215).

In *The Celling of America,* Adrian Lomax discusses "segregation" in terms of deprivation, especially of reading and writing privileges. When prisoners occupy "the hole," their reading privileges are severely curtailed and prisoners "must wear handcuffs and a waist chain while using the seg library." Furthermore, "they only let us have pens for two hours a day. We can have pencils all the time but good luck trying to get a guard to sharpen one for you" (194). In a short story, produced by a woman prisoner, she describes the difficulty of reading in this solitary space: "Segregation. The hole. There was very little light and the air was dank. The walls oozed. . . . I was trying to read the time away, holding the book open toward the light that came through the food slot in the door" (Rosenberg 214). Even in this horrendous solitary setting, imprisoned women have accessed their creative urge to produce writing in the constrained spaces of a prison cell. For instance, in the collaborative essay, "Sestina: Reflections on Writing" by the Bedford Hills Writing Workshop, a group of women writer/prisoners reflect on what writing has meant for them:

> The writing workshop has had a profound and lasting impact on each of us. Some of our writing is taken from personal experience, both in and out of prison, a lot of it comes from the pain of being incarcerated, away from family and especially children. Sometimes the writing just comes from a place never visited before. We all agree that the workshop has made a distinct difference in how we see ourselves. (114)

But prison writing space is different from my own. Susan Rosenberg's story "Lee's Time" describes her space in stark contrast to the space of the privileged white woman academic in her study or office, or even at the kitchen table with the kids yelling: "I went to my cell. Since my cell will never be my home or 'house,' as the police like to call it, I don't keep a lot of things. But I do have a big knitted blanket which I crawl under, trying to get warm and calm down so I could think" (212).

Solitary space, solitude, a private room to write, the time in this room, a womb, a containing, silent space in which a sheltered, precious process occurs, the pleasure of being alone to write and think— writers desire these treasures. At the Faculty Writing Group at my college where we gather to discuss strategies for producing academic writing and to share how our writing is going, we use an interrogative refrain—where is the time; where is the space? How can we produce between classes in the fifty minutes when we guiltily lock our office doors and let the phone go to voice mail, writing phrases as we watch the computer's clock tick at the bottom of the screen. How dare we put that Do Not Disturb sign on the door? And how can we discipline our students and ourselves not to ignore that message? How can we go into solitary, obtain our own privileged version of a High Security Unit in which to work?

I'm at home, thinking about all the books I've been reading on women and work, the design of work space, the ideology of inspiration, the gender dynamics embedded in the histories of women's work in America, the history of housework, the theories of women and economics, the feminist critiques of Marx, the critiques of feminism by scholars of color, the disciplines of Foucault, the various testimonials about writing process from various classes and races of women writers, the sociological and psychological analyses of the psychic and cultural scripts that bracket women repeatedly, and the appalling literature documenting the prison system now. I'm at home, alone, at my beautiful hand-painted desk, trying to finish this draft, writing, glancing up at the clock, writing faster because someone will be coming home in an hour or in thirty minutes or in five minutes. The car will grind in the gravel and dinner will not be ready, not even started, not even considered. And I'm far away, though the clock has tethered me so that I will be able to rise and welcome home the ones I love—my great interrupters. And with this interruption, I think of Terri Apter who says that "having it all is not having all of everything, but finding out what is most important and learning to lift these things of importance out of their usual leaden trappings" (115). But more important, I conclude that my many advantages as an academic woman are pirate treasure, relying on a class structure that provides me privileges at an invisible cost to others and that the sweetness of my solitary herspace is the reflection of that terrible inequity.

WORKS CITED

Alcoff, Linda and Laura Gray. "Survivor Discourse: Transgression or Recuperation?" *Signs* Winter 1993: 260-290.

Apter, Terri. *Working Women Don't Have Wives: Professional Success in the 1990s*. New York: St. Martin's Press, 1993.

Bedford Hills Writing Workshop. "Sestina: Reflections on Writing." In *Doing Time: 25 Years of Prison Writing* (pp. 114-118). Ed. Bell Gale Chevigny. New York: Arcade Publishing, 1999.

Chevigny, Bell Gale, Ed. *Doing Time: 25 Years of Prison Writing*. New York: Arcade Publishing, 1999.

Chopin, Kate. *The Awakening,* Second Edition. Ed. Margo Culley. New York: Norton Critical Edition, 1994.

Faith, Karlene. "The Politics of Confinement and Resistance: The Imprisonment of Women." In *Criminal Injustice: Confronting the Prison Crisis* (pp. 165-183). Ed. Elihu Rosenblatt. Boston: South End Press, 1996.

Gini, A. R. and T. J. Sullivan. *It Comes with the Territory: An Inquiry Concerning Work and the Person.* New York: Random House, 1989.

James, Joy. "Introduction." Special Issue on Prisons. *Radical Philosophy Review* 3:1 (2000): 1-7.

Jensen, Derrick. "Crimes of Punishment: An Interview with Christian Parenti." *The Sun* October 2000: 4-13.

Kirsch, Gesa. *Women Writing the Academy: Audience, Authority and Transformation.* Carbondale: Southern Illinois University Press, 1993.

Le Guin, Ursula. *Dancing at the Edge of the World: Thoughts on Words, Women, Places.* New York, Harper Row, 1989.

Lomax, Adrian. "Report from the Hole." In *The Celling of America* (pp. 193-196). Ed. Daniel Burton-Rose, with Dan Pens and Paul Wright. Monroe, ME: Common Courage Press, 1998.

Nagel, Mecke. "A Week in Ithaca's Court: Chronicling Domestic Violence." *The Cobbler* August/September 2000: 5.

Olsen, Tillie. *Silences.* New York: Dell, 1965.

Rich, Adrienne. *On Lies, Secrets, and Silence: Selected Prose 1966-1978.* New York: W. W. Norton, 1979.

Rosenberg, Susan. "Lee's Time." In *Doing Time: 25 Years of Prison Writing* (pp. 206-216). Ed. Bell Gale Chevigny. New York: Arcade Publishing, 1999.

Showalter, Elaine. "Chopin and American Women Writers." In *The Awakening,* Second Edition (pp. 311-320). Ed. Margo Culley. New York: Norton Critical Edition, 1994.

Woolf, Virginia. *A Room of One's Own.* New York: Harcourt Brace, 1929.

– 8 –

Car, Kitchen, Canyon: Mother Writing

Claudia Mon Pere

Ken, my eight-year-old, is in the tree house with his good friend, sweeping out dry leaves and setting out bowls of fish crackers. Angela, my thirteen-year-old, is working on her paper on cults. She's finished her research on the Web—so at last the computer is mine—and I've convinced her to use books, too, so she should be occupied with the library books in her room. I settle down with my notes—after a busy week of teaching, finally, some glorious time to write!

I'm ten minutes into revising a short story when Ken comes in.

"Mom, either me and Danny are crazy, or there's a dead rat by the garbage can."

There is indeed. The body's nearly eaten. (Raccoons? Possums? The cats? We live in the Oakland hills and there are plenty of possibilities.) But the head and tail are intact, being poked gingerly by the boys' long sticks. I get rid of the rat, make the boys wash their hands, return to the computer.

Soon my daughter enters to tell me maybe I'm right, maybe there are kooks on the Internet. She's been reading sixteen pages she printed earlier, realizing the writer is in prison, where he's railing against the government, urging readers to accumulate a hefty supply of weapons. Concerned, I spend thirty minutes with her, reviewing her materials.

Finally I'm back to my short story, working quickly because soon I have to take Ken's friend home. I'm in the world of Bass Lake now—an elderly woman in an unhappy marriage, fishing with her grandson in the rain. I have the woman's husband watching through the cabin window, angry that they won't come in. A sudden retching sound catapults me back to my house in Oakland. The cat is crouched over the heating vent, throwing up.

"To write is a solitary and singular act," (xvii) says Margaret Atwood. Indeed. As a mother who teaches full-time, commutes an hour each way to work, and writes, it is the solitary part that is a challenge. As other working mothers know, one copes by doing two things at once whenever possible—talking on the phone while doing dishes, paying bills while supervising children at a park, grading student papers while waiting at the orthodontist, and writing while driving.

I have been writing in my car ever since I've had children. (No accidents or even near misses. The traffic jams are so frequent and so long.) And I have a pretty good sense of what can and cannot be accomplished in a moving vehicle. No complete sentences or organization of ideas. But words, images, a line or two of poetry, a plot idea—these come to me and I sloppily record them with my right hand while my left hand holds the steering wheel. In my drive to and from Santa Clara University, I pass dead animals, emergency call boxes, shredded tires, right-lane-must-exit signs, fields of wild mustard, discarded shoes, the Goodnight Inn with its sign blinking vacant, crows and pigeons and seagulls and occasionally a snowy white egret in a bit of field surrounded by computer companies, jackknifed trucks, a hot-tub wholesaler, a small cemetery nudged up against some shabby apartments. At various times these images have made their way into my poems and short stories.

What about the focused solitude that is so critical in order to move beyond the image, to shape words and ideas into something meaningful?

When I was younger, solitude and loneliness and fear were synonymous. I was the oldest of six children and my mother was seriously depressed. Sometimes my father, a patient and loving man, had to whisk her away in the middle of the night to the hospital, leaving me in charge. Although I remember times when my mother seemed happy, she was often overwhelmed by the energy and arguments and illnesses of six children. She retreated to her bedroom much of the time. We had a parade of baby-sitters, and I worried constantly about what my mother was doing alone in her room. Sometimes she'd scream and throw things. Often, we heard low, sustained weeping.

Other times it was quiet. She and my father were avid readers, and probably at times she was simply reading.

I grew up in the 1960s, and our family went through problems typical of that period, with some serious struggles with alcohol, drugs, and mental illness. It seemed to me that when a person was emotionally healthy, he or she remained part of the daily fabric of life in this busy household—helping with chores, visiting with the constant stream of priests, antiwar activists, civil rights workers, relatives, friends, neighbors. If a family member withdrew, wanted to be alone, I worried that he or she was doing something destructive.

I wrote a lot as a child, most of it in a social context. My siblings and I loved to play church and school, and I often wrote little scripts, which we'd act out. Horror stories were my forte, and my sister and I formed a club in which we'd spy on neighbors and write up elaborate stories of their imagined misdeeds. Fast-food places were a new phenomenon, and when we rode our bikes to McDonald's we were shocked at how many people could be served so quickly. I returned home and wrote a tale of a fast-food restaurant that ran out of beef, so they ground up children, stuffing them into giant loaves of French bread for fancy parties. Our family loved to hike in the Sierra Nevada Mountains, but the trails were sometimes too much for the younger children. So my sister Julie and I would run ahead, creating fairy and elf houses out of bits of bark and wildflowers and stones. Then, when the younger ones caught up with us, we'd read aloud fantasy poems we'd composed, which the elves had supposedly left behind. Essentially, then, my writing was social. I wrote alone only when unhappy.

At school I was plenty alone, in the way of many shy and anxious children. You find them at lunchtime hiding out in the library or lingering in the rest room to use up time. This seemed such a wickedly enforced aloneness—a kind of solitary confinement—and I grew to want nothing more than friends. By high school, a sensitive teacher got me involved in drama, speech, and debate. I began to see I could have friends. I never wanted to be alone! I continued my social writing—protest songs I sang with friends; debate speeches my partner and I wrote together; and, late at night, anxious little poems in my journal.

Once or twice a week on mornings I don't teach, I write. I take the children to school and then, if I'm planning to work on a short story, I go to my exercise class, a fine group of spirited women. We wear sweats over our imperfect bodies and joke a lot. If I'm planning to work on poetry, I need a more contemplative mood, so I walk in my neighborhood canyon. It is an urban canyon, houses and basketball hoops and cars parked in driveways. But there are plenty of trees— oaks, eucalyptus, Monterey pines. Ivy spills down hillsides. The blackberry bushes take over in places, splotching the ground purple when berries ripen and fall. Deer dash across the road, and the morning birdcalls are rich and varied—trills, squeaks, coos, hums, and one that sounds like a schoolchild's pink eraser.

When I return to my home, I sit at the kitchen table with my fiction journal or my poetry journal, do some informal writing and browse through past entries. Or I get straight to work developing or revising a draft. Sound distracts—a neighbor's power tools, a barking dog. But clutter is all right. The table is rarely empty. Now, for example, it contains: three cat collars that need to have bells attached and name tags filled out, a Little League form that is overdue, a new walkie-talkie and defective batteries—or maybe it's the walkie-talkie that's broken—mutual fund brochures, a photo of my poetry class I've been meaning to get framed, and a jar of tomato sauce with a lid I can't unscrew.

I push this accumulation to the end of the table. There's a maple outside my window, the branches bobbing in a light wind. On the deck a crescent jay investigates a red M&M. When my writing freezes, I look out at these things and they help me move forward.

There is a public kind of solitude I need when I write fiction. I have rarely sat alone and conceived of a character or story line. Usually, my initial ideas for short stories spring from public encounters or observations of strangers nearby. An aggressive teenager passes me in a car and flips me off for driving too slowly; a man kneeling in church hunches into himself in quiet despair; a middle-aged man at a baseball game tells and retells the story of his schizophrenic brother to his buddy; who clearly wants him to just be quiet and watch the game; a teenager in punk attire tells her mother she looks pretty as the mother tries on a new dress.

Really, these events are nothing special, just part of the dailiness of life. And yet what a look they give us at human frailties, yearnings, possibilities. Sometimes I can ignore such things, going about my business of picking up a prescription or getting gas for the car. But when I am in the thick of working on a story or am fiddling around with ideas for a new one, my skin prickles with the possibilities I find in the public sphere. Grocery shopping, in particular, is difficult then. Everything is a story, every person a character with his or her own delights and sorrows: the produce men arguing over how to stack apples, the young lesbian couple holding hands in front of the frozen peas, the arthritic woman fumbling with her wallet while the clerk waits patiently. I'm distracted from my shopping by the possibilities of these people's lives. I jot down descriptions and snatches of dialogue, follow someone around a bit, forget where I've left my cart.

When my daughter was a baby, my mother was diagnosed with breast cancer. She died two years later. When my son was a baby, I became the university's director of composition for three years. I place these facts side by side, for they both impacted my writing significantly. My mother, who had been so troubled when I was growing up, had gone back to college to study art and was creating a prolific number of beautiful oils and mixed-media pieces. She'd also been seeing a new therapist and was on new medication that made her much happier. She and my father took a few trips, taking obvious delight in their relationship. That she should get breast cancer was devastating. During this same time, my toddler daughter was burned when a pot of boiling water fell on her. Even before this, I'd been an anxious mother. Angela had colic as a baby, cried and cried and slept little. And during my pregnancy, I'd gone into preterm labor while out of the state and had to be rushed to a hospital, then spent the last two months of my pregnancy in bed.

With my mother's death and my daughter's burn, I sensed loss and danger everywhere. My husband had to be gone a lot, working long, demanding hours at his law firm. My overprotectiveness toward our daughter and his long work hours put a great deal of strain on our marriage. I returned to writing poetry during this period, with the vibrant cool shock of plunging into a mountain lake after miles of dusty switchbacks. I wrote in bits and pieces, mostly in the car or at night on my daughter's floor.

Because Angela had difficulty sleeping, she had an elaborate bedtime routine, the last part of which involved me lying down on the floor next to her bed and singing to her. Eventually she'd fall asleep, but she'd wake up and call for me intermittently. So I'd rest there on the floor for a long time, jotting down images and lines of poetry, squeezing up close to the hummingbird night light so I could see. Often, I fell asleep like this and once woke up on the floor to a warm nuzzling on my nose. Opening my eyes, I saw a rat peering at me. I screamed, Angela screamed, and eventually I realized it was only Tasha, our pet rat, who'd escaped from her cage.

If I'd had little solitary writing time with one child, when I had Ken and began directing the university's composition program, it was nearly impossible to write poetry. Because I taught in the field of composition and rhetoric and was running a writing program, I felt that was where my writing energy should go. I was writing conference papers, book reviews, and a few collaborative scholarly articles. I enjoyed the field of composition and rhetoric, and writing poetry seemed a guilty pleasure I didn't have time for. Between interviewing and hiring writing instructors, doing classroom observations, assessing and developing curriculum, teaching, and doing academic writing, time for my poetry grew slimmer and slimmer. A blade of grass! A filament!

This troubled me greatly, so I set aside a few mornings a month when I could work at home on my poetry. It took a great deal of practice to ignore the things outside my room. "A house," writes Alice Munroe in her short story, "The Office," "is all right for a man to work in. He brings his work into the house, a place is cleared for it; the house rearranges itself as best it can around him. Everybody recognizes that his work exists. He is not expected to answer the telephone, to find things that are lost, to see why the children are crying or feed the cat. He can shut his door. Imagine . . . a mother shutting her door and the children knowing she is behind it" (60).

I tried to explain to Ken that I'd be working at home and his sitter would play with him. There were loud scenes with him sobbing and flinging his body against the door. A skinned knee, a broken Popsicle—oh, the things he thought only I could fix. So I pretended to leave the house.

"Goodbye," I'd say at the front door. "I'm going to work. See you this afternoon." I'd wave to him, briefcase in hand, slippers on my feet, and sneak around the back. I worked out a system with the sitter so I could enter other rooms occasionally without Ken knowing. If the two of them were in the kitchen, for example, and I needed a cup of coffee, I'd fling three or four crumpled pieces of paper into the room. This was the sign she should move to another part of the house.

"What's that?" he'd ask as the paper flew into the room.

"Oh, sometimes paper just does that," she'd say.

One summer I went to the Squaw Valley Writer's Conference and had a blessed week in which to write poetry. We were expected to write a poem a day, setting it out by the front door to be picked up by someone who made copies for the next morning's workshop. I stayed in a house with six other women. I wrote intensely, alone in my room or on hikes during the day. At night we shared a typewriter, read drafts of our poems aloud, went to readings and parties. My clothes were mom clothes. The other women were single, younger, writerly looking. They fixed my hair, lent me a gauzy blue skirt for a beach barbecue where we ate chicken and potato salad with Galway Kinnell and Lucille Clifton, poets I'd long admired. Not long after the conference, I was given a leave of absence from Santa Clara University to get an MFA degree in creative writing.

I have always treated my house with a sort of benign neglect. This has not been a conscious rejection of domesticity, but rather a lack of time to attend to it beyond trying to keep the house somewhat clean. But the things outside each window, now those I could describe in size and shape, texture and color—particular branches on which the cats like to rest, the tiger-striped spiders that spin webs on the eaves each fall, the little bugs that look like flecks of flying rice darting around the birch, the endless variations of moon—a squint of white on a Wednesday at 2:00 a.m., when I am up writing; another evening, a full round rich yellow like some otherworldly fruit.

But sofas and stoves, window coverings and floors, stereos, vases, jewelry boxes, portable telephones, batteries and lightbulbs, yo-yos and roller blades—how much there is and how it crowds and breaks down and refuses to stay organized! In the two years I wasn't teaching and was getting an MFA, I spent a lot of time home alone writing. I looked closely at my indoor surroundings. The cats had shredded the edges of the living-room rug. The rear burner of the stove worked only on high and the front right burner didn't work at all. A CD had been stuck in the CD player for four years. Photographs and artwork were piled in a corner, waiting to be framed. Oh, my, I thought, with a bit of shock. Am I going to turn into one of those eccentric people who is found dead some day, buried beneath piles of yellowed newspapers in a house full of broken-down appliances?

My children are getting better about helping out with chores. And there is one aspect of domesticity that feeds my writing—doing the dishes. We do not have a dishwasher and I have resisted buying one. I love the feel of my hands in warm water, I love the instant success of this household chore—plates smeared with potato and hamburger grease are clean and shiny in minutes, like a little magic act. And when I am alone with the dishes, my mind takes off. I figure out how to complicate a character; I decide three scenes should be merged into one; I think of a line or two of poetry.

Several months ago I learned that Don, my husband of twenty-one years, wants our marriage to end. "You have to learn how to breathe again," my friend Susan told me. My senses seemed alien. Sounds were too loud or too soft. Sight was distorted. I looked at my beloved canyon and the trees were a garish green, flattened into one dimension. "What is your husband's birth date?" an insurance adjuster asked, and I couldn't form the words to answer.

It was difficult for me to feel anything except through the filter of narrative. In a department store rest room, I saw a mother nursing a baby and hated them for how content they looked. "It was the year she hated mothers and babies," flew into my mind as the possible opening for a story. This happened over and over again, whenever I felt lonely, angry, or depressed. I couldn't get myself to sit down and write, but I was writing fiercely in my head. An incident at a cemetery kicked me out of the story mode. I'd driven with my son to a nearby cemetery to see the tulips blooming, something our whole family had done each year. A few minutes earlier, Don and I had been talking about lamps. He needed some for his apartment and I needed some too, and I jokingly suggested we shop together. Instead, I took Ken to see the tulips. As we drove through the cemetery, I pointed out the different varieties, all with ridiculously cheerful names. But he kept interrupting.

"Where do they bury the children?" he asked.

"Well, there are mostly adults here," I answered. But he pointed at some tombstones, the dates clearly showing children were buried there.

I finally convinced him most people don't die until they're old. I tried to get back to the flowers. "Ken, look at these yellow tulips," I said. "Aren't they something?"

"Why do you think we're here about the flowers?" he asked. "This is about the dads who go away and die."

I am blessed to have close women friends with whom I teach, who are also mothers. We laugh together and comfort one another when things get rough. We're all struggling to balance our teaching selves, committee selves, writing or research selves, and family selves. I sometimes miss the collaborative writing in composition and rhetoric that I did with these women. We'd brainstorm ideas over coffee or lunch, huddle together in front of a computer screen to write a conference proposal, enthusiastically share books and articles, pour over drafts together. Sometimes a child or two would tag along. We'd pull out paper and crayons, fluff up an extra pillow, inquire about Girl Scouts or gymnastics or baseball or ballet before getting back to work.

None of my creative writing colleagues has children. Writing poetry and fiction is a solitary endeavor. In spite of writers' conferences and groups (I am part of a wonderful one whose members are women I met in the MFA program), ultimately a writer has only paper and pen for company when he or she is trying to create. And for women, in particular for mothers, there's not much of a literary tradition in which to place our work. The poet Pattiann Rogers points out that "there are few fine, serious and complete, artistic accounts in our literary tradition of the experience of mothering rendered by those actually involved in carrying out the endeavor" (165). And Deborah Tall remarks on the ambivalence of motherhood as expressed by writers she admires, such as Sylvia Plath and Adrienne Rich. I remember the surprised delight with which I first encountered Brenda Hillman's poem about combing lice out of her child's hair. Or Kim Addonizio's poem, "One Day My Daughter Will Learn About Anne Frank." Such tenderness, wedded with complexity. And Rita Dove's magnificent collection, *Mother Love*. Such works have given me a kind of permission to let my children enter my writing.

Their influence creeps in. "You need remedial math for mothers!" shouts Angela in frustration one day when I'm struggling to help her with geometry. Later, the image of a trapezoid enters one of my poems. Ken loves baseball and is teaching me to improve my catching. "Take it like it's flying candy," he instructs me about the ball as my mitt fumbles again. "Don't wait for the candy to come to you. Just pluck it out of the air. Like this." I do; then record his words for a later poem.

Often my writing has nothing to do with the children. But their lives are so entwined with mine, it is good to know this part of me that is a writer has room for them.

I try not to let interruptions bother me, and I take my solitude when I can, knowing the best plans can be altered by croup or head lice or a child's distress over a low grade or a trip to the principal's office for wearing green nail polish. Deborah Tall, noting the gaps between books by Ellen Bryant Voight, remarks that "now, her children grown, how many rich poems tumble from her" (192-193).

Ken and Angela are spending the night at their father's place for the first time. They leave without crying, Ken with a bag of stuffed animals and a Mark McGwire poster tucked under his arm. I cook dinner for only myself for the first time in many years and eat the spaghetti without tasting it.

In difficult times, clichés seem so apt—the heart heavy as a stone, news hitting someone like a ton of bricks, one's legs feeling like Jell-O. "Keep track of everything," my writer friends have been telling me, "and some day you'll turn this into art." Perhaps. Now, it's difficult to record such details.

I think about how fearful I was of being by myself when I was a girl, then how I craved solitude when my children were very young. I look at my watch, realize the children are probably in bed now listening to their father read them a story. I wander around the house, look at my mess of writing notebooks, journals, fragments of poetry and story ideas written on the backs of checks, calendars, receipts. I think—*this is crazy!* Next to the television, I find a magazine contract I still need to sign with a wad of pink gum stuck to the corner and think—*idiotic!* In the closet I discover one of the cats has had another accident, has urinated on a new suitcase. *You fool!* I think. *What makes you think you could possibly keep at it as a writer and teacher and, now, a single mother?*

Write! I demand. *Write now while you're all by yourself.* But I can't, so I tell myself the writing will come later, when I am not jolted by the solitude of Tuesday and Friday evenings. I sit at the piano, instead, thinking of my grandmother, Angela Erro Mon Pere, who played so beautifully my father still talks about her rendition of "Claire de Lune." Married to a difficult man and the mother of four children, she struggled to find time to play. She'd be a page or two into a Chopin prelude, and a boxing match in the backyard would erupt in violence. (My grandfather was a lightweight boxer and got his sons involved in boxing too.) Or someone would burst into the room needing help with homework or wanting to pound on the piano keys. She eventually gave up playing.

In a box by the piano, I have some of her old sheet music—dusty, yellowed, crumbling. She wrote her name on everything, and now I read the endless variations of her signature, from the flowery Miss Erro on the cover of *Forty Daily Exercises* to Angeline Erro, Angela Mon Pere and, finally, on the cover of Czerny's *The School of Velocity,* Mrs. J. V. Mon Pere.

I can't find the Debussy, and the Schumann looks too difficult. Although I took ten years of classical piano as a girl, I haven't played for a long time. But here's *Tchaikovsky's Album for the Young.* I try the first piece, "Morning Prayer." The notes are halting, my fingers stiff. I play "The New Doll," "Sweet Dreams," and "The Peasant Plays the Accordion." By the end I am smiling, and the notes are crimson flickers, airbound, whirling through night into my children's open window three miles away.

It is December now. There are holiday traditions to reframe in a way that allows celebration and honors loss. One moment I feel strong and capable, standing on a ladder and stringing lights. Another moment I fling the Christmas tree across the room because, after forty-five minutes of wrestling with it, I still can't get it to stand straight.

The fragile structure I built that allowed some regular writing time is crumbling as I wade through financial statements and material on mediation procedures, educate myself about divorce law in California, drive the children and myself to therapists, make small home repairs that my husband used to do, carry on at work. But, interestingly, I pay more attention to my indoor surroundings. I hang a kite up in a dark corner, put bright yellow candles in candleholders that have remained bare for three years. Move the living-room couch. For the eighteen years I have lived in this house, I have felt claustrophobic in the living room, have wondered how it would look if the couch were moved away from the wall. It was an idea my husband scoffed at, so I never tried it. Now, the couch moved, the room opens up in a remarkable way. It's still small, so there's some awkward maneuvering to get in past the piano. And there's no longer space for the end table and its lamp, so the room's a little dark. But one can sit on the couch now and see trees instead of a wall.

Ken and Angela are furious at first. "This is too symbolic," says my daughter. "The new independent woman!"

"Honestly, I didn't think of it that way," I say. "I just want to see the trees outside the window. But you're probably right."

Many critics have pointed out the emblematic nature of rooms in Virginia Woolf's writing, not only the widely known *A Room of One's Own,* but also the recurring images of rooms in her novels. C. Ruth Miller comments that "Woolf's choice of rooms as symbols of consciousness, identity and isolation may be due to the fact that she was repeatedly impressed by the extent to which they express the individuality of their inhabitants" (83). This is a notion I've resisted. Sometimes it simply felt too obvious, not an idea worth pursuing. But I am beginning to think, instead, that it was too painfully true and made me uncomfortable. What does it imply about my marriage that it took me so long to move the couch? Or that the portrait my husband commissioned to have painted of the two of us sat in the bedroom corner, unframed, for a year and a half until—the marriage over—it's now in a box? It's tempting to read the furniture and rooms in my house as a text, from the queen-size bed that I have difficulty sleeping in nowadays to the antique dresser in the computer room. I bought it with money I'd received for a short story. In a room filled with the chaos of Angela's current research on immigration, the paint and poster board for Ken's penguin project, piles of my manuscripts in various draft stages, it's a reminder I've carved a piece of that room for myself, a reminder that something concrete—and lovely—can come from the mess.

I have wondered during the past few months if my marriage would have succeeded if I hadn't written; if the writing was too major a distraction in a busy, complicated family unit full of commutes, my demanding job, a husband working long hours, two children passionate about sports, and involvement with our church and the children's school. "We're always on the edge," Don complained frequently. "Everything's frantic and disorganized. Something's got to give."

I have wondered if my passion went the wrong way, spilled into my stories and poems (and my children, of course) instead of into my husband. But I cannot imagine a life without writing any more than I can imagine a life without my children. When I am tempted to dwell on memories of my early married years or to fear the future with its seemingly endless responsibilities and financial uncertainties, I remind myself that I am here in the present and that it is to be lived and nurtured, not gotten through. The poet Jane Hirshfield writes "it is up to the writer to recognize everything that happens to her as a gift, to love each thing that comes under the eye's contemplation, inner or outer" (212).

When the fiction writer Roy Parvin was speaking to my students recently, he encouraged them to examine their stories for recurring images, such as the snow that links his novellas. I thought about most of my short stories. Dishes. Dishes are under my "eye's contemplation." And little plastic army men. And laundry and teenage fashion magazines and pediatric cough syrup and basketballs and braces.

When I was in my first MFA workshop, a young man remarked about a story of mine: "Yeah, I guess it's a good story. But really, who cares what happens to a middle-age housewife?" At the time, his comment scalded me. The Western canon's preoccupation with male stories of war, politics, crime, travel—plots grounded in large-canvas emotions of revenge, betrayal, heroism—can seem to validate those kinds of narratives at the expense of the more familiar domestic world. Yet a novel such as Woolf's *Mrs. Dalloway,* with a protagonist who is an upper-class housewife, with settings in a park, flower shop, and home, encompasses the range and complexity of what it means to be human. In life itself, the world of home and family enacts, on an intimate scale, the rivalries and hostilities, hopes and losses, passions and sacrifices that frame our larger world.

As writers, we create credible ideas and scenarios when we speak with authority. And we speak with authority about that which we know and care most deeply. When my children are older, I will read and travel more, will do volunteer work beyond the confines of my church, will attend lectures without having to scramble for child care.

For now, my stories will be set in houses and grocery stores, schools and backyards.

In the little bit of writing I can manage these days, my poems come with difficulty. They are like limpets—unmoving, clinging stubbornly to my personal life no matter how hard I try to write about other things. Sorry, I tell my poetry group, I have another marriage poem. But my fiction ideas are fast and furious, just jottings for now, but tethered, thank goodness, to the world outside myself. The 7-Eleven clerk, a large, pasty woman with frantic eyes, seems to have a crush on the man who delivers bread. I enter her world gladly, accumulate imagined details about her life. She will wait patiently in these journal pages with the others: a girl trying to save her mother's third marriage, a man obsessed with his neighbor's noisy peacocks, a veterinarian who has taken to rummaging through garbage bins. Over months and years, these characters will accumulate full inner lives and a narrative form and structure. I will tend them when I can, and it will be a slow, often frustrating process. But they will grow. And like my two children, I have no doubt they will make me alternately surprised, sad, delighted. And awed at what they have become.

WORKS CITED

Atwood, Margaret. Introduction. In *The Paris Review Interviews: Women Writers at Work* (pp. ix-xviii). Ed. George Plimpton. New York: Modern Library, 1998.

Hirshfield, Jane. *Nine Gates: Entering the Mind of Poetry.* New York: Harper Collins, 1997.

Miller, C. Ruth. *Virginia Woolf: The Frames of Art and Life.* New York: St. Martin's Press, 1988.

Munroe, Alice. *Dance of the Happy Shades and Other Stories.* New York: Penguin Books, 1968.

Rogers, Pattiann. "Degree and Circumstance." In *Where We Stand: Women Poets on Literary Tradition* (pp. 160-167). Ed. Sharon Bryan. W. W. Norton and Company: New York and London, 1993.

Tall, Deborah. "Terrible Perfection: In the Face of Tradition." In *Where We Stand: Women Poets on Literary Tradition* (pp. 184-194). Ed. Sharon Bryan. W. W. Norton and Company: New York and London, 1993.

Between the Study and the Living Room: Writing Alone and with Others

Eleanor Berry

For the past twenty years or so, I have written in a house of my own—more exactly, in a succession of houses owned jointly with my husband, who is also a writer. Though I have worked at writing in various spots in these houses (bedroom, kitchen, living room, porch, and deck), in each of them I've had a space primarily reserved for my writing. Most often, as in our present house, it has been a relatively small room, generally one that had been used by the previous owners as a children's bedroom. For my study I like to have a small space that wraps closely around me—a small space within a larger open space. I've described such a space in a short poem called "Interior with Window." Though the inspiration for the poem was a room where I stayed during a women writers' conference, the imagery also applies to the rooms that have served as my study in the several houses where my husband and I have lived:

> With your life contracted, for a retreat's
> interval, to a small room
> (chair, table, bed, walls painted
> gold and orange with brown trim),
> in its small enclosure from which you look out
> at a wide space open
>   to all the changes
>   of the sky,

My thanks to Jane Bailey and Lois Rosen, and to Richard Berry, for their helpful comments on earlier versions of this essay.

like a creature denned in the midst
of field or forest, like
a poet in a small poem with quirky
patterns of sound and movement,
you can compose
a sense of home. In such a made place
that curves about you as snugly
as any shell around its occupant,
while you inhabit it or even do no more
than reconstruct it in your mind, you can
gather yourself
    to begin again
      again.

When I wrote this poem, I was not thinking of Gaston Bachelard, and
it had been many years since I'd read his 1958 book *La poétique de
l'espace* (in a 1969 paperback translation that I'd bought remain-
dered). Nonetheless, the imagery of the small room felt as a home and
serving, even when simply remembered, as a site of regeneration echoes Bachelard's discussion of the value of intimate, sheltering spaces
to nurture daydream and creativity. The poem instances his claim that
"all really inhabited space bears the essence of the notion of home"
(5). It also exemplifies the tendency, remarked by Bachelard, to com-
bine images of human inhabitation with those of animal—here, the
den and the nest (to the latter Bachelard devotes an entire chapter).
And it speaks of the situation of the small inhabited interior space in
the midst of an immense natural world, suggesting the dynamic dia-
lectics that Bachelard sees between house and universe, the correspondence he perceives between immensity of world space and depth
of inner space. I will return to Bachelard's phenomenological reading
of the house later in this essay, but I want first to consider another association that the imagery of "Interior with Windows" has for me and
may have for readers—to Virginia Woolf's little book of 1929, *A
Room of One's Own*.

    In this book, to recall it briefly, Woolf expounds, in the voice of a
quasifictional narrator, on her reasons for concluding that "a woman
must have money and a room of her own if she is to write fiction"
(4)—or, as she adds later, poetry. She calls on her contemporary fe-

male audience to work toward creating the conditions within which a female counterpart to Shakespeare ("Shakespeare's sister") would "find it possible to live and write her poetry" (199). Writing poetry in the various small rooms that have served as my study in the houses where I have lived with my husband, I have been one of the many beneficiaries of Woolf's articulation of the need of such spaces for women writers.

Much of the thinking about the woman writer or, more broadly, the female artist, that is explicitly elaborated in *A Room of One's Own* is already implicit in the fictional world of *To the Lighthouse,* published just two years earlier. Indeed, it seems to me that the analysis of the situation of the female artist dramatically represented in *To the Lighthouse* is even richer than that laid out in *A Room of One's Own,* and conveys an aspect of her needs that is not taken into account in the polemical work. The novel's representation of the character of Lily Briscoe vividly conveys aspects of a woman artist's struggle that make it vitally important for her to have a work space of her own. At the same time it implies her equal need—one not discussed in *A Room of One's Own* (though arguably implicit there as well)—to share her work in progress with others.

As she begins a painting, Lily is beset by self-doubt:

> Such she often felt herself—struggling against terrific odds to maintain her courage; to say: "But this is what I see; this is what I see," and so to clasp some miserable remnant of her vision to her breast, which a thousand forces did their best to pluck from her. And it was then too, in that chill and windy way, as she began to paint, that there forced themselves upon her other things, her own inadequacy, her insignificance, keeping house for her father off the Brompton Road. . . . (23)

Lily not only fears that her powers of rendering her perceptions in paint are insufficient, but worries that the lowliness of her socioeconomic position limits the interest and value of her perspective. She is also quite susceptible to critics' opinions on the relative value of different styles and techniques, as well as to others' failure to acknowledge the role of artist as a viable role for a woman. Despite her self-doubt, she does manage to get started on a painting, but when she looks at it, after having left it for the duration of a walk with her friend William Bankes, she all but repudiates it:

> She could have wept. It was bad, it was bad, it was infinitely bad! She could have done it differently of course; the colour could have been thinned and faded; the shapes etherealized; that was how Paunceforte would have seen it. But then she did not see it like that. She saw the colour burning on a framework of steel; the light of a butterfly's wing lying upon the arches of cathedral. Of all that only a few random marks scrawled upon the canvas remained. And it would never be seen; never be hung even, and there was Mr. Tansley whispering in her ear, "Women can't paint, women can't write. . . ." (56-57; ellipsis Woolf's)

Confronted with what she has been able to achieve to this point on her canvas, Lily doubts both her ability to convey her vision and the validity of the vision itself. Fortunately, however, Charles Tansley's blanket dismissal echoing in her mind is silenced by the supportive, nonjudgmental response of William Bankes, who looks at the canvas analytically, and quietly discusses her intentions for her composition with her, thereby overcoming her sense of isolation. At the end of her conversation with William Bankes, she reflects,

> This man had shared with her something profoundly *intimate*. And, . . . crediting the world with a power which she had not suspected, that one could walk away down that long gallery not alone any more but arm-in-arm with somebody—the strangest feeling in the world, and the most exhilarating—she nicked the catch of her paint-box to, more firmly than necessary. . . . (63; emphasis mine)

"Intimate": for me, this word instantly evokes Bachelard's *Poetics of Space*. It is "the values of intimacy"—primarily daydream and the creativity associated with it—that, thirty years after Woolf published *To the Lighthouse,* the French philosopher would make the subject of this late work of his. If we read the above passage of Woolf's novel in the manner that Bachelard examines numerous passages of poetry and fiction—for what they reveal of the human imagination of intimate space—we can say that it shows the transformation of an artist's intimate space of creative work when another person, a sympathetic one, enters it. The passage shows this transformation to be salutary for the artist. Such a reading of the passage may be complemented by a feminist reading, taking it to show that, besides financial independence and a work space of her own, away from the demands and expectations of family members and others with claims upon her, a woman artist needs the opportunity to share her work in progress with people disposed to support her creative endeavors, who will approach the work analytically and comment constructively.

Though this need is not discussed in *A Room of One's Own,* one of the work's premises suggests an argument for it. She identifies self-confidence as the primary prerequisite for life: "Life for both sexes . . . calls for gigantic courage and strength. More than anything, perhaps, . . . it calls for confidence in oneself" (59). If self-confidence is essential for life's struggles generally, it is perhaps even more essential for self-revelation in an aesthetic medium. When it flags, such self-confidence may be restored by another's supportive comments on a work in progress, pointing out what it has achieved and suggesting how it may be further developed. This is what William Bankes's questions and comments offer Lily Briscoe. Through her representation of his interaction with Lily and her painting, and of the effect of this interaction on Lily's attitude toward herself and her work, Woolf conveys the value for women artists of getting responses to their works in progress from sympathetic and intelligent viewers, auditors, or readers. Besides money and solitude, then, the woman writer may need society; besides an income and a room or house of her own, she may be sustained by a writers' group—such, in fact, is part of my argument in chapter. First, though, I want to consider more fully what significance a room or house of her own may have to a woman writer.

When I was a child, my mother—thinking, perhaps, of Woolf's book as well as of her own childhood as the fourth of six children—attempted to impress on me how fortunate I was to have a room of my own. At the time, I tended to think that I would have been much happier if I'd had a sibling with whom to share a room. Even after I became an adult and left my parents' home, it was a long time before I grasped Woolf's point that women need independence comparable to that routinely enjoyed by the male intelligentsia of her time to have comparable opportunities for creative work. In Bachelard's phenomenological reading of the house, on the other hand, I immediately recognized an articulate mirror of my experience. My upbringing as the only child of reclusive parents had left me with a habit of solitude and accustomed me to a space of my own in which to daydream, to think, to imagine, to write. In Bachelard's description of what he claims as a universal human experience of spaces of solitude, I recognized my own experience of such places:

> [A]ll the spaces of our past moments of solitude, the spaces in which we have suffered from solitude, enjoyed, desired and compromised solitude, remain indelible within us, and precisely because the human being wants them to remain so. He *[sic]* knows instinctively that this space identified with his solitude is creative. (10)

The rooms where I have been alone are strongly associated in my mind with daydream and with creative work—the writing of poetry—that is closely connected to daydream. As I was excited to discover, Bachelard valorizes daydreaming, declaring, "Thought and experience are not the only things that sanction human values. The values that belong to daydreaming mark humanity in its depths" (6).

Daydream or reverie articulated in poetry Bachelard takes as a means of deep connection between one human being and another; in particular, poetry arising from daydreams associated with houses— which he identifies as primary sites of daydream—he sees as a peculiarly powerful connector, the poet's images, derived from her reverie, evoking readers' own daydreams of the houses where they have lived. My poem "Interior with Window," reproduced at the beginning of this chapter, can be taken as an instance of such poetry; its imagery will, I trust, remind readers of rooms in their own experience of intimate space. When I think back over my poetry of the past twenty or thirty years, I realize that I have written a good number of poems arising from daydreams of the rooms and houses in which I was working. I realize, too, that I respond strongly to such imagery in other poets' work, and even to images of poets' work spaces in illustrations and on book covers. I am deeply moved, for instance, by Adrienne Rich's evocation of a farmhouse in Vermont—the scenery, objects, and memories that surround the speaker in part III of *An Atlas of the Difficult World:*

> Two five-pointed star-shaped glass candleholders, bought at the
>   Benjamin Franklin, Barton, twenty-three years ago, one chipped
> —now they hold half-burnt darkred candles, and in between
> a spider is working, the third point of her filamental passage
> a wicker basket-handle. All afternoon I've sat
> at this table in Vermont, reading, writing, cutting an apple in slivers
> and eating them, but mostly gazing down through the windows
> at the long scribble of lake due south
> where the wind and weather come from. . . . (7)

Likewise, the black-and-white photograph of Denise Levertov's desk, its surface covered with open books and papers, beneath a cityscape seen out the window, on the cover of her collection of essays *The Poet in the World,* induces a daydream whenever I let my eyes linger on it.

The value Bachelard sees in the house is a positive one: "the house shelters daydreaming, the house protects the dreamer, the house allows one to dream in peace" (6). In contrast, the use that Woolf sees in "a room of one's own"—one with a lock on the door—is a negative use: it allows a woman writer respite from the demands of her family. Where Bachelard speaks of the value of the house in terms of what it closes *in,* Woolf speaks of the value of the room in terms of what it closes *out.* Woolf's and Bachelard's views are not necessarily contradictory, however, but complementary. Combining them, we achieve a fuller sense than either affords alone of what a room or a house of her own may provide for a woman writer.

Such a rich sense of the ways in which a house of her own may prove generative for a woman writer can be found in May Sarton's 1973 *Journal of a Solitude.* Sarton's solitude, as the book makes clear, was a chosen solitude in a commodious house of her own. The ways in which she represents her house and study as functioning correspond both to the ways laid out by Woolf and, especially, to those set forth by Bachelard. The house serves, albeit (as we shall see) imperfectly, to demarcate the limits of others' claims on Sarton's time, and also to represent publicly the autonomy and achievement possible for a single woman and a lesbian. Beyond that, it serves as just such a site of creative daydreaming as Bachelard envisages. One of Sarton's entries proclaims,

> Today I feel centered. . . . have a fire burning in my study, yellow roses and mimosa on my desk. There is an atmosphere of festival, of release, in the house. We are one, the house and I, and I am happy to be alone—time to think, time to be. . . . I have put the vast heap of unanswered letters into a box at my feet, so I don't see them. And now I am going to make one more try to get that poem right. (81)

It strikes me that Sarton would almost certainly have agreed with Bachelard's view that "the house is one of the greatest powers of integration for the thoughts, memories and dreams of [hu]mankind" (6). I think she would also have agreed that "[w]ell-determined centers of revery [sic] are means of communication between [humans] who dream as surely as well-defined concepts are means of communication between [humans] who think" (Bachelard 39-40). Indeed, she says as much herself: "From my isolation to the isolation of someone somewhere who will find my work there exists a true communion" (67).

However, as Sarton's *Journal of a Solitude* makes clear, her house doesn't function as a place of creative daydream without her active and repeated efforts to make it such a place. Speaking of returning home after a weekend away, she dwells on the difficulty of reordering both herself and the house around her, insisting, "The house is no friend when I walk in. . . . [T]here are no flowers. A smell of stale tobacco, unopened windows, my life waiting for me somewhere, asking to be created again" (32). She proceeds to "put out birdseed, tidy the rooms, try to create order and peace around me even if I cannot achieve it inside me" (33). Elsewhere she characterizes what she calls "'the usual' days" in her house as "the most creative and most precious within their inexorable structure" (83) and indicates clearly that she makes a deliberate effort to give them such a structure. The reference, in my "Interior with Window," to "compos[ing] a sense of home" reflects my own similar sense that a space needs to be at least minimally arranged and adorned to acquire the feeling of an intimate space conducive to creative work. The space of creative reverie is, as I call it in that poem, a "made place."

Even when she has her house and, particularly, her work space pleasingly arranged, however, Sarton cannot always find within it the centeredness, the strong sense of self, that seems to be, for her (as I know it is for me), a condition conducive to, even necessary for, productivity. Early in the journal she muses, "The ambience here is order and beauty. That is what frightens me when I am alone again. I feel inadequate. I have made an open place, a place for meditation. What if I cannot find myself inside it?" (12). This passage reminds me of the sense of inadequacy that Woolf's Lily Briscoe feels as she tries to paint in the midst of the quite overwhelming domesticity and so-cial/intellectual life of the Ramseys. It has been my experience, too, that solitude in a room or a house of one's own—even self-chosen solitude in a commodious house—does not always afford relief from a sense of inadequacy. The record of Sarton's journal suggests that, sometimes, such solitude may even exacerbate it.

A house of her own, by Sarton's account, may not even give the woman writer a reprieve from the demands of others. "It may be out-wardly silent here," she says of her house in Nelson, New Hampshire,

> but in the back of my mind is a clamor of human voices, too many needs, hopes, fears. I hardly ever sit still without being haunted by the "undone" and the "unsent." I often feel ex-hausted, but it is not my work that tires (work is a rest); it is the effort of pushing away the lives and needs of others before I can come to the work with any freshness and zest. (12-13)

This sort of difficulty Sarton sees as greater for women than for men. "It is harder for women" than for men, she says, "to clear space around whatever it is they want to do beyond household chores and family life. Their lives are fragmented . . . this is the cry I get in so many letters—the cry not so much for 'a room of one's own' as [for] time of one's own" (56, ellipsis Sarton's). Even though I have no chil-dren to claim my attention, I generally have more difficulty giving my writing the time it needs than my husband seems to experience in tak-ing time for his. A home work space of my own doesn't, of itself, au-thorize me to claim time for my own writing. However, the presence of another writer in the house, devoting his time to writing, does help legitimate this use of time in the home for me. And having my writing taken seriously by fellow writers and other readers I respect likewise helps authorize me to take time for it.

Ironically, the letters from other women bewailing the fragmentation of their lives contributed to the fragmentation of Sarton's own life. Her journal refers frequently to the time and effort needed to respond to those letters. Nonetheless, though she would postpone answering them to work on a poem or other writing project, she was firmly committed to being responsive. Similarly, as a teacher of writing and a writing consultant, I have often taken time to respond to others' writing that might have been spent on my own. In this, I have been driven in part by a sense that my commitment is to writing broadly, not to my own writing exclusively, and in part by a sense of responsibility to the individuals who have been my students and clients.

In *A Room of One's Own,* Woolf predicts that women's books will tend to be shorter and more concentrated than men's, "and framed so that they do not need long hours of steady and uninterrupted work" (*Room,* 135). Such a prediction seems implicitly to recognize that, as Sarton's *Journal of a Solitude* evidences and my own experience corroborates, rooms of their own and incomes they can live on will not keep women writers from being distracted. It's not clear whether Woolf was assuming that women's roles would continue to entail interruptions or whether she believed women constitutionally inclined to briefer periods of focus than men. In either case, though, she seems to be implying that work produced amid interruptions, by one with multiple objects of attention, can be as valuable as work produced in long periods of undisturbed concentration, albeit of a different character.

Sarton's discussion of women's susceptibility to others' needs, even when physically removed from others, is echoed by Mary Catherine Bateson in her book *Composing a Life,* exploring the improvisatory careers and personal lives of herself and four women friends. Likewise, Woolf's implicit valorization of women's books that do not require long periods free from interruptions for their composition is made explicit in Bateson's challenge to the assumption "that work shaped in response to multiple commitments must be inferior work" (177). Bateson discusses women's multiple commitments and distractability, and asks, "[W]hat if we were to recognize the capacity for distraction, the divided will, as representing a higher wisdom? . . . Perhaps," she tentatively concludes, "the issue is not a fixed knowledge of the good, the single focus that millennia of monotheism have made us idealize, but rather a kind of attention that is open, not focused on a single point" (166). This jibes with my own sense of positive value in my diffused attention, including awareness of household needs and concern to care for animals and plants and to respond to students and fellow writers.

Though Bateson speaks approvingly of a female "heritage . . . of responsiveness and interruptibility" (a heritage of which Sarton, for all her complaints about the demands of her mail, is definitely a part), she acknowledges that "[t]here are tasks that really do require extended narrow concentration" (179). Writing autobiographically—as she does in *Composing a Life*—she might regard as such a task. In fact, she mentions that "increasingly I do my serious writing in our [her and her husband's] studio in New Hampshire, a single room with a loft, perched over a stream" (a situation for a dwelling that Bachelard would certainly see as highly conducive to reverie). Bateson adds that, partly because they take much less time with meals when they're separate, she and her husband "prefer to be alone when [they] have intensive work to do" (124). My husband and I, likewise, are much more inclined toward elaborate meals and leisurely mealtimes when we're together than when we're alone, so each of us values occasional periods when the other is away for sustained work on projects, especially in their final stages. On the other hand, as I've mentioned, my knowledge that he is in his home office, working on his writing, generally helps me, in my study, to focus on mine. For me, as appears to be the case for Sarton and may be true for Bateson as well, it is not pure solitude, but a rhythmic alternation of solitude and understanding companionship that nourishes writing, especially, perhaps, autobiographical writing.

What is entailed in autobiography, and how do its particular demands affect a writer's needs? Woolf seems to assume that autobiography is self-expression and that self-expression is inferior to art. Though she anticipates Bateson in questioning the patriarchal value of single-minded focus, she seems to accept without examination the patriarchal hierarchy of literary genres, with autobiography at the bottom of the hierarchy and poetry at the top. Thus, she speculates that, with the woman writer attaining a higher level of education, "[t]he impulse toward autobiography may be spent. She may be beginning to use writing as an art, not as a method of self-expression" (138). The genre that Woolf identifies most with art is poetry. She concludes her discussion of the imaginary novel *Life's Adventure* by the imaginary author Mary Carmichael—a construct of a novel by a contemporary woman—by forecasting that in a hundred years, given adequate income and rooms of their own, women will be writing poetry (164). To Woolf, the notion of autobiographical poetry would probably have seemed paradoxical. Nonetheless, the impulse to poetry and the impulse to autobiography may be fused.

Autobiographical writing (whether in prose nonfiction, fiction, or poetry) entails doing something that, as Robert Coles says in a passage quoted by Sarton, " '[n]ot everyone can or will do' "—giving one's " 'specific fears and desires a chance to be of universal significance' " (60). This, as Sarton reflects,

> takes a curious combination of humility, excruciating honesty, *and* (there's the rub) a sense of destiny or of identity. One must believe that private dilemmas are, if deeply examined, universal, and so, if expressed, have a human value beyond the private, and one must also believe in the vehicle for expressing them, in the talent. (60; emphasis Sarton's)

Much of the poetry I write could accurately be described as autobiographical, and I have found that to be able to write such poetry I need to bring to it more than a sense of the rhythmic possibilities of English syntax crosscut by lineation and line-grouping, more than an ear for the sounds of the language and an eye for the shape of text on the page, essential as these are. In addition, I do, indeed, need to muster humility, honesty, and a sense of worth, to summon belief in the value to others of my personal experience and of the power of my writing to convey that experience. To help me to do all this, I depend on both solitude and society—on my work space within my home and on the responses of fellow writers to my work in progress and the example of their work.

In "Seasonal Growth," a poem originally written about twenty years ago, I celebrate the solitude of a home work space of mine. To signal the influence on the poem of Bachelard's *Poetics of Space,* which I must have first read about this time, I use a quotation from it

as an epigraph: "[I]n the daydream . . . , the recollection of moments
of confined, simple, shut-in space are experiences of heartwarming
space, of a space that does not seek to become extended, but would
like above all still to be possessed." In a dedication—"With thanks to
Kathleen Dale, whose writing of her own frosted window and a bego-
nia in front of it helped prompt this poem"—I acknowledge my debt
to a fellow member of the writers' group in which I was participating.
Here is the text of the poem:

> 1
> This morning, only light,
> diffused as through sheer
> curtains, enters from the outside.
> For the first time since last winter,
> a film of condensation on the storm
> windows of the study cuts off
> the view of the house next door.
>
> Though I know I should seal
> around the frames that let the warm
> inside air leak out and its vapor
> condense on the cold panes
> of the storms, I love
> the seasonal growth of this membrane
> that, admitting only light, leaves
>
> the inside to itself, the room
> to its own objects solely.
>
> 2
> This early in the season, the dew
> spread across the panes
> in the night dissipates quickly
> in sunlight. Later, deeper
> into the winter, it will have hardened
> to ice and shrink only slightly
> when the sun strikes the glass.
>
> Gradually, over the weeks
> of winter, it will thicken and change

from featureless translucence
to a frond-patterned
white brocade. Then set
a pink geranium on the sill,
and its red nubbins of buds will seem

little by little to melt away the rime
through the lengthening days of March.

The impulse to this poem sprang from reading work by another member of my writing group at the time—as it happens, the one at whose house we regularly met. (We chose her house as our meeting site so that she would not have to take her baby out in the evening or to find a sitter for her during the meetings. While we met, the baby would be in bed in a room off the living room where we gathered.) Through meeting regularly at this writer's house, I developed a sense of her in her home work space that resonated with my mental picture of myself in mine. Ultimately, my poem "Seasonal Growth" emerged from a reverie about a home work space of mine induced by images in her writing.

These images blended with thoughts stimulated by Bachelard's *Poetics of Space*. In particular, my poem seems to reflect the influence of his treatment of winter as enhancing the imaginative value of the house as shelter, or, at least, to accord with his theory. "A reminder of winter strengthens the happiness of inhabiting," writes Bachelard. "In the reign of the imagination alone, a reminder of winter increases the house's value as a place to live in" (40). The poem also accords with his comments on the imaginative value of a house in the country as opposed to a city dwelling. According to Bachelard,

> [A] house in a big city lacks cosmicity. For here, where houses are no longer set in natural surroundings, the relationship between house and space becomes an artificial one. . . . Moreover, our houses are no longer aware of the storms of the outside universe. . . . In our houses set close one up against the other, we are less afraid. (27)

The study that is the setting of my poem was a room in a city house, from which another house, close up against it, could be seen out the window—except when the frost simultaneously curtained out the neighboring house and made a natural world of winter cold visible in its place. The frost on the windows thus converted the study into an intimate human habitation in the midst of a natural universe, a refuge of warmth surrounded by cold. I am not sure whether Bachelard's contrast of city houses with country houses influenced me, perhaps sensitizing me to the transformation in my experience of the study when the frost asserted the presence of the natural world and concealed the nearness of other human constructions, or whether my imagination simply responded as he might have predicted. In any case, since Bachelard quotes many passages of poetry as evidence of the imaginative experience of the house as intimate habitation, the imagery of these various passages must have mingled in my mind with that of my friend's writing.

Even this brief account of the origin of a poem of mine suggests that the society of a writers' group may complement the solitude of a home of one's own in many and complex ways. The operation of writers' groups outside academe has recently been studied, under the rubric of "the extracurriculum of composition," by compositionist Anne Ruggles Gere. In a 1994 paper, "Kitchen Tables and Rented Rooms: The Extracurriculum of Composition," Gere speaks of how the members of the Tenderloin Women's Writing Workshop in San Francisco "take strength from finding that their experience is worth expressing" and of how the members of a writers' group in the small farming community of Lansing, Iowa, "gain confidence and begin to think of themselves as writers" (76). I, too, have found that doubts about the validity of my vision may be assuaged by seeing that fellow members of my writers' group take an interest in what I am trying to convey—even as Lily Briscoe's anxiety about the distance of her vision from a fashionable etherealized style of painting is relieved when William Bankes takes an interest in what she is trying to do on her canvas. Another way in which writers' groups can help writers to take their experience seriously as material for writing is by affording them regular exposure to a range of different personal visions and regular occasions for witnessing other writers' doubts about the value of their own perspectives. Through writers' groups, writers also get serious attention to their work from fellow writers on a regular basis; this can help them maintain the self-confidence that is indispensable for the struggles entailed in transforming their experiences into works of verbal art. Regularly witnessing the self-doubts of other writers in my writing group and regularly receiving their serious attention to my work have definitely helped me to believe (at least intermittently!) that I have worthy material for writing, and to maintain sufficient self-confidence to persist in wrestling with it.

Such periodic reflection of one's achievement through the eyes of others may well be valuable to creative work generally. Mary Catherine Bateson quotes an electrical engineer, Alice d'Entremont, one of the five women friends whose lives she explores in *Composing a Life,* talking about the roles she has played with creative people (in this case, computer hardware and software developers) with whom she has worked on projects. Creative people, says d'Entremont,

> can get discouraged, and then you want to be there to talk with them about the latest problem and make them able to go back to it. . . . [C]reative people . . . really want to finish their creations. They need those little helps when they've lost confidence in what they're doing, and they need to hear from somebody else that they are on track. . . . Frequently, when you're exploring some blockage, . . . it is like holding up a mirror, so they can see what they have achieved, and that's more important than the actual advice you give. (d'Entremont quoted in Bateson 182)

A writers' group can function in exactly this way for a writer—reflecting her work back to her so that she can see what she's managed to do when she's too close to the work to see it directly, for herself. A writers' group can also help her to solve problems she encounters in her work by exposing her to others' ways of working and by giving her experience figuring out how the same or similar problems might be solved in other writers' works in progress. In addition, writers' groups can stimulate a writer to persist in the difficult work of realizing the potential of a particular piece and in the larger and more difficult work of developing as a writer. The three writers' groups in which I have participated for extended periods at different times in my adult life have all functioned in these several ways for me. In addition, the sense of being among others engaged in a common enterprise helps to dispel the loneliness of working in solitude.

The dynamics of a productive alternation between solitude for writing and the responsive society of a writers' group is beautifully captured by Mary Tallmountain, a writer and member of the Tenderloin Women's Writing Workshop referred to by Anne Gere. Tallmountain explains that she writes down everything the other group members say about her writing; then, " 'at some point in time, when it's quiet and spiritually proper, when my mind and whole system are attuned to the writing, I go through it' " (Gere 76). Writers go home from a writers' group meeting with constructive criticism from a number of different readers; sifting through the various suggestions and responses may help them, back in solitude, to imagine readers for their writing and to adopt a reader's perspective on it. Over time, growing familiarity with the group members' different ways of approaching texts may give them new critical tools to use in revising work on their own. Thus, criteria of various other writers, whose reactions to mine and other group members' writing I've observed over many meetings, have certainly become part of what I consider in evaluating my work by myself.

Besides helping writers develop and maintain the confidence, discipline, and critical skills needed for writing, long-lasting writers' groups with a stable core of members can, I have found, become spaces for cross-fertilization among writers. As I listen to my fellow writers reading their works in progress, their images, rhythms, structures, and turns of phrase lodge like pollen grains in my mind. Once I'm back in the solitude of my study, these various elements of their work mingle with the preexisting stuff of my thought, contributing to the shape of new pieces. And I've seen that, from time to time, work of mine has inspired other group members in a similar way. The solitudes in which we write are thus filled with the voices of each other's works. Serendipitously, sometimes, the works that members bring to a group meeting will seem to speak to each other, as if in conversation. After such a meeting, that conversation will continue in my head, and I'll find myself developing new pieces as contributions to it. The conversation of the living room is thus extended into the solitude of the study. The stimulating and encouraging voices of this conversation may even be strong enough to drown out the distracting voices of others' needs and expectations, which, as we have seen, also penetrate that solitude.

It is perhaps no accident that all three of the writing groups in which I've participated intensively have met in members' living rooms. The first of these was a group of women poets, all of us members of the Milwaukee Chapter of the Feminist Writers Guild; this was the group that met at the house of the member with a very young child. The second, a group of poets of both sexes with no affiliation to any organization, was started several years later by two of us who had been members of the first group. It met in the living room of my husband's and my house in rural Wisconsin, roughly halfway between the cities and suburbs where the other members lived. My present group, a group of writers living in or (as in my case) outside Salem, Oregon, meets in the living rooms of several members whose houses are more or less centrally located, tending to alternate among three of them. I have found that sharing and discussing writing with fellow writers in their homes or mine implicitly validates my working at writing in my home, counteracting my uncomfortable awareness that such work may look like idleness to nonwriter neighbors and visitors. In addition, bringing a piece of my writing from my study to a living room, moving it from a space of private meditation to a space of conversation, helps me to assume an audience's perspective on it and also to conceive it as part of a large company of writings by many different hands—as I need to do in revising and editing.

Whatever the literal space in which a writing group meets, the group itself constitutes a sort of space for the writer. When a group is functioning effectively, it constitutes what I would call a *space of permission* for its members. When, in the months following her death, I began to write about my mother in poems filled with anger at her for the undiagnosed and untreated anorexia with which, as I had come to see, she had spent most of her adult life, my writers' group helped me find the courage to break through the powerful inhibitory force that my mother's extreme privateness exerted even after her death. Similarly, when I tried to find ways of writing about intense encounters with students that had occurred in my teaching, my writers' group encouraged me in my efforts to find language for relationships outside the commonly treated categories of lovers, friends, and family. When, in more recent work, I have experimented with incorporating into meditative poems something of the analytical language of my prose criticism, as well as with the use of prose "interchapters" between poems in a larger text, my current group has supported my experimental departures from conventional lyric or narrative poetry. Generally, the groups to which I've belonged have helped me to shed a succession of old poetic skins and to continue developing as a poet.

The social space of the living room, the permission-giving space of the group, is complemented by the solitary space of the study, the space of brooding, to which the writer returns to compose and revise. According to Bachelard, "the dream house must possess every virtue. However spacious, it must also be a cottage, a dove-cote, a nest, a chrysalis. Intimacy needs the heart of a nest" (65). For me, the spaciousness of the living room, of the view from the windows, must be complemented by the snugness of the study. A similar dual need is reflected in Sarton's thoughts about the possibility of renting a large, old house on the seacoast:

> I saw it yesterday, and am imagining myself into it, feeling a little clumsy. It is far grander than Nelson, but without Nelson's distinction . . . built in the 1920's, is my guess, solid and comfortable, with a superb outlook right down a golden meadow to the ocean itself. I roved about it trying to find a nest where I could work, and it is just that I wonder about. But I have an idea that a rather sheltering paneled room on the third floor might work. (144; ellipsis Sarton's)

Likewise, when my husband and I were considering the possibility of buying our present house, much larger than our previous one, I wasn't at all comfortable with the idea of living here until I'd found a small room that I could envision as my study—a small room in the heart of the house, with a view of a natural landscape.

In the small room that I make my study, I like to have houseplants—which, of course, require my care, so constitute something of a distraction, but are much less insistent in their demands than people. Whereas my husband likes to have music while he is writing, I prefer silence—not so much for itself as to be able to hear noises from other parts of the house and from outside: our dog moving from one favorite spot to another, the furnace or the dehumidifier turning on and shutting off, the rhythmic tapping of hammers from across the pasture as neighbors build a new barn. This is, perhaps, again to invite distractions, but, in accord with Bateson's notion of entertaining multiple concerns simultaneously, I am most comfortable working with my attention diffused. Though things that catch my attention may distract me from my writing, they often instead enter into it fruitfully.

The study with the frost-prone windows referred to in "Seasonal Growth" was one of three work spaces I used regularly in the small Milwaukee bungalow that was the first house my husband and I owned. Sometimes I worked at a desk in the dining room, a spot used for paying bills and other domestic business as well as my writing, and definitely *not* closed off from family obligations. Sometimes I worked in a small room, occasionally used as a guest bedroom, entirely separated from the rest of the house—a single finished room at the far end of an otherwise unfinished, open attic. Although this room appealed to my imagination as a sort of nest at the level of the tree-tops, it would get uncomfortably hot in the Midwestern summers and correspondingly cold in the winters, and its distance from the rest of the house made me uneasy. The room with the frost-covered panes, on the other hand, was a small bedroom in the middle of the main floor of the house. It was not a room of my own, however, but a study shared with my husband and more his work space than mine.

In our subsequent houses, my husband and I have been able to have separate rooms for our work as writers. In the next one, a house in the country with something of the compactness of a boat afloat in its four acres of former hayfield, I chose as my study a small room in the middle of the daylight basement. A room of my own, it allowed me to be away from most household concerns without being completely cut off from them. The washer and dryer were right across the hall, and I found that the sound of those machines steadily doing their work usually stimulated me to attempt comparable productivity. For breaks, folding clothes and creating a small bit of spatial order proved conducive to ordering words. Like Sarton, I found it helpful to have order around me when I was writing, but, also like Sarton, I generally didn't feel driven to do much housework beyond what was needed to make my immediate surroundings orderly.

My present study is a small room in the middle of one of the legs of the "L" that is the layout of our current house. It has a picture window out of which, as I enter the room, I see a beautiful view—across pasture to the long ridge of low mountain. But that view into the distance, with the added interest of cows, horses, and occasional deer, is not what I see from my desk, which I've placed not beneath the window but beside it. Thus, in order to look out, I have to turn my head; when I do so, my field of view is completely filled with nearby fir trees, a sight that tends to return me to reverie rather than distract me from it. Of course, though, I am sometimes distracted by such sights as the motion of the tree limbs in wind or sunlight glistening on wet boughs, but, unlike Annie Dillard, who, in her account of *The Writing Life,* describes taping an unchanging picture over a window facing a changing scene and choosing windowless rooms in which to work, I have no desire to eliminate all distractions.

One of the first poems I wrote in this study meditates on an occasion when I was distracted to the point of getting up from the desk. It is titled "New Year's Day":

At the early end of the dimming afternoon, a sudden flare
of reflected light on the east wall of the study
catches my eye, startling me from my desk to look
out the window toward the westward-sinking sun
slipping beneath the lid of cloud, to blaze briefly
before disappearing for the night behind McCully Mountain.
As its disk emerges, the flare on the wall broadens
to a wide diagram, in light and shadow,
of the south-facing window, projected slightly skewed
across the walnut-stained closet doors. For a moment,
that image holds steady in brightness, then gradually fades
and cools from tawny to bluish.

So the New Year's Day is over
that begins the first full year in western Oregon
for us who grew up in southern Connecticut. On the verge
of late middle age, we've left the long winters and slow springs
of Lake Michigan, where we came in our twenties and stayed
a quarter century, to arrive at this place where new growth
starts up with the rains in October, and in the woods,
not the tall firs and the cedars alone, but the clumps
of long-fronded sword ferns on the forest floor
and many broad-leaved forbs and shrubs, remain green year round.

Even now in mid-winter, long, green grassblades
stream out in the current of the seasonal creek
like wind-blown hair. After so long in the upper midwest,
such a climate is strange, but seems hospitable,
offering us all these obvious metaphors
for how we might hope to live
the rest of our lives.

In this poem, as in "Interior with Window" and "Seasonal Growth," a small room, a space of solitude, a "nest" as Bachelard would have it, is a site for beginning again. Writing is always beginning again. In a small room at the heart of the house, with a window looking out on an open space, with occasional, indistinct sounds of my husband working at his writing in a room nearby, and with the living-room conversations of my writers' group echoing in my head loudly enough to be heard over the voices that induce self-doubt and discouragement, I am best able to summon the resources for thus repeatedly beginning anew.

WORKS CITED

Bachelard, Gaston. *The Poetics of Space*. Trans. Maria Jolas. 1964. Boston: Beacon Press, 1969.

Bateson, Mary Catherine. *Composing a Life*. New York: Plume/Penguin, 1990.

Dillard, Annie. *The Writing Life*. New York: Harper and Row, 1989.

Gere, Anne Ruggles. "Kitchen Tables and Rented Rooms: The Extracurriculum of Composition." *College Composition and Communication* 45:1 (1994), 75-91.

Levertov, Denise. *The Poet in the World*. New York: New Directions, 1973.

Rich, Adrienne. *An Atlas of the Difficult World*. New York: Norton, 1991.

Sarton, May. *Journal of a Solitude*. New York: Norton, 1973.

Woolf, Virginia. *A Room of One's Own*. New York: Harcourt, Brace and Co., 1929.

_____. *To the Lighthouse*. 1927. Harmondsworth, Middlesex, England: Penguin, 1964.

SECTION III:
WOMEN WRITING HERSPACE—
PERSONAL TAKES ON HOME

It is important to theorize herspace and to show how it manifests in women's literature and in women's writing lives. But beyond discussions of what the creative process requires and how the subjectivity of solitary women is constructed, the love affair of solitary women with their own houses provides a refreshing alternative to the usual heterosexual love affair. In the minds of many, a house is a provoking substitute for a man, and the transformative possibility of this provocation is precisely why we have included the essays in this final section. Also, the trend of women choosing herspace over the usual heterosexual arrangement speaks to women's shift away from a historically oppressive paradigm of dominant culture: that women must be dependent on men. Although women without men are still regarded suspiciously in a culture that worships the romantic couple in their nest of material bliss, increasingly women are claiming their own space, buying their own houses, and living singly in order to ensure that they will not be diverted from their own fulfillment. These home-owning women who have chosen not to participate in the heterosexual economy do not make central to their identity the support and happiness for others. In fact, as two of our lesbian contributors attest, owning one's own space is a political act affirming values outside of the heterosexual order. The number of women claiming herspace is increasing. This section is an exemplification and affirmation of their joys.

In a 1999 radio broadcast on National Public Radio, Elaine Korry reported that home improvement businesses are targeting single women who have bought houses because this segment of the population is growing so fast. Korry goes on to cite the U.S. Census Bureau:

single home-owning women comprise 57 percent of all single women (*Morning Edition,* September 30, 1999). On October 21, 1999,
The New York Times published an article by Julie V. Iovine on the
same topic. In "When a Single Woman's Home is Her Castle,"
Iovine's focus, also, is the change in marketing strategies used by
companies that sell building materials, tools, and other do-it-yourself
accoutrements. This recent and dramatic change by these retailers is
based on reported dramatic shifts in the population of the United
States. Iovine writes that the number of women who own their own
homes has increased dramatically. There has been a 33 percent in-
crease in women living by themselves because they marry older, develop careers, get out of marriages, and outlive their male counterparts. The U.S. Census Bureau estimates that there are 30 million
women living by themselves. Iovine goes on to say that more than
half of women living alone own homes. These statistics, she argues,
call into question the common notion that the space we call home is
defined as the container of a nuclear family (2). Iovine quotes "Ms.
Roth, a Manhattanite," in her article as saying, "Virginia Woolf had it
wrong. Why settle for a room, when you can have the whole house?" (6).

Also, a morning television news program reported that 20 percent
of homes purchased in 1999 went to single-women buyers. Featured
in this telecast was an interview with a woman in her midtwenties
whose burning desire and goal, she said, was to purchase a house—a
house of her own.

And, in July 1999, Terence Riley, chief curator of architecture and
design at New York's Museum of Modern Art, was quoted in *House
Beautiful,* a popular "shelter" magazine, in an article about demo-
graphic shifts in housing in the United States. Riley stated, "25 percent of all households in this country have a single dweller, as opposed to eight percent just after World War II, or virtually zero under
the Puritans, who actually forbade solitary living" (42).

This section of *Herspace* documents the love affair of solitary
women with their homes. These spaces nourish the mind, and women
who occupy the space and write about that occupation reflect the
ways that spaces nourish. Herspace has supported them, and they
have fallen in love with it, with the character of this space that contains so much of themselves.

WORKS CITED

Filler, Martin. "MOMA Comes Home." *House Beautiful* (July 1999): 40t.

Iovine, Julie V. "When a Single Woman's Home Is Her Castle." *New York Times on the Web*. October 21, 1999. Online: <http://www.nytimes.com/library/home/102199single-houses.html>.

– 10 –

What to Make of Missing Children
(A Life Slipping into Fiction)

Jan Wellington

It's early January, and I've just finished puking in a snowdrift. We did a lot of that in college—regurgitating—in communal toilets, in kitchen sinks, on tests, in snowdrifts outside the gym where the dances were held. Inside, the dancers sweated and splashed in puddles of beer, the drunkest plunging out into the snow to puke and hopefully not pass out. Rumors of perfectly preserved student bodies exposed during spring thaw were part of our college mythology. The snowdrift I've resorted to this January morning is by the road to the train station. My rank breath is like steam engine smoke in the frozen air as I groan and turn back to the road, where Hope, my friend and soul mate, has planted herself at the edge of a drift with her thumb out. Her royal stature and halo of red curls soon win us a ride with an elderly couple, in whose slippery back seat I manage not to vomit.

Once on the train, fortified with peanut butter crackers, I feel better. I alternate between looking at Hope looking at me with her wide, green eyes and staring out the window at the white world blurring by. I think about the Wind—wishing he were here, wishing he hadn't let me come. The Wind is my name for Adam, the man who planted the two-inch thing in my womb that is making me sick. I call him a man because of his talented sperm, but otherwise he's a boy. I call him the Wind because he's always in motion, long hair streaming as he strides. Of course he's motionless on occasion, like the time I first noticed him in Russian 101, daydreaming with his head on the desk, that ravishing hair twining around his arms. After I gave him my barely used body on the dorm-room floor, he gave me a rueful smile and wafted off to lie with another girl. The reason he isn't here is because I never told him.

Hope is the only one who knows my secret—the reason I've had to dash out of morning lectures, running for the toilet, and for the haunted face I see in the mirror. Though I've pummeled my belly red with my fists and even introduced a coat hanger up my vagina in a frantic moment, the face is still there. As for the thing inside me, the thing that sticks knives in my nipples and fogs up my hazily glowing future, I think of it as the enemy—the thing that will ruin my life if I let it.

"Shouldn't you tell him?" Hope asked when I told her.

"I'm afraid to," I answered.

"What do you think he'll do?"

"I think he'll say, 'Let's get married.' We'd have to drop out, and we'd probably end up sleeping on a stained mattress on the floor in Brooklyn." (At the time, before I lived there, Brooklyn is where I imagined the losers lived.) "He'd have a crappy, dead-end job and it would kill him . . . after all, he's the Wind."

"But what about you?" Hope asked.

"I'd be stuck with a life I'm not ready for. This isn't supposed to happen yet—it's part of the far-off future—a later chapter." What I didn't tell her is that I was afraid the Wind would say "Get rid of it" and never come back. I still hoped he would, if only to retrieve the gray sweater I'd stolen from him. I'm wearing it now on the train, on the way to get my abortion. Absently, I stroke my fuzzy arm, imagining the hand is his and that he loves me—a comforting delusion. The truth is, Hope is the only loved one who knows and—lucky for me— besides being tall and beautiful, she's the queen of comfort.

In the days before I really needed her, we'd joke about the way we felt sometimes, sad or depressed for no particular reason, and blame the feeling on little, amoeba-like pests that invaded our optimism. We called these enemies "globules of impending doom." To fight them, one sought out comfort—the kind found in a bowl of homemade split pea soup at Sadie's, the local luncheonette with checkered tablecloths and baskets of crackers. It was August and warm, so we walked the three miles to town between sultry fields of Queen Anne's lace and gnarled trees fattening with apples, grasshoppers ricocheting off our feet. We talked about the future, when we'd both be famous writers.

We'd publish slim volumes on thick paper, give readings at bohemian bookstores, marry whimsical, sensitive men, name our daughters after each other, issue our collected works. We diligently saved the notes we wrote to each other in class and the letters we penned when apart—evidence of budding genius we'd leak to each other's biographers when the time was right. Or maybe we'd write our own lives.

The clinic turned out to be a tan brownstone on an upscale side street in Manhattan. Above the door was a sign that said Women's Center, a comfortingly neutral name, yet appropriate, considering what went on there. This was in the days before pro-life protests and doctor-snipers, and aside from a lone, middle-aged woman walking her schnauzer, the street was empty of life. Inside, the waiting room was packed with women of all descriptions—girls, mostly—girls with their mothers, girls with their lovers, girls with their sisters and friends. After signing in, I sat down with Hope to wait, each of us watching the other waiters, imagining their stories and thumbing through worn magazines. Was I nervous? After all this time, I can't remember, or maybe I've blocked it out. I must have been anxious— I've never liked to wait. When at last they called my name, Hope squeezed my hand and I stood and followed the attendant.

The rest went quickly, or so it seems in memory, with its habit of collapsing time. A series of halls lined with anxious girls, blue paper shoes that flap when I walk, a narrow table, a nurse's face, the doctor vacuuming between my legs. I concentrate on breathing, as a woman in labor would, but it doesn't hurt—all I feel is vibration. In fact, I feel great—triumphant—proud of myself for saving my future without my parents finding out, alone but for Hope and the promise of a bowl of soup. As we leave the clinic, I notice others leaving, too. Leaning on their mothers, lovers, friends, they are weeping—a tribe of vacuumed women, mascara streaking their cheeks like initiation marks. Smugly, I think, "I don't belong to their tribe." I don't wear makeup and I'm feeling downright high.

I dropped out of college at semester's end. I'd taken to cutting classes and hiding in my room, skipping meals and making off-hour forays to the dining hall for peanut butter sandwiches I gorged on back at the dorm, topping off the meal with a birth control pill. That year I'd just begun to lose my teenage fat, but now I put it on again. I stayed in my room, scrawling furiously in the pages of my journal and then burning them one by one in the candle I used to light my cigarettes. Again and again, Hope would come to the door, tapping her light signal knock and calling my name, but I didn't open up. Finally she'd go away, and the hall would be quiet. There were times, though, when I felt a presence on the other side of the door. Later I found out she *had* been sitting there, keeping vigil, saving up the comfort I refused. Then it was May and I went quietly home with my parents. I spent the summer on the sofa, glued to the television, watching the Watergate hearings unfold corruption so enormous it made me feel positively clean. I cheered the good senators and booed the evil president—just looking at his hunched-over shoulders and shut-up face, you could tell he had a secret.

In the years that followed, I lost track of Hope. We both got married and eventually divorced. I lost three children I wanted with a passion to early miscarriages—spontaneous abortion, they call it, as if the fetus makes a snap decision. Hope found a good man to make up for the first mistake, remarried, and had a red-haired son whose first few years I followed from afar, thanks to the photos she sent. After I recovered from the bomb blast of my marriage, I went back to school and ended up with a doctorate in English. As lives often do, ours diverged so slowly we hardly noticed the gap until we'd grown so far apart, we couldn't recognize the friends we'd been—cohorts in genius. She had kids; I had words. Well, no . . . to be totally honest, more often than not, I had writer's block. Over the years, I've swept up the shards of untold lives and moved on, becoming intimate with distance in the process. Aside from the stray big bang, it happens slowly, blindly, the way a stream wears away stone until, suddenly, you notice the canyon. As the physicists put it, distance is practically the twin of time.

Then, shortly after my fortieth birthday, I find out I'm pregnant again. It's an accident—I hardly know the man, the latest episode in the serial disaster my love life has been. The test is positive, and I'm elated. "Forget the father," I think. I'll go on welfare, sleep on the floor. Quit failing to write—at least for a while—and focus on the other life inside. Now, when I vomit, I'm thrilled. Then, I begin to bleed.

Although they know my history, the hospital people are hopeful. I try not to be, but hope can be contagious. In the darkened ultrasound room, the technician points out the head and budding hands of my inch-and-a-half-long daughter. (I'm sure it's a girl.) All I can see on the screen is a blizzard, but I nod and smile, struck by the strangeness of seeing my womb on TV, inside out. Then, in the middle of the storm, I notice a flashing point of light that reminds me of a quickly blinking pulsar. "What's that?" I ask. The woman says, "It's the heart." In an instant, the room expands and I'm falling an immense distance, upwards toward the pulsing point of light, which I reach for. Touching it, I'm ravished.

Over the weekend, the bleeding increases. Back in the dark room on Monday, ghostlike figures cluster around my spread legs and squint at the screen. Do what they can with their instruments, all that is visible in the blizzard is darkness.

While they fill my prescription, I sit in the waiting room and start to cry. Through the downpour I notice people staring, no doubt wondering who died. I hate being stared at, but I can't stop weeping for the death I'm carrying. A riddle bobs in my brain: "When is a womb not a tomb? . . . When it's a slaughterhouse." To clear my mind, I close my eyes and focus on space. Scraps of science float through the ether, and I recall what I read somewhere about space and time— about the enormous distance the light from a star must travel to reach us, and the eons it takes. It occurs to me that the pulsar I spotted in the womb on the screen could have died before I ever saw it flash.

The hot flashes I'm having now remind me I've entered that limbo they call "the change of life," as if it were the only one that mattered. I have dreaded the time I would know for certain I'd never have a child of my own, but now that it's here, I'm glad to be sure. Last week my sister Merry had her first baby after losing one the year before. I'm genuinely thrilled for her, even though now I'm my family's only childless child. I can't help thinking of the two events—my menopause and my sister's baby—as partners in the crowning irony of my life. When I'm in a really metaphysical mood, I feel the hand of an even sterner justice. At times like this, I crave a bowl of homemade split pea soup. But since the change of life began, peas give me gas.

Did I mention I first got pregnant around the time that *Roe v. Wade* was passed? In hindsight, this, too, seems ironic—or perversely appropriate, at least. Irony, after all, isn't meant for the young and innocent: it wears a mask only experience can penetrate. While I'm on the subject, here's something else that recently occurred to me. My parents brought us up to value candor, openness, and truth—in their book, only murder was worse than a lie. But they also believed in protecting the young from ironies such as death and sex, even if it took a lie ("your grandmother is getting better") or the weird logic of omission (sex, though it doesn't exist, is bad). I would do it differently—teach my children, if I had them, that sex happens, that it's good, but it isn't the twin of love. The trouble is, children may listen, but they seldom hear.

I know better than to blame my parents. They were raised in silence on certain subjects and simply kept up tradition, doing the best they could, a best that is always flawed. It was beyond them, I think, to imagine their children rutting, moaning, coming, as it's beyond a child to imagine its parents having sex, unless it has caught them in the act. I've heard that, to a child, sex looks like murder. Who knows—if I'd I seen them in the act, I might never have slept with the Wind. But seriously . . . what if I'd told them, or him? I wonder about it at the supermarket, in the checkout line, when I see a woman wheel past on her way out with a child in her cart—a little girl with a halo of curls and eyes that stick to mine. I'm stuck at the checkout between loaded carts and can't quite reach her, though I know she's mine.

* * *

The truth is, I haven't hit menopause yet, nor has it hit me. Not long ago, at my forty-sixth birthday party, I drank a lot of wine—not enough to make me vomit, mind you—but enough to bring on hot flashes. Recalling that my mother entered menopause around this time, and being in a sentimental mood, I imagined my time had come. Other factors, including the birth of my sister's baby—which really did happen—and a long-dormant wish to write fiction, converged, resulting in the story you've just read.

These hints of genesis were far from the upper story of consciousness when I began it. Happy to be writing poems again after a lengthy drought, I wasn't especially prose minded at the time. A few days after my birthday, though, the snowdrift memory that opens the story occurred to me and wouldn't leave me alone, so I sat down and started to write. What emerged was clearly autobiographical, or so it seemed. I sensed that the time had come to address some of the losses that have shaped who I am—a woman who lives alone, teaches at a university, and, at least in the summer, is blessed with abundant time and space to think about life, and to write. The story of the first big loss proceeded apace, until at some point—I'm not sure where—I began to feel uneasy with the truth-telling venture I'd embarked on, as if I were exposing too much of myself. The me I saw on paper looked bloated and out of focus. More or less concurrently, I noticed as I wrote that where I liked my story best, it had the ring of fiction. What made it sound that way is a long story in itself, but for now suffice it to say that, on occasion, I heard myself sounding like a character from J. D. Salinger. Perhaps in attempting to retrieve my lost eighteen-year-old self, I slipped unwittingly into a fictional voice I'd loved as an adolescent. The ease with which I did this suggests that, in the heat of composition, the gaps between present and past, fiction and fact are as easily spanned as a river at its source.

A week or so earlier, I'd been writing a poem about a recurring nightmare, hoping to put it to rest, when I was halted by a similar disease. What I did then was turn myself into a man named Joe—a simple matter of altering a name and some pronouns—after which the poem wrote itself. So, taking a cue from that success, I did the same with my story. This time, though, rather than overtly transform myself, I remained nameless and instead renamed the other players in my life. Picturing my redheaded college friend, the name "Hope" instantly came to mind. Almost as instantly I said to myself, "Fool—what are you letting yourself in for?" The critic in me knew all too well the unsubtle pitfalls of allegory. But the poet in me insisted I continue, and as I reread what I'd written, overlaying my friend's name with "Hope," I understood that that's who she'd been all along. Emboldened, I submitted to temptation and renamed the father of my first lost child "Adam" in honor of the archetype status he deserves. (I'd always called him the Wind.) Changing a detail here and there, attending to transitions and allowing images to echo, I became a shameless autobiographical liar. Nonetheless, the story remains true.

In order to get on with a story that needed telling, I'd had to make a pact with myself to think of my life as someone else's and let the fiction unfold. As with the poem, so with the story: in the process of writing, I gave birth to another self. Why did I need to? Perhaps, in the face of the plentiful solitude I live and write in, I had to find a way *not* to be alone. Having become too close to myself for comfort—or, for that matter, vision—I needed a way to step outside the too-familiar me and get a better look. I suppose you could say that, living alone so long, I've become farsighted, psychologically speaking. From this perspective, my fiction of premature menopause is not a lie, but a step into the future.

Now it's time to step back again about five years to my last miscarriage, an event I wrote about in the story you've just read, and look at what I was reading and writing at the time. But first, a digression on solitude.

I believe I'm right in thinking that the human losses I've experienced have converged to form a steep-sided psychic trough it's hard to climb out of in order to connect with people in the flesh—especially those who might open old wounds, such as children and men. Call the trough a foxhole: a defensive solitude. But in another sense, I've lived in the trough for a very long time—may have been born in it. Call it a womb: a protective, nourishing solitude. An introspective, oversensitive child, I fell in love with poetry at the age of ten, and a particular brand of poetry at that. Digging up a scrapbook of favorite poets I'd put together in the fifth grade, who do I find there but Wordsworth, Shelley, and Byron. A fragment from the latter, pasted carefully on a time-rippled page, hooks my attention:

> There is a pleasure in the pathless woods,
> There is a rapture on the lonely shore,
> There is society where none intrudes
> By the deep sea, and music in its roar.

This flash of music from the past suggests that, whatever I knew or imagined of peopled solitudes[1] or rapture at the age of ten, even then I carried the seeds of a romantic loner—an alienated soul to whom solitude is a badge of (and buffer for) difference. Also telling is the picture I pasted below the poem—a photo from a magazine of deep woods in which, in the lower right-hand corner, a man in a polo shirt is walking. The really telling thing is that the man is looking at someone now outside the picture, his left hand cut off. What I'd done is clip a photo of young lovers walking hand in hand in the woods, circa

1963, and chopped them apart to illustrate the poem. The woman, I suppose, I trashed. But for the demands of composition, she could have been the one I saved. Or perhaps the man is meant to be Byron, whom I kept as a soul mate for myself. Whatever the case, I've clearly been a longtime romantic.

Speaking of which, here are some words from another romantic— or, rather, two of them in one: "[s]ympathies . . . exist (for instance, between far-distant, long-absent, wholly estranged relatives assert- ing, notwithstanding their alienation, the unity and the source to which each traces his origin) whose workings baffle mortal compre- hension." They were uttered by Charlotte Brontë and her character Jane Eyre (*Jane Eyre* 249). It was *Jane Eyre* I was reading in the pro- cess of losing my last child, and as I lived through the novel and the loss, I perceived affinities—wombs, tombs, endangered children— everywhere. Obliged to write a paper at the time, I produced an essay whose title speaks for itself: "What to Make of Endangered Children: A Pregnant Reading of *Jane Eyre*." An experiment in critical autobi- ography, it proved too close to the bone to expose to the world back then. It's worth unearthing now, though, for what it says about wombs and tombs, solitude, writing, and life. As it turns out, though es- tranged from each other by time and space, both Charlotte and I have wrestled with the uterine paradox—the problem posed by the womb and the brain, spaces with the power to strangle and to nurture.

During the miscarriage process—a process that lasted longer than the story suggests—I was engrossed in the story of Jane.[2] Since I met her first as a preteen, she has, through many readings, remained (along with Holden Caulfield) a close fictional relative, one whose life I entered and lived beneath the covers after bedtime by flashlight: the shy, isolated child reading in a curtained window seat; the woman crossed in love, whose soul mate's call bridges impossible distance; the girl and the woman who burns for more. This time, she was the girl who, locked in a red room, sees a ghost in the mirror—her ghostly self; the girl imprisoned in a "cradle of . . . fog-bred pesti- lence; which, quickening with the quickening spring," brings death to one she loves, the girl who reminded her she must bear her fate.[3] The woman who dreams of portentous children and labors through multi- ple passages to birth her unfettered self. The fictional character who, when she suffers "an unutterable wretchedness . . . which kept drawing from me silent tears" is me, crying in the waiting room, soon to write, "[f]earful . . . of losing this first and only opportunity of relieving my grief by imparting it, I, after a disturbed pause, contrived to frame a meagre, though, as far as it went, true response" (Brontë, *Jane Eyre* 52, 56). This is not me, of course, but Jane . . . or both of us, proving Patrocinio Schweickart right when she writes, of the "intersubjective encounter" of reading, "there are no safeguards against the appropriation of the text by the reader" (52, 53).

Appropriation or meagre response, my "Pregnant Reading" included an episode I left out of my opening story but will tell now in the interest of truth: it happened at the hospital, after I learned my child was dead, before I cried. Back then, I wrote, "The doctor comes in and I tell him I have to go home; I need to smash something and don't want to do it here. When he earnestly suggests I hurl the book I'm holding, I recoil and clutch it to my breast. It's a book about Charlotte Brontë's life." Another reader, Carol Bock, observes that "[a]n emphasis on the author's life experience and on the supposedly confessional aspects of her work may well serve important needs within the community of Brontë readers . . ." (150). In my case, the shocks of affinity I'd experienced while reading and bleeding had made me want to know more about the dead woman who seemed to be writing *my* life. Given the unsafe position I was in at the time, it was, perhaps, inevitable that I would appropriate Charlotte and her alter ego by losing (infusing) myself in (confusing myself with) them.[4] Now, with the benefit of distance, I am better able to recognize and manage "the contradictory implications of the desire for relationship (one must maintain a minimal distance from the other) and the desire for intimacy, up to and including a symbiotic merger with the other" (Schweickart 55). With the benefit of distance, I can look back at that scene with the doctor and see that throwing the book would have put me in the position of Jane's persecutor, John Reed, who, in a fit of proprietary pique, hurls Bewick's *Book of British Birds* at her, wounding her mouth: I would, in effect, be throwing the book at myself, endangering my ability to speak.

Instead, reading about how Charlotte and her siblings grew in the desolate wilds of Yorkshire, reveling in the solitude of shared imagination, I wrote,

[w]hat can I learn from the womb/tomb of Haworth parsonage that grew you, Charlotte, a place they say you never escaped? That your mother died there of having children, leaving six youngsters who dwindled into four who turned inward and, nourished by reading, created and populated fictional kingdoms with names like Glass Town, Gondal, and Angria (my favorite). Of this collective inward existence, your friend Mary Taylor remarked, "You are like growing potatoes in a cellar." (quoted in Peters 27)

On the surface, this doesn't sound like a situation conducive to growth or health. In fact, I've learned since then that the picture of childhood isolation and deprivation long drawn by Brontë biographers is itself a persistent fiction.[5] It's true, though, that by the age of thirty-three Charlotte was the sole survivor of this close-knit band of siblings. Visiting her at the parsonage, another friend, Elizabeth Parkes, would observe, "there is something touching in the sight of that little creature entombed in such a place, and moving about herself like a spirit, especially when you think that the slight still frame encloses a force of strong fiery life, which nothing has been able to freeze or extinguish" (quoted in Peters 311).[6] Her home may seem a tomb and her body ghostly, but her mind remains vital, a hothouse kindled by spirit. A womb within a tomb. Some, however, have declared its fruits unnatural or damaged.

Biographer Elizabeth Gaskell observed that the stirring tales Charlotte and her siblings birthed and transcribed in tiny volumes verged on madness: "[t]hey give one the idea," she writes, "of creative power carried to the verge of insanity" (quoted Barker 789).[7] Over a century later, critics continue to tell a similar story:

[t]hese narratives of sexual obsession and adultery, barely concealed incest, parricide, and matricide run rampant, provide us with an uncanny glimpse into—shall we be blunt?—childhood neurosis. Telling the same story of love, betrayal, adultery, and murder again and again, the Brontë children drew on their own wounds and losses, as well as on their readings in the gothic fiction of their own and past generations. (Hoeveler 186)[8]

What I like best about this diagnosis is the suggestion that fiction is born of the messy union of "real life" and other fictions present and past, and that "real life" itself is generated by the union of fact and fiction. To my mind, we're all the children of incest, along with what we write. What I like least is the cloak of unwellness in which observers have enveloped Charlotte. I shudder when I read that, "overwhelmed by her sense of inadequacy" (she couldn't keep her sisters from dying or her brother sane), she "denied her needs, repressed her anger, and withdrew into a womblike world of fantasy"—a world of sex, adventure, and sublimation for which she felt increasing guilt (Moglen 240). Perhaps this reading angers me because it hits close to home and I rankle at the accusation. Having spent the better part of my life reveling in that "womblike world," I resist theories—fictions—that smack of sickness and sin. Although, perhaps, unqualified to pronounce them "wrong," I still say they feel untrue. Worse, when paired with Charlotte's ostensible lifelong fear of pregnancy and birth,[9] the sum is the sin of murder.

Charlotte Brontë, it's generally agreed, died with a child in her womb, suffering from a condition called hyperemesis gravidarum, in which the nausea and vomiting of early pregnancy, rather than subsiding, are especially severe and continue until the mother dies, along with her child. Although they tend not to anymore, doctors once blamed the condition on the mother, whose unconscious rejection of her child (so they say) leads to a species of passive-aggressive murder-suicide. As I read while losing my own child, Charlotte died pregnant, "sickened by fear. It was the last of her neurotic illnesses; the last of her masochistic denials." The final verdict: she "could not bring to birth the self she had conceived" (Moglen 241). Something similar has been said of Charlotte's character Jane, whose ambivalent dreams of threatened, hampering children are symptoms of "dissolution of personality" (Gilbert and Gubar 359); or they represent separation anxiety, a "way of describing the danger that the self will become something other than itself" (Homans 90). It is true that Jane, on the eve of her marriage, harbors fears about the leap into a new existence, the birth of a new self with a new name and (less explicit) a new, penetrated body. It is also true that Jane resists the efforts of her soon-to-be husband to "master" her into a false, aggrandized version of herself. Nevertheless, she describes herself as "an ardent expectant woman—almost a bride" (323). For Jane, marriage to the man she loves means expanded, intensified life. Yet the death of the author herself has been predicted in Jane's dreams, which supposedly embody Charlotte's ambivalence about assuming the "responsibilities of mature womanhood" (Moglen 240). Though I myself have been talking about the stimulating permeability of fiction and fact, present and past, mental leaps such as this one disturb me.

Lacking conclusive evidence, I choose to let the jury stay out on the state of Charlotte's anxieties seven years before her marriage. (If forced to take a stand, I'd say I believe her anxiety—if she suffered it—would have paled in the face of expectation, as it did for Jane.) I also choose to read Jane's dreams as portents—not of her own or Charlotte's self-abortion, but of separation from the soul mate for whom she burns but refuses to accept on terms her sense of principle rejects. Their union thwarted, the ardent woman reverts to the "cold, solitary girl" (323) whose love, she tells us, "shivered in my heart, like a suffering child in a cold cradle" (324). In short, I read her dream children as fears that the self will remain in solitude and *fail* to become something other, larger, than itself. As the writer of fiction knows, when the self—itself a fiction—becomes something other, it grows. As a reader of Charlotte's fiction, I inhabit foreign yet familiar wombs and tombs, and my own solitary life-and-death struggle is peopled with sympathy and hope.

Less sympathetic was George Henry Lewes, who, in response to the part in Charlotte's novel *Shirley* in which a woman abandons her baby, exclaimed, "Currer Bell! If under your heart had ever stirred a child, if to your bosom a babe had ever been pressed,—that mysterious part of your being, towards which all the rest of it is drawn, in which your whole soul is transported and absorbed,—never could you have imagined such a falsehood as that!" Lewes, for all his glowing prose and his life with a brilliant novelist,[10] remained in the dark about women's imaginations. I shouldn't be too hard on him, though: like my parents, he was raised in a different time.

For that matter, so was Charlotte. Acknowledging the distance between us, I'll nonetheless venture a guess or two, authorized by the sex we share. In fact, it doesn't take sex to see she conceived of feelings, thoughts, and fantasies as living things that are engendered, are born, and grow. They can even fall victim to imaginative murder—as when Jane Eyre declares, " I strangled a newborn agony—a deformed thing which I could not persuade myself to own and rear . . ." (272). Unwilling and unable to persuade myself that this is a portent of the author's murder-suicide, I see instead a woman's refusal to imagine the loss of love.[11]

Of other inhabitants of her mental womb, Charlotte wrote at nineteen,

> Succeeding fast & faster still,
>   Scenes that no words can give
> And gathering strength from every thrill
>   They stir, the[y] breathe, they live
> They live! they gather round in bands,
>   They speak, I hear the [tone]
> The earnest look, the beckoning hands
>   And am I *now* alone? ("Long since as I remember well," Lines
>   249-256)

Despite her doubts, Charlotte *did* find the words in which to embody her brainchildren, peopling her solitude with characters who live to stir this reader's mind. Later in the same poem, she writes of the images that wax and wane in the womb of the mind,

> They come again, such glorious forms
>   Such brows, & eyes divine
> The heart exults, the life-blood warms
>   To see, to feel their shine
> Oh stay! Oh fix! Oh start to life
>   Flash out reality
> Methinks a strange commencing strife
>   Of dream and truth I see. (Lines 281-288)

Charlotte, in these remarkable lines, labors to birth a prospect more glorious than the one she faced as a budding spinster in 1836. The "commencing strife" between imagination and reality—between the aspirations of a woman of genius and the limited field before her— would prove an ongoing tug of war. Just how possible it was to imagine abandoning her offspring is revealed in exchanges with the literary men she approached for advice. As Robert Southey tells her in 1837, "Literature cannot be the business of a woman's life, and it ought not to be" (quoted in Barker 262). Edified, she tells Hartley Coleridge—another who would try to herd her back to the narrow fold—that she intends to "commit her characters to oblivion, despite what it cost her" (Fraser 138). Thankfully, Charlotte—although she was a liar—*wasn't* that sort of killer. Far from repressing her mental kin, she recreated them in her own maturing image.

As her character Jane declares, "it is a madness in all women to let a secret love kindle within them, which, if unreturned and unknown, must devour the life that feeds it" (190). The unrequited mind, writes Charlotte in a hopeless moment, becomes a "narrow cell;/ Dark— imageless—a living tomb!"[12] In better moments, though, the mind was a womb. Deprived in "real life" of the object of her desires— whether flesh-and-blood soul mate or dark, potent Byron of the brain, the active principle denied women of her time—she made him out of words and married him. Through every threatened abortion, he survived and gained a new name. In an early incarnation, he is her alter ego, Zamorna, of whom she writes, "[h]e's moved the principle of life/ Through all I've written or sung or said."[13] Later he is Rochester—partner, child, and father, burdened with a mad, locked-up wife. After shoving the hopeless part of herself off the roof of Thornfield and refining the part that locked it up in a crucible of fire, she writes their reunion at Ferndean, where "to talk to each other is but a more animated and an audible thinking" (476). Actually, that was Jane. She, Charlotte, and I—romantics all—have lusted after the seemingly unattainable, often in the form of a man.

My pregnant reading showed me this, and I wrote,

> I recognize this man. He is the fathers of my missing children, the dark complement I conceived, mated with, and found insufficient in the flesh: a hoped-for soul mate who in "real life" proved a faulty embodiment of the Byron in my brain. In one incarnation, he's the Wind. In another, he's my husband, who, though he looked the part, insisted he owned me and enforced his claim with violence. I survived his atrocities by imagining myself a fictional heroine whose plight I'd written and so could erase. Our child—conceived at the height of his violence and my terror—died. This was a chapter I didn't write.

Another chapter I didn't write concerns the father of my last lost child—another faulty embodiment who pressed so close, I buried him between the lines. In writing the story this essay begins with, I skated over him again, dismissing him with the phrase, "forget the father," which is what I preferred to do. I rationalized the omission as Charlotte did when she omitted eight years of Jane Eyre's life, informing her readers, "this is not to be a regular autobiography: I am only bound to invoke memory where I know her responses will possess some degree of interest . . ." (115). Like Jane Eyre's, my autobiography was "irregular"—a fiction that justified my obscuring what didn't interest *me*. Now I suspect it's in my interest to remember this particular man.

We'd known each other about a month and were infatuated. We had a mutual birth control slipup. When I told him I was pregnant, he talked as if he were thrilled—even came up with names for our child. But when I started to bleed, he disappeared. After it was over he returned, explaining he'd had to get away alone and think. I yelled something trite but heartfelt, something like, "That's great, but you left me alone when I needed you most!" I suggested he disappear permanently, which he almost did until now, when his absences remind me of solitude's Janus-faced potential for comfort and pain. Now I suspect that, if and when I invite another mate to share my solitude, he won't be a loner. (I'm *certain* he won't be Byron.) Disappointing as "real life" can be, even fiction has its limits. It can't be counted on to reform the flesh-and-blood escape artist or abuser, or to save a child who is destined to die. But, in the reading and writing, it *can* people our solitudes by bringing the buried, unimagined, unexamined parts of us—our selves and our others—to light.

Charlotte's last chapter begins with her late marriage to the sturdy, un-Byronic clergyman whose persistence chipped away at her romantic side. What began the chipping process was solitude itself, that womb/tomb whose double nature she'd long understood. On one hand, it was a place of escape from the tedium and stress of irksome realities that quashed her fantasy life. "Delicious," she writes, "was the sensation I experienced as I laid down on the spare-bed and resigned myself to the Luxury of twilight and Solitude." Here, "[t]he room is quiet, thoughts alone/ People its mute tranquillity."[14] On the other hand, this private place could cloy. "One cannot live always in solitude," writes Charlotte; "[o]ne cannot continually keep one's feelings wound up to the pitch of romance and reverie." Furthermore, while voluntary solitude was one thing—imagination's breeding-ground—enforced solitude was another. Once "isolated by destiny," deprived of the siblings who nourished her and the hope of romantic fulfillment, she found herself imprisoned with spectres and sickened. Up to a point, writing was consolation—"hope and motive," she calls it—but ultimately, an overdose of solitude poisoned her spirits and threatened to paralyze her pen.[15]

After her marriage, Charlotte's fictional pen was less active than in times past. Now, however, solitude was not the cause. Loneliness relieved by the presence of a flesh-and-blood mate in the house and occupied by flesh-and-blood concerns, her need to spawn mental companions may have waned along with the time and space they demand. I refuse, however, to accept the verdict of the writer who insists that "Charlotte's marriage to Nicholls blighted the great powers of Currer Bell . . ." (Peters 399). And, for personal reasons—gut feelings, call them—I reject the notion that she and her flesh-and-blood child succumbed to guilt, fear, or the Muse's cosmic revenge. A man once wrote in a story born of observing the women in his life give birth, "[y]ou think of the womb as a place for transients, but it's a whole other life in there. It's a lot to give up" (Updike 96). Speaking as a woman who gave up that flesh-and-blood "other life," by fate and by choice, and almost abandoned her brainchildren, I agree. As for Charlotte, I believe because I choose to that if not for biology's fatal throw of the dice, she would have brought to birth the tale she'd begun before she fell ill—and others as well—lured by the ideal pleasures of imagination.[16]

* * *

As I mentioned earlier, though I've long been a writer, I'm also a longtime sufferer from writer's block. Seeking the origins of my impotent pen, I've entertained several explanations. Once I imagined I had nothing to say, until I recalled I had a life. Then I imagined my life was not worth writing—that I'd spill my guts and hate them, or be laughed at. It even occurred to me that my desire to write was a fiction, belonging not to me but to someone I'd read about. Once or twice I came close to the truth: that to write fluently, freely, fearlessly, you have to write every day, and every day write a lot. This I did only sporadically, and as a result I hated the little I wrote and stopped. Lately, though, like a certain mechanical rabbit, I keep going.

Along the way I've admitted that, as a teacher of writing, I can't afford to be a hypocrite and must practice what I preach. This practice has sparked the intuition about fiction that freed me to write what you're reading. It has even freed me to abandon the fiction of fiction from time to time—to return to my story's beginning and substitute "true facts" for some of its unifying inventions. For example, I once described my PhD as an MFA to sanction my character as a bona fide creative writer. The true facts are messier, and better: after starting graduate school at age thirty-seven with a concentration in literature, I was so shocked and baffled by post-New Critical literary theory (deconstruction was in vogue) that I switched to creative writing and recovered the poetic self I'd almost lost. By the time I earned my master's degree, I'd reconciled with theory—some of it, at least. This was a fortunate reunion since, for practical reasons, I returned to the literary critical fold for my doctorate. Now I trust the mingled voices of instinct and experience when they remind me that *all* writing is (or should be) creative, and that genres, like people, seldom live in total isolation—and shouldn't.

My students deserve a lot of credit for nudging me out of my classifying box into the messy realities of writing. As a fledgling teacher, I was often baffled by their difficulty in making what I, in my "superior wisdom," considered the clear-cut distinction between fiction and fact. Mnemonic devices helped with the labeling process, but not with knowledge: we'd get entangled in language, debating the meaning of terms like "real," "true," and "fact." At one especially frustrated point, I passed the buck to others, declaring, "If the book says 'essay,' it's nonfiction; if it says 'short story' or 'novel,' it's fiction." We all knew this was a cheat. Then, of course, there's the complication posed by poetry and drama, autobiographical fictions such as *Jane Eyre,* and writings such as this one. Ignoring the generic label's list of ingredients, a large faction of readers will insist that if there's an "I" in the text, it's the author. They seem to need to believe it—to make a connection with a "real" person like themselves en route to connecting with a text. And, as I've been hinting all along, there's a sense in which they're right. So, what I tell my students now is that selves have many faces and voices, some of which are masks that speak the truth in lies. As for what to call a particular face or voice, it's a pact we make, with a wink.

Another student habit that baffled me was the propensity of many, when asked to engage in literary analysis, to ignore or misinterpret instructions. Some would embroider characters, invent relationships, or predict the future, often in ways that were dubiously (or not at all) supported by the texts they were writing about. Others would pen a personal narrative that grew out of their sympathy with a writer or character—saying, in effect, "this happened to me, too." Their urge was not to take apart but to supplement. The voices of professors past buzzing in my brain, at one time I'd pat these rebels on the head ("I applaud your inventiveness, your willingness to enter into a text") and then brandish the rod of correction ("You haven't followed instructions"). In doing so, I felt like a traitor to us all. Wasn't my own abiding impulse to wax poetic over, around, and under a text, weaving with fluid logic a family of strangely related fabrics, engendering a fascinating bastard? (In past parlance, a "natural child.") Hadn't I often, for practical reasons, stifled that impulse and felt cheated, imprisoned, false? Yet I can't ignore the "real world" value of clearly making and supporting a point, and I certainly can't ignore the permeability of academy and "real life." Romantic that I am, I wish the world as a whole gave better credit to poetry . . . or that credit were never invented. The debate about what constitutes "valid" reading or writing in an academic setting being far from settled, I settle for instilling in students a sense of situation, helping them learn how to read, write, and think in multiple ways and giving them credit for pushing the envelope. I retain a subversive faith that academe is neither a factory nor a tower, but a womb for the mind—a space that nourishes change, development, revision.

That's the wonderful thing about writing—doing it, reading it, thinking it: its openness to re-creation. Unlike life, it allows us to change the past and, in doing so, to alter the future. Once, in a melancholy, fanciful mood, I blamed my writer's block on the fact that none of my embryonic offspring lived long enough to develop the hands they needed to wield a pen. Though appealingly poetic (and correctly cognizant of writing's *un*solitary nature), this trope doesn't help, so I try again: The part of Charlotte Brontë called Rochester lost a hand but gained a righteous voice called Jane. And again: Since fiction has declared I'll never give birth to a literal child, I'd better tend to the other ones. Call it compensation, sublimation, or what you like— there are many ways to touch the heart of what you love.

Though I love to travel, mentally and otherwise, I'm a homebody at heart. Wherever I've lived—and I've moved a lot—I've made for myself a separate space, a place that pleases me aesthetically, is private, nurturing, and safe. Figurative or literal, fictional or real, this place is my green world, my Ferndean, my curtained window seat. This womb of my own is the place I long to return to whenever I'm away, which is seldom for long. Among its attractions is the fact that I needn't dress up, or at all. I'm free to arrange and rearrange the furniture however and whenever I want. Sometimes, though, an excess of solitude turns me in on myself until, trapped, I begin to go mad, paralyzed and blind. Then, the womb is a tomb. Should this fatal transformation threaten, I go out or invite someone in. I can do it literally, in the flesh, or emblematically, in fiction.

I might read or write about a woman pacing a corridor, "safe in the silence and solitude of the spot," relieved "to let my heart be heaved by the exultant movement, which, while it swelled it in trouble, expanded it with life; and, best of all, to open my inward ear to a tale that was never ended—a tale my imagination created, and narrated continuously; quickened with all of incident, life, fire, feeling, that I desired and had not . . ."(Brontë, *Jane Eyre* 141). From behind a door in this corridor comes a madwoman's laugh. Having escaped the lunatic's house but lost the mind she desires, our heroine suffers the exile's solitude, finds her kin, claims her inheritance, re-produces the lost soul mate. Mining the womb of his mind, she masters him, restores his vision, bears his fictional children. Of this fictional heroine's ending, it has been said, "[q]ualified and isolated as her way may be, it is at least an emblem of hope" (Gilbert and Gubar 371).[17] Perhaps, after all, Jane's ending is not as bleak as Gilbert and Gubar would have it: perhaps it is neither least *nor* last.

* * *

As it turns out, it is not. Not long after I wrote what I thought was this essay's *finis,* I landed in the hospital with an intestinal obstruction. At a loss to explain the cause until the great god CAT scan spoke, my doctors at last informed me that the culprit was a large uterine fibroid which, in its eagerness to claim new abdominal territory, was crowding out the other residents of my nether regions. The solution, they concurred, was an immediate hysterectomy. Needless to say, given my longtime investment in my womb, I was (as the politicians put it) "shocked and dismayed."

"Why not just take the tumor out?" I inquired.

"Because," asserted Doctor One, "it's easier to remove the whole uterus." Turning an incredulous gaze to Doctor Two, I was met with what he must have thought was a more considerate response:

"After the childbearing years, a uterus is really good for nothing but cancer."

"You need to be a woman for a while," I replied.

Thankfully, my gynecologist is a sensitive and sensible woman who advised me to load up on fiber, drink gallons of water, and wait and see. After a year of waiting, though, during which I came to feel as if I were living on a planet with twice the gravity of ours, it became clear that the tumor would have to go. Having given me all the options and concurred with my choice to keep my uterus, my doctor scheduled the big event. Imagine our shock and dismay, then, when the managed care company in whose hands my fate rested refused to approve the surgery unless I had my uterus out! I can say without hesitation that I had never known fury until that moment. Thankfully, my gynecologist is an eloquent and feisty woman who managed to persuade my health care provider of the error of its ways. Awaiting surgery, in my relief I meditated on the meaning of "managed care" and concluded the following: in the process of managing their clients' care, such providers often manage *not* to care.

Who, after all, need care about a bundle of muscle the size of a fist, or—once it ceases to yield its wonted fruits or fails to—need care about what it means to the woman it inhabits? Far from assuming it means the same thing to every woman—or even that it means much at all to each—I still insist on a woman's right to bodily sovereignty.

Having read this chapter, of course, you will have a sense of what a womb means to me and understand why I insisted on retaining the traitorous organ. In short, for all its failings in the literal child department, my uterus has been fruitful: has, even as it generated the "unnatural fruits" that spelled, perhaps, the death of one sort of hope, helped articulate another. Buried deep beneath inscrutable strata of skin, fat, and intestines, or revealed to the startled eye of technology as a miracle of heraldry enthroned in the flaring pelvic bones, its banner of fallopia and ovaries rampant, it generates tales that bring unexamined selves to light. In short, it generates redemptive fictions.

I can't help thinking now what might have been had Charlotte Brontë lived in a time in which medical science, with the flick of an IV (and good insurance) could have set her stomach to rights, saving her child and her life. Nor can I help thinking about what might have been had someone told me my fibroids (which I've had and known about for many years) might have been responsible for the losses I've described. The outcome of these thoughts I'll save for a future fiction and merely observe yet another irony experience has brought to light: now that my womb, in its recently achieved, splendid solitude, may well be receptive to literal children (or so the doctors say), I find that I don't want them. No matter that my dear, ever-hopeful mother has called to tell me of the woman she saw on TV who had a baby at fifty-one—I don't want one. I find, after all, that I'm too fond of my writing solitude to give it up. And, if you'll permit me one final irony, I'll admit that, having taken an indignant stand and defended my womb's right to exist, I'm prepared, should a *real* need arise, to give it up. For all the sound and fury I've expended on its explication and defense— or, rather, because of it—I'm ready to admit that what I thought was adamant conviction was itself just another fiction: that is, a truth on the verge of metamorphosis, awaiting the birth of another self.

NOTES

1. From "Childe Harold's Pilgrimage" 4.178.594–97, in which Byron elsewhere refers to solitude as the place "where we are least alone" (3.90.843). (The passage I read as a child had been excerpted and anthologized as the short lyric, "Solitude.") Versions of the term "peopled solitude" were popular in the Romantic era. Byron, for instance, writes of "a populous solitude of bees and birds" ("Childe Harold" 3.102.950). Ferguson glosses the concept as the natural wilderness to which the Ro-

mantic consciousness was wont to retreat: a space where objects, forces, and creatures could serve as sympathetic reflections of the individual's state of mind (114). In this essay I suggest that both the womb and its metaphorical counterpart, the imagination, can be considered such spaces.

2. At the time I was experiencing a rare condition known as cervical pregnancy, in which the embryo implants itself in the cervix or neck of the womb, an inhospitable place for development. I learned I was pregnant in the sixth week, shortly after which light bleeding began to occur. After the embryo died early in week ten, I was given the drug methotrexate to encourage "inversion"—the dissolution of the "products of pregnancy" within the body—and monitored for another month.

3. *Jane Eyre* 108; ch. 9. This quotation refers to the typhus epidemic that swept through Lowood Institution, where Jane was sent to school, and to the death of her friend Helen Burns from consumption while the epidemic was in progress. The character of Helen is based on Charlotte's oldest sister, Maria, who fell ill at the Clergy Daughters' School the Brontë girls attended (the model for Lowood) and returned home to die.

4. "To understand a literary work," writes Georges Poulet, "is to let the individual who wrote it reveal [herself] to us in us" (from "Criticism and the Experience of Interiority," quoted in Schweickart 52). Discussing Mikhail Bakhtin's notion of reading as dialogue, Morson and Emerson caution us that, "to understand an author in the richest way, one must neither reduce him to an image of oneself, nor make oneself a version of him" (56). They write that "true understanding both recognizes the integrity of the text and seeks to 'supplement' it. Such understanding 'is active and creative by nature. Creative understanding continues creativity, and multiplies the artistic wealth of humanity" (Bakhtin's "From Notes Made in 1970-171" 141, quoted in Morson and Emerson 56).

5. The children's mother, Maria Brontë, died of uterine cancer in 1821, when Charlotte was five. Afterward, they were cared for by their father, Patrick, and their aunt Elizabeth Branwell, with the help of devoted servants. The fiction of the Brontës' deprived childhood was begun by Charlotte's first biographer, Elizabeth Gaskell, who was both misinformed and intent on explaining to critical readers the wild, supposedly "improper" nature of the sisters' novels.

6. Charlotte's older sisters, Maria and Elizabeth, died in 1825. Her brother, Branwell, and sisters Emily and Anne died within an eight-month period between 1848 and 1849, when Charlotte was approaching the age of thirty.

7. From a letter to Charlotte's publisher George Smith, written in July 1856.

8. Besides fiction, the Brontë children read religious works, poetry, biographies, travel books, and periodicals. According to Barker, the highly reputed *Blackwood's Magazine,* "a potent miscellany of satire and comment on contemporary politics and literature," had a decided and enduring influence on their literary development (149). I believe that Hoeveler's statement—which is rather gothic in itself and based on long-standing misconceptions about the Brontës' childhood—exaggerates the effect of their "losses" on their juvenile writing. Barker, for instance, argues persuasively that, "[t]hough the loss of their mother at such an early age could not be anything other than a personal tragedy for the children she left behind, its influence should not be exaggerated. . . . Her loss, terrible as it may have been at the time, did

not permanently blight their young lives" (111). I also suspect that Hoeveler underestimates the extent to which these juvenile tales, which the children acted out, served as a form of imaginative play.

9. Re: Charlotte's fear of pregnancy and birth, see for example Moglen 21.

10. Lewes' *Edinburgh Review* excerpt from January 1850 is quoted in Peters 273. Lewes and novelist George Eliot (Marianne Evans) lived together as man and wife from 1854 until his death in 1878.

11. Homans acknowledges that this is one of several possible interpretations of Jane's dream children (92). Both she (300) and Peters (407) suggest that the anxieties reflected in these dreams may relate to Charlotte's fear of loss of her writing self: a theory I find worth pursuing (and do, in this section of my essay)—though not, like Peters (405) and Moglen (240), to the brink of the literal grave.

12. Lines 65-66 from "Frances," published in 1846. According to Neufeldt in his notes to *Poems,* this poem blends the fictional world of Charlotte's juvenilia with her real-life disappointed love for teacher Constantin Heger (446).

13. Lines 150-51 from the 1836 poem "But once again, but once again."

14. On June 29, 1854, Charlotte married her father's curate, Arthur Bell Nicholls. Their marriage—by all accounts a happy one—ended with her death on March 31, 1855. Quotations are from a journal manuscript written while Charlotte was a teacher at Roe Head School in 1836 (Barker 236) and from her 1837 poem "The Teacher's Monologue," Lines 1-2.

15. Quotations are from an 1838 story in which Charlotte, as narrator, interrupts the plot to question her own fiction (Barker 291) and from Barker 556 and 601, referring to the paralyzing loneliness that interfered with the writing of Charlotte's final novel, *Villette.*

16. When she fell ill in January 1854, Charlotte was in the process of reworking a story (which became known as "Emma") she'd begun the previous year (Barker 768).

17. It could be argued that, unlike Charlotte Brontë, I—a woman alive in the twenty-first century—have little excuse for failing to grasp "that existence more expansive and stirring." A child of the 1950s, however, I too imbibed an ideology of women's domesticity that decades of "liberation" have yet to totally erase. I, too, got the message that my worldly options were to teach children and/or nurse the sick— and then only until I found a spouse. Like Charlotte and countless other women, I was unimpressed with the options. (Perhaps this helps explain why, as a ten-year-old, I trashed the photo of a woman; why Charlotte's early heroic personae were male; and why even now I sometimes need a man's voice to tell my tale.) At any rate, ambition made us opt for the wider sphere of literature as antidote to that haunting, enforced solitude known as the "woman's sphere."

WORKS CITED

Barker, Juliet. *The Brontës.* New York: St. Martin's, 1994.
Bock, Carol. *Charlotte Brontë and the Storyteller's Audience.* Iowa City: U of Iowa P, 1992.

Brontë, Charlotte. "But once again, but once again." *The Poems of Charlotte Brontë: A New Text and Commentary* (pp. 184-192). Ed. Victor A. Neufeldt. New York: Garland, 1985.

_____. "Frances." *The Poems of Charlotte Brontë: A New Text and Commentary* (pp. 302-308). Ed. Victor A. Neufeldt. New York: Garland, 1985.

_____. *Jane Eyre.* 1847. London: Penguin, 1966.

_____. "Long since as I remember well." *The Poems of Charlotte Brontë: A New Text and Commentary* (pp. 171-181). Ed. Victor A. Neufeldt. New York: Garland, 1985.

Byron, George Gordon, Baron. *Byron.* The Oxford Authors. Ed. Jerome J. McGann. Oxford: Oxford UP, 1986.

Ferguson, Frances. *Solitude and the Sublime.* New York: Routledge, 1992.

Fraser, Rebecca. *Charlotte Brontë.* London: Methuen, 1988.

Gilbert, Sandra M. and Susan Gubar. *The Madwoman in the Attic: The Woman Writer and the Nineteenth-Century Literary Imagination.* New Haven: Yale UP, 1979.

Hoeveler, Diane Long. *Gothic Feminism: The Professionalization of Gender from Charlotte Smith to the Brontës.* University Park: Penn State UP, 1998.

Homans, Margaret. *Bearing the Word: Language and Female Experience in Nineteenth-Century Women's Writing.* Chicago: U of Chicago P, 1986.

Moglen, Helene. *Charlotte Brontë: The Self Conceived.* New York: Norton, 1976.

Morson, Gary Saul and Caryl Emerson. *Mikhail Bakhtin: Creation of a Prosaics.* Stanford: Stanford UP, 1990.

Peters, Margot. *Unquiet Soul: A Biography of Charlotte Brontë.* Garden City, NY: Doubleday, 1975.

Schweickart, Patrocinio P. "Reading Ourselves: Toward a Feminist Theory of Reading." *Gender and Reading: Essays on Readers, Texts, and Contexts* (pp. 31-62). Ed. Elizabeth A. Flynn and Patrocinio P. Schweickart. Baltimore: Johns Hopkins UP, 1986.

Updike, John. "Grandparenting." *The New Yorker* Feb. 21, 1994: 92-97.

The Little Gray House and Me

Claudia A. Limbert

When I was a child growing up in poverty in the Missouri Ozarks, I enjoyed drawing. In particular, I would draw a house that I drew as any child would when asked to depict his or her idea of "home." It was a little gray house with a dark roof, white trim, a big brick chimney on one end, and a sidewalk right up to the front step. I drew endless versions of that house, but they were basically the same and they all meant "home" and "security" to that little girl in that time and place.

After high school and after a brief stint in a cloistered convent, I married and had four children. From our wedding day, our marriage was a very unhappy one, and I felt trapped by it and our lack of money. Often my husband chose to be jobless and I worried about how to feed and clothe the children.

There was little that I could do about it with only a high school education. It wasn't until I was thirty-five and my children ranged in elementary school from first through fifth grade that I was able to enroll as an undergraduate, taking advantage of a series of scholarships. Through additional scholarships, I received an MA in fiction writing and a PhD in English literature. It will probably not surprise anyone that, during that time of grueling scholarly work and an increasingly unhappy marriage, I continued to draw pictures of the little gray house of my dreams. Calling upon memories of some New England beach cottages that I had seen, I also began to draw what the floor plan would look like. And, at some point, I would always draw a picture of stairs with a cat sitting just halfway up, the cat my husband wouldn't allow me to have.

By 1988, my children were either completing college or well on their way to becoming independent, so as soon as I got my PhD that spring, I filed for divorce. One of the last comments my husband made to me before I left him was that, no matter how hard I worked or how hard I tried, I would never escape poverty. I remember how he commented with some satisfaction that I would end up in one room in a flophouse, trying to cook on a hot plate.

Although I am sure that he has long since forgotten that conversation, I never will. And, for some time, I believed him.

I left that marriage with only enough money to move a few pieces of furniture and my books to my new apartment halfway across the country. I was a lowly assistant professor of English at a small Penn State campus, making the typical low salary of such a position. I remember spending the first two weeks of my new job with only fifty cents in my pocket.

During those first two weeks, I also remember going to an animal shelter and adopting a two-year-old, wildly colored calico cat, whom I would name Emma, a cat who had been so unloved and mistreated that she wouldn't meow, purr, or even allow me to touch her for six weeks. When I think back on it, I realize that I adopted Emma because she needed me just as much as I needed her.

The moment that I received my first small paycheck, I began to squirrel money away in what I called my "house" fund, because I wanted to have my very own little house and not just a series of apartments that would cause me to end as my ex-husband had predicted.

Then, through a lot of hard work and a series of opportunities, I began to advance through the university. Within ten years, I was appointed as the campus executive officer at a Penn State campus and I had accumulated just enough to make a down payment on a house, plus a bit extra to make any needed renovations.

For six months, I looked at houses. None were right. They were either too large or too small or too far from campus or too expensive. Sometimes they didn't feel right. I remember going to look at more than one house where I would refuse to go past the entryway because it just felt unhappy inside. As time went on, I began to think that I would never find the right house for Emma and me.

As I was about to give up, I found a house only two blocks from campus that had been built in 1948—a house that would become my little gray Cape Cod.

To begin with, the little Cape Cod house was not gray when I first saw it, while I was taking a walk one day. It had been painted a peculiar color that had become washed out and chipped over the years. My daughter, irreverent soul that she is, called it a "pukey orange-brown." (And she wasn't far from wrong.) The trim was painted a dark green and the peeling garage door that led under the house was that same dark green. Old cloth awnings sagged over most of the windows, giving them a hooded, secretive appearance. There were three nice maple trees that came in papa bear, mama bear, and baby bear sizes, each bearing at least one bird's nest, but the "shrubbery," as the realtor would later call it, was either dead or needed to be put out of its misery as quickly as possible. One owner at some point had surrounded the foundation with clear plastic and what would later seem like tons of small stones. From the street, I could see the gigantic weeds that had grown up through that plastic.

There was a "For Sale" sign pounded into the front yard.

As I think back on it, I doubt most people would have even looked twice at that little house. Actually, most people hadn't even looked at it once, because I learned that it had been on the market for some time. Yet I remember continuing to feel drawn to the little house that crouched so uncomfortably on its hillock of a lot. There was just something about it that called to me. Its roof beam was straight as an arrow, it had good lines if you could look past everything else that was wrong with it on the outside, and there would be plenty of space for me to garden.

I called and asked to see the house. As I stood on the grass with the realtor, peering up at the little house's uncompromising one-and-a-half-story exterior, I thought to myself, "This house needs me now just as my cat Emma needed me then."

The outside was indeed a mess with that awful paint and the sagging awnings blocking any possible light that might enter the windows. And I noticed that, almost hidden by the awnings, the house still had its original single-pane, metal crank-out windows; they were in bad shape and could be counted on to let heat out in the winter and rain in during the warm months.

I continued to walk around the house, still followed by the anxious realtor. On the upper floor, there was only one full-sized window and two tiny hatchlike ones. The tall chimney and the steep roof looked sound, but a tiny porch on one side with a door opening onto it from the living room had a floor that was rotting. Across the back of the house stretched a huge, sagging deck that was also in very bad shape and covered with sodden green indoor/outdoor carpeting.

I took a deep breath. "May we go inside?" I asked the realtor.

I will never forget my first step inside the entryway. Immediately, I felt at peace. The living room had a fireplace with wooden bookshelves built into one end of it and a long mantle with a huge plate-glass mirror over it—all very nice. The roughly stuccoed walls with their curved doorways were in good shape but a curious tan color. The oak floors were intact but in bad condition; in places, I could see where the windows had been left open and rain had damaged the floor. But a big plus to the lower level was that no previous owner had ever painted the golden oak staircase, the doors, or any of the trim. Even in the dark room, they glowed with warmth and quality.

The kitchen received light from two sides and there were plenty of wooden cupboards that were in good shape. But the linoleum and the yellow countertop were chipped, burned, and stained and their edges finished off with metal strips. The wallpaper was just as wildly patterned as the wallpaper that I would find in every other room throughout the house. The finish of the porcelain sink had long since been scrubbed away; it was badly chipped and the faucets were old. The refrigerator crouched beside the back door that led out onto the crumbling deck with its sodden carpeting.

I entered the bathroom and almost gave up at what I saw: more wildly patterned wallpaper, wall tiles in several colors, and a bright aqua plastic bathtub. There was little lighting, an old toilet, and a badly water-damaged vanity that almost blocked the doorway. Behind the door was a large linen closet with a big hole in the door. And, although I didn't know it then, beneath the floor were rotted joists, the result of years of water leaking down around the shower and toilet.

I went on to the front bedroom where I noted yet another pattern of wallpaper and more stained carpeting. The light fixture had a fan and that was about all the room had going for it.

I thanked the realtor and said I would think about it. As I left, I remember realizing that my head was being very practical and saying, "Don't even think about buying that house" while my heart was saying, "You need that house and that house needs you."

That evening I sat at the kitchen table in my apartment and added up columns of numbers as I tried to figure out how to afford the changes it would need. Finally, I went to bed, but all night I dreamed of that poor little house.

During the next week I went back to see it on two other occasions. I kept thinking about it and sometimes during meetings I would catch myself drawing floor plans for the upstairs or pictures of how the outside could look given some attention.

Finally, I called the realtor and negotiated the price. Then I went to several banks and bargained for the best mortgage rate. The result was that I bought the house, scared to death at the immensity of such a commitment but feeling deep inside that Emma and I were supposed to live in that house.

Finally the day came when the owners handed me the keys to my house. It was a crisp September day when I first entered the house by myself. Gently, I shut the front door behind me and leaned against it, closing my eyes. Once more, I felt the peace of the house surround me.

I opened my eyes and the first thing I noticed was a stray beam of sunlight that cut across the living room's oak floor and landed on the stair wall. Then I looked around. It was going to be beautiful. I could feel it. Yes, the things that looked horrible before still looked horrible, but the things that had looked good now looked even better.

I began the same circuit of the house that I had taken before. How much bigger the living room was than I had previously thought when all that heavy furniture had been there. Yes, the kitchen needed a lot of work, but there was an honesty about it that I loved.

The house gave me my first surprise when I walked into what had been the children's bedroom. It was now empty of bunk beds and everything else. I turned on the light and gasped in pleasure. From floor to ceiling were solid slab cherry walls with lovely simple moldings along the ceiling. And, stretching all across the back wall, was a handmade, built-in cherry desk, with cupboards and drawers below on either side and, above, built-in glass-fronted bookcases. Looking through the window that was over the desk, I could see the beautiful large maple tree and knew that I would hang bird feeders there. The ceiling fan was missing some lampshades, but the fan was made of wood. This would be the office I had always wanted.

After months of construction and renovation, March 11 dawned. I got to the house before the movers and walked into my little gray Cape Cod. All was quiet and smelled of paint and new things. That was when something very curious happened. Emma and I had moved several times before and, each time, when I would let her out of the bathroom, she would quickly hide somewhere—often for several days—only venturing out cautiously before reluctantly settling in. I expected the same from her when I opened the bathroom door that March 11.

But Emma totally surprised me. She strolled out of the bathroom door, taking a moment to stretch each leg and her tail. Then she rubbed against my legs before setting off confidently to explore her new home.

I went back downstairs, back to the front door, leaned my back against it and closed my eyes—just as I had that September day on my first visit to the house after the owners had moved out of it. This was the moment I had been putting off, as well as the moment I had been waiting for—when I would know whether I had either done the right thing or had made a big mistake.

I opened my eyes and my heart leapt. I looked around me. The house had been transformed into the little house I had always imagined. And my calico cat, Emma, sat tidily halfway up the stairs, just where I had pictured she would sit in those pictures I had drawn as a little girl. The once dark rooms were now full of light and air, and the house had come alive.

That night I just lay in bed, Emma curled up in a warm ball on my chest under the comforter. I listened to the house. I could hear the whoosh as the warm air from the furnace began to circulate in the room. I could hear the odd creaks and pops that any old house makes. I could hear the deep rumbly purring of my cat. I knew that I had done the right thing.

And I can tell you this. My job is a busy one and one that I love. However, by the end of a typical day, I don't have one drop of energy left in my body. I pack up my briefcase, shut down the computer, and turn off my office lights.

Then I walk the two blocks to my little gray house.

As I approach the house, I see that Emma is sitting in her basket on the bookcase under the front living-room window, flanked by the scented geraniums and the rosemary plant. She sees me and stands up and rubs her face against the window pane. I get the mail out of the mailbox at the bottom of the front steps, purposefully taking my time so as to prolong the joy of the moment.

I walk up the front steps and slip the key into the lock.

I push the door open and then close it behind me.

I am home. It is a far cry from the flophouse where my ex-husband suggested that I would end up. My little gray house shelters my body and my mind. It is my sanctuary, my own space, my home.

– 12 –

The Colors and the Light

Maria Brown

As a single woman home owner my sense of home has been shaped by my experience growing up. My siblings and I were part of the child welfare system by the time I was four years old. We lived in a series of brief foster care placements that summer. At the time, they were still trying to find a treatable diagnosis for my mother's mental illness, and she was in the hospital for several months at a stretch. While we were away, I was somehow convinced that my parents had died, and from what little I could remember of my mother and her anger toward me, I was sure that I had something to do with it.

When we did go home in the fall, our life continued to be volatile. During my fifth year, Mom had many other stays in the hospital as they experimented with the drug lithium in an attempt to treat what they now know is a bipolar disorder. For me, the next few years were a time of fear and unpredictability, with a mother who was, at best, absent, and at worst, violent. When she was home, I was never sure what to expect from her; when she was away, I was always afraid that I had seen the last of her. I was never able to relax with her or to feel safe in our house.

We always rented houses, and we moved several times before I was thirteen. The houses were shabbily furnished; I don't think my mother had the energy to personalize them through any kind of decorations. The walls were always bare and white, and the carpeting was always durable and ugly. I shared a room with my two younger sisters. With six children in our family, there was no privacy for any of us. Crying was just not something that my parents could tolerate, but I had so many upset feelings; I was constantly looking for some privacy so that I could release them.

By the time I was thirteen, we were back in the system again. My father had left, after several months of manic behavior from my mom, and it took us about four more months to get ourselves removed from the home as well. I had pushed for placement in foster care, in the hopes that there would finally be some peace for myself and for my brothers and sisters. I did not want to be separated from them or from my parents, but life had become so intolerable that I saw no other way to survive. But life in my new home was also volatile. My foster family was very vocal, very demonstrative, and often vented their feelings by yelling and cursing. After a year I was also subjected to emotional and sexual abuse, which lasted until I left my foster home for college at age seventeen. This house also had no privacy; locked doors were regarded with suspicion and mistrust. I did have a room with its own separate entrance, but the key was always kept inside the house, so that anyone else could come in at their own discretion. I spent a lot of time as an adolescent attempting to carve out little pockets of privacy and safety. I was often anxious and on edge, became anorexic at fourteen, and turned to smoking, drugs, and alcohol soon after.

Because I craved safety and peace, but had never experienced either, I made many mistakes in my search for them. For many years I thought I had found safety and peace in drugs and alcohol and in relationships, but all of these things eventually left me feeling empty and ashamed, and even more abused than before. I also attempted to control my life through anorexia well into my twenties, but again, I only felt more and more out of control.

By the time I got sober at twenty-four, I was getting sick of the tumult in my life. I had figured out by then that the answer to my problems did not lie in drug use or drinking, or in starving myself. It took me another few years to come to the realization that relationships also would not create the safety and peace that I was looking for in my life. At twenty-six I resolved to someday buy a house of my own. I knew, and finally accepted, that I was the only person who could create the peace, safety, and stability that I needed. I had spent my entire childhood being shuffled around from parents to foster parents, from one bad living situation to another. As an adult, I continued to live my life like that, choosing living situations that were dependent on other people making them work. I longed for a place that I could call my own, a home that I wouldn't have to give up, where my sense of security would not be dependent on someone else's reality. Of course, it was six years between realizing that the desire existed and making it happen, but I never lost sight of the desire itself during that time.

I had no idea what the process of buying a home would be like, having never seen my parents purchase one. I felt strong doubts as to whether this was something that I could actually do on my own. At first, I hoped that I would find a lover with whom I could make such a commitment. It eventually became apparent, however, that I needed to do this for myself and by myself. I was never going to have the security and stability that I wanted if I waited for someone else to make it happen. One valuable thing I did learn is that even though I was purchasing the house alone, I had many people in my life that supported my process and offered unlimited encouragement along the way. My home-owning women friends also provided, and continue to provide, practical and invaluable guidance in dealing with all aspects of searching for, purchasing, and maintaining my home.

I questioned my ability to buy and maintain this home at first. Lori, my lover, and other people close to me, spent a great deal of time encouraging me to trust my instincts. As I continually make the decision to do the work, mistakes and all, I discover that my instincts are good.

When I was a renter, even buying curtains was stressful. It didn't seem prudent to invest any money or energy in anything that felt like it could be lost on someone else's whim. Just unpacking all my belongings felt too risky some years; getting attached enough to any space to change more than the curtains didn't seem possible. But once I knew this house would really be mine, I spent days looking at different colors, different combinations of color, fantasizing about the moment when I could begin painting the walls of my living room. Lori and I made preliminary trips to several home-improvement stores to price materials. We watched many hours of home and garden programs on cable. I shopped for colors and tested combinations. By the time I closed on the house, I had a list of cosmetic changes that I was eager to make.

I spent my first night after closing on the living-room floor, on an air mattress with Lori. The house was completely empty, and I felt on the verge of a great adventure. I was so excited I could barely sleep. In the morning, the contractor arrived to sand and refinish the floors. Now *that* is an expense I will never regret. For months I walked around my house, savoring the glow of those floors, the honey color of the wood, the clarity of the finish. By the end of that first day I had already spent $400 on materials for painting supplies, gardening supplies, and basic home-maintenance tools. I was excited not just about getting started on the work to be done, but about the fact that I felt capable of it!

My first week was spent putting in a bed of wildflowers, cleaning the house, and painting the kitchen and living room. Lori and other friends would stop by in the evenings to help, but I spent the days there alone, adjusting to the new feeling of home ownership. The living room is perfect now: bright white walls, except for the feature wall, which is the most beautiful shade of blue that I have ever seen. Cool Bluette is the name of the color, and it makes the whole room glow with the most peaceful light. My favorite thing to do is to come home and watch the light change in my living room as the sun sets or to open all the soft, white, gauzy curtains on a Sunday afternoon and watch the light fill the room, and feel my spirits lift with the growing brightness of the walls. Feeling this inspired by my home is a constant reminder of how much I have grown in the last few years. I am always amazed to have a home that I look forward to returning to, and a space that fills me with such hope and peace.

Since I was a child, I have had this fantasy of creating the perfect bedroom. I started two years ago, buying the furniture I wanted, one piece at a time. But this summer I finally got the colors I wanted. I painted my bedroom this June—pink and white. Actually, it's a lavender-pink, Lyrical Pink, and it changes with the light, so that any time of day it can look like a completely different color. I love it! And what I love the most about it is that it's mine.

Of course, no home is ever really finished. I have many "projects" to do around the house. The living room and kitchen I painted before I even moved in, but I just didn't have enough time to paint all the rooms at once. This summer I gave the bedroom a face-lift. Now I am reminded every morning of the fact that I have really made myself a home here, and I find such joy in that.

Perhaps in the spring I will redecorate the bathroom. It has a lovely black tile floor, and the walls will be the same luminous white as the living room, with black stencils of dancing women. I'm not in any hurry, because I want it to be perfect. That's one of the things I love about owning a house, even as I find it unsettling: the idea that I can take as long as I want to fix something, because I'm not going anywhere. It's comforting and yet frightening at the same time. But as frightening as it is, I enjoy the knowledge that I finally have control over my home and how my home makes me feel.

One of the great ironies of my life has become very clear to me since I settled into my sweet little home. I have always believed that if I could just find a home of my own, I could finally begin to heal from the abuses of my earlier years. But it was the process of deciding to take charge of the desire to make a home, the searching for and purchasing of the house, and the process of both physically and emotionally claiming my little house that have ultimately enabled me to truly heal.

I've been living here over a year now. Normally, I would already have looked around to see if there was a better apartment to move into, or made a dreaded yet necessary move, packing, unpacking, adjusting to new surroundings. I sort of miss the process, even though I hated it. So instead, I painted the bedroom and hired painters for the exterior of the house—change and stability all at once. I think this stability is something I can really adjust to.

– 13 –

A Woman's Place

Anne Mamary

On the day I moved in, my mother and I climbed into my new house through the dining-room window. With friends outside waiting to unload a rented truck and the person sworn to deliver the key nowhere to be found, we made use of the worn cement steps that might once have led to a kitchen door, a room long since demolished. No one, not even people with neighborhood memories dating to the 1940s, seems to remember when the steps stopped leading to a door or onto what that door might have opened. Whatever their forgotten purpose, those steps were welcomed on a sticky August day, as we coaxed the swollen storm window from its frame, nudged the window up, and clambered into the house through the window—a window that revealed itself to be an excellent spot for cat conversations, one beast moaning outside, as only cats can moan, and one in, as well as for feline entrances and exits when doors are simply at the wrong place.

No husband carried me across the threshold into the red brick house. I moved with a lanky black cat and piles of books into my early-nineteenth-century house in a little North Country town for a teaching job at a small undergraduate college. It was my work that led me to the house, and the work of women before me that made it possible for me to buy a house in my own name and to live there alone. It was also my work, the ways in which I refused patriarchal thinking and being, which, in the end, made it impossible for me to afford to stay in my house. For although banks and neighbors were long past judgment at a single woman buying and living in a house—a house that fits me as perfectly as any structure of brick, tin, wood, and glass can fit a person—the college, one of patriarchy's dashing sons, expected to carry me across the threshold, expected wifely loyalty in thought, word, and deed in return.

Colleges, institutions in patriarchal systems, still operate on the model that faculty have wives at home doing the invisible work that allows the faculty member to appear the "independent" scholar. At school, secretaries, cleaning, maintenance, and bookstore staff work, often literally or figuratively invisibly, to support the work of the academic. Faculty are freed, then, to teach, write, and study as if this work happened on its own, the faculty member not hampered by the "tedious" chores of everyday life. At home, wives also work, often unsung, to "free" the faculty member for academic pursuits. This model relies on wives' loyalty, not only to particular men but to the values of the larger university and patriarchal systems.

Mrs. Huddleston lived for forty years in my house; or rather, I lived for three years in her house after I bought it from the Flemmings, who bought it from Mrs. Huddleston some years after her husband's death. Mrs. Huddleston and her son came to visit Don and Betty Peckham, my neighbors, their neighbors, the second summer I was in the house. Betty brought them over to meet me and to see the house. The son, then fifty-five, moved with his parents into the house when he was a boy of five. He recalled summer nights half a century ago, sleeping on the screened porch, gray floor cool. Upstairs we stopped to talk in my study. Its ceiling slanting cozily over my desk, the room has an oak floor that shines in the morning sunlight. Across the hall, my bedroom, running the full width of the house, is brightest in the afternoon. With windows at floor level, the bedroom offers a drowsy cat warm pools of light. On cooler days the cat might slip across the hall to another small room, to dream under the twin bed's blue comforter.

Betty, the Huddlestons, and I looked out the study window, out of the original brick two-story house, over the old tin roof on the one-story addition. The tin roof is of the oldest style, metal folded and crimped over joints so that nail holes are not exposed to rain, ice, and snow. Roofers have told me it may well be seventy years old or more. I pulled out a photograph of my father standing next to me in front of the house, next to the For Sale sign, and gave it to Mrs. Huddleston as a reminder of her house and the one who would look after it. Later I would send her a jar of currant jelly to remind her of the vigorous currant bushes we could see from the study window. Looking out across the tin, we could also see Mr. Huddleston's anemometer, a curious weather vane of an apparatus, small metal cups spinning in the June breeze. In the kitchen is a display, attached to the instrument, that tells indoor and outdoor temperature, wind speed and direction, and atmospheric pressure.

Mr. Huddleston was not a professor; she was not a faculty wife. He was an agricultural expert for the cooperative extension and made things grow in the backyard gardens. She raised children, kept house, processed and preserved the garden's offerings, and taught home economics. The floor-to-ceiling yellow pine cabinets in the dining room are still known as Mrs. Huddleston's sewing wall to longtime town residents. The thread closet dwarfed my tiny collection of, say, thirty spools, with its capacity for more than ten times as many. What a kaleidoscope of colored strands she must have tended.

Like the sewing wall, the kitchen cabinets still remind me that this was Mrs. Huddleston's room. Mr. Huddleston built them of the same golden pine he used for the sewing wall and, it seems, exactly to her specifications. She was shorter than I am, her countertops reminded me, when I stooped, shoulders tightening, lower back clenched, to roll piecrusts or put up currant jelly, steaming from the old electric stove. Some of the lower cupboards have doors that look like they would swing open just as expected; but they surprised me, as I pulled on their handles, when they rolled out deep, long drawers with bins for sacks of flour and slender shelves perfectly crafted to hold cookie tins. Two tiny Alice-(that is Mrs. Huddleston's first name, too)-in-Wonderland cupboards are perfect for boxes of tea or tins of cocoa. And some of the kitchen's cabinets have not offered up their intended purpose, their loyalty to their first mistress preserved.

When I write that husbands carried wives across the thresholds of their houses or that the university demands a wifelike loyalty of its women faculty members, I am not overlooking the actual lives and contributions of wives. The women who lived in my house and the neighboring women were not chained in their homes; their lives are and were not ones of cartoonish abject drudgery and servitude, although they certainly did their share of hard and tedious work. But their work and lives (and those lives included creativity, skill, and connection, friendship and nurturance with and from other women) allowed their husbands to go off to work, some at the university and some at other places, to appear (and, often, actually) to make "important" contributions, and to return home to clean houses, cared-for children, supper on the table, and loving support.

Feminists in the academy have helped to acknowledge the important work of women in their own homes, recognizing that care for a home and for children and other adults, sometimes along with paid employment, and sometimes not, is valuable, is difficult, is skilled—is work. In philosophy, the discipline in which I do my academic work, feminist ethicists have critiqued concepts of "justice" and "individual rights" for their hegemonic masculine assumptions and roots in Western masculine experience. Women, some feminist thinkers have argued, often frame ethical thinking through a lens of connection and care—frameworks with roots in feminine experience. It is important and humanizing to recognize care and affection, to acknowledge familiar and intimate relationships between and among people, for, in patriarchy, such relationships are pushed away, muted, devalued. According to the rules of hegemonic masculinity, men *are* their jobs, like Mr. Huddleston was an agricultural expert and others are college professors. Women may do many things, some for pay, but, in hegemonic patriarchy, they are more defined by their relationships to other people.

January 8, 1998. The North Country awoke to the crack of tree branches snapping under the weight of several days' freezing rain. Whole trunks toppled in the night, dragging power lines down with them across roads, onto the roofs of houses. Trees snapped like carrot sticks; the entire power grid did too. My alarm clock stopped at 6:20 a.m.; so did the furnace. In the country, people might have had woodstoves for warmth, but electric pumps no longer carried water into houses and milking machines couldn't pump milk from dairy herds. Many farmers lost hundreds of animals in the days after the power went off.

By some miracle, the phone lines were unaffected, although the windowless grocery stores, relying on electric light and cash registers, dispatched employees with flashlights and battery-powered calculators to help people find candles, batteries, and food that didn't require cooking. I ventured to the store the first afternoon without electricity for paper plates and sauce. My neighbors, Ginny and Steve Cohen, had an older gas stove without an electric pilot, and they put on a spaghetti supper for anyone who cared to brave icy roads and sidewalks. Ginny, out walking three of her many dogs, brought me a plant and warm wishes the first week I lived in my house. She and Steve showed that same generosity of spirit on a cold January evening when the setting sun did not herald rising street lamps and warmly lit windows.

The next morning, Nancy called early, and I ran downstairs from my knotty-pine floored bedroom, through the chilly house to answer the old rotary phone in the kitchen. Without electricity, cordless phones are just plastic.

"There's hot water and coffee on the gas stove, and we need help eating frozen waffles that are quickly thawing," she beckoned. Every morning for the eight days we were without power, Nancy's voice on the phone called me out, called the Flemmings out, and we drank from steaming mugs to warm up during the day. Later in the week, the three longtime friends cooked vats of orange marmalade from the box of Florida fruit that had arrived in the mail the week before. Tropical sweetness in a cold, icy winter.

After tea that second morning without power, I walked around the splintered town, scrambling to stay on my feet, the roads smooth as mirrors and the sky ladling out liquid ice. In the gray of the morning, the Chinese restaurant was the only business open on Main St. With their gas stoves, they were cooking food that would soon spoil, and piping-hot rice offered a perfect antidote to the weather. By the time I got home again, I'd snapped many photographs and my coat was covered in ice like plastic wrap. I'd forgotten I had no place to warm up. The Peckhams were on their front porch, drinking coffee cooked on a propane camp stove. They tried to drive out of town by the main road to catch a flight from the Syracuse airport and had been escorted all the way home by the state police, as driving was officially disallowed. I told them about a route out through the Adirondacks that someone else had just taken successfully. Off they went, while I went inside to my bed and all the blankets I could find.

The philosophers and psychologists who propose an ethics of care seek to recognize women's experiences and contributions in a patriarchal system dominated by a dualist view that codes men's lives public and women's private (and, therefore, perhaps not worthy of serious consideration). I think the care discussions are valuable, especially for their recognition of women's work. At the same time, pitting "men's justice" against "women's care" can reify the very system a focus on care calls into debate. Naming what women have achieved in patriarchy and how women have navigated patriarchy is important. It is more important still to do something about patriarchal structures on a more fundamental level. My commitments are to moving from describing women's experiences, women's reality in patriarchy—from describing and validating "what is"—to thinking and living a way out of patriarchy and its demands on women's lives and intellectual creativity.

Out the back door, the one leading from the kitchen past the steps to the basement and outside to the nineteenth-century carriage house-turned-garage, I entered the almost magical, creative world of gardens, cats, and neighbors. All around the house grow flowers and flowering bushes and trees. Nearest the driveway, in the full southern sun, columbine sends forth delicate ballerinas in mauves, purples, and rose each early summer. In fact, columbine seems scattered all over the neighborhood—the wild, uncultivated kind of columbine—growing from building foundations, compost piles, and popping up in the middle of the tomatoes. Moss rose in a splash of shades volunteers every year, and the antique rose bush offers a pink bouquet from spring until early December in the warmth of the southern sun and the protection of the house.

During the ice storm, I wanted more than ever to be close to the protection of my house. And I felt protective of it, too; not in the sense that I had to guard against intruders, but rather that we were going through the discomfort together. The cat also was confused, sitting on top of heat vents, cold metal against his soft belly. He burrowed under the blankets, making a pretty good space heater. People with hot-water heat drained their radiators and pipes to prevent them from freezing. When I went into the basement to check on the pipes, I discovered that it was surprisingly warm. The gas hot-water heater kept running throughout the storm, kept the basement, foundationed with thick stone slabs, warm enough to prevent frozen pipes. And every afternoon when I was chilled through, I took a long, hot bath, reading Brother Cadfael mysteries, in the bone-warming tub, under the bathroom's tin walls and ceiling. Ellis Peters' tales of a twelfth-century Welsh monk threw into even more vivid relief my dependence, my whole town's dependence, on electricity and our fragility without it.

Meg and Jeff, and their three boys, Dan, Pat, and Mike, had a night of games in front of their fireplace, inviting in neighbors who may not have known one another before the power went out. Steve Cohen and I played old tunes, him on the accordion and me on the violin, in the shelter mostly inhabited by senior citizens. Many sang, and some just listened, one woman snug on her mattress on the floor, her cat curled up in the crook of her knees. The best part of the ice storm, aside from the truly dark nights and the heavy full moon reflected in icy snow, was neighbors, friends, and strangers looking out for one another and doing things together. It was also comforting to hear Lamar's voice over the public radio station, broadcasting by generator. She played, "I Want a Woman with a Chainsaw," that Susan, herself handy with all sorts of saws, pulled from the station's collection.

Under the ice, between my house and Don and Betty Peckham's house to the north, is a shared summer perennial garden. The Huddlestons chose the bulbs for the side nearest the Peckham's, the side best seen from my kitchen and dining-room windows, and the Peckhams picked the bulbs for the side nearest my house but in their line of sight. It is especially splendid in late spring, after the daffodils and tulips have heralded winter's end with a dizzying array of colors, for then the world is awash in purples. While lilacs, in plum, white, and palest orchid, sweeten the air, the perennial garden, for a magical, golden week, blossoms purple with irises. Plum, lilac, grape, violet, amethyst, mauve, mulberry, hyacinth, lavender. Cool, mellow, regal, variegated purple. One of my deepest joys in my house is intimacy with its walls in a way I never felt close to apartment walls, and the cyclical pleasure of seasonal delights in the garden. Repetition, familiarity, anticipation, and still, every year, the surprise of newness.

One of my colleagues said to me that wherever I went I'd find friends; another house is out there for me too. We were talking about a friend of mine who had a dissertation-year fellowship at the college, and who had turned down the offer of a second year to move south to be with her boyfriend. I had to understand, stressed my colleague, that the friend in question was a young, heterosexual woman, and that her relationship was very important to her. Of course I understood; that idea is hardly new or unexpected. But I did not understand why I was to find a nutmeg of consolation in the idea that I'd find new friends, a new house, that I'd make it wherever I went.

One reading, of course, is that I am perceived as resourceful, independent, easily befriended. But I don't think of friends as easily interchangeable. Nor is this house, are these neighbors, blithely to be tossed aside when the winds of fate toss me, perceived as essentially unattached and solitary, to wherever they will blow next. But it is this house, 16 Church street, and these neighbors, this location within easy driving distance of my mother's home, of morris dancing with the Harridans, of which I am especially fond. I hadn't planned to buy a house when I moved north. But this house chose me, this particular house. I am very protective of my solitude in my house, of my time writing and growing plants in the large, bright bay window of winter afternoons at the piano when the low-slung light falls perfectly across the music. And I am very attached to my friends, particular individuals who cannot be replaced, even as new people come into my life. Somehow, though, these connections carry less weight than one person carried in the life of my friend leaving the college.

When I refuse to act the part of woman in patriarchy, some patriarchal women's "care" quickly evaporates. Quite apart from the fact that many women faculty members work a second shift at home—either cooking, cleaning, and caring for themselves, or doing those things both for themselves and for children and other adults—the academic world demands, in either blatant or subtle ways, that women be loyal to the ideology of white, heterosexual patriarchy. In other words, it requires a sort of wifely subordination of a woman's own thoughts, goals, and desires to those of the white and male academic world. Even women who call themselves feminists often demand of themselves and other women a kind of "loving support" of individual male colleagues, male students, and hegemonic male academic discourse, ideology, and commitments. This is not surprising, for it reflects the white patriarchal order of things, an order as familiar and accepted to many as the air we breath. But I do not accept it; it is painfully familiar, but not the stuff of life for me.

I delight in caring for flowers, in sharing their beauty with my neighbors. When Don had hip-replacement surgery and couldn't bend to reach brown earth, I missed his calm presence and went calling with coffee cake, streaked purple with juicy July black raspberries. At my job at the college two women colleagues and I recognized a campus culture that kept women students from reaching to their own voices. And so we began, under the auspices of the college's program for new students, a residential and academic experience for women only. Our hope was that we could facilitate multicultural feminist transformations, that we could work toward women connecting across differences of race, sexuality, ethnicity, class, and ability; that we could work toward blossoms rarely seen on campus.

For all of our students, our work was about fostering students' senses of themselves as creative, smart, funny, intellectual, embodied women, not in relation to protecting, nurturing, comforting, or trying to impress men. For the students from dominant groups, by race, sexuality, ethnicity, and class in a variety of combinations, our work was about recognizing the double-edged results of connections to men of those dominant groups. That is, we hoped to illuminate how privileged women's privilege comes from acting in complicity with the rules of the privileged culture, oftentimes to the detriment of women and men from marginalized groups. Like gardening, the work is both difficult and rewarding, leaving all involved changed in the end.

When I center women's lives, women's own lives, clearing the air, trying to breath freely, women and men with patriarchal loyalties lose their footing, feel faint, lash out. Some women rush to defend their own particular men, as if my attempts to live with women in the center negate their lives. Perhaps there is a grain of truth to that fear. I hope that I do not judge women's personal choices; I do reject confinement to cages of least resistance. Maybe the simple example of my life, with my cat, plants, and books, alone in my house, surrounded by friends, shines a light on some loss for some women who see themselves reflected primarily in their care for individual men, or in their care for the collective history of men.

Some gay men, who, like other men, define themselves as "not women" cannot stand the reality of a woman who is not, primarily, their buddy, confidant, or comrade in arms. As it does to gay men, hegemonic masculinity, in varying and painful ways, excludes men of color, working-class men, Jewish men, and a host of men marginalized by conviction or birth from the ruling class. For all too many men, whether privileged or marginalized, resisting such exclusions takes the form of trying to gain full access to hegemonic male privilege. For many, the very idea of patriarchal prerogative is not the issue; access to it is. And, sadly, some women with either male or female life partners fear that their relative comfort as token "others" is made less comfortable by a woman not seeking token status, not seeking another adult to share her house, not banging on the big door and hoping to slip in.

When "care" evaporates or is selectively withheld, I am confronted, again, with the double-edged realities of privileged women caring for privileged men and children. If such a woman puts her own life first, or if she puts women of color or lesbians or poor women in the center of her commitments, she may well lose the financial or emotional support of an individual man, with potentially devastating consequences. But history has shown that white, affluent women have "cared for" men of their station to the direct detriment of women of color, some of whom may have been employed to "care for" the children and/or houses of the privileged family. And some heterosexual women have "cared for" their husbands and their own limited visions to the erasure of lesbian existence. In some forms, women's care can lead to the maintenance of patriarchy and of racism.

Many of the students who participated in our women-only living/learning experience learned that lesson too. Many of them hope for fundamental shifts in the game rather than for admission on equal terms; they carry the connections and shifts in consciousness with them even now, on the eve of their college graduations. As my friend Mary says, they are like grenades scattered across the campus ready to explode lies of gender and race. I am exceedingly proud of them as they navigate through the sometimes hostile realities of life on their campus. I know, with sadness, that our multicultural feminist work can't protect them from rape or the nearly invisible racist, heterosexual patriarchal haze permeating academic life. When one white woman spoke out about the white fraternity brother who raped her, she ran, crash, into a wall of institutional silencing. When another white woman, set up by her black boyfriend for rape by another man, decided to speak out, the wall was not quite as strong. The perpetrators were banned from campus for the last few weeks of their senior year, until graduation took them from campus and out of the college's concern.

Of course all young campus men who rape should be punished for their violence. The fact of unequal punishment shows how racism is alive and well and how white male institutions can still use the myth of "protection" of white women to brutalize black men. Although the two men in this case were not harmed and were, in fact, protected quite well, their white counterpart was protected utterly. The white woman who tried to name his crime was forced to attend classes with him and to see him on campus every day. There is no reward for white women who don't protect white men.

The white woman who, betrayed by her own lover, made the difficult decision to come forward was offered a modicum of protection. But I don't believe it was offered based on a shift in the college's interests between the first rape discussed and hers. Instead, the men's punishment reflected, I think, the college's view of the woman as its metaphorical maiden daughter, violated by only provisionally accepted black men. Her "victory," no matter how small, was really no victory at all. She was never a priority, valued for herself, in the college's scheme of things.

Between my house and the Halls' house, to the south, was an old mossy maple tree. It came down one July night when a thunderstorm shrieked through town, in ten minutes yanking trees from the ground by the roots as if they were no more abiding than beets. Amelia, the ten-year-old across the street, lost her box elder—her reliable old swing, a round of wood on the end of a rope hung from that tree, and its limbs ferried her from the ground to the porch roof—in those ten minutes. Amelia's mom, Elisabeth, and I were glad no one was hurt and marveled at the fact that I'd gone to the store for cat food in the moments before the storm and returned home to find the maple felled where not only my car had been but also the cars of my mother and friends, Meredith and Kristin, who had just left after a weekend visit. Amelia and I mourned the passing of our leafy friends.

In the days after the trees toppled, Amelia's father, Peter, and his friend cut up the trunk with chainsaws. I wasn't home when the village came around to haul off brush, so Don and Betty, Peter and Elisabeth, Nancy, and Beth and Craig from down the street quickly dragged branches and limbs from my driveway to the curb. The next day, Susan came by, and we loaded sections from the trunk into her truck—solid maple for the woodstove. Don and Betty claimed several sections for campfire seating, and John took care of the sections Susan couldn't use. Neighborly care.

Our students, fifty young women of a remarkable (on this campus) variety of backgrounds and experiences, faced harassment all over campus, but especially from the all-male fraternity next door. Those men themselves chose a single-sex living environment; they courted young women in single-sex sororities. They also recognized that our students were up to something different. Our students' living together was about putting their own lives first; it was about women learning, with much effort, how to value differences of all sorts and to understand structures of privilege and oppression that work against women's alliances and friendships. The furious, sustained strength of the young men's reaction pointed to the power of those brave, smart, strong, tender young women's lives.

When a woman faculty member teaches, writes, or interacts with colleagues in ways that seek to open nonpatriarchal ways of thinking, teaching, or interacting, her position on the faculty may be threatened, especially if she is not tenured. Although charges of "essentialism" are often leveled at such women, those accusations are often a silencing strategy. The real issue is often that the woman in question is not playing the expected part of "caring" woman. That is, even with advanced degrees, publications, and teaching credentials, women are expected to be the intellectual (if not physical and emotional) supporters of the ideas and frameworks of men. Arguing with and challenging those ideas still keeps the ideas central and attended to. Shifting attention to women-centered scholarship and teaching breaks the "caring" role and, in my case, made it impossible for me to be hired as a permanent member of the faculty.

I bought my house with money earned teaching three sections of summer school and with help from my parents. My initial appointment at the college was for three years, with the knowledge that after a fourth year (away) there would be a tenure-track line in gender studies. During my year away I lived in the small city where I grew up, close to my family and friends. It was a hopeful and restorative year. Then I went back to the college for an interview for the tenure-track position. Despite many positive comments about my lecturing skills, good teaching evaluations, and the support of many students and faculty on campus, the committee canceled the search after their first choice went elsewhere. The college did not pull the line. There was no other emergency making hiring someone impossible, except that the someone, like the women in our single-sex class and residence, offered too great a challenge to the gender order on campus. My biggest consolation is knowing that I, with colleagues and students, did work at the college so powerful and so important that it could not be allowed to continue.

During the summer after I was not hired, I spent several months living in my house, writing, gardening, visiting with friends. I discovered then, as I am discovering now, that my work in academia, the kinds of writing I'm required to teach, the patterns of thought I am obligated to unravel for students, has an effect on the kind of writing voice I can summon. It is not enough for women to have credit and houses and jobs in our own names. It is not enough to be admitted to the institutions that may once have excluded us on the existing terms of those institutions. I want more (and risk being called selfish, ungraceful, and unwomanly in my desire). A transformation of thought, a flowering of speech as riotous as early-summer apple blossoms on a tree so old no one remembers what sort of apples it bears—but an apple tree still, not a stick laden with picture-perfect fruit.

Wanting more, one risks the judgments of other women, who giggle, "women multitask; women are communal," even as they look puzzled after reading some of my ideas. The patterns don't fit; I am not enough like their picture of woman—excluded, then, from the giggling. What I want are words such as Nicole Brossard's when she writes,

> I am talking here about a certain angle of vision. To get there, I had to get up and move, in order that the opaque body of the patriarchy no longer obstruct my vision. Displaced, I am. And not like the girl who didn't quite make it but like someone they missed their shot on when they once had her in their sights for the bead of a rifle will never have at its disposal the powers of a mirror. This displacement gives rise to all others. (79)

It's a difficult task, this displacement. Students must have the language and the tools to navigate their academic lives. I am obligated to help them acquire those tools. Displacements make many students uncomfortable, the ground beneath their feet no longer solid, but slippery and ice-covered. Others already have a new angle of vision, and others hunger for it. It's not always easy, moving in hostile worlds;

trying to come back out, one finds oneself changed often in ways un-welcomed.

Neighbors, two older men, neither of whom I would have met at the college, talk with me in our gardens about the changes happening there daily. Don's garden and mine are a shared plot, the dividing line marked by a wooden post and the end of his neatness where my chaos begins. John has one large cultivated area in his backyard, and he purchased the vacant lot running the combined width of the Peckham's and my yards, replacing an abandoned rubbish pile with renewed life. Our three gardens are surrounded by a common fence against rabbits and other seedling nibblers. They are very different, Don and John, and we are all three different from one another. John grew up on a farm in Maine and has an enormous garden, which provides enough food for local food pantries in the summer and for Dotty, himself, and many neighbors. John spends hours gardening each day, after going to the office at five in the morning, teaching and working with students. He uses no black-plastic mulch, the way Don and I do, and controls weeds, as my grandfather did, with frequent cultivation.

Don is very encouraging, and he grows lovely produce, including mountains of rhubarb that make an appearance in his and Betty's famous punch at their annual Church Street picnic. When I found myself frustrated at not getting the garden in the shape I would have liked, he reminded me that he'd had many, many five-year plans in his years on our street, and that not one of them had been entirely finished. Both men have an obvious love of our private yet shared gardening worlds. Many children in the neighborhood have played among the cornstalks and eaten the sweet kernels outside in the glow of a late summer sun. Both men, in different ways, cared that I joined them in the garden, in watching the sky for rain after a long hot spell, in sharing whatever we grew and in simply being neighborly.

Anne and Catherine and I made pesto each summer, enough bright green paste, pungent with garlic, cheese, and strong basil pulled by the armload from the garden, to last the entire winter. When Meredith, Kristin, and my mother came to visit, we ate noodles robed in green. So simple and so satisfying. Meredith, my mother's college roommate, gave me some All-Clad cookware, a "house-cooling" present of sorts. She said that she had waited too long to give her own daughter, my lifelong friend Kristin, such "serious" cooking tools, thinking that she would wait for a wedding and the presumed need, then, for a daughter to possess serious kitchenware. But she recognized, she said, that we, Kristin and I, had need for such things now, for ourselves.

Although I don't see myself as having postponed marriage for a career, I did appreciate the sentiment nonetheless. My house, my writing, my work, my gardening, my dancing, my friendships—these are not temporary diversions until "the real thing" comes along. These are my life now, for myself. When I use the solid, lovely All-Clad, I think of my house, of Meredith, and am reminded of what is possible and of what remains to be done.

WORK CITED

Brossard, Nicole. *The Aerial Letter*. Trans. Marlene Wildeman. Toronto: Women's Press, 1988.

– 14 –

Reframing My Life

Mary Rose

Picture this. A woman wrapped in a blue robe, her blonde hair carelessly pulled back behind her ears. Two small boys, in red and blue pajama suits, who no doubt wakened early, for it is Christmas morning. The older child, aged three or four, has silvery blond hair, just as the woman had when she was young. The three of them sit together on the floor, and the woman reads to the children, the younger boy tucked in her lap, his brother distracted by a new collection of toy cars. A man, older than the woman and wearing a red-plaid robe, sits nearby in an oversized blue chair. On the table beside him are a mug of coffee and a plate of jule kage, Christmas bread that the woman made from his mother's recipe. A folded newspaper lies in his lap. A fire glows in the red brick fireplace and bookcases line the walls, full of books and beautiful objects that the man and the woman have collected together. The Christmas tree is decorated with brightly colored lights and ornaments, and in among the presents and the mounds of wrapping paper on the floor, you see the rusty reds and deep blues of an Oriental carpet. The young mother smiles as she meets the viewer's gaze.

The traditional gold frame dominates the image and demands too much attention for itself. The blue mat matches the blues in the lithograph, but the color confines the picture space. Step closer and you can see that the acid in the mat is starting to burn the fine rag printing paper, leaving a faint brown stain, the color of newspaper left too long out in the sun. The woman in the lithograph does not know, for how can she possibly know, that in twenty years she will come to understand that the artwork of her life has the wrong frame. She will leave the man who sits in the blue chair, and the house, with its double

261

lot at the edge of the city and its garden to which she devotes so much of her time. She will move off the hill, from where she now looks down and sees the city lights, down onto a city street, where there are sidewalks and a corner grocery and long, narrow lots, and the only reason for a double lot is because the house next door burned down.

1991

On the first night in my house, I was just settling into bed when two friends arrived with a bottle of champagne, and we drank a toast to my new life. "Now don't you wish you'd done this years ago?" one of them asked. "No," I answered. "This is just the right moment for me. The frame fits."

Enter my house and you may still find the ghosts of Chester and Emily Larrabee, who built the house and moved in as newlyweds in 1892. In this once prosperous neighborhood, now among the poorest in the city, the Larrabees lived in fashionable elegance, with oak moldings and pocket doors and a pair of carved griffins guarding the oak sideboard in the dining room. One day a man knocked on my front door and told me that Emily was his grandmother and he has memories of playing secret games with his cousins in the cupboard under the stairs. Helen Larrabee lived in this house all her life, and I bought the house from her estate. The house accommodates both my living and my working, but my working takes the lion's share. The spaces that the Larrabees filled with seven children I have filled with miter saws and molding samples. The master bedroom has become my workroom, furnished with tables, banks of drawers, and shelves and bins for storage. My upstairs office, with its tiled fireplace and maple mantle, was once a cozy sitting room. Children slept in attic bedrooms, from where they could call down to their mother in the kitchen through a hollow tubing in the wall. Now the tube holds wires that connect with fixtures lighting up an attic storeroom, where I keep my inventory of antique picture frames. Downstairs in the front parlor, where the Larrabees entertained their company, I entertain my clients. When I take customers up to the attic to look at merchandise, we pass by my frame collection, empty frames hanging on the wall of the oak stairway.

My framing business has always been homework. I began it in the basement, when the boys were young. I remember how they sat on the red-carpeted basement stairs when they came home from school and told me about their day. Back then I did not look upon my work as a career. I let my husband frame my life. My business was a second income, a glorified hobby, which paid for vacations and trips abroad. It was confined to the edges of the house and the edges of the marriage. My shop furniture was custom-built for the basement space, made so it could be disassembled and moved when my academic husband advanced in his profession.

My basement business has come upstairs into a workroom full of light. While the afternoon sun pours through three windows that overlook the street, I am reframing the lithograph of the family scene, just as I am reframing my life. Lying on the table, out of its blue mat and gold frame, see how the image spills out into its aesthetic space. See how the buckling paper relaxes, as I cut away the border of masking tape, which has fixed the print to the mounting board. Paper needs room to expand as it absorbs the moisture in the air around it. When I put it in its new mat, I will take care to hinge the print at the top of the paper only, so it can hang freely. The mat will be made from neutral materials and a neutral color. I will select a frame that is strong enough to protect the mat and the artwork, and which complements the image, perhaps one from my antique inventory. The best framing, I always tell my clients, is framing that respects the artwork and lets the image speak for itself.

1992

The ephemera on my refrigerator door betrays my heart: a Margaret Atwood poem ("Men and their mournful romanticisms, that can't get the dishes done. . . ."); an English landscape painting by David Hockney; a cartoon from *The New Yorker* ("Wait! Come back! I was just kidding about wanting to be happy."). There are postcards a good friend sent from Germany, photos of my dog, an obituary of a favorite poet. But what catches your eye is a photograph of the artist Matuschka titled "Beauty Out of Damage," her white dress cut away to reveal the place where her breast used to be. My experience with breast cancer was a powerful survival test of my solitary life, a test that I passed, but only with the considerable comfort of family—sons, brother, cousins—and the daily attention that I received from friends. Their remarkable support helped me find the strength to make difficult choices. As Audre Lorde writes in *The Cancer Journals:* "To this day, sometimes I feel like a corporate effort, the love and concern of so many women having been invested in me with such open-heartedness." A friend accompanied me on visits to doctors, took notes, and sat with me as I panicked under the bone-scan machine. Another drove me hundreds of miles to a consultation in Philadelphia. A third was waiting by my bed when I came back from the recovery room. "Want to see the scar?" I asked, taking her aback. My neighbor took care of my dog, and my older son stayed with me when I returned home. When I finally had enough of the telephone that never stopped ringing and the get-well cards that multiplied on the mantle, I called my Canadian cousin at her Muskoka cottage and told her I was coming to visit. I put the dog in the car and drove six hours, slept the whole of the following day, and let my cousin take care of me. I learned to ask friends for help. Others helped without my asking, like the women who got together and gave me three months of house-cleaning services. Inside the new frame of my life, I managed my illness on my own authority. Back in the house on the hill, I slept in the spare room whenever I was sick. I slept in the spare room whenever my husband was sick. This time I was in my own room, and I even got breakfast in bed.

1993

"Do you live in that big house all by yourself?" he asks, stopping to watch me weed the daylilies that edge my front walk. "Sort of," I tell him, a neighbor boy who knows only cramped apartment living in one of the big old houses on the street. Even I sometimes find it hard to believe that I am the sole proprietor of a house with fourteen rooms, not counting the basement and the attic, with thirty windows, two staircases, three fireplaces, and porches front and back. Whatever compelled me to possess this queenly Queen Anne, who sometimes seems to possess me with her constant demands for attention?

When people come to my house for the first time, they are captivated by the way the ample spaces flow from room to room through wide oak-framed doorways. They marvel at the narrowly tapered spindles on the stairway railing, the carved leaves and flowers on the mantle in the sitting room, the way there is hardly a square corner in the whole downstairs. Even if I live here for ten years, I will still be giving guided tours.

My house has been a group project from the beginning. Before I moved in, friends helped me take layers of old wallpaper off the walls in the downstairs parlors. In the spring friends came with trowels and shovels and perennials from their gardens, and together we resurrected Helen Larrabee's flower bed. Now the city is helping me with $20,000 in loans and grants, and I have employed electricians and plumbers. Plasterers walk around on metal stilts repairing sagging ceilings, and I am getting a new furnace and insulation in the walls. A builder is remodeling the kitchen and replacing the rotting stairs on the back porch. On the wall of the garden house, I am trying out the five period colors that I will use to paint the outside of this "painted lady" next summer.

I live on the kind of street where passersby offer to dig out my snowbound car and won't refuse the cash. I leave my deposit bottles at the curb for an elderly Vietnamese woman, who comes by with her shopping cart on trash days. My neighbor mows my lawn to supplement his night-shift job, and the men who sit out all day on the porch at #13 across the street keep a watchful eye on my property.

My lifestyle has an openness and informality that it never had during my marriage. My old way of entertaining, the one that I learned from my mother's example in the 1950s, left me alone in the kitchen while my husband played host to guests over drinks in the living room. I was always on the edges of our dinner parties, on the periphery of conversation. Now my guests are in the kitchen, and I am inside the frame. My entertaining, large or small, is a group effort, and preparing the meal is part of the entertainment.

1995

Four women are walking together in the woods. Their five dogs disappear into the thicket and reappear at the edge of the lake, which is just icing over, and then race off again. There is a dusting of snow on the ground and a pileated woodpecker high up in a tree above the path, his tap-tap echoing across the water. It is a sunny Thanksgiving Day morning, and three of the women have made arrangements to have dinner with friends or family. The fourth, whom you may recognize, looks forward to a solitary afternoon, with a long hot bath in her old-fashioned cast-iron bathtub and then a nap, afterwhich she will settle down to writing.

As the woman confronts the loneliness in her solitary life, holidays have been the biggest challenge. The traditions that filled her home-maker years, Thanksgiving dinners of turkey and cranberry sauce, roast beef and Yorkshire pudding on Christmas Day, were thrown into confusion when she moved out of the house on the hill. In her new life she has had to find new ways to frame the holidays.

Her two sons took years to feel comfortable in their mother's house. Familiar furniture in unfamiliar surroundings was a constant reminder that the definition of their family had forever changed. "Home" for them meant the house where their father lived, and at their mother's house they felt like visitors. They never wanted the picture of the Christmas family scene to change.

As the woman lingers behind her friends to watch the woodpecker at work, she remembers the first Christmas that she spent alone. On Christmas Eve, which is her birthday, she made an elaborate roast beef dinner for her two sons. Delayed by a shopping trip with their father, they came late, not dressed for the formal occasion that the woman had envisioned, and she was hurt and angry. At the end of a tearful argument, the older son surprised her with a birthday present that he had been patiently holding behind his back: three beautiful long-stemmed roses.

A dear friend once told the woman that the best cure for loneliness is solitude, and time has proved the truth of that. But she surprised even herself today, when she suggested that her sons have Thanksgiving dinner with their father so that she could celebrate the day alone.

1996

The setting is the garden. The occasion is the garden tour. It's a picture-perfect day. Some visitors are drinking lemonade on the patio, while others walk slowly around the garden, notebooks in hand, for they are eager gardeners all, and they have come to find inspiration for their own gardens. In the sunny perennial border, repeating clumps of pale blue irises and yellow evening primroses appear behind an edging of wispy coralbells and mounds of white candytuft. In the shady garden, under the pussy willow tree, pink and white *astilbe* consort with deeper pink foxgloves and pale lavender *Phlox divaricata*. Above the wall at the back of the garden, early yellow daylilies are blooming, while below them in the vegetable garden grow the familiar dark green leaves and red stalks of rhubarb plants and new plantings of parsley and sweet basil. Everywhere there are roses, a semicircle of *Rosa bonica* along the edge of the patio, low-growing fairy roses in the perennial border, and pale pink blossoms cascading over the latticework fence that frames the garden.

Helen Larrabee would be pleased, for the star of the show is her old-fashioned climbing rose, towering ten feet high inside its modern wrought-iron trellis, and covered with masses of single deep pink flowers with yellow centers. The pink and white peonies, with fragrance that can fill a room, are in pictures that I have from the 1950s, when Helen's garden was in its prime. In early spring hundreds of pale lavender naturalized crocuses appear in wide circles around the yard, shadow gardens of the gardens that Helen planted and then abandoned when she could no longer manage all the work.

My garden was what I most hated to leave when I divorced. It was my territory, where I was left to make decisions without argument. I could move my plants around as often as I wished each season, always striving for the perfect arrangement, and no voice told me that I was being irrational or wasting my time, as happened so often in the other rooms of my life. Sometimes in the early spring I go back into the woods behind that house, when nobody is home, and I pick large bunches of narcissus blooms, majestic creamy white Mount Hoods, and tiny white and yellow Cheerfulness, just the way I imagined that I always would. My labors for the past six years have been to reproduce the beauty of that garden here. The gardens are not the same, for my old one was shaded by massive oak trees, and here the sun makes everything grow ten times as fast, making ten times the work; or perhaps I just feel that way, because I am no longer the young mother who tended that other garden.

In winter, downy woodpeckers eat suet from the feeder outside my kitchen window, and cardinals, brilliant red against the snow, come looking for sunflower seeds. In the springtime Baltimore orioles, indigo buntings, and common yellowthroats are backyard visitors. My neighbors in the apartment house behind me hang their washing out all year long, their white sheets blowing in the winter wind, but I keep that luxury for warmer weather. All summer I enjoy solitary breakfasts at my table under the willow tree. I could never be without a garden and the peaceful solitude it offers up. It is my sanctuary, a thousand miles away from the ugly side of the street.

1997

They just up and left. Only the animals stayed behind, the keeshonds and the scrawny, limping, tan-colored cat. Sue and Billy were living across the street at #11, watching Barbara's kids while she was in jail. Barbara's father took care of the bills, and Sue did errands for him, feeding her drug habit at a crack house in the next block. One day Sue and Billy dropped the kids off at their grandfather's, stole his ATM card, took $4,400 out of his bank account, and no one has seen them since.

Barbara grew up on the street. She married Hank and had five kids before the age of thirty. Hank beat her and was irresponsible around the house, and she threw him out. Once she told me how, when she was young, her family used to rent a cottage in the summertime on a lake across the Pennsylvania border, and how someday she would like to do the same thing for her kids. Barbara has black hair and a round face and tattoos on the pale skin of her upper arms. She has been dealing drugs for twelve years.

It wasn't easy for the police to get solid evidence on Barbara. She was selective in her clientele, and she didn't keep the drugs in her house. I felt sorry for her kids, with their "Dare-to-Keep-Off-Drugs" T-shirts, when the news of their mom's arrest was in the paper. The judge sent her up north for six months of rehab. It turned out that Barbara was part of a major drug ring, led by Dominicans from New York City. In a massive drug sweep called Operation Golden Road, Barbara got six federal indictments. Her friends Ann and Cindy were arrested as well, all of them white women, single mothers with young children, who lived in the neighborhood, whose kids go to the Neighborhood Watch Christmas parties.

Cindy's apartment was shut up with her dogs inside for two weeks before Billy got in to clear it out. He piled up all her stuff in his front yard across the street from me, and set up a permanent yard sale. "Operation Golden Road has been good to me," Billy told the city code officer, who came in answer to neighbors' complaints. His two keeshonds and Barbara's dog, Blackie, ran loose twenty-four hours a day, intimidating people on the sidewalk and keeping the neighbors awake at night. Billy explained that the dogs had fleas. "I don't want no fleas in my house," he bellowed. The neighbors signed a petition to get the dogs picked up, and when Billy didn't show up at the hearing, the dog warden had Blackie put down. Billy sent a tearful child of Barbara's over to knock at my door. "You killed my dog," he said, while Billy watched from the curb across the street.

The mess in Billy's yard grew exponentially, and finally the police put out a warrant for his arrest. That was when Sue and Billy disappeared.

"I can't believe what they did to my house," Barbara said, when she came home on parole. The code officer wouldn't let her move back in until she cleaned up the place. I saw her over there every day, hauling old bikes and mowers and wrecked furniture out of the backyard and putting mounds of garbage bags out on trash days.

Now Barbara has a steady job. She told me that when she goes to work at five in the morning, she sees drug dealers going down the driveway of #22, and she doesn't like her kids out so early on their paper routes, when the dealers are out. She used to deliver back there, she said, and she isn't talking about newspapers.

1998

"Whereever are you calling from?" I said, groping for the light switch. "It's 12:30 at night."

"Oh, I'm terribly sorry," a man's voice answered. "I've seen an antique frame on your Web site that I want to buy. I'm calling from China."

I have 500 visitors a month at my new place of business. I learned the rudiments of HTML and Photoshop, and now I hardly ever have to leave my house to sell my merchandise. I photograph the frames with my digital camera in my attic darkroom, and I play with the images on my computer screen, cropping and adjusting colors. Then I e-mail the images to clients or post them on my Web site.

I have been selling antiques frames for several years. I wrote an article about picture frames for photographs, which appeared in a national magazine, and it brought me private clients from across the country. Two or three times a year I load frames into the back of my Toyota wagon and drive to New York City, where I sell to prestigious Manhattan frame dealers, setting up my display on the sidewalk for them to see. But it was my Web site that allowed me to shut down my custom framing business after twenty years and specialize in selling antique frames.

When clients walk through my virtual door, I don't have to be presentable, and my hours are completely flexible. Sitting in my upstairs office, "You have new mail" pops up on the computer screen. It's an old client wanting a frame or a note of thanks for a frame just arrived or a new visitor seeking information. People tell me that they like my Web site, because it is easy to move around in, and they learn a lot about frames when they visit. On my home page I have a photograph of a man selling picture frames. It was taken 125 years ago, when the frames were new, and the man worked in Endicott, a town just west of here.

1999

When Zeke and I walked in my neighborhood, people moved to the other side of the street. When we met the crossing guard down on the corner of Main St., he asked, "Are you walking that dog, or is he walking you?" Little kids wanted to pet him. "Does that dog bite?" they asked. When we went to the park, people stopped and said, "What a beautiful dog."

Zeke was a Chesapeake Bay retriever, with short, curly, auburn-colored fur. At ninety pounds, he was large for his breed. He looked especially handsome in the autumn, when his coat blended with the turning leaves. A friend told me that the two of us looked like a picture out of *Country Life*. Zeke was a lively three-year-old when I adopted him, toward the end of my marriage. It was an important gesture of independence for me. Dogs had not been "allowed" in our household. Too impractical, my practical husband thought. Zeke had a dominating nature, and the vet advised me to have him neutered. "Just like what you do to all your men," my husband said.

I could not have moved into this neighborhood without having Zeke for security, or lived alone so contentedly without his companionship. I called out to him when I came home; it was a good way to break the silence. When I read or watched TV in the evenings, Zeke would curl up on the floor at my feet. He always came with me to answer a knock at the door, and he had a formidable bark. I never felt nervous walking in the neighborhood or hiking in the woods with Zeke at my side.

This year we traded roles, and I took care of him. As his arthritis grew worse, our walks around the block slowed. Zeke would pause frequently and look around, taking in the smells, resting his tired legs. When my neighbor around the corner, the youngest in a large Hispanic family, passed us on his way to school, he would ask, "How old is that dog?" Zeke had an audience until the day he died, at age fourteen. Friends helped to bury him in the garden, and I threw purple lilacs on his grave. It was a beautiful day to die, warm and sunny, one of the happiest and the saddest days of my life.

2000

You don't hear the gunshots. You don't hear the man yell, "I'm going to kill you, nigger." Only when daylight comes do you hear about the bullet hole on Carol's front porch and the marks on the driveway at #15, and the flattened tires. Five or six bullets in all. By the time the policemen got there, whoever it was had disappeared.

The following day, drinking coffee out on your front porch, you read about the second shooting. The gunman lives around the corner, and you look over and wonder which windows are his. It's the same gun, the paper says, and this time it was an accident, but reckless nonetheless. The bullet shattered the arm of his girlfriend, who lives at the other end of your street, and lodged in her abdomen. The picture shows a policeman holding up the weapon, a Chinese-made AK-47-style assault rifle.

In the daylight everything seems ordinary, with neighbors mowing their lawns, and painters working next door. A Vietnamese family bought the house, and the man arrives with egg rolls that his wife has made for you, in gratitude for your neighborly assistance. He was a POW in North Vietnam, he tells you in his halting English, and they moved on the street to be near their Vietnamese friends. Together you watch his son, whose English is fluent, skateboard with the neighbor kids from #11. It was their mother who made the first 911 call, she tells you, when you go across the street to talk about the shootings. She was getting ready for work, and her son was just about to start out on his paper route. "Get away from that door," she shouted, and pulled him back.

Your writing group meets that evening, and when they ring the bell you hustle them inside, shutting the door quickly against the fear. You have tea in your front parlor, which you have reclaimed for living now, with a sea grass rug and a couch, and a huge old carved chair, which you bought at auction. Then the four of you move to the table in the dining room to write together. The first topic is "Don't Park Here," and you write about the gunman who parked himself on your street.

Picture this. A feast of ham, cheeses, baskets of bread, platters of vegetables in colorful arrangements, and jule kage, Christmas bread made from an old Swedish recipe. Eggnog in a silver punch bowl at one end of the dining table, and opposite, a crock of hot mulled cider, with floating cinnamon sticks and orange slices. The walls of the room are covered with rich red-and-gold-patterned wallpaper, and the oak wood of the sideboard and the fireplace mantle glow in the candlelight. A crowd of people, young and old, stands around the table in animated conversation. Through a wide doorway you see another room, where there is a Christmas tree and people gathered by a piano singing carols. In the center of the composition, a woman is blowing out the candles on her birthday cake, and her two sons are standing beside her. She is sixty today, and she is giving the same Christmas Eve party that her mother gave for her when she was growing up.

The framer used museum quality materials to frame the lithograph, and the paper hangs freely from hinges at the top. This time she chose a wide cream-colored mat to give the composition ample breathing room. The antique frame is narrow, gilded, with a delicate beading on the inner edge, in the Federal style. Its soft gold color harmonizes well with the gold accents of the wallpaper and the candlelight in the picture.

WORK CITED

Lord, Audre. *The Cancer Journals*. San Francisco: Aunte Lute Books, 1997.

An &/or Peace Performance

H. Kassia Fleisher &/or Joe Amato

(BRIDE'S SIDE)	*(GROOM'S SIDE)*
Who wants to go first? **No you go first.** **No you go first.**	**You go first.** **No you go first.** **No you go first.**
"I say, I have no title (again)"	"(I love) collaborating with the enemy (I love)"
Here's what I have to say: my problem is not collaboration so much as heterosexual marriage. Or, heterosexual marriage as experienced by two people born during the second Eisenhower administration.	Beginning, as always, with some end in mind, to get over— poetry? exceptions grate against, disproving laws, utterances, whatever and without shopping around
What I have to say is that collaboration is supposed to be a groovy thing because it collapses our greedy little capitalist notions of authorship *Mine! But in a collaboration between men and women, the authorship of the woman is already collapsed swooning.*	A prose is a prose is a prose— We've filed our works & filled our days together many ways, or both ways and you want us 2 to work it *out?*

Text in bold addressed to each Other; Otherwise to the audience/reader.

Literary history says, *Well, he really rewrote that whole novel for her. Well, she really got most of those ideas from him. Well, I can't remember the name of the little book she wrote, but he's the greatest literary genius of the twentieth century!*

Jacquie Fox-Good says, "The death of the author roughly coincides with the birth of the female author."

A friend at a university press asked us recently whether a book on collaboration would be a good idea—and we yawned, silently, on cue. On the q.t., you should know that we collaborate, in part, by *not* collaborating. We eat together, yes, and our bodies have been known to enjoy roughly identical rhythms.

I'm sorry—did I interrupt you?

Were you saying something?

But I will not say here what I really have to say here. I said what I really have to say and read it to my husband-collaborator and he said, "Isn't it interesting that your piece is an attack on me, and my piece is completely self-deprecatory."

But *work—together?* Yes & no. However, we (he alleges) shall endeavor to create the illusion of same, if not the "peculiar illusion of collaboration" to which Elizabeth Hardwick once referred:

Carolyn Heilbrun says, "And above all other prohibitions, what has been forbidden to woman is anger, together with the open admission of the desire for power. . . ."

Virginia Woolf says that "very few women yet have written truthful autobiographies."

You pick up 1 side of the desk, I pick up the other. We decide who walks up the stairs backward, and who carries the brunt of the weight. Or we've done this before, and we migrate to our customary ends. The 2 of us lift the desk, and move it up the stairs.

And you'll note that now I'm quoting people, quite scholastically. This is what one does when one has a PhD and is not

But each of us needs to get a grip. So get a grip on it—we write for different ghosts, gravities, we hoist the same object encouraged to shout at the top of one's lungs. *This is really pissing me the fuck off!*

Say it with me now: To dialogue with Them, use Their Language.

[3 beats]

Nancy Miller says, The life of the female mind is "not coldly cerebral but impassioned."

I'll say.

Myra Jehlen says, A "female tradition" of autonomy is marred by "no tactual independence but action despite dependence."

I say, I am not a postfeminist. *I'm a postal feminist.*

The OED says that "husband" descends from housebond, from the Old Anglo Saxon. "Peasant owning his own house and land. The master of a house, the male head of household." Also, "housekeeper; one who manages his affairs with skill and thrift."

The OED says, The word "wife," means *woman*. "In later use restricted to a woman of humble rank or of 'low employment,' esp one engaged in the *sale of some commodity.*"

with different hand-holds, hands. Our digits do different work.

We are not 1.
We are not 2.
boohoohoo
hoohoo.

[3 Beats]

I think it fair to observe that I usually leave the burden of sense-making to my partner's hypotactic talents. I think it fair to observe that she usually leaves the burden of nonsense-making to me. I think it fair to observe that We are not 1. We are not 2. boohoohoo hoohoo.

Yet (2 ways): I suggested (for months) that we screen *The Shining* in preparation for this piece, hoping to incorporate the film's various overtures toward cognitive architecture, writer's block, the stereotype of writerly solitude—in particular, Duvall interrupting Nicholson, and his response (to which Kass might relate, I thought, owing to her similar reaction at times to me)—into our seemingly all work & no play presentation. Kass insisted (finally) we watch the film early (she has trouble sleeping after suspense or horror films, much to my dismay), so I popped in my bootlegged copy (taped during a promo for

The Housebond interrupts my reading and says, "You're using the wrong source. The OED isn't comprehensive. You have to use this."

I say, For just a damn minute, and only for a minute, let's quit the fucking quoting and deal with the spirit here.

He says, There's that anti-intellectual side of you again.

I say, There's that anti-intimacy side of you again.

Whadayamean *my* problem?

I say, He owns and I sell. *Title.*
I say, *Title to what*?
The Housebond says, "You stink at titles. Leave the titles to me. I'll come up with a title for your book."
I say, I have no fucking time to think up a better title right now because I'm consumed by an insatiable obligation to perform my Consumption Management duties.

Which is to say, *We are out of fucking milk again! Someone has to go to the store. SOME ONE OF US has to go.*

The En-Titlest says, I love to cook. I'll cook dinner! But—we're out of milk. What should we do??

The En-Titlest says, The car needs work. The trash needs taking out. The computer has

Showtime) and we both nearly fell asleep.

Simultaneously, or nearly.

It was 1 long goddamn day of collaboration, believe me.

What's your problem anyway?

Well that's something worth reporting, or repeating, or repeating, I thought. After all, the film *has* made an appearance here—just *now.* Are you still awake? Stop listening so intently for a message in the throttle, or the forms of address—you're interfering with our concentration. I don't know about you, but I can't keep up with the weather these days, or Stephen King. Is the point on which I think this body needs to focus. Do you have any idea, any idea at all how fucking EASY this could be? As undiplomatic as it may be to say so *en anglais, mesdames et messieurs,* saying so in any case, *avec plaisir,* however signed, must be a *contretemps,* no? Yes, there *are* dominant effects, but of course. . . . On a given (collaborative?) occasion, e.g., I talk twice as much as she, she produces 25% more writing.

Wasted words on my part (or so I'm advised).

crashed. I'll get right on it.

What say we have a nice continental breakfast—café au lait, jus d'orange, gender rolls.

I say, I have no fucking time to think up a better title right now because I have to swallow fertility drugs to elasticize my ancient fucking eggs so we can fuck and breed a pestilence that will suck milk from my breast *Not yours!* and then the only writing that will matter *in the house WHO owns*? will be that of The Bond Holder because he will have to Win the Bread— assuming he stops to buy any on the way home—and thus is ink semen and not breast milk—and by the way, bodily fluid mechanics have never been my thing, which means, I suppose, that I will be a dread-full mother.

If I do say so myself—

Excuse me, are you cutting me off?—
—are you *shittin'* me?

I say, Yes, Virginia, the worst thing a heterosexual woman writer can do is squeeze her writing desk into a virginal corner of her lover's bedroom—*a site of contesting membrains.*

Knock knock. Who's there?
The Bond Holder says, Inter-**Kass?—What was it that Gertrude Stein said to her French friends, Kass?—that America is the oldest country because it was the first to enter the 20th century? Kass? Kass!**

No I'm just asking you a question.

It's just a question—what in the hell is *wrong* with you?

Hence, some questions remain: Is it working? And *how* is it working? And what might be the context (historical, cultural, social, familial, blah blah blah) for evaluating the success of—?

And those questions shall continue to remain, suspended like lyrical balloons over my (i.e., "his") economically comic head. And in contrast to her persistently poker-faced delivery—an upstaging gesture if there ever was.

Another question remains: are we working—together? She & I? You & I? Us? Do you find the noise level excessive, or do you take pleasure in diverting your attention so, in having it so diverted? A survey will be distributed at the end of our presentation.
(Not to worry. The thought crossed our minds, but 1 of us—

ruption is the way of the 20th century—get used to it! My mother says, Don't say bad things about your husband. It's bad taste.

Gandhi says, Strive for avoidance of bad taste.

I say, Avoidance tastes bad, striving tastes good.

Winston says, What do you want, good grammar or good taste?

I say, I strive every day for the fucking truth about what goes on here only to find out that the truth is taboo.

I tell the Angel in (his) House, This isn't about my husband and me, and you fucking well know it. It's about the definition of Housebond. *Who owns the words we pile up around here?* I say, I can't talk as I like and that's as old as the hills.

The Bondsman, James Bondsman, says, It's about genre. Me Poet, You Prose. Me Nonsense, You Sense.

I say, *I am a highly sensitive person.* Me and Emily and Virginia. Which is now a condition, pathologized, *you poor thing, are you feeling again?? where's your Prozac??* He says, What in the hell is wrong with you??

I forget who—was opposed, so we scrapped the idea. And along with it, your empirical say in these proceedings.)

Let us not to the marriage of 2 minds admit collaboration, and let us appropriate, presently, an unadulterated thought on or around which to end this torturous exposition. Not my thought, of course, or her thought—and certainly not our thought or thoughts—but the thought of another collaborator, thought (at least) long dead.

Before we conclude on said thought, though, it's worth noting that the enemy of your enemy is not necessarily your friend. I mean, she or he could be your lover. Also, dichotomies would no doubt disperse here were it not for the problem of the numeral 2 and how it manifests itself among those historical, cultural, social, familial, blah blah blah contexts, as above (i.e., pertaining to those questions that shall continue to remain).

To wit, not 2 months before his death in Cortland, NY; not 1 hour from my birthplace; not 2 months after I turned sixteen, unremitting:

He says, This is how I talk.
I say, Bully for you.
People say, Two heads are better
than one.

I say, Two contradictory goals
intellect versus intimacy can
make for interesting magnetic
poetry, but in whose terms? I
say, I hear literary history
breathing down my neck and I
do as I choose; but with what
freedom to choose?

What say we agree that my identity politics are at risk in the
house *The home is the most dangerous area for women.* The
house is *his* bond.
My word is my bondage.

You don't say.

Bigod, I must have been full of
shit.

* * *

Afterword

Victoria Boynton

This collection began with two women talking at home. Over the past twelve years, Jo and I have come to think of our homes as gendered *herspace,* places that each of us has occupied in significant ways and into which each has invited the other. As nontraditional graduate students, each of us had had experience with a variety of homes in which we lived and worked as writers and thinkers, as wives and mothers, and as single women. But we also experienced the herspace of our lives differently, as I shared space with my family while Jo did not. So for these conversations I went to Jo's home more than she came to mine because, in her space, we could depend on quiet and insulation from others; her children were grown and she lived by herself, and so she controlled her space in a way that I did not. In addition, she has a knack for making space beautiful and thus inviting for our collaborations. Since she had her space to herself, we could spread out at her dining-room table or sit comfortably in her overstuffed chairs in her beautifully appointed living room without interruption. Sometimes she would come to my house, sit at the small kitchen table and eat, surrounded by everybody's old mail and books and crumbs from children's breakfasts. My space has been crowded, hers has been elegantly spare; my space has been populated, hers has been profitably empty; my space has been comparatively chaotic, hers ordered. But this duality is deceptive and contradictory: herspace is not as simple as this series of oppositions implies. We know the contradiction when we recognize the urge toward the other's space, her environmental otherness. Though each of us has chosen herspace for good reasons, each longs for the herspace of the other. We discuss the roots of these longings as social results stemming from gendered desires for connection, from intense socialization processes, from commitment to intellectual and artistic projects, from desires for autonomy, from heterosexist and capitalist and historical pressures, and from complex mixtures of all these and more.

Through these years, Jo and I have spoken often to each other about our scholarly struggle to produce as feminist women in a tradition that has defined us as homebound while ironically denying us our own space within the home. We are to occupy the spaces of others in order to make "the home" habitable. Those herspaces that are actually designated for women at home have been defined as factories of comfort—the kitchen, the sewing room. Even art in conventional herspace supports the family. It is intended to enhance the social atmosphere of the home and to teach children skills, not the least of which is to learn to signify and display to others one's cultural status. This mother-art does not require solitude but ensconces her further in her conventional setting. Invoking quaint pictures of the homemaker-mother may seem to some an identity citing from a dead past. However, these histories of clichéd conventions, underwritten by the binary oppositions that support gender relations, are, unfortunately, not exhausted; as we attempt to occupy space in new and more productive ways, these histories of space occupy us. Jo and I, in this collective project, have tried together to understand how these conventions have shaped us as women, i.e., how we have been molded by the invisible hands of historical and immediate complexes of cultural forces.

Our identities as academic women have been at the center of our meditations and conversations over the years. We have spoken about what we need to write, what helps us write, how various configurations of space and time influence our writing—our successes and our struggles with it, what we need to keep it going, to keep ourselves going, to overcome the "bad" inertia, and to use the "good" inertia—in short, to move our intellectual projects along. Space is, for us and the other writers in this volume, highly significant in this life we are lucky enough to be leading. The confluence of women's writing production and space—especially solitary space—is the definitive juncture of this book. Many of the essays in *Herspace* chronicle how a writing woman on her own learns to nourish herself and to find not only sustenance but delight in living alone. Authors also speak about the longing for this solitude, especially for wives and mothers to whom domestic relations are a matter of continual negotiation or coercion. As a writer, Carolyn Heilbrun articulates this longing in *The Last Gift of Time,* "Solitude, late in life, is the temptation of the happily paired; to be alone if one has not been doomed to aloneness is a temptation so beguiling that it carries with it the guilt of adultery, and the promise of consummation" (11).

Like Heilbrun, *Herspace* authors testify to the essential energy that resides in solitary space and the struggle to get it. They speak of their efforts to create spacial arrangements, composing an artistic rest area, an intellectual spot of purpose and playfulness. At times the essays occupy the very scene of "the home"—domesticated, feminized, decorated, shaped out of an interior aesthetic of comfort, even luxury. Yet these essays are not an advertisement for things; the things themselves, though carefully chosen, are not at the center of these essays. Interior arrangements and furnishings are not so much signifiers of class (a performance of economic position through the dominance of expense). Instead, the occupation and shaping of material space in these essays points to women's urges to define space for particular purposes and against others in an attempt to rework the meanings of woman-occupied space.

In the United States today, the aesthetics of interiors is inescapably tied to the consumerist genres of the decorating catalog, the home and garden magazine, and the eBay auction screens that encourage the citizenry to spend billions on ornament and atmosphere for living environments. However, this conspicuous display of purchasing power required to create striking physical effects in one's home environment is different from the solitary woman occupying a "home-made" herspace, especially because she has proved a traitor to the heterosexual fantasy of capitalism in which the idle woman spends "her" man's money on a display of status. The irony here is that as soon as women "own" their feelings about owning and occupying their own space (literally and figuratively), they become conscious of this new position as a sign of privilege, social inequity, and complicity in a nasty global capitalism that promotes consumerist values. The fact of women commanding the nerve and the capital to own their own homes and, furthermore, delight in and produce out of those solitary spaces, defies the heterosexist fantasy of the man and his homemaking wife in their packed nest of luxury, which stands in poorly for love. This familiar image negates the reality of an un- or otherwise-coupled individual as well as negating women's struggles with economics and family dynamics that have left them without space in their own homes—ironically "homeless." Narratives of women who have managed to shift out of economic instability into house owning to become productive solitaires certainly point out alternatives to the conventional narratives of women's space.

These essays also expand the idea of the house and "house-work," emphasizing that the house can function in ambiguous ways—as private, safe space in which to work and as overdetermined domestic space, in which women have to aggressively pursue herspace to do intellectual "house-work" seriously. Though the theme of relationships intrudes in discussions of herspace, our conversations have really not been about relationships, but about women, their work in their homes, their bid for solitude, and the exceptional examples that they set to loosen the matrix of gender.

Remarkable in this collection is the resonance of the personal, for whether the essay hinges on literary analysis or autobiography, the figure of the woman writer is central. Especially in relation to the space she occupies, this gendered, creative figure mirrors the *Herspace* author. But this figure is invoked in a variety of ways. Some cite other women's literary texts in which the solitary woman writes; others draw on feminist theory, joining it to theory about space and writing; some investigate examples of discrimination against solitary women, especially if they have chosen their singleness in order to create; some offer examples from film and photography that cite women in new and encouraging ways; some offer critiques of heterosexist ideologies; others give their essays over to the charms of the explicitly personal, filling them with the details of creating and inhabiting herspace as writers; and some authors write what Jan Wellington, in this volume, and others elsewhere have called *critical autobiography,* a mixed genre which slides between the personal and the academic, often occupying the fuzzy border between. In the last decade, particularly, feminists have claimed and theorized this mixed genre because it calls into question the clichéd binaries of the scholarly and the personal and complicates the autobiographical, with its tense and slippery relation to "the truth." This cross-genre essay is particularly suited for exploring how writing functions for solitary women writing about women writers in solitary space. These essays confess, through a rich variety of writerly personas and means, to the ecstasies and anxieties of a woman writing in herspace.

I would like to conclude this Afterword with a paragraph from my own essay: I turn to myself as a writing problem and as a political problem. Though I see this subject in relation to its larger contexts, I am making a home for myself in, through, and by writing. Significantly, my personal experience of writing is deeply connected to my sense of being contained in physical space—my writing setting, my gendered body, the *where* of myself, even as I feel my physicality inscribed as feminine and set in clichéd opposition to masculinized mentality. I turn to myself as subject, authorized in the project by such theorists as Linda Alcoff and Laura Gray:

> We need new ways to analyze the personal and the political as well as new ways to conceptualize these terms. Experience is not "pretheoretical" nor is theory separate or separable from experience, and both are always already political. A project of social change, therefore, does not need to "get beyond" the personal narrative or the confessional to become political but rather needs to analyze the various effects of the confessional in different contexts and struggle to create discursive spaces in which we can maximize its disruptive effects. (283-284)

Alcoff and Gray's *discursive space* which can create a *disruptive* politics begins, for me, with an interrogation of my own identity as it manifests in set urges, ideological concretions, and cultural scripts. This interrogation doesn't stop with myself, doesn't stop with my own temptations and urges and compulsions, but asks, "Who else is out beyond me? Who else holds a pen? Out of our solitary writing space, can we reach one another, pens in hands? Can I extend beyond my own *discursive space,* my own writing desire and my own middle-class upbringing and privilege to hear other voices, other desires? What products might herspace have?"

WORKS CITED

Alcoff, Linda and Laura Gray. "A Survivor Discourse: Transgression or Recuperation?" *Signs* (Winter 1993): 260-290.

Heilbrun, Carolyn. *The Last Gift of Time.* New York: Balantine, 1998.

T - #0091 - 270225 - C0 - 212/152/17 - PB - 9780789018205 - Gloss Lamination